THE
SILKEN
ROSE

CAROL MCGRATH

ACCENT

First published in 2020 by Headline Accent
An imprint of HEADLINE PUBLISHING GROUP

2

Cataloguing in Publication Data is available from the British Library

ISBN 978 1 7861 5727 0

Typeset in 10.5/13pt Bembo Std by Jouve (UK), Milton Keynes

Printed and bound in Great Britain by Clays Ltd, Elcograf S.p.A.

HEADLINE PUBLISHING GROUP
An Hachette UK Company
Carmelite House
50 Victoria Embankment
London
EC4Y 0DZ

www.headline.co.uk
www.hachette.co.uk

Carol McGrath taught History and English for many years in both the state and private sectors. She left teaching to work on a MA in Creative Writing from Queens University Belfast, then an MPhil in English at Royal Holloway, London, where she developed her expertise on the Middle Ages.

Praise for Carol McGrath:

'Powerful, gripping and beautifully told. A historical novel that will resonate with the #MeToo generation. Carol McGrath bewitched me with her immaculate research, vivid characters and complex tale of politics, power and love. I could smell the secrets and taste the fear that stalked King Henry's court. Clever, intimate and full of intrigue, I loved it.' – Kate Furnivall, author of *The Liberation*

'A very well-researched tale of a fascinating period.' – Joanna Courtney, author of *Blood Queen*

'*The Silken Rose* dives into 13th century England with the relish of a peregrine's stoop . . . Temptation for any fan of scheming behind the arras and swooning courtly love!' – Joanna Hickson, author of *The Tudor Crown*

Also by Carol McGrath

Mistress Cromwell

The Daughters of Hastings trilogy

The Betrothed Sister
The Swan-Daughter
The Handfasted Wife

For Elysium
Time passes and princesses grow up

THE FAMILY TREE

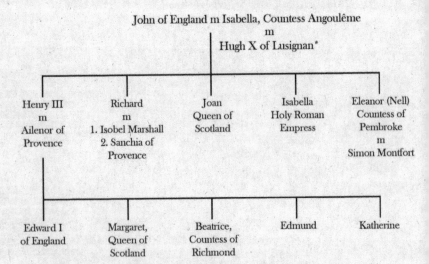

John of England m Isabella, Countess Angoulême
m
Hugh X of Lusignan*

Henry III m Ailenor of Provence	Richard m 1. Isobel Marshall 2. Sanchia of Provence	Joan Queen of Scotland	Isabella Holy Roman Empress	Eleanor (Nell) Countess of Pembroke m Simon Montfort

Edward I of England	Margaret, Queen of Scotland	Beatrice, Countess of Richmond	Edmund	Katherine

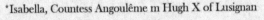

*Isabella, Countess Angoulême m Hugh X of Lusignan

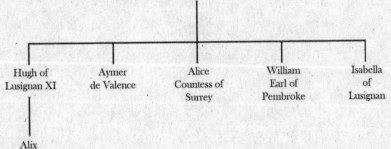

Hugh of Lusignan XI	Aymer de Valence	Alice Countess of Surrey	William Earl of Pembroke	Isabella of Lusignan

Alix
and others

Les Heures Bénédictines

Matins:	Between 2.30 and 3.00 in the morning
Lauds:	Between 5.00 and 6.00 in the morning
Prime:	Around 7.30 or shortly before daybreak
Terce:	9.00 in the morning
Sext:	Noon
Nones:	2.00 and 3.00 in the afternoon
Vespers:	Late afternoon
Compline:	Before 7.00 as soon after that the monks retire
Angelus Bells:	Midnight

Arthur and Guinevere

'At the King's arrival the town resounds with the joyous welcome which they give. Silken shifts are taken out and hung aloft as decorations, and they spread tapestries to walk on and draped the streets with them, while they wait for the King's approach . . . And the lady came forth dressed in an imperial garb, a robe of fresh ermine, and upon her head she wore a diadem all ornamented with rubies. No cloud was upon her face but it was so full of joy that she was more beautiful, I think, than any goddess.'

Chretien de Troyes (d.1191), 'The Knight of the Lion'
Project Gutenberg, *Four Arthurian Romances*.

Chapter One

The road from Dover to Canterbury was mired with winter mud so progress was slow. Ailenor, Princess of Provence, had never seen such weather in all of her young life. She tugged back the oiled canvas that served to keep out the worst of the rain and peered from her long, box-like carriage into the January landscape. A collection of gaunt faces stared back; figures huddled in heavy cloaks, watching the golden lions of Savoy and Provence pass through Canterbury's southernmost gate into the cramped lanes of the city.

Domina Willelma's rhythmic snores competed with the splashing of hooves moving laboriously through the gateway, the roll of wheels belonging to sumpter carts, the cracking of whips and the protesting snorts of an escort of three hundred horsemen. All the way from Dover, thirteen year-old Ailenor had listened to rain rattling on the curved roof of the carriage. With a hiss, it occasionally dripped through a minute crack onto the box of hot charcoal that warmed her feet.

She let the curtain drop and withdrew into her furs. Was this country a place of eternal deluges? *It's so different to my golden Provençal fields on which sun shines winter and summer.*

A tear slid down her cheek. She instinctively drew her mantle closer. This was not what she imagined after Richard of Cornwall, King Henry's brother, had visited their castle of Les Baux last year and she had listened to his thrilling tales of romance. England was

1

not the magical land she visualised when she wrote her best poem ever, set in Cornwall, verse that Prince Richard admired. Nor was it the luscious green country filled with wild flowers she dreamed of when Henry, King of England, sent for her to become his bride.

She shivered in her damp gown. She had not wanted woollen gowns and underskirts. Rather, she desired velvets, silks and satins, and the finest linen for under-garments. But after two days' travel over the Narrow Sea and on waterlogged roads she understood the need for warmth. Her mother, Countess Beatrice was right. She was now to dwell in a land where winter never ended and summer was but a distant prayer.

The carriage jolted to a halt. Uncle William, the Bishop Elect of Valence, thrust his head through the heavy hanging.

'We are approaching the Archbishop's palace. Prepare to descend.' He almost fell off his horse as he pushed his neck further into the carriage to waggle a long finger at Ailenor's senior lady. 'Waken that woman at once. Order her to tidy your dress.' With an impatient grunt, he withdrew before Ailenor could reply.

'Domina Willelma, wake up.' Ailenor gently shook her lady's shoulder. 'Uncle William says –'

'By our sainted Lady, my child, forgive me. Why have you permitted me to sleep?' Lady Willelma sat straight up, her dark eyes wide awake.

'Because, dear Willelma, you have hardly slept since we left Vienne and that was three weeks ago. We've almost arrived.'

'I'm neglecting my duty to your mother.' Willelma fussed about the seat and opened the tassels of a velvet bag. My mother, Ailenor thought, a leaden stone invading her throat, tears gathering again. If only she were here. She would make jests and have me laugh at it all. How can I face this awful land alone? A heartbeat later her lady was holding a comb. She plaited Ailenor's luxuriant dark hair – Ailenor let out a wail of protest. Willelma tugged again and it hurt. She coiled the plaits into crispinettes which felt uncomfortably tight.

Dragging a mantle lined with ermine from the travelling chest, Willelma wrapped it around her shoulders and pinned it closed with a jewelled brooch. 'I feel like a wrapped-up gift, not a person,' Ailenor said, her voice almost a screech.

'There, much better.' Domina Willelma sat back and tossed the cloak Ailenor had been wearing to one side. 'Servants can look after that now.' Ailenor had no choice but to compose herself, though she wanted to shout, 'Turn about. Take me home.' It was too late.

A jolt and the carriage stopped. Uncle William opened the carriage door. They had pulled into a vast courtyard. Ailenor allowed Willelma to arrange her flowing mantle. A servant raced forward with a carpeted step. Placing her foot down on the top tread, Ailenor descended onto slippery cobbles, her arms flapping outwards as she tried to steady and balance. Above the courtyard a pale midday sun reached awkwardly through fat grey clouds.

'The sky is clearing,' she said, seeking something polite to say, though she did not feel like showing off fine manners today.

'Indeed,' said Uncle William. 'The Archbishop is here to greet you.'

The English Prelate, Edmund Rich, picked his way forward stork-like, his hands extended. Ailenor managed a smile, bent her knee, and kissed his ring. Glancing up, she looked into the most austere face she had ever seen in her thirteen years.

'No need, my lady,' he said, raising her. 'Welcome to Canterbury. You will wish to rest and refresh yourself before meeting the King. Come, come.'

Ailenor took a quick glance around. Noticing the sumpter vehicles rattling into the courtyard, her courtiers and servants descending from painted boxes, and others climbing off horses, she turned back to the Prelate. '*J'espere que vous avez beaucoup des chambres.*'

The Archbishop smiled thinly, his chin thrusting forward like a stork's reedy beak. 'Indeed, indeed, my stewards will escort your retinue to accommodation close to your own. Perhaps your domina will select those ladies who are to accompany you to your apartment.'

Domina Willelma called out four names as Ailenor caught her arm and said, 'I need all my ladies.'

'It's only for a short time. They will all accompany you to your wedding, all of them. For now four of those ladies will suffice.'

Uncle William frowned and Ailenor knew she had no choice. She would be compliant today but later she would decide who stayed with her. The damsels who were to remain with Ailenor gathered behind her as servants dragged two leather chests from a covered wagon. These coffers held linens and clothing for her wedding on the following day.

With the Prelate leading, they hurried into the warmth of the Archbishop's palace, a vast stone building of several storeys connecting houses, towers, and exterior staircases. The Archbishop led them through an immense pillared hall where nobility stood in clusters waiting to see their new Queen. As she passed, they bowed and curtsied. Ailenor inclined her head and raised it, determined to appear every inch a queen. Where was the King? Why was *he* not here to welcome her?

'Where is the King, my husband?' she asked.

'He is with God,' the Prelate said, eyes glancing heavenward.

'With God?' She stared at the Archbishop. 'In Heaven or on earth?' she asked.

'The King is at prayer,' he said, his tone deferential, clearly towards God and the King, not her. She looked straight ahead. No one would be dismissive to her once she was queen, not even her husband. The Archbishop raised his hand, jewelled rings glinting in the candle-light, glittering stars on his finger bones. He stopped their procession and signalled to a lady whose countenance appeared both serious and sad. She wore a simple grey velvet gown and close wimple with confident elegance.

'My lady, Princess Eleanor, the King's sister, will escort you to the women's quarters and see you and your women are comfortable.'

The Princess bowed. 'Welcome, Lady Ailenor, welcome to England.'

Ailenor, her deportment erect despite her exhaustion, returned the obeisance. 'Thank you,' she said.

At once a body of ladies surrounded Ailenor and guided her to a wooden staircase. The palace was such a strange place. It smelled damp and as she climbed towards the dimness beyond, she imagined all sorts of strange creatures lurking in corners. Halfway up, she turned and looked down, her eye seeking out Uncle William amongst the scattering throng below. She glanced at Willelma who wore an impassive expression. She must do likewise. Climbing again, following the sister of the strangely missing King, sensing all nature of perceived things watching from the shadows, Ailenor slowly mounted a second staircase towards the unknown.

Her chamber was spacious and, unlike the gloomy staircases and corridors, was well-lit with wall sconces which cast light over rich hangings and a large curtained bed with an embroidered coverlet. Ailenor looked out of a large window onto a garden. A robin was flitting from one pollarded tree to another. She breathed more easily to see the sky and the walled garden below it patterned with winter herbs. Willelma directed servants to unpack Ailenor's two leather chests and she felt even better as she watched familiar mantles and her linen tumble out, gowns and mantles hung on a clothing pole, her under-garments neatly folded into a wall-cupboard. But when the most important item, the cloth of gold wedding dress, was lifted from its linen wrapping, the maids drew back, and Domina Willelma looked dismayed, her dark eyes surprised and her nose wrinkling. Ailenor came close to the bed and immediately recoiled. 'What is that disgusting odour, Domina Willelma? It stinks.' She tentatively touched the creased silken fabric. 'It's ruined. I can't wear that.' She burst into tears.

'We can air it, hang it with lavender. I am sure it will have just been the damp, my lady.' Domina Willelma said in a soothing tone as she examined the silk pleats, peering into every crease and crumple. 'Praise God, no stains.'

Princess Eleanor touched the gown and calmly called one of her ladies over. 'Ann, take Lady Ailenor's wedding-gown to my chamber. Have it hung with lavender and fennel.'

Willelma dabbed Ailenor's eyes with a linen cloth and placed a protective arm about her charge. '*Merde*,' Ailenor muttered into her domina's shoulder. 'Will it ever be the same again?' Her father, who could not afford to, as he was an impoverished count, had spent a fortune on new clothes for her wedding to Henry of England. This union with the great English King was as prestigious for her family as that of her sister Marguerite's marriage to the King of France. It was important everything was perfect. Now her wedding dress reeked of wet hay. She had been right to feel unease in this palace. Its shadows harboured malevolence.

She watched uneasily as Princess Eleanor's lady whisked the gown away. Frowning, Domina Willelma laid out her new burgundy tunic with flowing sleeves trimmed with gold embroidery. Ailenor was not consoled, not even when Willelma leaned forward, sniffed and lifting her head announced, 'It is fresh and uncorrupted, my lady. You can wear this tonight with the gold slippers.'

'I may be wearing it tomorrow if my wedding dress is ruined.'

'No,' said Princess Eleanor. 'Your wedding gown will smell sweetly. I promise.'

'I hope so,' Ailenor said, trying hard to regain her poise.

Princess Eleanor indicated a comfortable winged chair by the fire. Ailenor, exhausted by her uneasy welcome to Canterbury, sank back into soft cushions. The King's sister took the straight-backed chair opposite and called for refreshments, which soon arrived on a silver tray as if ready all along. The Princess poured two cups of hippocras and offered one to Ailenor, saying, 'They will serve your ladies in the ante-chamber. They must be famished.'

Servants discreetly vanished. As she sipped her honeyed wine, Ailenor felt the Princess studying her. Raising her eyebrows she said, 'My lord, the King, was not here to greet me. When shall I meet him? Surely he is not always at prayer?' She was reminded of Marguerite's husband, King Louis, who was so religious there was no time for anything else. Marguerite had confided to her sister when her retinue had paused in Paris, 'Not even love-making. How will I ever give him a son?'

'Soon.' Princess Eleanor said, and offered her a dish of warm pasties. They had not eaten since dawn that morning. Ailenor bit into the crust and, at once, a velvety smoothness caressed her tongue.

6

The pasty was light and tasted of cream, chicken, and eggs mixed with herbs. She felt a smile of pleasure begin to hover about her mouth. The warmth of the fire, the Princess who was kind, the honeyed hippocras which she sipped slowly, savouring it, and the delicious pasties restored her sense of excitement. All would have been as all should be if only Henry, himself, had greeted her instead of the pious Prelate and the King's sister.

'I'll take you to my brother when you have refreshed and changed your gown,' Princess Eleanor said. Ailenor helped herself to a second pasty. She glanced at the candle clock on the table. 'There is no need to hurry, Ailenor. The King will escort you to the Archbishop's great hall for supper. Do not feel overpowered, because only a few of our friends will join us tonight and, after you have dined, we shall show you the cathedral where you are to be married.' Princess Eleanor stood and added, a natural cordiality radiating from her, 'I'll leave you to your Domina for now. Rest and do not feel anxious. I'll return later to fetch you.' She touched Ailenor's hand lightly and floated from the chamber as if she walked on air.

She is truly a princess, thought Ailenor looking after her. I like the Princess already. But the King should not have kept me waiting.

The candle clock burned down. The supper hour approached. Dressed in her burgundy gown, her hair combed yet again and plaited into crispinettes, Ailenor waited for Princess Eleanor's return with an impatience that caused her to fidget. Why should she have to wait?

At length, Princess Eleanor returned and said the King would receive them. Ailenor stood, held her head high, ran her hand along the skirt of her burgundy gown and tried to imagine she was simply attending her mother in their hall at Les Baux, wishing with all her being the Countess was in attendance on her now. Slowing as they turned corners, they negotiated two dim narrow corridors.

'You must call me Nell,' the Princess said as she escorted Ailenor and her ladies along yet another dimly lit passage to the King's waiting chamber. 'The family always calls me Nell. Too many Eleanors.'

Ailenor nodded. 'No one will change my name. I am to be a

queen. It would not be fitting.' She added, 'But I do like Nell.' Nell smiled.

Ailenor's heart pulsed as they approached the great doors behind which the King waited. She was sure Nell could hear it beat like a drum that could not stop drumming, in a frantic fairy-tale manner. It felt like it could not stop dancing. Everything she had longed for during her long journey through France and over the sea was to happen at last. Would her betrothed love her – would he even like her?

Doors flew open. They entered the great chamber. Pages stood about the walls dressed in livery, displaying on their chests three lions wearing crowns. Uncle William stood by the King's chair, his face inscrutable. Her throbbing heart leapt and her hands felt clammy. Domina Willelma and Nell stopped walking.

Henry rose as she approached. Measuring her steps with care so they were even and she appeared to glide, she proceeded alone until she stood still, several paces before the King. He was of average height and stocky like Beau, her favourite dog. I hope I have stopped growing, she thought anxiously. I am too tall for him.

Henry wore a long green velvet coat trimmed with pearls that flared out from his waist. An expensive scent of sandalwood wafted towards her as he stepped forward to meet her. His hair was flaxen and fine and it fell to his chin where it fashionably curled under. She tried not to stare at his face. His eye! *Mon Dieu*, it droops. She lowered her own gaze and sank into a deep obeisance, her gown sweeping the tiles as her mother had instructed her. She imagined she heard Countess Beatrice whisper in her ear, 'Remember he is your betrothed but he is also your king. Show him your most refined obeisance when you first meet.' She had practised hard to her hound in their sun-baked courtyards scented with lemons. Beau had always barked approval.

'Ailenor, rise,' he said. As he raised her, their eyes met. His were a pale blue, at least what she could see, with that drooping eyelid. Closer, she saw she was correct. She was almost his height. 'Come sit with me.' His voice was musical, gentle, and he spoke in elegant

French. There was nothing to fear from this man who was, of course, twice her own age.

He took her hand and led her to a chair beside his own. Uncle William smiled at last and, with a bow, withdrew to a cushioned bench on one side of the room. Her ladies followed Nell to another bench opposite. The King snapped his fingers. Within a few moments a procession of pages advanced with gifts. One by one, extravagant offerings were laid out on a table to her side for her appraisal. First, she was presented with a sapphire brooch for her mantle, a necklace of creamy pearls, and an enormous ruby set into a gold ring.

The King leaned over and slipped the heavy ring onto her middle finger where it sat beside her sapphire betrothal ring. She held her finger stiffly. 'It is overly large for such a little finger but we can have it adjusted. The ruby belonged to my grandmother, Queen Eleanor, Countess of Aquitaine.'

Other gifts followed: jewels in tiny coffers and lengths of silk in baskets. A selection of gowns and tunics arrived, carried into the chamber by long-coated men whom she thought must be tailors. Her father could have spared his own coin because when the pages held the garments up, she saw at once they would fit perfectly. As she touched the silks and velvets she remembered a gown had been borrowed from her wardrobe by Prince Richard when he had visited them in the summer. They've allowed for me growing. Finally, servants delivered belts for her new silken tunics, and purses with the treasured gold and silver embroidery that across France they called Opus Anglicanum, English work.

She heard her ladies' gasps of astonishment as so many gifts arrived.

Tears threatened. She blinked them away. 'My Lord King, I know not what to say. I have only one present for you, an Arab stallion called Caesar. He is a lovely creature, white as snowfall with a grey nose. He is a good horse but nothing as generous as all this.' The words poured from her mouth in a rush as she stared at the fabrics, jewels, gowns, and tunics.

'Hush, little princess.' He took her hands in his own. She smelled

9

his sandalwood scent again. 'I shall love Caesar and look forward to meeting him,' he said, smiling. 'It pleases me to give you gifts. I expect nothing in return.'

The stallion had been transported all the way from Aragon by a distant relative who bred horses. The bridle and reins were finely tooled and the saddle was studded with jewels. She hoped desperately that Caesar would please the King and whispered a prayer to St Bridget, her name-day saint, 'Please let the King love me.' Henry squinted over at Uncle William with a smile hovering about his mouth.

'Come,' the King said, taking her hand. 'It is time we presented you to my closest friends. Come, Bishop William, you too. My chamberlain will take all of these to Ailenor's chambers.'

If this kind man remained generous and was always good to her and her family, Ailenor thought, she would be content with her royal husband. He was not as handsome as French Louis. He was not King Arthur either, but he would be devoted to her, unlike the King of France over whose heart, Marguerite insisted, the Queen-mother Blanche ruled. Ailenor had met Queen Blanche, who reminded her of a beady-eyed spider. There was no queen-mother in England. Uncle William had explained how Henry's own mother, Isabel of Angouleme, had run away to France many years ago to marry her first love, Count Hugh of Lusignan – an old scandal. No, Henry must be ruled by one heart, hers.

On her wedding morning, Ailenor's ladies, those permitted to attend her, bathed her in rose-scented water and dried her with perfumed cloths. She was anxious for her gown, until, at last, it arrived. Gently she held a handful of pleated golden skirt to her nose, feeling relief.

'Nell, it's as if it had never smelled foul. You have saved my wedding dress and saved me, too.' She wanted to hug Nell but drew back. Instead she said, 'Will you ever marry again?' It was a forward question and she should not have said it. She bit her tongue. Uncle William had explained how the King's sister had been widowed at sixteen. She was once married to William Marshal, son of the great

10

knight of the same name who managed the kingdom of England when Henry was only nine years old and a king.

The Princess's violet eyes filled with tears. 'I cannot, for I took a vow of chastity after my husband died.' Her voice became a whisper. 'William was a good man, son of a great man. I was only ten when we married but I came to love him. Now I don't think of marriage. I must not.' Nell seemed so sad, Ailenor wished her runaway tongue had not taken her over. Nell touched Ailenor's gown. 'I shall wear plain garments all of my days and never wed. I swore it in front of the Archbishop.'

'A bride of Christ but not a nun. A ring but no earthly husband. And no other jewels.' Ailenor looked at the gems laid out for her to wear that day. 'It is unfair to gaze on others wearing these and not to possess any of your own.'

Willelma, who was lacing her gown, groaned. 'Stay still, my lady.' Ailenor ignored her and reached out to touch Nell's finger on which a plain ring declared her loyalty to Christ. 'I hope we are to be friends,' she whispered to Nell.

'I hope so, too. Your wedding dress is so beautiful.' She smiled again. 'You will be much admired, Ailenor.'

They clasped hands for a moment and, Nell's mood restored, Ailenor spun around so her golden pleated skirt flowed about her legs. It made her feel beautiful.

The wedding took place at noon. The fair-headed King, whose crown made him appear much taller than she was, was clad in a long cloth-of-gold coat embroidered with golden lions, jewelled, and trimmed with ermine. He was handsome. Over and over, at the previous evening's supper, he had admired her beauty until she glowed in his praise. She had enchanted this king who had not been there to greet her when her carriage entered the Archbishop's courtyard, that absent king who would never again treat her in that way.

Before she had set out for her long journey through France, Countess Beatrice had engaged in an intimate and slightly embarrassing conversation with her daughter.

11

'Fourteen by Candlemas. Soon you will be old enough to be bedded. Your duty will be to bear your husband a son.' She had coughed and coloured. 'And daughters, of course.' Beatrice had four beautiful girls and no sons. Ailenor smiled to herself at her mother's hesitation. 'Your compensation for the marriage bed is that like your sister, Marguerite, you are to be a queen of a great country. Perhaps you will be the greater queen.'

She demurely assented. 'Yes, Mama.'

'You give him your body without complaint. He will penetrate you. You have seen cats and dogs copulate.' Ailenor had reddened. She had. This was the bit that worried her. It seemed strange and brutal. Even so, it was expected and she demurely said again, 'Yes, Mama.'

'Painful to begin with but you'll get used to it. You might come to enjoy it. Let him think you do. In bed, make him the centre of your world. It is how you bind him to you. Just don't confess that to a priest.' Ailenor knew priests thought that women led men astray with their sinfulness. She determined that even if she never enjoyed it her husband would not fault her.

Oh yes, she would never complain. They would have sons. She would be a great queen.

Ailenor lifted the pleated front of her wedding gown as they stepped into the great west porch of Canterbury Cathedral. Her gold silk gown shimmered and she was aware of how perfectly it fitted below her small breasts, its sleeves, trimmed with ermine, falling to her feet. When she stood beside Henry in his cloth-of-gold she murmured, 'Look, my lord, see how we match.' He inclined his head.

In the Cathedral porch, Archbishop Rich's scribe read out the long list of lands, tenements, towns, and cities that Ailenor was to possess as her dower. Considering she had brought nothing to her marriage other than her intelligence, her love of poetry, and the luxuriant beauty that had won the heart of the man by her side, this dower was generous. Whoever said that daughters could not bring greatness to their families? Yes, she was grateful to Henry.

If only her mother could see her today in her pleated gold gown, a circlet of gold on her flowing dark hair. If only her beloved papa could have heard the dower promise and further promise of estates, castles, and ten thousand marks; such a great sum. Her head high, she processed into the Nave for her wedding mass.

After the ceremony was over, while kneeling on an exquisitely embroidered cloth, from the corner of her eye she glimpsed Uncle William, Bishop Elect of Valence, smiling at her from the side, pleased as a hawk that had just made a kill.

During the feast that followed, Ailenor sat beside Henry, delighting in every moment of his obvious adoration. From his spoon she sampled frumenty of hulled wheat and milk of almonds with a little venison and saffron, tiny morsels of duckling, crayfish set in jelly, salmon from the river, capon in lemon, carp from the Archbishop's own fishponds, roast swan, a minute portion of pasty of young hare and peacock, minced kid, blankmanger of mince with cream and almonds, parmesan pies gilded in a chequer pattern with banners of England and Provence set on top, wafers served with hippocras, fruit, a variety of hard cheeses Henry said were English and which tasted sharp, plus compote and custard tarts.

When the subtlety was placed before them, a tall castle of marchpane with windows of coloured sugar, turreted towers and a moat with a perfectly crafted ship in full sail upon it, Henry broke off a bit of silver marchpane from the tallest tower and, popping it into her mouth, whispered, 'I wonder, can I make you happy?'

She swallowed the delicate sliver of marchpane and looked into his eyes. 'My lord, you have raised me up. All I wish in the whole world is to please you.'

'When we enter London, smile in this way, you will win the hearts of a difficult people.'

Ailenor's smile turned into a frown. In Provence their people never questioned her father's authority. This was not the way God intended people to behave. 'Why are they difficult? You are their king. How foolish.'

'The merchants overreach themselves, as do many of my barons.'

He lowered his voice. 'They wish to control my power. They forget that a king is closer to God than they. But smile at them as you smile for me and you will win even the hardest of hearts.'

I shall smile. They shall know that I am their queen, she thought to herself, and they shall never disobey me either.

Princess Nell and Domina Willelma were approaching. Nell touched Ailenor's sleeve. 'It's time,' Nell said in a quiet voice.

Ailenor rose to her feet. Nell drew her up the staircase to her bed-chamber that had been prepared for their wedding night.

They washed her hands and feet with rose water. They cleaned her perfect white teeth with a soft twig and gave her liquorice to sweeten her breath. As soon as her Domina slipped her shift over her shoulders, Nell took her hand, drew her towards the bed, and drew back the covers. Henry entered the chamber clad in a night robe embroidered with golden lions and acanthus tendrils. His favoured nobles stood by the door peering in. The Archbishop followed Henry into the bedchamber and solemnly proceeded to bless the marriage bed with prayer and a sprinkling of holy water. As if this throwing of water could make her marriage fruitful. She *would* be fertile because she wished it so.

She knelt beside Henry to say her prayers with him and they were put to bed.

After the chamber had emptied and they were left alone, Henry drew her close and buried his face in her hair.

'Do I please you?'

'My lord, I am the most fortunate of women.' He did please her, and he smelled of musk and some exotic spice she could not identify. She forgot the drooping eye because she was used to it already. His body appeared firm and his breath smelled of cloves. He excited her.

'We will not do this, not for some time, my sweet. Not until you are a woman. I would never wish to hurt you.'

'But, my lord, I *am* ready. I love you. My duty is to bear you an heir.'

'You are still a child. What would you know of love?' He seemed amused.

'I have read the poets, listened to their songs of love. As for the rest, I am a willing pupil,' she said firmly.

'Let us be companions first, get to know each other and, little by little, discover what follows.'

'As you wish, sire.'

Was there a mistress? Could there be a boy? She had heard of such things.

He climbed down from her bed and left her after dropping a kiss on her forehead. Ailenor thought about him long past the midnight Angelus bells' peals. She would bind him to her somehow. There would never be others.

Chapter Two

Ailenor stepped onto the blue ray cloth of silk spread out for her husband and her to walk upon into the magnificent abbey church at Westminster.

On the previous afternoon they had ridden in a grand procession of nobles and City aldermen from the Tower, where they lodged, to Westminster Palace. Tapestries were hung from windows as well as garlands of winter greenery tied with colourful ribbons. Crowds threw silky rosebuds at the great procession. Trumpeters sounded gilded horns. Lamps flickered like a thousand golden stars to light the route along the Cheape to St Paul's, out of the great Aldgate where they turned onto the Strand and rode forward to Westminster, which they reached as dusk descended.

The walls of her chamber in the palace at Westminster were decorated with ancient stories. Her ante-chamber was green, Henry's favourite colour. Her favourite legends had been painted on his chamber's walls as well. How had he known the stories she loved? When she asked, he told her he loved those legends also. On their first evening at the palace, as they shared a private supper in the King's chamber, he told her what was to happen on the following day.

'I shall be preceded by three earls,' he said as he placed a little fish on her plate – she was so entranced she could hardly eat a morsel. 'They carry the swords of state. My treasurer follows, and my

16

chancellor who carries the stone chalice for the holy anointing oil. Two knights will bear our sceptres. I walk before you into the cathedral under a canopy of purple silk and you, Ailenor, you will look magnificent under your own purple silken covering. It will be held up with silver lances and gilt bells on each lance, and will chime sweet as Heaven's angels as you step forward.'

'But I do not walk alone, do I?' she had asked, her heart beating faster and her appetite diminished. She felt her stomach cramping and she prayed to St Beatrice that her courses were not descending early. Her flowers, as her mother called them, would render her unclean. She found she was biting her lip. All had been worked out ahead. She was not due for at least another week.

Henry glanced at her plate. He said, 'Ailenor, you must eat or you will faint tomorrow and we can't have that.' Ailenor dipped a morsel of bread into a sauce which tasted lemony and tried to swallow. 'You will not walk alone into the church nave.' Henry lifted another tiny fish onto her silver dish. 'Two grand bishops shall accompany you. One is to be your Uncle William.'

She felt queasy as she reached the church door where she paused for Archbishop Rich to read the first prayer. He looked severe and frowning. She had disliked him in Canterbury and she had not warmed to him as they travelled to London. It had only been because she'd insisted and complained to Henry that her damsels were returned to her, and only once they reached the Tower was accommodation granted to the ladies from Provence in her own chambers. Edmund Rich was stern, always so stern. She heard that he wore a hair shirt under his gown, and that he whipped himself. She glanced around, feeling relief. Uncle William was close enough to ease her passage through this foreign ceremony. What would she do without him? How would she manage if her people were sent home to Savoy and Provence? They must all stay, all her damsels and all her clerks.

She tried hard to concentrate on the Archbishop's prayer but it was tedious and long. He was reciting the names of women who had borne sons in the line of David, the endless royal line that led to Christ. Her ear caught at particular names such as Sarah, Rebecca,

Rachel, and the Virgin whom she loved with all her heart. She whispered her own prayer, 'Blessed Madonna, please give me a son, too. It is what they want from me.' Remembering Henry's reticence to deflower her, she murmured, 'And may it happen soon.' She felt Uncle William's white gown twitch by her side. He was smiling. Perhaps he had heard her words.

He nudged her gently. 'Walk forward, Ailenor.'

They moved inwards to where the church was ablaze with colour. The greatest nobles of the land were pressed into the nave, clad in gold, furs and silks; everything seemed gleaming in the soft candlelight, perfumes and incense mingling with the sour scent of perspiring humanity. She took a deep breath. Before she stepped to the high altar, Uncle William said into her ear, 'Remember to prostrate yourself.'

The Archbishop recited more prayers containing hopes for her fruitfulness and her kindness, and after that, the rest of the ceremony followed in a dreamlike trance. Someone – she could not discern who – removed her gold circlet. She felt the warmth of holy oil, the chrism, trickle onto her head. She was a queen, sanctified and anointed by God's archbishop, and as Queen she possessed powers bestowed on her by God, power which she intended to use to help her family. After all, she had made her parents a promise to remember Savoy and Provence, and this promise she must keep.

Like Queen Esther of the Book, she would intercede with the King for the well-being of her people. She had already done so that morning, pleading before Henry on her knees for the life of a criminal. Archbishop Rich had chosen the fortunate man for her royal intercession. She would have preferred to have been able to choose but she was a stranger to this different land.

A heavy crown of golden lilies was placed on her head. A sceptre was placed in her hands. The Archbishop recited, '*Christus vincit, Christus regnat, Christus imperat.*' At last it was over.

She wondered if she could survive the feasting that would follow. All she wished to do now was retreat to her bed chamber, wrap herself in her coverlet, close the curtains, and sleep for a week. Her belly still ached and she was exhausted. Instead, when they returned to her apartments, Nell guided her to a couch where she was to rest before the feast began. Closing her eyes, she lay down, thankful her courses were not quite yet pressing down on her after all. Not yet. Nell kindly massaged her hands and feet and bathed her face with lavender water.

'I cannot eat. My belly aches,' she said, folding her hands over her stomach.

'A maid will bring you a hot stone wrapped in cloth for your pains and I'll send for a hot posset. You must attend the feast, Ailenor, if only for a while,' Nell said with sympathy creeping into her voice. 'The feasting is for the court, the clergy, and the people. You won't be expected to stay long.' Ailenor gratefully sipped the sweet drink when it arrived, then closed her eyes and dozed. When she woke up she was clutching the hot stone to her belly. She felt better and, to her surprise, a little hungry.

Smiling graciously, as she knew she must, Ailenor prepared to enter the hall. Her ladies fell into step behind and processed with her through the enormous doors. The hall was packed with nobles placed below the high table of state.

As trumpets sounded everyone rose to greet her and the King's steward led her to a throne-like chair beside Henry's. She sank onto a soft cushion for which she was thankful. Henry leaned over and whispered, 'You need not stay long, little queen. I have ordered refreshments to be sent to the great chamber for you and your ladies.'

'I shall stay awhile, my lord, and enjoy it too,' she replied brightly, despite longing to return to her apartments.

She found herself alert again as a striking dark-haired knight served them. A golden-headed page, almost as handsome as the knight, poured her wine. The knight had hair blacker than her own, glossy as a jackdaw's coat. He seemed mysterious and self-assured. He emanated confidence and power. He was charming. He was like Launcelot of the Lake.

'Your Grace,' the noble servitor said, 'may I offer you a portion of larks' tongues in aspic?'

She glanced up into the nobleman's dark brooding eyes and could not refuse, even though she had no real desire for larks' anything. She accepted the tiny pink things that looked like miniature mushrooms and using her eating knife pushed them to the side of her golden dish.

'Who is he?' she asked Henry in a low voice, as the knight moved along the table to stand behind Nell.

'Simon de Montfort-Amaury, a Frenchman.' Henry spoke into her ear. 'He's impoverished and not popular here but I like him. I'm going to make him Earl of Leicester one of these days. He's been petitioning me for the honour. Apparently he has a claim; thinks he's Leicester's rightful heir.'

Ailenor had no idea where or what Leicester was or about what claims there were. She asked an obvious question; at least she thought it such. 'Has he a wife?'

For an intake of breath, Henry frowned. 'No, he's unwed. If he serves us well, perhaps I can award him a countess when I make him an earl.' Henry smiled, his eyelid once again making him look as if he was winking at her. She laughed.

'You are delightful when you laugh, my queen, but I hope you laugh for me and not for Sir Simon. I shall have to send him to the Tower dungeons and have unmentionable things happen to him if he dares look your way.'

She took his hand and boldly raised it to her lips. 'My Henry,' she said. 'Only ever you, of course.'

A moment later she watched the handsome steward serving Nell. He was lifting a small gleaming fish onto her plate. He placed an adornment beside it, a posy of herbs tied with gold silk. Nell glanced up at the knight and smiled. Ailenor's heart fluttered for them both. *Could it be a token? Would Nell accept it?*

I am living in Camelot with my very own King Arthur and his knights. As Henry was distracted by a juggler who balanced plates on a pole wound round with golden ribbons, she lifted a chicken wing to her mouth. *Nell deserves her knight for she is kind and I must write a song about them. The knight desires a widow dressed in grey wool. But, he knows that she possesses the most beautiful smile of all the ladies at court, surpassing all the jewelled creatures dressed in furs, silks, and velvets dining here today. He tempts her away to a forest dell and wins her heart.*

Ailenor wanted to compose her song at once. She thought herself very clever having discovered what was possibly a secret love affair at court already. It was too sad. Just as in all the best love stories, his love would be unrequited because of the Princess's vow. She belongs to Christ. Yet how could she refuse such a fine knight? Ailenor turned away, tears in her eyes. *And I must not say anything for that would spoil it. There must be a way for them to love each other.*

She listened to musicians play an assortment of instruments as course after course of colourful platters circulated the hall and tried to forget the intrigue she had noticed. She liked the swan dressed in his feathers, and the boar's head with an apple in his snout that was pierced with cloves. She tasted a sliver of both. Finally, it was enough. If she stayed longer she would faint. She leaned over to Henry and tapped his arm. 'May I leave now, my lord? My ladies have not eaten a morsel. Domina Willelma has been standing for an hour.'

Henry nodded. 'Go, my sweet. I shall join you later.' *Did he intend to come to her after all?*

As she rose she glanced down at her cushion. It had felt soft and warm. The roses embroidered on it had golden hearts. Nell rose from her place. Ailenor noticed a silver plate with a fish spine and a posy of herbs and for a moment she forgot the cushion. Nell was smiling, though she left the posy on the table as she joined Ailenor. *So, I am right. Nell does like the dark knight.*

Halfway to the side door, Ailenor stopped. She said to one of her attendants, 'Lady Mary, could you fetch my pillow, for I would not want it to fall into the Lord Chamberlain's hands. The embroidery is exquisite.'

Nell said quietly, 'I know many of the royal embroiderers. I shall examine the stitching later.'

Lady Mary returned and Nell took possession of the cushion for Ailenor.

Once they reached her ante-chamber, Ailenor granted permission to her damsels to dine since they had not eaten all evening. They fell on the food laid out for them on a long table with the hunger of wild beasts, picking up morsels with their fingers, cramming pasties and little tarts into their mouths without ceremony. Yawning, Ailenor asked Nell and Willelma to prepare her for bed.

She was so exhausted; she thought she could sleep for a month. Even though she was tired, she waited for Henry's tap on her door. There was wine on the side coffer and a dish of honey cakes placed beside two small goblets. But Henry did not come that night. She was his queen. Had he forgotten her already? A tear fell onto her cheek. Turning to her pillow, she drifted into a lonely sleep, hugging the embroidered pillow to her chest.

In the morning, she realised her flowers had fallen and it was as well Henry had not come to her. She was spared embarrassment.

Henry apologised for not coming to bid her goodnight after the coronation. 'The nobles squabble like children,' he said when he visited her on the following morning. She lay in bed, feeling unwell. 'It's a tradition that the plate from the coronation feast goes to those who served us so I had to settle a dispute between two of my nobles over who could have our golden dishes.'

'I would have banished them both from my presence.'

'I said they could each have one and in return they must give me the weight in coin.'

'Will they?'

'If they don't I shall have a castle from each of them.' Henry was laughing. 'My nobles must obey their king.' She frowned. He lifted her hand and planted a kiss on it. 'And their little queen, too.' With a rustle of his mantle, he withdrew from her chamber, leaving her to the ministrations of her ladies.

The rain which had paused for the coronation fell with a vengeance during the following week. Ailenor's courses had come and gone and she shook off a melancholy that accompanied the fuss with rags and a soft belt to hold them in place. She ate and dwelled privately with her women.

On the eighth day, Henry burst into her ante-chamber where she and her ladies were reading poems together. He first asked her how she fared and looked down at her little book. 'We are moving back to the Tower. If these downpours continue we'll soon be flooded. It happens in the palace here. You will find many books to entertain you in the Tower. I have a library.' He looked concerned. 'Are you well enough to be moved.'

'Yes,' she said, as ever glad to see him. 'I am happy to go there.'

He smiled down on her. 'Then I am happy too.'

A day passed with the fuss of preparation to move out of the palace at Westminster. This time, rather than riding through the City, a royal barge carried her downstream. They passed under a great London bridge that was covered with tall buildings, their gables jutting over the river. She peered up through slanting rain.

Pointing up, she asked Nell, 'Do people live on that bridge?'

'Yes. Hold on to the boat rail. It can get rough as we shoot the tides under the bridge.'

'It's thrilling,' Ailenor said, peering all around her at the rushing murky waters, welcoming the expectation of danger. Life in a damp palace where all she did was stitch, sing ballads, and pray day after day was turning monotonous. It would be fun to shoot rapids.

'Not if you pass under as the tide surges in. This is nothing,' Nell warned.

Timing was precise. The boatmen understood the river's moods, particularly during heavy rains, and they knew the exact moment they could navigate forward. They passed safely beneath the bridge. Ailenor, who had held her breath, breathed evenly again as the barge arrived in calmer water.

Ailenor's apartments adjoined the King's own in the Wakefield Tower. It was a relief to return there where they had slept on their first night in the City. The weather was continually dreary with rain falling in sheets, rattling windows. Her scratchy woollen gowns felt damp. A musty smell clung to all her clothing no matter how much lavender her ladies used to make the garments smell sweet. She doubled over with laughter when Henry told her last time the rivers flooded Westminster his knights had had to ride their horses through great puddles to reach their chambers.

Here, safely in the Tower, she enjoyed a bedchamber freshly painted with a mural of summer roses and climbing vines. Her feather bed felt soft, its heavy curtains protecting her from draughts. Henry had prepared for his queen's arrival in England here, too. The decoration surpassed those in the palace at Westminster, where her bed had been so uncomfortable that after her coronation she was pleased to gift it to the Lord Chamberlain.

'Henry,' she said, delighted with her queenly apartment, 'I shall name this the Rose Chamber. Thank you.'

She spontaneously embraced him. He held her close and spun her around. His steward placed a gold goblet and silver platter with gold shields engraved on it on an enamelled table by the window.

'For you, Ailenor.'

'You must stop giving me presents. I have nothing more for you.'

'You give me your beauty, and you gave me Caesar.' He laughed. 'I shall show you my menagerie. I even have a creature called an elephant.'

He was watching her face closely for a reaction. She would not show the fear she felt. She clapped her hands. 'Show me. I'm not frightened of wild beasts, my lord.'

'Really, you are not? Lions – a polar bear that fishes in the river. You must see that, too.' He grinned. 'So, if you are not afraid, shall we affright your ladies?' he said with mischief in his eyes. 'Let us not prepare them.'

In that moment of understanding, she loved him. She longed to confront fear, because in confronting terrors it would make her a leader amongst women and a stronger queen and brave. She would be like one of King Arthur's fearless knights, like the dark knight who watched Nell. Though she never spoke of him to Nell or to

Henry, she was sure Nell liked him, too. *I shall watch and wait. They love each other yet they cannot declare that love.*

'Yes, let's surprise my damsels,' she said.

Some days after her ladies had seen the lion, shrieking and clutching each other in delight and fear, Ailenor asked Nell to discover the embroideress' whereabouts, the one who had embroidered her coronation cushion. Her damsels disliked the cold English winter. There were endless complaints. They needed distractions and a ferocious lion was not enough to interest them all. Nell told Ailenor the girl's name was Rosalind Fitzwilliam, and she was a tailor's daughter. The tailor, a wealthy widower, worked for Richard of Cornwall, Nell's own brother. It would be an easy matter to send Rosalind a request to come to the Tower and receive commissions.

Nell said, 'The family lives in the City, in Paternoster Lane, close to St Paul's.'

Ailenor peered out of the window down at the river. 'The rain has stopped, Nell. All is drying out. Send for her.' Ailenor thought for a moment. 'I want to learn some of her skills. Do you think she might teach me? The winter here is endless. My friends are bored. I want my women to remain with me. I want them to be busy and happy here.'

'I can see all this. Their faces are as long as winter's staff.' Nell glanced over at Willelma who was mending one of Ailenor's fragile veils. 'The girl would be honoured, I am sure. We shall ask her.'

Nell sent a royal messenger for Rosalind who, accompanied by her father, came to the Tower on the following Thursday. The tailor was a little plump and his hair was beginning to grey at the temples. Despite his stiff pose, Ailenor noticed how his eyes twinkled and liked him at once. He introduced his daughter and withdrew.

The quivering girl fell onto her knees in front of Ailenor's chair. She was small. Her plaits beneath her cap were golden, her skin white and clear, and the fingers clutching her simple gown long and delicate. Ailenor liked the English girl at once.

She glanced over at the long-nosed ladies who had accompanied her from Provence. She was tired of their complaints. Only that morning, one young lady had burst into tears and said she could not serve Ailenor any longer. Her sister needed her to help with their mother, who was unwell, and she missed her sister. Others followed suit with various grumbles. It was cold, which was untrue because her apartment was comfortable and fires burned constantly. When she pointed this out to them they found other complaints to make. The food was too heavy and they had little fruit except endless stewed apples. The gardens were soggy underfoot and without flowers. They were homesick and there was no fun to be enjoyed. Even the troubadours were forgetting to sing. England was dull. That morning, she had said firmly, 'There are earls' sons here without wives. They are very wealthy.'

Domina Willelma added with a frown, 'Where will you all find husbands if you return to Provence? You must be patient. Summer will come soon enough.'

Ailenor said with a snap in her voice, 'I have a mother and father and sisters, too. I am determined to be happy. You must be also.'

She would bring summer to them by creating rooms for them filled with beautiful fabrics displaying embroidered and woven images of stories and song. Her chambers would become their indoor gardens. She would create joy, even on the most miserable winter's day. Her ladies would forget Provence. And now she would encourage them to learn new embroidery techniques, but only if this girl who seemed so frightened of her would teach them. It would keep them busy.

She did not dare suggest to Henry that she hold courts of love in his hall as her mother, the Countess, had in Provence, or that her troubadours sing ballads of love and betrayal in case he disapproved. He watched over her with sharp eyes like one of the hawks that sat tethered to a perch in his bedchamber. At the coronation feast, she had admired Sir Simon. Henry had not liked that. It might be risky to upset him. Embroidering tales of love with silver and gold threads and with pearls and semi-precious stones might be a less treacherous occupation.

'Rise,' she said to the embroideress in stumbling English. 'Do you speak French?'

The girl scrambled awkwardly to her feet.

To her surprise, Rosalind spoke perfect French, '*Oui, ma grand-mère etait Français et aussi ma mère. I speak both French and English.*'

Ailenor clapped her hands. 'Bien. I intend to improve my English. I hear that it is occasionally spoken at court these days. I want to know what people say.' She smiled. 'Particularly if they think I cannot hear them. What is your name?'

'Rosalind, Your Grace. Rosalind Fitzwilliam.' Ailenor, of course, knew the girl's name but wanted to put her at ease.

'Do you know why you are here, Rosalind?'

'No . . . no . . . I do not, Your Grace. I -I . . .' The girl was tripping over her words.

Nell quietly intervened. 'There is no need to stumble over your words, Rosalind. The Queen won't devour you. We saw the King's elephant some days past and the beast was so big we were all afraid. It spat water like a fountain from its long, long nose. As if these rains have not brought us more than enough. And we heard the King's lions roar. There is something to truly affright you.'

There were chuckles from Ailenor's Provençal ladies. Ailenor stared sternly at them. Her mother had advised her to take no forward behaviour from her women. 'When you are a queen, Ailenor, begin the way you mean to go on. Take no nonsense from anyone.' Surely this laughter at the expense of a girl her own age, her subject, was unacceptable. She kept her gaze steady. The women dipped their heads to their embroidery frames. Domina Willelma spoke sharply in French to three of the Queen's ladies seated on stools. Their faces reddened as they composed themselves. Ailenor snapped her fingers at English Mary, her newest lady. Mary was sensible enough not to laugh in such a frivolous manner. She always displayed humility. She liked this wife of one of Henry's gentlemen of the bedchamber. 'Lady Mary, kindly bring me the cushion.'

The lady disappeared through a low door and reappeared with the rose-covered cushion. Ailenor held it out with both hands and said, 'Is this all your own work, Rosalind?'

'It is.' At last the embroideress appeared confident, as if on seeing her own familiar work she became a different person, a girl who knew who she was and that she possessed a unique talent. She smiled at Ailenor showing even white teeth. Her blue eyes widened.

Ailenor nodded. 'I can see you care about your work. Would you be able to embroider more? This is so fine. I would like four rose cushions, roses with golden hearts embroidered on velvet just like this one. How long will it take?'

The girl studied her embroidery for a few moments. She ran her hand over the silken roses. She did something Ailenor thought peculiar. She lifted the cushion to her nose and inhaled. 'It smells of attar of roses, the perfume I think you favour, Your Grace. They will take me a few months to stitch. It is detailed work.' In a halting voice, she added, 'But I'll need coin to purchase silks and velvet. Gold thread is expensive.'

'You shall have it. And if the King agrees, I may request hangings for my bed.' After she had spoken, Ailenor frowned. Already she had gleaned that, whilst the King was hard-pressed for money, their wedding had been expensive. There were whispers amongst Ailenor's English ladies that he was profligate and, on overhearing these murmurings, it occurred to her that the King had amassed great debts on her behalf. The coronation feast, the improvements on her apartments and the gifts he showered on her were extravagant. She found herself turning to Nell and saying, 'Princess Eleanor, will coin be released from His Grace's wardrobe, or may I have a loan, perhaps?' She loathed having to ask the King's sister this but her own allowance had not been settled. Biting her bottom lip, she blinked tears away. She was humiliated and should never have mentioned money. Rosalind glanced away. The girl was embarrassed, too.

Nell said, 'I shall see that Rosalind has a purse to purchase her threads and velvet. She will be paid for her work. Think nothing of it, Your Grace. It is a gift.'

28

'Thank you,' she said into the air which, for a heartbeat, had crackled with tension.

She promised herself to do Nell a service in return. And she knew exactly what. Nell must not remain prisoner to the ridiculous pledge made to Archbishop Edmund of Canterbury. She had once heard that such an oath made under duress could be annulled if His Holiness, the Pope, was generously approached. She would speak about Nell's oath to Henry. She must!

She smiled and said, 'Rosalind, return to us when your commission is completed. If we like the cushions, perhaps you will teach my Provençal ladies English embroidery.' She pointed at the embroidery frame by which her ladies sat. 'This embroidery shows Sir Galahad. Next, we plan to work on the story of Gawain. Do you know these stories?'

'Ballad singers tell them at our guild feasts.'

'They are thrilling tales,' Ailenor said with enthusiasm. 'Return soon.'

Nell ushered Rosalind towards the door into her bower-chamber. She overheard Nell say in a quiet voice, with discretion, 'I shall send you a purse to take care of all your needs. It is an honourable commission and more will follow. Attend it well, Rosalind.'

Rosalind nodded. 'I am honoured.' She added, with just a hint of hesitation, 'Does the Queen really want instruction in English work?'

'We shall see,'

Ailenor saw the Princess smile at the tailor, the girl's father, Master Alfred, who hovered by the doorway as Nell said, 'Good day, Rosalind. I shall send the purse to your father's house.'

A week later Henry swept through the maidens' chamber seeking Ailenor. She was discussing with Willelma about how the ladies would celebrate her birthday in the hour following Vespers. The pittancer had promised Willelma dates, candied oranges, and pears he had purveyed from Gascony, all of which he had kept aside from the coronation feast. When Henry approached Ailenor, she dipped a curtsey, all her damsels including her new English ladies following her lead.

'Rise, all of you.' He waved them away and took Ailenor's hands in his own. 'My love, I have not forgotten.'

She drew an excited breath. 'My name day,' she whispered. 'I am fourteen today.'

He withdrew a purse from his mantle and placed it into her hands. 'You must spend these sovereigns as you will, sweeting.' He leaned forward and removed her circlet and veil. He slipped a fine golden chain over her head. She glanced down. It contained a cut emerald set around with pearls. It was even more beautiful than the other jewels he had given her. It gleamed like the eyes of a magical sea creature and when she touched it, its facets as smooth as satin.

'It is too generous, my lord,' she said.

He shook his head. 'Once, long ago, it belonged to my mother. Like you, she is very beautiful.' For a heartbeat he looked sad. 'A pity she is far across the sea, but I have you and now you are more precious to me than she.'

Moments later he was gone. Ailenor gave the purse into Willelma's care. Now she had money of her own and her first thought was to pay Nell back for the loan she gave her.

Chapter Three

After Ailenor told him her ladies had felt homesick for Provence, Henry made more effort to make them happy. He welcomed her Provençal attendants into their retinue with smiles and attention, learning their names and addressing them personally. He especially welcomed her beloved Uncle William. Ailenor wrote to her mother, Countess Beatrice. She wrote to her sisters Marguerite and Sancha. Little Beatrice was still very young, so she sent her youngest sister a poppet for which she had stitched a gown just like one of her own.

Gradually, Ailenor accepted the changes in her own life. She liked the deference shown her by the English ladies in her train. She enjoyed sitting with Henry on feast days at the high table looking down on his stuffy barons. Nell was often in her company, as was Sir Simon and Richard of Cornwall whose wife was the great William Marshal's eldest daughter, Isabel. Ailenor considered Isabel possessed of an ethereal fragility. Sometimes as she watched how Isabel ate like a bird and moved light-footed as a wood nymph, she wondered if this older, beautiful woman would vanish like an angel, there one moment and the next not. Earl Richard's wife's countenance bore a sadness that caught at Ailenor's heart, though she never understood why Isabel was sad until Nell explained that Isabel had recently lost a child.

Although Ailenor's birthday had passed, intimacy had not yet come into her and Henry's marriage. Gradually, morsel by tiny morsel, she began to want more than a meeting of lips. She felt a weakness in her legs when he kissed her and she began to return his desire with a hunger for prolonged kisses, the sort priests disproved of. Women were Eves, temptresses, or else they imitated the Virgin and were mothers. Priests frowned upon desire. Could she ever dare hold a Court of Love here to pose the question – *why should a woman not feel desire?* No, she dared not; not whilst the frowning Archbishop Edmund visited them with a frequency that bothered Ailenor. Henry loved Edmund because he was a truly pious man, a piety Henry determined to emulate. Whilst her religious devotion – praying at shrines, learning about Henry's favoured saint, Edward the Confessor, giving alms to the poor, and endowing nunneries and chantries dedicated to the Virgin – was an honest display of piety because she *was* devout, priests' opinions on the subject of desire could not be the whole truth. She possessed a passionate, earthly nature and it confused her.

That winter, Ailenor, Henry, and Uncle William often dined privately together, discussing poetry, pilgrimage, and Jerusalem – the centre of the known world. Ailenor listened closely when they discussed Henry's finances and how he depended on a treasury ruled by his barons. When William recommended Savoyard administrators, able clerks whom Ailenor had brought to England in her train from Provence, to reform the Treasury, Henry agreed to try them. She encouraged him.

'Your uncle is knowledgeable and wise,' Henry said as they entered the Great Hall at Westminster one evening after Vespers. 'I hope he will stay with us.' Ailenor glanced across the hall to where her uncle was standing by a pillar surrounded by courtiers. They were all laughing and Uncle William seemed to be accepted by them. 'Indeed, I might find William a bishopric here,' Henry remarked. 'If he is not settled in Valence, Winchester could suit him. After all, he is only Bishop Elect of Valence.'

She said with excitement at Henry's suggestion, 'I think he would be pleased to consider Winchester. My mother's brothers are all knowledgeable but Uncle William is my favourite of them all.' The thought of having her favourite uncle by her side caused Ailenor's heart to leap as if a March hare was jumping about inside her. 'Please persuade him, Henry.'

Smiling, Henry folded his arms. 'He is a man of genius. I'll ask him.'

Ailenor felt herself grow taller. Her small chest puffed out with pride. She decided to chance her good fortune further. 'What about my ladies and my escort and my advisors and secretaries, my priests and doctors?'

Henry nodded. 'There's plenty of space in our castles for them all.'

'Thank you, my lord.' She threw her arms about his neck and he held her close.

'Grow up soon, my love,' he said into her hair.

'At my age my mother was chatelaine of many castles.'

'As are you.'

'But you know what I mean.'

'We shall give England a son soon enough. You are young for childbearing, my sweet. Too risky.'

She dropped her head and remained silent. It was difficult to say it to him but she was strong and she was sure she was ready to carry his son.

Her days passed pleasantly with dancing, feasting, and embroidery in the company of her new English retainers and all her friends from Savoy and Provence. The sun shone again. New growth sprouted on the trees around the Tower and flowers grew amongst herbs in the garden. Spring was filled with promise. Henry would love her completely soon. They walked in the garden hand in hand, prayed together, exchanged gentle kisses and shared a plate when the court set down to dinner.

In March, Rosalind brought Ailenor the embroidered cushions. Her father, Master Alfred the tailor, once again accompanied his daughter to the Tower. Learning that he was waiting out in the draughty corridor, Ailenor called him into her presence.

The tailor knelt before Ailenor and when she told him to rise, he stood to attention like a guardsman, straight-backed. She admired the new cushions and sent Willelma to place them on chairs and on her bed. Turning to Master Alfred she said, 'I need a tailor. You are a tailor. *Bien!* I want you to make me bed curtains and, you, Rosalind' – she smiled at the girl by his side – 'must embroider them with English flowers – marigolds, daisies, pansies, *une tapisserie* of flowers of fields and the woods.'

Master Alfred bowed, his greying hair falling untidily about his face. On coming up he smiled broadly, displaying a set of even teeth. 'It would be an honour, Your Grace. I'll need to measure your bed-rail.' He whipped a rule from out of a battered leather satchel.

Ailenor nodded at Lady Mary. 'Mary, assist him. You, too, Willelma.'

After they had pushed through the arras to the bedchamber, Ailenor turned to Rosalind. 'Let us wait in the window seat. I love to watch the river.'

The embroideress appeared ill at ease. She was awkward and unsmiling.

'Come.' Ailenor led the girl to a wide window bench. She said, 'Now, sit.'

Rosalind immediately moved to the other end of the bench as if Ailenor was about to cast a wicked spell on her. Yet, once seated, the embroideress seemed to relax and for a moment it felt as if they were simply two curious young girls idly viewing the world outside together. A gently warming thin March sun slanted through the glass. Soon, they became engrossed watching the many small boats bobbing up and down on the river below.

'It's huge,' Ailenor said after a brief silence. 'There are ships, docks, merchants, travellers, visitors from all corners of Christendom, so says my husband, the King.' She studied Rosalind whom she was sure was not much older than she. 'How many summers do you have, Rosalind?'

'I shall be fifteen soon.' She paused and added, 'My mother died when I was born. She was an embroideress too.'

She looked younger than Ailenor yet she was a year older. It was sad not to have a mother. Countess Beatrice was far away in Provence but she was alive and well and wrote to her daughter every month. 'I'm sure, Rosalind, your mother is an angel in Heaven watching over you. My mother said this when my grandmother, whom I loved dearly, died of the flux.' The next question slipped out. She had not intended to embarrass the girl. Tact was not her best attribute and sometimes, as when she had asked Nell about marriage, words tumbled from her mouth. 'Do you have a betrothed?'

Rosalind shifted on the widow seat, her face colouring. 'My father wishes me betrothed to Adam de Basing's son, Jonathan.'

'Do you mean the royal grocer who appoints tailors and dress-makers and buys spices and other goods for us? A good marriage. Your families would be matched in wealth.'

'My father believes so.' Rosalind dipped her head. She looked tearful.

'You don't wish to marry his son.'

Rosalind shook her head. 'I fear Jonathan's mother. And I've seen him kick dogs in the street for no reason. He is cruel.'

'Ah, is there another?' Ailenor said, clapping her hands, and almost but not entirely regretted her words.

The girl shook her head.

Ailenor was about to question her further, but instead she said, 'I can keep you very busy. My ladies need instruction in English embroidery. Could you attend me here once a week, well, maybe until we set off on our summer progress? Perhaps on a Monday?'

Rosalind brightened. 'I have hoped for this all winter. I have thought about it. But it is a distance from St Paul's steps to the Tower. My father would have concerns.'

'I'll send a boat for you and an escort. We shall pay you well.' She smiled to herself, recollecting her embarrassment over payment on the previous occasion Rosalind had come to her. On her birthday, Henry had settled an allowance on Ailenor as well as giving her a Master of the Wardrobe to organise her household and to her delight, she owned several river vessels and a larger merchant ship which would bring her goods from France. 'I'll speak to your father today if you're agreeable.'

'Thank you, Your Grace.'

'And I'll ask him to delay your betrothal for a year. Master Alfred cannot refuse his queen.' Rosalind's wide smile convinced Ailenor she had saved the girl from an unwanted courtship. There was a rustling from behind the arras. 'And here your father is returned to us.'

Alfred's pleased face appeared through the curtain followed by his plump body, his hand holding a knotted measuring rope.

'When will they be ready?'

He tugged at his beard as if considering this. 'They should be ready by Michaelmas.'

Ailenor nodded and drew a long breath. 'Master Alfred, I wish to learn the skills possessed by your daughter.' She swept her hand along her gown. 'Also I shall need my new gowns embellished. Rosalind might like to embroider these.'

Master Alfred's eyes twinkled with pleasure. 'Your Grace, we are honoured. As you may know, I am tailor to Earl Richard, the King's brother, and for my daughter to be an embroideress to the Queen is indeed a privilege.'

Ailenor judiciously hesitated as the bells for Nonce rang around the Tower. When they stopped clanging she said, 'Your daughter tells me she is to be betrothed. May I ask that this is delayed for a year whilst she is my embroiderer? Would this be agreeable to you?'

Ailenor noticed how the girl dropped her head as if she was studying the stout leather boots on her feet.

'Well.' He turned to Rosalind after a short silence. 'Would you like to embroider for Her Grace?'

Rosalind nodded and another heartbeat passed before she said with confidence, 'Yes, Papa, if you are happy to delay my betrothal, I am indeed content.' She turned her earnest eyes to Ailenor and smiled. 'Thank you, Your Grace. Thank you from the bottom of my heart.'

'In that case, Master Alfred, it is agreed.' Ailenor inclined her head momentarily. 'I'll send for your daughter on Monday next. She'll come by wherry to me, accompanied by a royal guard.'

Master Alfred beamed with pride.

Ailenor considered she had handled the likeable tailor well. Next time she met him, she must find more reasons to keep Rosalind safe from an unwanted betrothal. What would Queen Guinevere say were she listening from Heaven? She would approve. A queen is benevolent and always considerate towards her subjects.

The calends of May approached and with it plans were made for Henry to show her his kingdom, or a part of it. He promised to escort her to King Arthur's grave in Glastonbury. She could talk of nothing else for days and insisted they read stories of Arthur over and over. Together, she and Henry read French and Norman legends. They pored over painted illustrations in a book of stories and discussed them, growing closer and closer every day as spring tumbled towards summer.

The sun shone daily. The night sky was filled with brilliant stars. Each morning, she fed a blackbird that scratched at the thick glass window with its yellow beak, insisting she lifted the catch, push the window open, and place crumbs on the narrow ledge. As she crumbled a piece of manchet loaf and indulged the persistent creature Ailenor mused to herself. Henry loved her and she loved him back. They were Arthur and Guinevere.

She climbed from her bed on May Day filled with anticipation as the journey drew nearer. Somewhere beyond the wall a cockerel crowed. Church bells rang for Prime. Ailenor spun around and around making herself dizzy until she had to stop. She valued this early morning time to herself without her damsels. Her gowns hung on rails in an annexe to her bedchamber. What could she wear this May Day? How could she *ever* possibly wear all of these satins, velvets, and fine woollen gowns in so many lovely colours and trimmed with embroidery and fur? How could she choose?

She stared at the rails and muttered, 'I hope I don't grow taller before I've worn them, or wider.' She touched her budding breasts. 'They are growing. That is good and bad both. Good as Henry will desire me, but it's bad because my gowns will soon be too tight.'

Glancing towards her door, she convinced herself she heard

Domina Willelma's steady snores. On an impulse she dragged out gown after gown and held each up to herself. She had never possessed such luxury, never in Provence, nor such jewels.

She allowed gown after gown to drop onto her bed and spill onto the carpet, covering the floor straw. As the sun's rays slanted through her high glass window, bathing them with summer light, their hems shone with jewel colours.

Her own embroidery lessons had begun that spring. Each Monday, Rosalind had been ferried along the river from St Paul's, east to the Tower or west to the Palace, when she taught Ailenor and her ladies English embroidery. Often she embellished the Queen's gowns with gold and silver threads stitched into birds, flowers, and tendrils with woodland leaves. Ailenor decorated belts and purses and took pleasure in her own skill. These joined the pile on the bed and floor. How can I decide; I cannot. They are all beautiful.

Pushing open her window, Ailenor thrust her head out. No waiting blackbird yet. Glancing downriver towards the great bridge she watched a pair of swans gliding towards her. They mate for life, she thought to herself. 'It will be so for Henry and me too.'

A sharp voice cut across the room. '*Diable*, Your Grace, come away from that window at once. You will catch a chill.' Then, 'What by the Sainted Virgin is this?'

Ailenor spun around to see a horrified Willelma staring at the piles of damask, silk, and woollen gowns. Her other ladies were trying to conceal laughter behind raised hands.

She snapped, 'Mary, close the window. Sybil, help me into my crimson gown.'

Willelma lifted the gown before Lady Sybil could reach it. Holding it up, she said to Ailenor, 'A messenger came from the King. He wishes to discuss the summer progress with Your Grace, after you have broken your fast.'

'I must not keep my husband waiting. Sybil, please fetch my sleeves, the pair with the gold heartsease flowers I embroidered myself, and a belt to wear with my gown.' She turned away from Willelma. Her senior lady would not treat her as if she were still a child in her father's

38

court. She was a queen and a married woman. Provence was becoming a memory.

A yellow sun shone from a sapphire sky on the morning they set out on the summer progress. Ailenor sat erect on her grey palfrey, Bella, impatient for them to begin their journey. Pennants and banners – her banners and Henry's entwined – flew in the breeze, displaying griffins, dragons, and golden lions. She anticipated their journey west, pausing at various important castles and manors on the way. Henry wished to introduce the people of England to his queen. Once they visited King Arthur's grave at Glastonbury, they would ride to Gloucester and turn east into the Midlands before returning to London. He had sounded out strange names she had never heard of such as Thame, Watlington, Wallingford, and Stroud, Berkshire, Wiltshire, Somerset, and Gloucestershire, held her close and told her he loved her.

She glanced back at the sumpter carts in which her collection of leather coffers were filled to the brim with silks and velvets, soft shoes and boots, delicate veils, sarsinette fillets, and golden crespines; another containing belts and gloves; a box of jewels and a collection of mantles, all variously trimmed with embroidery, marten fur, squirrel, and ermine.

Ailenor nudged Bella towards Earl Richard and Lady Isabel, who were already in position a little behind her. As the creature skittered about, Isabel was desperately clutching her reins. Richard had not noticed his wife's attempts to control her mare.

Simon de Montfort, dark hair flopping onto his forehead, rushed across the swathe to her sister-in-law's aid. His blue surcoat, which was slit down the sides, flapped about his colt-like long legs as he slipped around horses and carts. After he righted Isabel's mare, he moved towards Nell who was ushering a group of chattering maids into a line of painted wooden carriages. Nell wove her way through stable boys, carriages, and courtiers to her own palfrey. Sir Simon called out, 'Lady Eleanor, may I assist you to mount?'

Nell was smiling. Ailenor strained to listen but with the hubbub about them she could not hear Nell's reply. Even so she observed how Nell blushed as Sir Simon helped her onto her mare. How sad that Nell still wore dull colours whilst he was vivid in silk the colour of sky. Such a shame, for Nell possessed a beautiful face, her violet eyes shining. A small section of dark hair showed on her forehead beneath a plain white linen wimple.

Ever since Ailenor's Coronation in January, Simon had sought out Nell's company. On Candlemas Day Ailenor had watched as they walked together through the Abbey Nave at Westminster, solemnly holding candles lit for remembrance. On the feast of the Annunciation she observed how the tall, dark knight sat next to Nell. He amused them both with stories of his youth in France. At Eastertide he persuaded them to laugh at the glee-men and acrobats as they performed at the Easter Day feast in the hall at Westminster. Nell confided that day, 'He brightens my colourless existence.'

It was sad, Ailenor thought, that Henry's youngest sister was confined by a cruel promise. As their friendship grew she had learned how the vow had come about. Nell was persuaded by her friend, Cecily, to take an oath of chastity after her husband died. Ailenor was sure this ridiculous oath could be reversed because it was a promise made under duress. Nell and Sir Simon were destined for each other. Widows could choose a second husband for themselves, except Nell for whom marriage would be a matter of state. Ailenor never dared to confess her suspicions to Henry. He was the most devout man at court, but if Nell and Simon sought each other's company he would notice too. Already rumours were flying about the court concerning Simon's attentions to Nell. Uncle William had reported these to her with disapproval in his tone. It was only a matter of time before he spoke to Henry. If only she could help Nell and Simon, for surely they were in love . . .

Moments later, horns sounded. With a jingling of bells, they were away. Ailenor looked out for Sir Simon's dark head but he had already vanished. For certes, he would be riding with the King's men, guarding the rear. She kicked Bella's flanks and took her place beside Henry.

★

40

They rode in a carefree manner through lanes with hedgerows fat with hawthorn blossom and alongside verges smothered with celandine and primroses. Clumps of bluebells edged the woodlands. Lines of swifts criss-crossed the skies above the trees. The scent of fresh grass lingered in fields. When they entered villages, children sang and threw flowers at them. Ailenor opened her belt purse and, to the children's obvious delight, threw pennies back. The countryside, the jongleurs accompanying them with song, the pennants, the heralds, and the promise of several days hawking at Wallingford Castle where Earl Richard would host a great feast, lifted her mood into soaring heights. As they jogged along she became possessed by a mission. Nell must be persuaded to wear brighter colours this summer. Nell must be as happy as she herself was. Nell must marry the admiring knight.

All had been prepared for their arrival at Wallingford by Richard's steward. Shortly after they dined on their first afternoon, Ailenor and Nell seized a few moments of privacy. They chose a garden seat amongst cherry trees where they thought none would disturb them. For a while they sat in companionable silence watching tiny finches flit in and out of the foliage that climbed the castle wall.

'It will be a fine day tomorrow for the hunt,' Ailenor said after a while. 'Do you think . . .' She hesitated and lowered her voice further so her ladies could not hear her, though she need not have worried for the ladies were distracted by a troubadour who was playing his viol for them across the garden. '. . . I mean, do you think . . . listen, Nell, look, I have an idea. Could I persuade you to wear one of my gowns at tomorrow's feast?' There, she had been impertinent again and had spoken too impulsively. 'Nothing extravagant but something different to your grey tunics and gowns; a change.' Nell opened her mouth and Ailenor raced on. She couldn't help it. 'No, don't refuse. I was thinking of a deep blue silk I possess with a low-slung belt and a little jewelled dagger. I want you to have it. And, just think how it will send the bishops the message you have no intention of entering the cloister.' It was true. Nell had complained to her that just because she had taken a vow of chastity some bishops thought she should enter a nunnery and become an abbess. One such was William, Ailenor's uncle.

Quietly, Nell said, 'I promised to remain chaste but not to wear grey for the rest of my life.' For a moment, Ailenor and Nell both studied a pair of jackdaws as they flew cackling into the air like black cut-out shapes, stark against a deepening sunset. The birds hovered by the tall walls that edged the garden before roosting in a sweet chestnut tree.

Nell spoke again. 'If Henry sees that I am determined to embrace the world this summer, if I give up drab garments, for instance, he might recognise my need for a castle of my own as well as the fact I have no calling to the cloister. The Marshals have never granted me my widow's third portion and Henry is in possession of many lands belonging rightfully to my estate. Of course, he says he will look after me for the rest of my life and why would I want to be saddled with castles of my own.' She sighed. 'Ailenor, I do want my own manor. Henry does not need me at court as his first lady now he has his queen. Everything has changed.' Tears filled Nell's violet eyes. 'I want my own lands, to be independent, to be me.'

Ailenor touched her friend's hand and tried hard to understand Nell's longing for a castle of her own. It was the first time Nell had spoken of a longing for her own estates. If Nell left court she might miss her, Ailenor realised. She must not be selfish, and if Nell married her knight as she planned Nell could be mistress of her own castles. She had vowed to herself to help Nell return to the world and she determined to keep that promise. Ailenor's heart jumped when Nell added, 'And, Ailenor, I might discover that moment this summer to ask Henry for my own demesne.'

Ailenor had thought Nell was about to say she might discover love this summer. She took Nell's hand. 'I shall ensure that Henry lends you his support.'

'Thank you. I hope he listens.'

Isabel was gliding along a pathway toward them, faery-like, in that floating way she possessed. 'The blue gown?' Ailenor said in a very low tone.

'Yes,' Nell said. She squeezed Ailenor's hand and they stopped talking.

'Would you like to dine tonight in my bower?' Isabel asked when she reached them. 'The men are feasting in the Hall, where they are planning and scheming goodness only knows what. It will be the hunt tomorrow, I am sure. Are you both hungry?'

'Very much so,' Ailenor said, rising from the garden bench.

Domina Willelma, who had been overseeing Ailenor's unpacking, joined the ladies for supper. Isabel's ladies welcomed her and Ailenor's dwarf page, Jacques, begging him for rhymes and riddles, for Jacques was a wit.

'It's been long since the dinner hour. I'll have supper sent up at once.' Isabel hurried two of her maids to the kitchens.

The musician strummed on his viol. A trestle appeared, and a table covering, napkins were laid, spoons set out on the table, and benches drawn up. Dishes began to arrive as the ladies chose their places – eggs and rice in saffron, lampreys, fruits, cream, cheeses, and soft white rolls. When jugs of cider arrived, Ailenor, who refused the top place and ceded it to Isabel, exclaimed, 'It is just as it was in Provence, informal suppers and afternoon dining out in our gardens, fine weather and good company. Do not wait on ceremony because of me. We are all friends here.' She leaned towards her hostess. 'Thank you, Lady Isabel, thank you for your hospitality. I am honoured because you have made us welcome.'

'And why would I not?' Isabel said, her voice quiet, though there was no true enthusiasm in it.

Ailenor felt in her heart that Isabel, so delicate and so much older than she, ten years older than Richard, old as her own mother, Countess Beatrice, had not warmed to her yet. She determined to try harder to win her English ladies' hearts. It was not just Isabel who never betrayed her feelings but seemed distant. Apart from Mary and possibly Sybil, many were cool towards her. She thought it was because the ladies' husbands, the King's earls and barons, were unhappy with Henry. He could not see it, but Ailenor could. She wondered if they disliked Uncle William and some of her ladies from Provence too – well, apart from Willelma, whom clearly they did like. They enjoyed Jacques, of course, who entertained them, but he was lowly. They looked down their noses at the Alyses, Yolandes, and Christines who had accompanied her from Provence.

She longed to smooth the troubled waters caused by Henry's over-indulgence towards her attendants and his particular love for her uncle. She wanted her own people close. She wanted positions at court for them, but equally she did not wish to antagonise these difficult, powerful English lords. Henry needed their approval and their wealth because he liked to spend money on the feasts and pageants he held on saints' holidays.

Henry had told her what Earl Richard had said before they set out on the progress, " 'You will displease the London guildsmen and merchants, never mind the earls. You are favouring the Provençals. That does not sit well with the Barons' Council.' "

'And I said,' Henry retorted peevishly to her, ' "I shall choose my own companions." The Barons have tried to bully me ever since I was a youth. They are dullards. They will not get the better of me as they did my father. Richard is the wealthiest man in the kingdom and I shall make sure he spends a deal of his wealth on us this summer.'

Isabel, who was perhaps unaware of this earlier exchange between her husband and his brother, folded her hands with elegance, long fingers overlapping long fingers, and thanked Ailenor for honouring the castle with her presence.

Ailenor bowed her head to Isabel and as Isabel was instructing a servitor, turned to Nell, 'Are you riding with us tomorrow to the hunt, Nell?'

'I have my sparrow hawk, Sky-Lightning, with me.'

'Lady Isabel? Are you coming to ride and hunt?' Isabel had finished with the servitor. She looked tired, her eyes dull, and Ailenor wondered if she was with child. In Provence she had often seen women so, pale and listless in the early months. Her mother had warned her to be prepared for such feelings herself when her time came.

'No, Ailenor, I must oversee the preparations for tomorrow's feast.'

'You will be missed from our company, my lady.' She thought again of Nell and Simon de Montfort and immediately thought up another ploy to encourage romance between them. She looked right into Nell's eyes with as much innocent guile as she could summon up. 'I wonder, Nell, if you could be persuaded to play for us tomorrow night? Henry says you know many ballads, songs of *the greenwood*. I want to know more of this place.'

Nell shook her head. 'I cannot.'

Isabel smiled. 'What a good suggestion. Nell, you sing like a nightingale. I can provide a harp. I heard you long ago when you were married to William . . .' She paused. 'Never since,' she added.

'But if I have forgotten the words?'

Ailenor reached over the trestle and took Nell's hands. 'I am sure you will sing beautifully. If you forget words, just hum. That's what I do.'

She lightly clapped her hands and all the other ladies began to say, 'Please sing for us, Lady Eleanor. You must. We can practise after supper.'

'Bring me your harp, Isabel.' At last Nell agreed and smiled. Ailenor felt happy at her success in helping Nell back into the world. She scolded Jacques who had squeezed in beside her, telling him he must behave when Lady Eleanor sang for them all.

The next day, Ailenor and Nell rode out to the forest hunt side by side. Nell was a patient and calm huntswoman. Ailenor knew she could learn much from her. Whilst hunting, she must curb her own impatience because that way her own little hawk, Arrow, would become a better huntress.

The squires let loose small birds to tempt the hawks into the sky amongst the trees. Ailenor observed as Nell spoke gently to Sky-Lightning and up the hawk soared, high into the blue, above beeches, ash trees, oaks, and, when it reached a small lake, it captured its prey and descended towards them again in a graceful arc.

Sir Simon, who had been riding close to them all afternoon, twisted his black stallion around to face their mares. 'Well sent, my lady. I think you have a brace of thrushes for the kitchen.'

'Thank you, Sir Simon. She is a good hawk and shall be rewarded.'

Their falconer produced a dead mouse from his sack.

Ailenor said, 'Next time, my kill.'

'Can such a lovely lady kill?' Sir Simon asked.

'If I have to, yes.'

'I hope, in that event, I am far away.'

'Huh!' Ailenor laughed and rode ahead with Henry and Richard, leaving Nell to Simon's company. She cantered off to send her sparrow-hawk into the skies. This time she was successful. Soon she'd bagged a hermitage of thrushes and two wood pigeons. Her patience had been rewarded. All the way back to the castle, Nell, Henry, and Simon praised her sparrow-hawk. She beamed with pride and satisfaction.

'Henry,' she said, when she was alone with her husband. 'I think Nell is happier than I have seen her all spring.'

Henry poured her a cup of Rhenish wine. 'My brother serves good wine. We should visit him more often. What was it you just said?'

'Nell's an excellent huntswoman and she was laughing with Sir Simon, the whole way back to the castle.'

'Oh, was she? Interesting. Richard mentioned how our sister has changed. It's your influence, Ailenor. A joyful court makes for happy courtiers.'

'My people are content but I am not so sure about your people.' She saw his frown and moved their conversation back into safer territory. She played with the stem of her glass goblet and said with deliberate nonchalance, 'Nell has agreed to sing for us tonight.'

Henry started, nearly spilling his wine. 'It is a long time since my sister sang for anyone. If only she did not insist on wearing those dowdy colours. If only she had not taken that vow I could have made a splendid marriage for her. Bring coin into my coffers, castles into my sphere of influence, make an alliance. I could have found her a rich Spaniard.'

46

'A Spaniard would request a large dowry,' Ailenor said quickly. 'It was fortunate that I did not have to bring you one.'

Henry set his goblet on a table. 'No, it is I who was fortunate to find myself a sweet wife.' He reached out, removed her veil, and released her hair from its clasp. It tumbled to her waist. He began to draw his fingers slowly through it, a sensation she found soothing.

She smiled. Now was a good time to make her request.

'I think Nell would like to remain in England and if she could renounce her vow, you should marry her to one of your earls, to one with influence, to keep him loyal to us and through him others.'

'What a diplomat you are, Ailenor. A *petit* schemer too.'

'No, I speak sense.' She twisted her head to look up into his eyes.

He pulled her onto his knee. 'Richard thinks Nell should have her own castle. I hold lands that belonged to her dowry. The Marshals hold even more.' He smiled a benevolent smile. She was winning. 'Nell is my favourite sister,' he said. 'I shall grant her a castle, just in case we can dispense with that foolish vow.'

This was more than Ailenor had hoped. 'I think she was forced into it by Lady Cecily,' she said, careful not to mention Archbishop Edmund at all.

'I never liked that dowdy woman. Interfering dried-out stick of a wench.' Henry stood up and tumbled Ailenor from his knee. She steadied her balance, lifted her head, and kissed him on the mouth.

'Maybe we can do something about the vow.'

He raised his brow and frowned. Best leave it for now, she thought.

Gathering her loose hair into her hands she twisted it carefully and stuffed it into her crispinette which she snapped shut at the nape of her neck. She deftly replaced her veil and coronet. With a swirl of crimson silk mantle and green sarsinet they swept from their chambers, down the stairway, and into the Hall for the feast.

When Nell sat with her harp across her knee, Isabel turned to Ailenor, '*Belle*. She is beautiful. How did you persuade her to wear that silk tunic and a little jewelled dagger on her belt? *Bien*! Perfect.'

'I made her a gift of it.'

'Look at the admiring glances she is receiving. Tonight, your courtiers are her loyal knights.'

'They are, and she sings like a nightingale.'

'She would never lack suitors if she was free,' Isabel said. 'She was forced into that vow by her silly friend Cecily and Archbishop Edmund.'

'I heard.' Ailenor inclined her head to Isabel, whom she could not yet decide was friend or foe. She glanced along the table at Sir Simon. He was watching Nell with admiration as she sang a ballad in perfect pitch. Ailenor felt a shiver, as if the future was whispering a warning to her. *No, no, go away, shades of the night-time, be gone. Simon is a perfect knight, our friend, a loyal knight who would never become an enemy.*

There was a calculating gleam in his dark eyes as he watched Nell. A strange presentiment made Ailenor shudder. Simon's father had been responsible for the deaths of thousands of innocents, men, women, and children in Carcassonne. Cathars they were called, heretics, but children too; her father had once said *innocent children who never deserved such cruelty*. She knew, as she watched him watching Nell, that Simon, like his father, could also be a dangerous man. Simon was charming but what if his charm concealed a hardened nature? What if he ever became an enemy? Papa always said, *Keep your friends close and your enemies closer*. Would Simon of Montfort-Amaury ever become an enemy, because if he did, he would be formidable.

Walking through the cloisters at Glastonbury, Ailenor said to Nell, 'When we return to London, you are to have your own castle. It is to be Odiham. Is Odiham near London?' She looked into Nell's beautiful eyes. 'Dear Nell, I hope if you live there, you come to visit me often.' She glanced at her feet. 'Don't tell Henry that I have told you.'

Nell hugged her. 'Odiham! Mine? Truly? It is all I have wished for. It is almost an equal distance between Winchester and Windsor.'

The joy in Nell's eyes gave Ailenor even more pleasure than their visit on the previous day to King Arthur's grave. At once she decided on a project, another plan. Nell must have fabrics for her castle and new clothes for herself too. She would have colourful belts and golden crispinettes. And perhaps the embroideress, Rosalind, could design a cover for her bed and hangings for her garderobe.

Nell drew a breath. 'Ailenor, is this your doing?'

'I believe Richard requested this for you. I only said you would like it. Do you?'

'Very much.' Nell grasped Ailenor's hands. 'You must come for a feast on my saint's day.' She spun around. 'And I shall wear colours every day.'

'When is your saint's day, Nell?'

'My name day is the twenty-second day of November, the feast of St Cecilia.'

'The saint of music. It's only right.' Ailenor clasped her hands in delight at this jewel of information.

'Let's look at King Arthur's grave again.' Nell slipped Ailenor's arm through her own. Ailenor knew she had given Nell almost the best news she could ever give her.

In a companionable silence, their ladies trailing behind, they approached the grassy mound where King Arthur lay sleeping with his queen, Guinevere. Ailenor felt sure that now Nell would renounce her vow and marry Sir Simon. He would not be a popular choice with the barons but, even so, she sensed the glossy dark-haired knight's value to the throne.

She would nurture Sir Simon. If Ailenor had learned anything from her father, Count Raymond, it was diplomacy and a firm handling of his nobles.

Chapter Four

Rosalind
London, 1237

Rosalind's Papa was betrothed to a wealthy widow. Papa was in love. Not only did Rosalind want Papa to be content but she liked the twenty-eight-year-old widow, Dame Mildred, who was lively, kind, and pleasing company, perfect for Papa, perfect for both of them since Rosalind had a plan of her own for her future.

A blustery wind rattled the shutters of Rosalind's attic chamber. Holding her shutters ajar, peering out of her window at a storm that was whipping up leaves and shaking the wooden fence in the yard below, she wondered anxiously if Dame Mildred would cross the City that afternoon in such stormy weather. She slammed her shutters and secured them. Mildred must come. I have to tell them once they set a date for the wedding.

Cook was preparing a celebration dinner, selecting Papa's favourite dishes. The scent of ginger for the pork, mint for the lamb, and roasting meats drifted upstairs from the kitchen. She brushed her hair until it shone. Rosalind had turned fifteen and since the Queen regularly called her to court when she was at Westminster or resident in the Tower, Rosalind felt a new independence. She grew confident and wore her prettiest gowns when attending court. Sir Simon de Montfort's squire, Thomas, was waylaying her by the steps at Westminster Pier to help her from the wherry. They exchanged pleasantries when the handsome golden-headed squire accompanied her to the Queen's apartments.

Occasionally Papa reminded her, 'Adam de Basing will betroth his son to another if we hesitate too long. You cannot delay for ever. Anything could happen and this is such a good match. You will inherit the business once I am gone.'

She would say, 'The Queen needs me. I have gowns to embroider and I teach her damsels. I cannot leave her yet, Papa.'

Now that Papa and Dame Mildred anticipated their wedding day, all talk of Rosalind's betrothal was forgotten. Papa had met Dame Mildred in the spring of 1237. By autumn he was besotted. Rosalind smiled to remember how this had come about. Queen Ailenor had commissioned her to work on a coverlet for the King's sister. Princess Eleanor had removed from court to the castle of Odiham in Hampshire and needed new cushions, bed coverings, and hangings. When Rosalind returned to the Tower with the completed bedspread and Alfred with the curtains, they met Dame Mildred, who was trimming one of Queen Ailenor's gowns with crimson silk. Whilst Rosalind had withdrawn with the Queen to discuss further commissions, Mildred and Alfred fell into their own conversation.

On their return to Paternoster Lane, Alfred said, 'I promised Dame Mildred I would go to her Threadneedle Street workshop for trimmings.' His voice was somewhat coy. 'And you must purchase threads from Dame Mildred for *your* commissions.' Rosalind started at this request but nodded, keen to please Papa, whom she loved with all her heart.

After a few visits to Threadneedle Street that summer, Rosalind could see the widow, though plain of face and of middling stature for a woman, was of a good humour, sanguine and pleasant company, always fastidious, neat, and bird-like. In fact, when Dame Mildred smiled she was exceedingly attractive. She owned a thriving haberdashery trade. She was the perfect new wife for Papa. By September, Alfred announced he liked the buxom young widow enough to provide Rosalind with a mother. After all, he said in a confidential tone,

51

Mildred had inherited her deceased husband's excellent business. She had no children of her own. 'I hope to right this.'

'I hope so too, Papa,' Rosalind said, and gave her father a pleased smile.

Despite Rosalind's worried looks onto the windswept street below, Widow Mildred arrived with her maid in time for dinner.

'What a rushing kind of day,' she said as she threw off her mantle and took her satchel from her maid, shaking her head and saying, 'I am afraid we must stay the night, Rosalind. Can your housekeeper make up a spare chamber for us, do you think? Would you mind?'

'Of course not, Dame Mildred. You are most welcome.' Rosalind turned to see her Papa hurrying towards them from his workshop. 'Dame Mildred will be stopping tonight, Papa,' she called to him.

'Good, good. Tell Jane to make up the chamber behind the hall. It'll be warmer there.' He opened his arms and hands in an expressive gesture. 'Mildred, welcome, welcome, my dearest.' He planted kisses on both her cheeks. 'Your maid can share with our Jane tonight.' Releasing her hands, he winked. Blushing with embarrassment for her father, Rosalind clasped Dame Mildred's cloak to her, turned her back on the pair of turtle doves, hung it on a peg and sent Dame Mildred's maid scuttling off to instruct Jane, their housekeeper.

'I have something for you all,' the kindly Dame said as she produced a selection of small gifts, edible sugary fruit comfits, and sticks of barley sugar laid out in a row on a bed of dried camomile in a cedar box. 'For you, Alfred. You have such a sweet tooth.' She handed Rosalind a jar. 'From my own peach trees. I put them aside myself in August using my great-grandmother's recipe.'

'We shall enjoy them after dinner today,' Rosalind said and called for a maid to take them to Cook.

'Do give her this purse.' Mildred dipped into her cavernous satchel and smiled a broad smile. 'She is truly an excellent cook, Alfred.'

Rosalind squealed her delight when Dame Mildred made much of her, hugged her with affection, and presented her with a present of silver scissors and crimson and green ribbons for her hair. Would Thomas notice if she wore the ribbons in her long fair plait so they peeped prettily beneath her cap?

'Bring us mead, Rosalind, my love,' Papa said, interrupting her thoughts. 'We are celebrating.'

Affectionate greetings over and cups of sweet mead shared by the hearth, they sat down to dinner. By the third hour following Nonce, candles were lit, their glow lending softness to the hall's perpendicular angles, catching at the gold stitching on their wall hangings and causing the threads to shine, smoothing away wrinkles and allowing Albert and Mildred to appear youthful. The fire crackled and despite rain pounding against the closed shutters they were comfortable and dry.

Dame Mildred laughed in a pleasant manner, played with her spoon, and occasionally lifted dainty morsels of meat to her mouth. As they ate a savoury stew she recounted stories of her trading successes at London's Michaelmas Fair. Papa listened with total concentration until, too soon, he turned his full attention to his plate.

It was true, the food Rosalind had planned so carefully was delicious. Onions swam in a honeyed sauce. The mutton was soft. Cook had indeed surpassed herself tonight. The roast pork was served with a crisp golden crackling. Rosalind relaxed, listening with interest to an amusing description of a Frenchman who wanted yellow ribbons for his hat, and who pranced about Dame Mildred's stall in the Cheape, proud as a gander, but a gander, she said, that kept changing his mind. Rosalind felt herself frowning. Papa had not listened to a word of this story. Worse, his chin glistened with grease. Rosalind felt herself narrow her eyes. What if Dame Mildred thought Papa ill-mannered and course? What if Dame Mildred changed her mind?

Glancing from Dame Mildred to Papa, who was slowly moving another spoonful of gravy towards his mouth, Rosalind lifted her napkin and pointedly dabbed at her chin. Dame Mildred caught her eye. Amusement twitching about Dame Mildred's mouth, she lifted her napkin emphatically from her shoulder. Alfred moved another overfilled spoon, spilling the mutton gravy towards his mouth.

'Rosalind, we are decided on a Christmastide wedding. We'll celebrate throughout the twelve days.'

Another dribble of gravy oozed into his pointed beard.

Mildred leaned over and dabbed at Alfred's offending chin with her napkin. 'As you wish, my dear. Plenty of time. It is only October, after all.' She turned to Rosalind. 'What think you, Rosalind?'

'Cook will want to begin planning for a wedding straight away.' She must, thought Rosalind to herself. Ingredients for the feasting must be ordered now and baking begun. Aloud she added, 'The apprentices will be happy too. They enjoy festivals.'

Rosalind breathed evenly again. The Dame could have attracted any number of suitors but she'd chosen her plain-spoken papa. Now Rosalind would be free to take up the offer the Queen had made to her, an embroidery workshop of her own at Westminster. Once Papa and Dame Mildred were wed, she would be free to accept the Queen's proposal. The palace beckoned and with her father settled there could be no reason why she could not accept. The King, the Queen had confided, was so impressed with Rosalind's fine gold embroidery, he might even request a new altar cloth for one of his castle chapels.

'Windsor, I think,' the Queen had said. 'And I shall need you to stitch gold and silver thread and jewels, mostly pearls, onto my gowns.'

Rosalind pushed away her platter. She must tell them her news at once.

'My apprentices will be delighted if we marry at Christmas,' Dame Mildred was saying. 'I can see our union will be a large and joyful occasion for all of us, both our households.' Then, to her horror, just as she opened her mouth to reveal the Queen's proposition, Dame Mildred said, 'And, we must think about you, Rosalind.'

Papa nodded. 'Indeed. The de Basings . . .'

'No, I cannot.' Rosalind bit her lip so hard, she tasted blood. She studied Dame Mildred's face. Was the kindly widow trying to rid herself of her – but Mildred's face was innocent. 'No, Papa,' Rosalind said firmly glaring at her papa. 'The Queen needs me. It is an honour to please her. She liked the embroidered cushions last year. She is pleased with the bed-cover for the King's sister. She has commissioned more hangings for her bedchamber at Windsor.' She turned back to Mildred willing her support. 'Dame Mildred, I am too busy to be betrothed.'

Mildred reached over and patted her hand. 'No one should rush you. I only meant . . .' Rosalind breathed steadily again. Mildred's face was filled with concern. 'I was thoughtless. With my threads and trims added to your tailoring; with Rosalind's commissions, never mind all the other work you have, Alfred, why would you rush her to the church?' Rosalind breathed more easily. She smiled over at Mildred and nodded.

'Papa, I must accept the Queen's commissions.'

Papa shook his head at her. 'Rosalind, tell the maid to bring in the pies, cheese, and the preserved peaches. We'll say no more about it.'

Rosalind rose from the bench and sped with a lighter heart into the kitchen annex off the Hall. There was more to say because it was not over yet. She must tell them her latest news.

The maidservant served up a platter of cheese, figs, raisins, and the peaches and they began to eat again.

Rosalind drew a deep breath. 'There is something else, Papa.'

'Oh, and what is that, pray?'

'I have been offered a great honour by the Queen.' Two pairs of inquisitive eyes darted up from the figs.

She nervously twisted a ring – her mother's – a ring with a tiny amber stone. She stopped turning it and said, 'The Queen wants me to take charge of her embroidery workshop at Westminster. I shall have a dozen embroiderers.' This information was an exaggeration. 'We are to create altar cloths and other church items.' A further exaggeration. This additional detail only had a passing mention from the Queen. 'The King himself has commended my work. I shall be doing God's work.'

'You wish to accept?' Mildred asked gently.

Alfred frowned. 'Altar cloths are nun's work. I need Rosalind here.'

'No you don't. She could lose the Queen's goodwill if she declines. After all, Rosalind will have embroiderers under her own supervision, an accomplishment for one so young. The King and Queen will desire more church embroideries than the church embroiderers can possibly work with all the new chapels the King is building.' Mildred dished out the peaches. '*You* could lose trade from Earl Richard if you displease the Queen, you know. Earl Richard is a hard man. Counts his groats, I hear.' She reached over the table and took Alfred's large hand in her own little hand. 'I can provide you with two apprentices who show great promise as embroiderers. Let Rosalind go to Westminster if she wishes.'

Alfred closed his eyes. 'I shall miss her.'

'But you were going to betroth me. You would miss me if I married.'

'Go to the Queen. I can see you are set on it. Well, I suppose it may bring more work my way. You have my blessing.'

'The workshop won't be ready until after Christmas but the Queen wants me to select embroiderers soon.'

'Don't tempt any of my workers away from Paternoster Lane,' Alfred said, his grey eyes smiling again. This time his smile was open-hearted.

'Nor mine, my dear, though I would be hard-pressed to deny any one such a great placement.' Mildred was laughing. 'What a celebration tonight has become.'

'I may have to live at Westminster but I hope to be here often too,' Rosalind said quickly, anxious not to lose her beloved attic bedroom.

'And welcome you ever will be,' Alfred said, tears welling in his eyes.

It was time to distract Papa before he became too maudlin or mentioned the de Basings again. She poured him a cup of ale. 'Let us plan the wedding by the hearth,' she suggested.

'Thank you, Dame Mildred,' she whispered as they moved away from the table.

'Good luck, my child,' Mildred whispered back.

Rosalind breathed her relief. *Adam de Basing will soon find his son another wife.* For a heartbeat she thought of a fair-headed squire who was often at Westminster.

Chapter Five

'Welcome,' Ailenor said as Nell curtsied to her. The wassail log glowed, throwing out warmth and Christmas cheer. 'It is good to see you at court again,' Ailenor was unable to conceal her joy. 'I hoped you would come.' She studied her friend for a moment, looking for change in Nell's once-sad demeanour. There was a somewhat mysterious glow about her. Odiham suited her.

The grey cuckoo had altered into a bird of paradise, one of those exotic creatures knights carried back from journeys to foreign lands. Nell was wearing a rich velvet gown trimmed with fur. 'You suit colours, especially burgundy.' She reached out for Nell's hands and whispered, 'Dearest Nell, I have missed you.'

They clasped hands and kissed. The ring that bound Nell to Christ had moved position from her right hand to her left.

'Be seated,' Henry said to his sister.

'Between us.' Ailenor patted a comfortable padded stool.

Their page poured cups of wine and Henry, smiling, no doubt, mused Ailenor, thinking of a lucrative match for Nell to a Castilian lord, looked approvingly at his sister's rich clothing.

Ailenor found herself smoothing her hand along the folds of her new samite tunic. She patted her hair, neatly plaited at her ears, secured in intricately worked silver crispinettes below a newly fashionable pert pill-box hat. It held her crispinettes in place by a strap fastened under her chin, a recent fashion, a change from heavier veils. It represented a freedom with dress, generally denied a woman. Men never wore veils.

Henry took a plate of sweetmeats from his page, sent him away, and laid the dish on the low table by his side. Ailenor felt him smiling at her as she caressed the opals on the hilt of her little belt dagger, enjoying the velvet smoothness of the stones. He said, 'As you see, Nell, my wife likes to protect herself. As well she does not wear that in the bedchamber or I should never have conquered her.'

'My lord, I would not care to displease you there.' Ailenor laughed lightly.

Nell laid down her cup. 'I have something to say, Henry.'

'It must wait. I see Sir Simon coming this way.' Henry lowered his voice. 'I have decided on a New Year gift for him. He is to be my Earl of Leicester. Say nothing.'

'A good decision,' Ailenor said.

'It is to be a surprise. It's a secret. My barons are indifferent towards him. Can you keep a secret, Nell?' His eyes seemed to narrow as he studied his sister.

Ailenor noticed how Nell started. It was as if one of the puppies tumbling around their feet had bitten her friend with its sharp little teeth. Nell's hand shook as she picked up her cup. She tilted it, spilling a little wine on her gown. Dashing it away with a napkin, she said, 'It's only a drop.' Her cheeks were stained crimson like the wine.

Sir Simon paused by a pillar to speak with the nobleman who had been Henry's advisor for years, the powerful Hubert de Burgh who had married a Scottish princess when Henry's sister Joan had married the Scottish King. Henry's eyelid began to droop, a sure sign of discontent. The wealthiest earl in the land, Hubert was in and out of favour. At one time he had been accused of thieving from the treasury. He had endured sanctuary, hiding from those who were determined to arrest him, destroy him, and bring him to account.

To distract Henry, Ailenor, who had heard all about Earl Hubert's fascinating story, leaned closer to her husband. She thought she

58

knew what Nell wanted to say to him. Nell wanted to marry Sir Simon, and Ailenor hoped that Henry would be generous-hearted towards his sister. After all, Nell had created a bower for Henry and Ailenor in the bedchambers of her castle at Odiham.

At last *it* had happened, *it* being seduction. That September, all she had long desired occured. Her happiness was complete. They had retreated to the countryside during the months of July and August to hide away at Marlborough. Ailenor came to love the old rambling castle and the town's twisting streets. They hunted in the Savernake Forest, a royal forest, with their small band of courtiers.

The weather had been warm again that summer, the harvest had been bountiful, and the people of England seemed content. The court often dined outdoors. Some evenings she and Henry shared her bed for a little kissing and fondling whilst reclining with a book of hours on top of the coverlet. The book would on occasion slip to the floor and they lost themselves in love, arms and legs entwined, hearts beating fast. Yet, as they grew passionate Henry always held back at the last, saying they must wait. She was too young. She was only fifteen and he was past thirty.

She longed for him, but just as she coaxed her hawk to obey her, she applied the same patient tactic with Henry, wondering if he was embracing celibacy like Edward Confessor. At fifteen she did not consider herself too young to carry a child. She sensed that, though Henry tried to deny her, he was feeling the same sense of longing as she. She desperately wanted to give him a son or daughter.

On their return to London they had taken a detour to Odiham. Henry sent their courtiers on to Windsor, only retaining a guard of a dozen able soldiers and three personal attendants. They would proceed to Windsor as if they were in disguise, not a king and queen but simple nobility. They would not fly pennants displaying English lions. It would be a novelty not to be recognised.

'Where can we sleep, not, I hope, in tents or in the hedgerows like peasants,' she'd said.

'There's an inn. It's called The White Cross. The landlord knows not to make a fuss.' She let out a sigh of relief on hearing this.

Fortunately Henry, for all his scattering of alms amongst beggars and the poor, enjoyed his own comfort too much to embrace a peasant lifestyle. She would not have to camp in a field like a soldier's woman.

Nell met them in Odiham's courtyard. She had prepared, she said, for a greater court. 'You can be unpredictable, Henry. Where is your court?'

'I sent them on to their own castles,' Henry had said, taking Nell's hands in his.

Like an accomplished chatelaine, Nell knelt and washed her brother's feet before they entered her castle. 'It's a relief to be rid of them – bishops, earls, barons, the whole pack of them,' – he laughed at Nell's shocked face – 'just to be with my favourite sister.' He turned to Ailenor. 'And my wife.'

'I am honoured.' Nell faltered momentarily, it seemed, and said, 'I expect you would like to rest before supper. Your guard will be comfortable in the West Tower when they have unpacked your sumpter carts.'

'We only have one cart,' Ailenor said, unable to repress a giggle, delighted at the deception and at Nell's surprise. 'Nell, you see, we are concealing who we really are. You must keep our visit secret.' She looked at Henry. 'That is what you said.'

'As silent as our father's tomb, Nell.'

Ailenor accepted the rose water proffered her by Nell. She was to be happy here and this simplicity was not unlike her childhood in Provence.

'I have given you connecting chambers, Henry,' Nell was saying. 'Odiham is not a large castle.'

Ailenor slid her arm into Henry's as they followed Nell into her great hall.

They shared a cup of wine with Nell seated by the long arched window that overlooked yellow meadows beyond her castle. For a while they talked about the summer and the harvesting they had observed as they rode to Odiham.

'Our people are happy,' Henry said. 'This winter they will have enough to eat. That makes me happy too.'

'I'm told the harvest has been the best for years,' Nell remarked. 'I love my demesne. Thank you for it, Henry.'

Ailenor had noted then that Nell still wore grey and the ring binding her to Christ was firmly on her finger that September.

At length Nell set her cup down and said, 'The maids are carrying water up the stairway to your chambers so you can bathe before supper.' A smile played about Nell's mouth. 'Two bath tubs and curtains. Do you wish my maids to stay?'

'No,' Ailenor said quickly. 'I have Willelma and I don't –'

'One bath tub is enough,' Henry said quickly. 'It's a long way up those stairways. Just make sure we have plenty of water, Nell.'

Ailenor felt her eyes widen as she realised what was about to occur. Was Henry planning to make a whore of her, like those who lived in the stews over the river where bathing was a prelude to intimacy? Had Henry personal experience of what lay over the river? Was her husband accustomed to taking on disguise without her knowledge? It was nothing to do with celibacy, she decided. She would wait and see what his intent was. She loved Henry and knew he loved her back. Their companionship over the past year and a half had caused them to grow close, very close. They shared a love of music, poetry, and beauty. She learned to understand his adoration of Edward Confessor and appreciate the extravagant gold tomb he was planning for the English saint in Westminster's Abbey Church. Henry would create Jerusalem in his own abbey in England. Their first son would be named for Saint Edward, a truly English name.

Followed by her Domina, Nell leading, Ailenor climbed the winding staircase at Odiham with a beating heart, with longing and trepidation, wondering if the suggestion of shared bathing was to be a prelude to seduction.

She hastened into the bedchamber, tripping over her long-toed shoes. One almost slipped off. 'You have made it beautiful, dear Nell,' she exclaimed, utterly enchanted, as she grasped the doorpost and slipped the errant shoe back onto her foot.

'Ailenor, are you steady?' Nell asked.

'Perfectly. It's just wine and heat, nothing a bath won't help.'

Maids were filling an enormous wooden tub with pitchers of warmed water. They finished their task, curtsied and fled from the room. The tub sat in the middle of the rush-matted floor draped with linen sheets. Ailenor could hardly wait to sink into its soothing depths. A bathing gown so thin and fragile it was surely luminous lay on the bed. Her eye was drawn from the gown to the bed cover itself, which was embroidered with marigolds and daisies with golden hearts. She ran over to it and exclaimed, 'You have placed the coverlet I asked Rosalind to embroider as a gift for you over *my* bed.' She hugged Nell. 'You are too kind to me.'

'Henry is waiting through that low door.' Ailenor noticed an arched door set into the wall by the clothing rail. Nell turned to Willelma. 'There is a small chamber opposite for you, Lady Willelma.' Since Ailenor's baggage was already in the chamber, Willelma had begun unpacking as soon as the maids' clogs clattered down the staircase. Nell added, 'I shall leave you now.' She hesitated. 'Do you need help to undress? I *can* call for my maids.'

'No, we'll manage,' Ailenor said quickly. She wanted no one with her, no one other than her Henry.

Nell raised her hand. 'Come, Lady Willelma. Let me show you around my castle.' Willelma quickly laid a lovely blue tunic of light silk and matching under-gown on the bed and smiling a conspiratorial smile followed Nell from the chamber.

They were gone. All Ailenor could hear was the cawing of birds crossing the sky above the window casement and chapel bells ringing from the distance. She was alone with a large tub of hot water and her baggage half-unpacked. She deftly unlaced her own dress, undid her belt, and stepped from her under-gown. She kicked off her shoes and drew the thin cotton bathing robe over her head. She loosened her dark hair and feeling it tumbling down her back climbed two steps placed beside the tub and eased herself down into the bath. Water lapped about her, smelling of roses. A pot of soft Spanish soap sat on the tub's rim. She inhaled its aromatic scent and felt dizzy with delight. Her eyes closed and she did not realise Henry was beside her until she felt a splash of water on her face. Her eyes flicked open again.

'Make room,' he said in a coaxing voice.

Ailenor found she was gazing at his bulging manhood as she drew up her legs to grant him room. She had never seen Henry totally naked before. His body was a little plump. He was well proportioned, his shoulders broad, and as she had not grown taller during the two years of their marriage she knew they were of similar height. He leaned over and gently slipped her gown from her shoulders. He eased her up and tugged it off and threw it over the rim of their bath.

'I doubt you'll need it,' he said.

'My lord.' She tossed her head and said with a confidence she did not feel, 'I am yours.'

'Hush, Beauty. Let me –' He began to soap her breasts with the cloth provided and leaning over kissed her nipples – 'your breasts are those of a woman and your mouth tastes of strawberries and wine –' he gently kissed her lips, 'Come closer, come between my legs. Lay yours over mine.'

She slid further into the water. Her body relaxed as he stroked her gently with a sponge slippery with soap. She felt as if she were liquid, like the seductively spicy soft soap she could smell wafting in the steam that rose from the water as it cooled. She was lost for words. She began to lose herself completely to sensation as he caressed her, poured water over her, and washed and rinsed her long, long black hair. She felt filled with desire and taking the sponge from him slowly moved it over his body. He leaned back in the tub as if enjoying every moment. At last he said, 'Come, Beauty, we have a little time before supper.'

He dried her body and her long dark hair. In turn, she dried him, hesitating only for a moment as she came to his penis.

'Come to bed, my love. Come with me.'

He gathered her into her arms and laid her on the coverlet, slipped it from under her until she was lying with him upon a bed of fresh linen sheets smelling of lavender.

When he penetrated her, Ailenor did not feel more than a sharp moment of pleasurable pain. He whispered endearments into her ear as they made love and she kissed him, returning his caresses.

'Ailenor, I love you with all my heart and with my body,' he said when later she nestled into his arms, her head on his chest.

'I am not the first, I'll warrant,' she said. 'But I love you with all my heart too.'

'You are not the first, my love, but never have I taken a mistress, nor shall I ever have one. You are the only mistress and queen for me.'

The Hall was crowded and noisy with calls of Christmas cheer. Sir Simon had left Sir Hubert's side and was coming towards Henry. Ailenor stood, scattering a family of pups that had nestled by her chair. 'Come with me,' she said reaching out her hand to Nell. 'I have wine and wafers in my chambers. We can roast chestnuts. It is cold even though my fire has been lit all day, every day. Have they lit your fire too? I hope so. Let us leave Sir Simon with Henry.'

'Thank you. It *is* lit. The linen is clean and all is comfortable. My maids are unpacking.'

Ailenor looked down at Henry. 'May I steal Nell away?' she asked.

'Yes, indeed, my dove. I have much to discuss with Earl Simon.' He looked at Nell. 'The Earl will wish to greet you too, Nell.'

Nell blushed.

'They all admire my lovely sister. I believe Simon stopped at Odiham on his way to Winchester in September. He speaks well of the castle improvements. But, of course, you can converse with Leicester at supper. He will be seated with us.'

Sir Simon bowed low to the King and Ailenor and finally to Nell, his face inscrutable. Ailenor lowered her head to hide her amusement. The knight's confidence was remarkable. They exchanged greetings.

Ailenor gestured to Nell to follow her and left Henry to discuss what must be discussed with Sir Simon. If only he was asking if Nell's vow could be reneged upon as he wished to wed her. If only Henry would make it happen.

Chapter Six

Nell slipped into the courtyard between the palace and the abbey church, her heavy hood concealing her face. Silent monks and canons passed her on the path leading to the west door but they never looked her way. Inside the abbey, choristers practising plainsong for the Christmas services stared at their choir-master, paying her no attention as she stole through the nave. She hurried into a side chapel dedicated to 'Our Lady' where she fell weeping onto her knees.

Anxiety threatened to drown her with a profound sense of sadness and loss – sadness because she should relinquish her happiness with Sir Simon; loss because to deny her love was unbearably painful. Solace was not an easily won companion, not when you had sinned as she had sinned. Statues standing in the chapel's corners seemed to admonish her. The Virgin's usual serenity felt accusative. In her mind's eye she saw her own confessor, a stern priest who would never gainsay strict Archbishop Edmund Rich of Canterbury. If she confessed to her priest he would tell her to relinquish Simon. Their eternal souls would be damned. This was not what she wanted to hear.

Across the transept, she noticed an old monk sweeping. He coughed and coughed. *One day I shall be old too and must give an account of my life if I am to be permitted Heaven's grace, unless my vow of chastity is disaffirmed, reversed, and annulled.* Her mind swirling in turmoil, she bowed her head, twisting her prayer beads over and over, threading them through her fingers. A monk entered the chapel. Without a word he relit an extinguished candle. She noted the guttering of the candle as it flared up, smelled melting wax, and heard the whisper of his habit as he swept past her into the abbey nave again.

Her head remained lowered until she opened her eyes to study the middle finger of her right hand. She had removed the ring which bound her to Christ from her right hand to her left hand. If she wed Simon, she would remove it altogether. She was no true bride for Christ. Nell shuddered as she remembered the church wall paintings at Odiham – ladders and devils, vivid flames, curling whips, and vats of boiling water. She had only been sixteen when she had made her vow of chastity. She had not known then what it was to truly love a man as she did Simon. Could such punishments await her?

They had become lovers at last, when Simon visited Odiham on his way to and from Winchester. After the act of love, they'd wept together because of it. She had taken her vow of chastity before an archbishop, a binding promise approved of by the Holy Father in Rome himself and Simon, whom she knew to be a deeply religious knight, was as frightened of their passion as she. 'We must marry,' he'd said to her in the bedchamber where only a month before Ailenor and Henry had consummated their marriage. 'Live together as man and wife without shame. I love you, Nell, with all my heart. The vow was made when you were too young to know your own nature and your heart. We'll get it rescinded. There are ways.' He had been gentle, his tears mingling with hers. 'Henry will help us,' he had whispered into her fall of black hair. She'd lifted her violet eyes to his and placed her hand on his heart.

'God willing,' she had said. 'For I love you too, Simon.'

Could God understand that? Could He understand what it was to love and to desire children of her own? She felt a tear slide down her cheek as she remembered Simon's and her night of passionate lovemaking. She was not meant for the cloister.

She loved Simon and he loved her. Her brother's goodwill would be countered by the barons' fury. A princess could not marry without the Council's permission. Despite the chill that penetrated the cathedral her hands felt clammy and her rosary beads slippery. If only the Madonna would listen, understand, and intercede with God.

She began to pray her own prayer. Prostrating herself, she begged God's forgiveness as Christ had forgiven those who had crucified him. 'Forgive me, for I knew not what I did when I took a vow of chastity.'

She prayed to her name-day saint, Cecilia, to intercede for her. 'Life will be nothing without Simon de Montfort, but if I must give up my love and deny temptation as Christ denied his temptations in the wilderness, I shall obey your will.' Her tears washed the flags as she sobbed with a heavy heart.

'It was a promise,' she whispered into the stillness. 'One I should never have made.'

As Nell raised her head the Virgin appeared to lift her child as if offering Christ to Nell. Was it the sign she wanted? What *was* the meaning?

Nell returned to the chapel daily, hoping for another sign, but the Virgin remained serene, her great blue eyes looking down without emotion. Nell presented alms to beggars outside the church. She spoke to the old monk who swept the choir, wishing him 'Christ's Cheer.' But inside the chapel the Virgin remained still, her blue gown cloaking her in an ambience of calm.

Day following day, night following night, Nell wore an outer show of Christmastide cheer, particularly whilst in the company of Ailenor and her ladies. She could not confide her dilemma to Ailenor and deflected Ailenor's oblique enquiries as to the nature of her friendship with Simon.

Simon avoided her. He did not want to damage their cause by presenting the court with the opportunity to chatter about them. She felt her heart breaking into a thousand tiny pieces. Some days she felt everyone else's joy weighing down on her like a sack of stones. She felt like returning home. But if she returned to Odiham her departure would be questioned. As she watched Simon playing chess with Henry, dancing with ladies of the court, attending Christmas Masses with his companions, her pain cut deeper and deeper. The miserable state of affairs continued until the New Year's Eve feast. On this night of high spirits she felt Henry watching Simon and her with a curious expression crossing his countenance, his glance shifting from her to her lover. To Nell's puzzlement, Henry contrived to bring them together during the games that followed the feasting.

He drew her by the hand from her place at the High Table, saying, 'Nell, Simon will blindfold you for *catch-me*.' Her fingers tingled as Simon tied the dark cloth about her head, covering her eyes, and as he quickly kissed the nape of her neck and spun her around, a frisson of danger slid through her. She edged her way slowly away into the centre, her out-stretched arms groping air, hoping to catch him yet dreading it in case she fainted at his touch, but she caught Ailenor.

'Your knight has speed,' Ailenor whispered as Nell blindfolded the Queen.

Simon squeezed Nell's hand as they passed by each other in a dance and whispered, 'All will be well.' She remembered tumbled sheets, a full moon shining as holding hands they walked on the battlements at midnight and promised each other everlasting love, falling into joyful kisses, returning to her chamber to discover further passion.

Simon could lose all he had achieved if Henry was displeased. Her brother granted him the earldom of Leicester at Christmas and she must not jeopardise Simon's future by upsetting Henry, because that which was given with generosity could be taken away with displeasure. Recognising this, Nell remained discreet and cried into her pillow on New Year's night.

Snow lay about the palace in thick drifts. When many of Henry's barons departed Westminster for their own castles, Nell felt a sense of relief. There were fewer watching eyes. Occasionally she and Simon pressed hands. Often now, they exchanged glances. They pretended friendship. She waited and waited, hopeful that their strange situation as half-lovers could be resolved. Simon whispered to her on New Year's Day that Henry knew about their plight. Simon said he had told him. Henry was thinking about it. He had not yet spoken.

'Was he furious?' Nell whispered to Simon behind a screen that concealed a door to a small porch off the Hall that led into a garden.

He snatched a kiss from her. 'No, he's thinking of how it can be done.'

She took fleeting hope from Simon's words, but as days passed she despaired again and tried to avoid private conversation with Henry. Simon would speak for them both.

One night between New Year and Epiphany, Henry caught her as she sat playing with Ailenor's puppies by the fire in the Hall. He spoke in a low voice, so low no one could overhear. 'Do you love him, Nell?'

'I do,' she replied with honesty. Henry said nothing more nor, for once, did her bother's countenance betray his feelings. He moved on, giving her no resolution.

The diminished court threw snowballs at each other in the greater courtyard. After Henry's question, she knew she and Simon must talk but there was no opportunity to be private in a court that lived cheek by jowl. Without any decision, she wondered if now it was time to return to Odiham but she did not. She could not, not before Epiphany, not before the Madonna of Our Lady's Chapel gave her another sign or Henry did. He occasionally caught her eye but every time she tried to speak to him he waved her away.

She, who was always composed, began to nibble at her nails. She jumped at every odd sound or quick movement. It was a time of shadows. She thought she saw William Marshal's ghost on the stairway outside her chamber. His pale staring face looked as if the spirit carried with it a warning of great peril ahead. With a flicker of a candle in a nearby sconce her dead husband's ghost melted into the walls. Nell's dreams were haunted by memories of him aged and dying. She touched the ring that remained on her left hand and wept.

Ailenor drew her into her circle of happy ladies. Sensing that

Ailenor knew it all too and was sympathetic, Nell gradually relaxed. If Ailenor knew, why did she not confide her knowledge? Ailenor was learning to be a queen and she would not gainsay Henry. It would be a dangerous discussion. That was the nub of it.

At last Nell's chance to speak to Simon arose as courtiers tossed snow and laughed. No one looked their way. Simon drew his sport closer to Ailenor and her ladies and, at last, whispered in her ear as he swept snow from her mantle, 'Have courage, my love. Henry is coming around.'

'What did you tell him?'

'That you might be with child.'

'What?' she hissed into his ear. 'You know I've had my courses.'

'Look, my love, Henry is working out how we can marry without the Council's permission. He is adamant that no one knows, especially not Richard, and indeed not the Marshals. Gilbert Marshal and your brother Richard are not our friends. They resent me. Henry is waiting for them to depart for their lands. I had to say it.'

Nell felt tearful. 'I do hope for children but if Henry finds out you have deceived him . . .'

Simon drew breath and took her hand, raised it to his mouth and kissed her fingers. 'He will not. It won't be long, my love.'

She glanced about the courtyard to where the Earl of Cornwall was leaning against a wall talking with a pretty Provençal woman, one of Ailenor's ladies, and watching them with a frown creasing his brow.

Nell pulled away from Simon. 'Richard is observing us. If he discovers us, there'll be a scandal. He could ruin us both. He'll make our lives miserable if we wed.'

'Not if we are far away by then – in Kenilworth.'

'When, then, Simon?' She clasped his arm.

'Soon.'

She dropped her hand and thanked him loudly for sweeping snow from her mantle.

Earl Richard stepped away from the lady, pushed between them and hurried her into his own group of courtiers. Isabel was with child again, he said. Nell disliked the way Richard spoke of his wife, as if he had tired of her. He flirted with Ailenor's ladies and they flirted back. It was a great game of courtly love, one that was permitted Richard but not Simon or Nell herself.

'Are you not concerned for Isabel?' she said to him when later that day he had challenged her to a game of chess and seemed to be winning.

'Isabel is happy at Wallingford. She has no need of my company,' he said. 'Look out. Your rook is gone.' He seized her piece from the board. 'I wish Simon were gone too,' he growled. 'He does not deserve the title of earl.' His look was dark as he barked out Simon's name.

'Simon is pleasing company,' she said, feeling uncomfortable.

'He is a lowly upstart.'

Nell froze, a bishop in her hand.

'Concentrate on the game, Nell,' he snapped.

She slid her bishop sideways and captured his rook. From the corner of her eye she saw Simon talking with Henry by the great fireplace. Their heads were bent together, deep in conversation.

'Got you!' Richard glanced at her, triumph gleaming in his darkened eyes. 'You've lost him.' He held up her knight.

'When?' she said again in a very low voice when, later, she bumped into Simon on a narrow stairway that descended through the palace.

'I shall know tomorrow.' He drew her to him and kissed her deeply. Footsteps echoed below them. He let her go and in a louder voice said, 'Here are your scissors, my lady.'

'Ah, I thought I had dropped them here,' she said. He continued up the stairway as she hurried down, passing Gilbert Marshal ascending as she reached her chamber.

He waylaid her. 'I see you are not wearing the ring that honoured my brother's memory.' His tone was acid.

'It is overly tight,' she said, and fled into her chamber. She had removed the ring that morning in a fit of anger at it.

She threw herself on her bed and her thoughts at once filled with Simon, his hair glossy and black, his scent, which was musky, and the touch of his lips on her own. How she longed for him. She allowed a long heartfelt sigh to escape. Henry was unpredictable. They could wait years for his decision. After Christmastide her erratic brother might vent his fury on her and banish her to a nunnery in disgrace, particularly if he thought she was with child.

Earl Richard left for Wallingford. With his departure Nell breathed more easily.

The same night Richard had ridden off into a snowy landscape, there was a banging on her chamber door. Having just climbed into bed, she pushed back her coverlets and threw a robe over her night gown. Her fire had died down and the air felt chill. The knocking came again. It was more insistent.

'Who is it?' she called out. The Angelus bells were ringing. Her response was lost amongst the cacophony.

The person who had knocked waited until they stopped chiming. 'The King requires your lady's presence in the Painted Chamber.' The voice was that of Earl Simon's squire, Thomas. Why by the Blessed Virgin was Thomas requesting her to come to the King's chamber at such a late hour?

'Let him enter,' she said to her maid, who had risen from her pallet at the foot of Nell's bed and was standing by her side. 'Fetch my burgundy gown and mantle.'

'Wait in my lady's ante-chamber,' she heard her maid say in a shrill little voice to the squire. 'My lady must dress.'

Her hair was combed and plaited. She was wearing her best gown and had pulled a mantel lined with fur about her shoulders against the chilling air.

Thomas stood in the doorway. 'My lady, please hurry. The King is waiting.'

'My maid . . .'

'She may accompany you.' Thomas lifted a wall sconce and bade the women follow him. As they glided through dim passages and climbed down twisting stairways to the King's apartments, Nell questioned the squire.

'Explain this,' she said feeling her stomach heave.

'The King awaits you,' was all Thomas said in response.

As they approached the King's chambers Earl Gilbert stopped them. Nell looked away when he put out his bony hand. 'We have a habit of meeting in shadowy places.' His face was too near to her own, his breath stinking of sour wine. 'Visiting the King and Queen? The hour is past midnight,' Gilbert said with a saturnine smile.

A pool of moonlight slid in through a window of painted glass, casting eerie patterns on the corridor wall and crossing Gilbert's face with a lurid streak of red. He appeared devil-like. 'I am Henry's sister. If he requests my presence I attend him. Let us pass.'

'Sir Simon's squire accompanies you, my lady?' He was frowning now. There was a note of displeasure in his tone.

'That is none of your concern.'

'That we shall see.' Earl Gilbert, nevertheless, lowered his hand and granted them passage. She felt his cold eyes bore into her back as they proceeded to the Painted Chamber. She gathered her mantle about her and raised her head. In the sconce light Thomas looked at her with admiration in his soft blue eyes. She managed a smile and he nodded. She had handled Earl Gilbert well.

There were others, even at night, drifting about outside Henry's chambers, curious courtiers, sycophants, and pages. Guards stood by the doors of Henry's private apartments to prevent anyone curious entering the Painted Chamber. Nell, her maid, and Thomas were ushered inside. Time stilled. Candles lit about the chamber illuminated the beautiful wall paintings depicting Edward Confessor. The saint's crimson robes appeared more vivid than ever. Once they had passed into the Painted Chamber, a page guided them to Henry's bedchamber to the heavy arras that separated his private chapel from his bedchamber. She smelled frankincense mingling with rose. The scent of roses was drifting from Ailenor who stepped towards her from behind the arras. The Queen took her hand. 'Come, Earl Simon is waiting by the altar for his bride.'

Nell's heart raced. There was no room in the chapel for their servants, whom Ailenor bade wait outside. As Nell entered the chapel it was as if Simon, who looked around smiling, was a creature from Heaven, and not a mortal knight. He wore chainmail, which gleamed in the candlelight, and a short mantle of softest blue wool. His black hair touched his shoulders and his dark eyes as he turned towards her glowed with love.

Although a brazier heated the tiny shadowy room, Nell momentarily shivered as Ailenor guided her towards Simon. He looked down at her with reassurance and whispered, 'Are you well, my love?' She had no time to respond because Walter, the chaplain of St Stephen's, emerged from behind green velvet hangings to greet them both. Henry entered with the priest and stood by Earl Simon's side. He was wearing his favourite green and his ring jewels shone in the candlelight as he held his hands in a palmer's gesture. She could smell his favourite sandalwood perfume and ridiculously in that moment she wished she had been granted warning so she could bathe and anoint her own body with perfume. Henry never smiled, but after she and Simon clearly repeated their marriage vows, those the chaplain mumbled to them, he solemnly lifted Nell's hand and kissed it. She breathed more easily. Still unsmiling, Henry knelt before the altar with Simon and herself as Walter, the chaplain, said a brief garbled wedding mass over them.

Simon and she rose again as man and wife.

Before the palace stirred that morning they rode out from the courtyard, surrounded by retainers who would accompany them to Kenilworth. Others would ride to Odiham with news of their wedding.

Chapter Seven

1238

Ailenor was happy for Nell. Surely once their wedding was accomplished the nobles, many of them in their far-flung castles by now, would be accepting of the fact that her friend Nell and Henry's favoured knight, the Earl of Leicester, were married in the sight of God. She resumed her busy life, embroidering, reading, playing on her harp, and dancing.

A full week after the departure of the Christmastide court, Henry burst into Ailenor's solar, slamming her door behind him in a fury. The sudden draught caused fragile fabrics to drift to the floor tiles. His face, usually pale, was to Ailenor's horror blotched a fiery red as if he were stricken with the spotted fever. Ailenor's mouth fell open. As he approached her chair, the needle she was holding slipped from her fingers, a length of crimson silken thread clinging to her gown where it caught. She scrambled to her feet, almost tripping over the hem of her skirt. Her ladies dropped their embroidery. With wary countenances, they curtsied to the King and stood like a guard of frightened hoverflies around their Queen. How could she have displeased him? The unspoken question hung about her bower like an unpleasant odour.

'Whatever is wrong?' she managed to ask.

'Everything. Have your women pack at once,' he said, his tone angry. 'We sail for the Tower on this afternoon's tide.' He glanced around the women, his eyes resting on the embroideress, Rosalind, who was holding a square of linen in her hands.

'And as for you,' he said, 'you will return to your father's house.'

The girl curtsied. She looked terrified.

Turning to Ailenor again, he said, 'There's an army waiting at Kingston to attack us, Richard and Walter Marshal at its head. Traitors, the pack of them. No doubt they will infect the City burghers with their opinions. London, too, could rise against us. We must retreat to the Tower.'

'What has happened?'

Henry waved his hands which seemed to claw the air with a will of their own. Her damsels drew back. Ailenor stood erect and signalled to them to leave her. They ran for the window benches where they sat in a quivering row.

Henry said with a grunt, 'It's Simon and Nell. The earls want their marriage annulled. Send for your cloak at once. I shall wait for you in the Hall. Your ladies will follow with the sumpter wagons.' He swept out, shouting angrily they must be ready to depart before the tide turned. 'You have an hour.'

Ailenor spun around to face her ladies. 'They'll not dare attack the King. We had best do as the King says. Willelma, you will stay with me and travel on the river. Rosalind, go and tell your embroiderers to close up the workshop until you return. They can take sanctuary in the Abbey.'

Rosalind nodded and fled the chamber.

After a chilly journey down river, huddled in her cloak, Ailenor was safely ensconced in the Wakefield Tower. She remained quiet as Henry, huffing and puffing, called a council meeting to include his loyal knights who had remained at court following Christmastide, and her uncle, William of Savoy, who was his most trusted advisor.

Hours passed. The candle clocks burned low. The sumpter carts arrived in the inner courtyard during the hours following Vespers. Ailenor paced her chamber. She could not wait to hear any rash decision. She was Henry's Queen. If the crown was in danger she would have her opinion listened to. Nell's marriage must not be annulled. 'Willelma, take charge here. Send for wine and cakes.' Ailenor knew she looked fiercer than she felt as she glanced about the frightened women. She rested her eyes upon English Mary who was of sound sense. 'Lady Mary, come with me and wait outside the King's chambers in case I have need of you.'

Ailenor hurried from the chamber, Mary following. She swept forward along a dimly lit corridor. Sconces wavered as she strode past. Guards looked at her askance. Ignoring them she marched on. She would attend the King's Council whether or not she was welcome.

There were only a few knights present when, with a swish of velvet mantel, she entered the council chamber. Henry rose, hand on the hilt of his sword. He gave her a half-smile and ordered a chair to be placed between his own and Uncle William's at the round oak table. His left eyelid drooped, his eye almost concealed.

Ailenor drew her shoulders back and sat up straight, her neck rising from her mantle.

Henry addressed his knights. 'They come to threaten me, their King, whilst Earl Simon is at Kenilworth. They know my weakness. Simon should be here with us. He is an abler soldier than all of them.' He laid a long hand on an unrolled parchment sitting on the table and tapped with his middle finger. 'They send me this. Ultimatums!' Addressing the scribes sat against the walls, he said, 'Write to the custodians of all our ports from Norwich to Portsmouth. Write these words – *receive no orders from my brother, who has risen against me because I have married our sister to Earl Simon.*'

Silence followed, except for pens dipping into ink and scratching across parchment. When Henry's instruction was written down by ten monks, the portable desks hanging from their shoulders thumping, Henry lifted his seal from the council table and placed his stamp on each letter. 'See these are carried forth to the ports this night.' He dismissed the monks, and quickly called after them. 'Be at hand, Brothers, because I'll have more words to send out later.' As one, the scribes bowed, desks knocking against habits. They scurried from the chamber to seek messengers to take the letters to all the prominent East Anglian and Kentish ports.

'Uncle William,' Ailenor whispered, 'Is Richard intending a civil war? Is he threatening the Crown?'

William shook his head. 'We don't know yet.' He patted her hand. 'You are safe here in the Tower.'

Henry lifted the scroll from the desk. 'I'll warrant Richard wants money. That is what this is about. He has complained about having to return our sister's estates, those he had in trust for her. The Marshals are after the estates they still owe her as her widow's third portion. Her inheritance, her widow's portion, goes now to Earl Simon as he is her husband. Here, they list his shortcomings.' He tapped another scroll she had not at first noticed, by his right hand. 'The barons say he is ruthless. Are these men not hard-hearted that they would hold a king and his queen to ransom? I must do nothing of importance without the advice of my subjects, they claim.' He looked at Ailenor and with a hard smile, said, 'They complain, too, that I take advice from foreigners, mostly from Savoy like Bishop William, your uncle.'

'They *would* say that,' Bishop William protested. He stroked his beard and rapped his stubby fingers on the table. 'There is, of course, the matter of Princess Eleanor's vow.'

Henry was quick to challenge any hints of Church objection, even those of Ailenor's own most treasured Uncle William. 'That was a vow made when she was overly young to know her mind, taken under duress. Earl Simon will have it annulled.'

Uncle William raised his eyebrows but did not challenge. Ailenor nodded her agreement. It would mean a hasty journey to Rome to seek the Pope's blessing on their marriage, an official release for Nell from her oath, but Simon would go. He promised he would before they departed for Kenilworth. He would do anything for Nell.

The knights seated around the table began to discuss whether the vow was, in fact, made under undue duress by Archbishop Edmund. Ailenor thought it was and said so. They pondered how many knights they could call on to fight Earl Richard if he attacked. Henry shook his head. Their conversation went from knights to ships and ports, to exile and to sieges. As the night deepened, Gascon wine was served. Occasionally one of the company hurried from the chamber to seek the privy. Voices raised and fell. Henry's left eye angrily drooped more and more.

Ailenor puzzled how her father would settle such a quarrel. He may have lacked finance but he had castles and connections. He always called on her mother's brothers when his territories came under threat. His rule over Provence was absolute. Henry must flex his power more firmly, control Richard of Cornwall, and destroy Gilbert Marshal's rebellion. Henry might buy Richard off but if he did there should be conditions.

She leaned over and tapped Henry's arm. 'May we speak privately? I have a suggestion.'

Henry inclined his head and nodded. He rapped the table. 'I shall withdraw with the Queen for a while. Remain here until we return.' He turned to Ailenor's uncle. 'William, come with us.'

In the waiting chamber, Ailenor said, 'Earl Simon must travel to Rome at once, have Lady Eleanor's vow absolved. He must receive forgiveness and recognition from Pope Gregory for his marriage with our sister.'

Henry said, 'That has been agreed between myself and Earl Simon already.'

'Earl Simon should accompany Richard on the crusade Richard so often talks of though he has not yet taken the Cross. Many will gladly join a new crusade. What better to distract an enemy than a unified cause?'

Henry clasped his hands. 'Ailenor, you are right. A crusade, what a good idea. Money to finance it from both Church and Crown.' He smiled. 'I do not see why the Church cannot be taxed for a new crusade. I think there will be many monks and priests relieved to see Jerusalem freed from the infidel by English knights. Earl Simon and Earl Richard are leaders of men, the perfect warriors to take an army to Jerusalem.'

'A united cause,' said Ailenor, pleased they liked her idea so well.
'I'll put it to this council,' Henry said.

When they returned to the council chamber, Henry put her plan to the nobles. They all began to smile at last. This was a clever way out of an extremely difficult impasse and Ailenor found a smile hovering about her own mouth. She had made them listen to her. All her father had taught her was put to good use.

Henry elaborated on her suggestion. 'My brother will receive six thousand marks to lead a crusade. I shall support it. This will please them all – Cardinal Otto, the Papal Legate; Archbishop Edmund will support it; our earthly Father in Rome will be pleased with England. Earl Simon must accompany Richard to Jerusalem. It will take a year or two to organise, perhaps three, but I have no doubt there are those present who welcome a straight pathway to the Heavenly Kingdom.' He beamed at Ailenor. She clasped his hand under the table and raised her head in a queenly manner. Henry went on, 'A part of my sister's wealth must also be directed into God's work.' He let go Ailenor's clasp and raised his arms as if embracing Heaven. 'We shall rescue the Holy Lands from occupation. Christ's homelands will be returned to the faithful.'

His smile was, Ailenor considered, self-satisfied. It was, after all, *her* idea.

Yet she wore a serene demeanour and nodded. It would be a diversion from the unfortunate marriage. She had heard Richard talk of crusading and now his words would be made into action. What better to distract an enemy than a perceived unified cause? She moved her lips in hopeful prayer as she watched the council consider it.

Uncle William quaffed a beaker of Gascon wine and cleared his throat.

'There is the issue of the vow, Your Grace, we suggested –'

'The Queen suggests that Earl Simon travels to Rome at once, has the Lady Eleanor's vow absolved and receives forgiveness for and recognition from Pope Gregory of his marriage with our sister.' Henry narrowed his eyes, the droop having lifted slightly. 'He will have plenty of coin from my sister Eleanor's lands to buy Gregory's pardon and enough left over to go on Crusade.' Henry smiled again.

Clicking his fingers, Henry called for a scribe and dictated terms to be written to Earl Richard. These would be delivered by Bishop William.

That night Ailenor and Henry shared her rose bedchamber, still favourite of all her luxurious chambers. 'Henry,' she whispered, removing his shirt. 'The only way to keep our brother, Richard, away from our throne – and prevent him from seeing Earl Simon as too close to the throne – is for me to have a child. We must try harder.'

Henry kissed her as he reached for her and took her with passion. 'Are we sinful?' he sighed afterwards.

'No, this is our duty. If we enjoy it, God will forgive us, especially if we have heirs.'

She was Queen and she would bear her husband's children. Passion would result in beautiful children for the Crown, as their subjects expected of their king and queen.

'More than anything, I want a child, and, Henry, we must have children, lots of them.'

Later that month, Ailenor mused at how after receiving six thousand marks, Richard had withdrawn from Kingston. She was present when he made his peace with Henry and with Earl Simon, whom Henry had sent for, ordering him to Rome as soon as winter passed and the Swiss mountains were navigable.

'You will make over a portion of my sister's dower lands,' Henry said to Earl Gilbert at a meeting to discuss the new crusade.

Defeated and resentful, the Marshals retreated to their lands in the West. Ailenor cared not a jot about Gilbert Marshal's petulance. He had treated Nell abominably after his brother's death.

Simon travelled to Rome that spring. Nell, who was now with child, never journeyed to London, but instead passed her days away from public observance, at Kenilworth. Ailenor missed her company. They shared letters and she was pleased that Nell was to give birth soon. She looked with longing into the bitterly cold wintry landscape at bare trees and snow-filled clouds. If only she could conceive as well.

When Uncle William sailed for Italy in April to protect his Italian property interests which were under attack from the Emperor Frederick, Ailenor missed him also. She often felt lonely. Henry was busy ruling. She occupied herself by passing much of her day planning embroideries for her new chapel at Windsor, designing them herself, choosing fabrics and threads for them, and learning new stitches from Rosalind who, once the crisis with Earl Richard was over, had reopened the workshop at Westminster. When Ailenor was not engaged with embroidery, she wrote poetry. She read her best poems privately to Henry in her enthusiastic attempts to seduce him night after night.

Winter had edged into a chill spring but once June arrived the weather grew hot. The sunshine reminded Ailenor of Provence and her mood became joyful again.

Henry leaned on the thick windowledge of her chamber. July had opened with bad airs drifting from the river. He waved a strip of linen in front of his nose. 'There are multifarious airs here. We need to be away from the City to where we have gardens and streams, good hunting, and time. We'll pass summer at Woodstock. You, fair Ailenor, can write your stories of knights rescuing maidens from dragons and I shall devote myself to my own great plans.'

'Your plans?' Ailenor said from her bed, raising herself on one elbow, a poem discarded amongst their pillows. 'Which plans?'

'I intend rebuilding Westminster Abbey.'

'And . . .?'

'We shall conceive a child too.' Henry turned to her. 'I shall improve the castle at Windsor. We'll raise our family there, safely away from all bad airs.'

Ailenor climbed down from the rumpled sheets, stepped over the Turkey carpet, and stood with him by the window. She lifted her husband's hand and kissed it, smiling to herself. She would have children, a huge family of children. Hers had been a happy family. She was content and loved Henry. Nothing would disturb her and Henry's future joy.

'Come back to bed, Henry,' she said taking his hand. 'And yes, let us go to Woodstock.'

By September Ailenor was so delighted with Woodstock she could understand why Rosamund Clifford had been happy in this place. Old King Henry, her Henry's grandfather, had constructed a maze and a tower for his mistress at Woodstock. He imprisoned his wife, Queen Eleanor, in dank castles for years and years, because she had rebelled against him over control of her lands in Aquitaine and Poitou, siding with their sons against him. He only permitted his imprisoned queen to join him at Winchester for Christmases. The unhappy Queen never left this miserable imprisonment, until Henry's son, King Richard, freed his mother after his father's death, and returned her to his new court.

Ailenor began to write down the other Eleanor's sad story in verse. As she scribbled, she promised herself, I shall never displease my husband. Henry shall always be my true heart's love. I shan't ever, ever anger him.

Once they settled into the palace at Woodstock, Ailenor, as she had long wanted to, felt courageous enough to conduct a court of love in the garden. There, she, her ladies and courtiers debated loyalty, truth, requited love, and unrequited love. Troubadours recounted old tales, stories that had travelled from the courts of Persia and were magical and strange. Balladeers sang songs of England's greenwoods and moors where dog-headed monsters dwelled, and where King Arthur's knights had fought valiantly to vanquish them. At Woodstock her days melted into each other, all of them filled with pleasure. Henry visited her bedchamber night after night, growing more amorous as the days and nights passed. He loved her with true, genuine passion, as a true knight ought.

*

In September, their world of enchantment was shaken cruelly out of its summer dreaming. Ailenor dozed, her naked limbs relaxed and sated. Henry lay back against the pillows with an arm loosely around her shoulders. He muttered, 'I have ordered a new curtain wall with eight towers to encircle the Tower. It will be the most fortified castle in the land.'

'We'll be safer there if there's trouble again,' she said sleepily.

Henry's arm loosened; his eyes closed and he began to snore softly.

Ailenor sat straight up, her eyes wide open. A thump and harsh cry had cut into the night. She pushed Henry's arm away. 'Henry,' she said shaking him. 'Wake up.' Shouts came from the King's chamber. She could hear the crashing of overturned chairs, closely followed by the swish of swords. 'Henry, listen,' she said again in a frightened voice. 'We are under attack.'

Henry sat up. He pushed the coverlet away. 'What, by Edward's holy teeth, *is* going on out there?'

He climbed from the bed, pulled his night robe on and hurtled himself across the floor straw. 'Who's there? Where are the guards?' He shouted for his squires, yelling through the door, 'Alain, Guillaume, where are you sons of dogs? By Saint Edward's bones, is there no one left? Get in here the pack of you.'

Ailenor clutched their bed linen to her chin. Repressing an urge to scream, she stuffed a bundle of the lavender-scented fabric into her mouth. A breath later she pulled away her gag. 'Bar the door, Henry.'

Ignoring her, Henry grabbed a sword from the wall. He seized a shield with prancing lions and with his nightgown flapping about his legs, jumped forward.

One of the English ladies, Margaret Biset, burst into the bedchamber. 'My lady,' she cried. 'Are you safe?'

Her other women, led by Willelma, crowded into the doorway. Henry drew back still brandishing the sword. They screamed.

Squires and guards pushed through the women with drawn swords. One shouted. 'Where's the King?'

'Put up those weapons. By the Cross, what is happening?' Henry waved his grandfather's sword at them. 'God's blood, you are in your king's presence. By Saint Augustine, has the palace gone mad?'

The ladies screamed again and clutched each other. Willelma ran to Ailenor.

'There has been an attempt on your life, Your Grace,' the squire called Alain said. The guards surrounded Henry.

'My life?' Henry shouted. '*My* life!'

The squire drew breath. 'The rogue who entertained us at supper; the foolish fellow who pretended he was a king, tried to enter your bedchamber but you are here with the Queen. God be praised, because, Sire, you have escaped an assassin's dagger!'

'That idiot intended to kill me?' Henry laughed. 'Ridiculous! A beggar assassin?'

'We have captured him. Do we kill him now or question him first?'

'Question him.' Henry slowly lowered his sword and set the shield on the coffer by the foot of their bed. He shouted at the sergeant, 'Discover who sets him spinning. Keep him alive.'

'As you wish, Sire.' The sergeant's lip curled as he bowed, rose and ushered his guards out of Ailenor's bedchamber.

Henry followed the guard into the passage outside the chamber.

Ailenor tasted bile that rose from her stomach. She felt Willelma's arms encircle her. Another lady pushed a bowl to her. The chamber, usually so sweet-smelling, had been fouled by the sweating men. She heaved. Lady Margaret ran to the basin on a table by the window and poured water from an urn. She dampened a cloth and shook a few drops onto linen from a vial she took from her belt purse. She returned to the bedside where Ailenor was still heaving. She gently lifted her head and pressed the lavender-scented cloth to Ailenor's nose.

'Breathe,' Willelma insisted.

Ailenor breathed slowly, in, out, in, out, and finally found her voice. 'Lady Margaret, explain what has happened.'

She felt Lady Margaret gently place the silk bedrobe about her shoulders. 'I was at my prayers. I had just risen to leave the chapel. A figure entered the cloister. It was the mendicant the King gave his supper plate to after he had said a beggar should be as well-fed as a king. I followed him. He entered the King's chambers. Sainted Madonna, he was planning to murder us all. It was then I called for the guards.'

Ailenor looked up to see Henry had returned to her side. He had heard Lady Margaret's explanation. 'Lady Margaret, your devotion has been our protection this night. Thank you.'

'Go and rest, Margaret. Willelma, take my ladies away now. I have recovered my wits.' She turned to Lady Margaret. 'The assassin will be punished and we are safe thanks to your quick wit.'

A squire came to them with wine and wafers. Henry told him to leave it on the coffer and sent him away.

When Henry returned to her bed, he tenderly tucked the covers about her. 'Lady Margaret will be rewarded with a gold purse,' he said with firmness in his voice. 'I shall double the guards on our chambers. This must never happen again. Who knows what dangers lurk in the darkness?'

Sinking back down under the coverlet, Ailenor said, 'We cannot trust anyone. Must we always be alert to danger?'

Henry poured her a cup of Gascon wine. 'Sit up for a moment, my love.'

He held the cup to her lips. She gratefully sipped the ruby wine and when she felt it warm her queasy stomach she said, 'Let us try to sleep,' though she knew it would be difficult. She would lie awake until the sky lightened and birds began to sing.

After that night, Ailenor always kept a dagger under her pillow.

Chapter Eight

Winchester, Christmas 1238

'The fault must be with me,' Ailenor wailed to Willelma as she paced her chamber. 'Am I to be a barren wife? It's what they're saying. Have I offended God?'

'Nonsense, *cherie*.' Willelma clicked her tongue and tried to hush Ailenor, settling her against cushions and brushing out her hair with soothing strokes. Ailenor pushed her domina away and, scattering cushions, ran to the corner shrine dedicated to Saint Bridget, her name-day saint. She fell to her knees and wept frustrated tears. Was she wrong in thinking God would make her and Henry's ardour an exception because they needed a son and heir?

After her outburst she prayed daily, kneeling on chill tiles in the abbey at Westminster or her chapel in the Tower. She confessed her sins. She gave alms to the poor. She curbed any excess such as untrammelled desire. By Christmas, to her great relief, God had allowed her his blessing. They rode south to Winchester to celebrate Christ's Feast. She smiled and tossed pennies to the poor. God and his saints had listened to her prayers. At last, she was pregnant.

Henry loved Christmas and because she enjoyed the season too, and was with child, Ailenor was doubly joyful. They proudly circumnavigated the Hall at Winchester twice, her hands pointedly folded over her stomach, her head high, and her ermine-trimmed sleeves trailing over the rushes. She cared not if her ladies had to pick out camomile and dried stalks from the fabric later.

She felt herself smiling as she nodded greetings to the aristocratic Anglo-Norman wives who curtsied and wished her a joyful Christmastide. She felt their dislike. More Provençal ladies had joined her court who would steal potential husbands from English earls' daughters. She could read their thoughts and only kept with her those English women she favoured such as the Biset sisters, Lady Margaret and Lady Mary.

'Everyone is here today; well, everyone except for Earl Simon and Nell,' she said in an undertone to Henry. Nell and Simon's first son had been born in November. Brows had been raised when news of that birth raced throughout the court. Ailenor sighed. 'Simon is in Rome. Nell is recovering.'

'But, I was duped,' Henry said in an equally low voice. 'Nell cannot have been with child last December. No child takes eleven months to appear.'

'Maybe Simon just thought she was with child. I miss Nell.' Ailenor spoke through her teeth as she smiled at a group of abbots standing by a pillar. 'Order her back to court after she is churched.'

'A month out of childbed. I think not,' Henry said and patted his wife's belly. 'And we don't order, Ailenor, we invite. Come, now we have shown ourselves, we can retire until the Masses begin. You, sweeting, must rest.'

Ailenor groaned. Normally she enjoyed the Christmas Masses. As they exited the Hall, she said, 'Please forgive me. I cannot, I cannot endure them. The frankincense makes me nauseous. I'm so tired.'

She was not let off so lightly. 'Frankincense has a pungent scent about it. I'll order the priests not to wave it over you. You'll be seated today with a hot brick to warm your feet. We'll stay for the Midnight Angelus only.' That was the end of that. She must endure.

On Christ's Day, to Ailenor's approval, Earl Richard swept into the hall wearing a white tunic displaying a red crusader's cross. Ailenor wondered if his hand lay behind the assassination attempt the previous September. There was no proof.

'No, certainly not,' Henry said at the time. 'The madman, if that was what he was, has not incriminated anyone else. He will be punished.'

When she heard what this death was she said, 'That's a cruel death; limbs pulled apart by four horses. *Non*, terrible, terrible! How can you approve it?'

'It's just. The mendicant would not have hesitated to murder you in our bed, Ailenor.'

'Even so . . .'

She'd refused to witness that execution.

Watching Earl Richard walk about the Hall that smelled innocently of Christmas spices, perfumes and evergreens, she shuddered at the memory of Woodstock. He nodded amicably to everyone, his crusader cross stitched on his shirt for all to see.

Richard bounced into his oaken-armed chair beside Henry, who could not help but glance up at his taller, darker, younger brother with admiration. She found herself frowning. He may not be guilty of an assassination attempt on his brother's life, but he must be kept loyal to the throne. Over and over, she remembered her father's words, 'keep friends close and enemies closer'. She had not decided which Richard truly was. Henry's brother was ambitious and he was the wealthiest earl in the land. She had recently heard another rumour. Earl Richard kept a long-term mistress in Cornwall. He'd had children with this woman. Poor Isabel.

Henry leaned over, stared at the cross on his brother's gown and said, 'You are ready to go on crusade, I see.'

'When Earl Simon returns from Rome we shall make a final push to recruit.'

Richard and Simon had united. Placating Richard had come at a great cost to the royal coffers. Henry, Ailenor suspected, would not want to fund the new crusade from his treasury, not whilst he had new building plans. The Church would donate a crusading tax but it would take time to collect it.

'If only I could join you both,' Henry said with a sigh as a juggler passed by the table spinning plates on a stick. He threw a silver penny which landed accurately on a dish.

'You are the King and England needs you. The barons are ever dissatisfied.' Richard raised his aristocratic brow and looked at Ailenor. She knew whom he blamed for the barons' discontent. Her Savoyard clerks were not popular. They'd taken over the management of finance in many of the shires. The barons were not in control of the sheriffs as before. Henry's new foreigners were, and when they collected taxes money went into the royal coffers.

It was as well Henry remained in England, Ailenor considered. Whilst Henry would not join Richard's crusade, no matter how much he longed to go dashing off at the head of an army to the Holy Land, he was no warrior.

She said, holding Richard's gaze, 'Henry has plans to rebuild the ancient abbey at Westminster, create a New Jerusalem within England. The new Abbey Church will be Henry's Crusade.'

This and making heirs for the kingdom – a prince to follow him. The gossip in the City that she was not capable of giving Henry a child after over two years of marriage would dissipate once she gave them a prince.

'Indeed,' Richard said. 'I understand we can soon expect an heir.'

'We are hopeful,' Henry said, his pale blue eyes looking at her with love.

'When?'

Ailenor cupped her stomach, though at three months of pregnancy there was little as yet to hold, just a thickening and a constant tingling in her breasts which were growing larger at last. She *was* capable of bearing children – lots of them. She smiled at Richard. 'It is early yet but with God's grace, June is the month my midwives predict.'

She felt the air shift and glanced up. Silk rustled as Isabel of Cornwall slipped into her place. She greeted Isabel with genuine goodwill.

They had become friends after a difficult beginning. Isabel accepted her, even though Isabel was a Marshal and Henry viewed the family with suspicion.

Isabel arranged her skirts, accepted water from a silver basin to wash her hands and a towel from a page with which to dry them. After all was done, she said, 'Congratulations, Ailenor. Such good news.'

'God has blessed us, Isabel. We are content.' Ailenor wondered if Isabel, too, was with child. She looked very pale. 'Are you . . .?'

Isobel patted her hand. 'No, my dearest, just tired. We rode fast to get here in time for Christmas.'

'Thank God for fine Christmas weather.' Ailenor glanced towards the trestle where the court children had been placed that afternoon. The excited band of youngsters were chattering like magpies. She scrutinised the little gathering of cousins. One was missing. 'Where is your little Henry, Isabel? I don't see him.'

'In our lodgings with his nurse. I couldn't bear to leave him at home, Ailenor. He is too young for the feast, but maybe next year.'

'Your son will be a good friend to our children as they grow up.'

'Full cousins. I shall pray for a growing royal nursery. I have seen you tell stories to your ladies' children, Ailenor. You like children, I see?'

'I do, and I enjoy telling them stories.' Ailenor turned sideways towards Henry. As she did, she caught Isabel glancing at Richard. Would *he* pray for a royal nursery? Could it have been Richard who had spread the cruel rumour that she was infertile?

'When will you return to Berkhamsted?' she asked, returning her attention to Isabel.

'Saint Stephen's Day; Richard wishes to visit Nell to discuss recruitment for the Crusade. After this, he travels west to speak to the knights of Cornwall and Somerset.'

'Why?'

'The Crusade again, of course. He is enthusiastic. This will all take at least another year, maybe more. Crusades can take years to plan.'

'Ah, yes.' Ailenor wondered if, in fact, Richard was off to Cornwall to visit his mistress. Could it be that Isabel didn't know — or perhaps she knew about the woman and, as was expected of a noble wife, pretended not to know, or, worse, accepted her husband's bastards into her household? Henry's father, John, and his grandfather, the second King Henry, had both acknowledged some of their bastards. 'I hope Richard visits my family in Provence when he travels south.' Ailenor changed direction. 'Don't *you* wish to see Nell's Henry? Nell will miss Earl Simon this Christmas.'

'I shall wait until Nell is stronger and Simon has returned from his pilgrimage.'

'I miss them both,' Ailenor murmured.

Isabel laid her hand on Ailenor's. 'You'll see her at court soon, I'm sure.'

They turned their attention to the Christmas feast. Fowl was served and wine poured. Jesters performed tricks; musicians played; jugglers threw coloured balls into the air and caught them. Happily, Ailenor watched the children, who were shrieking with joy and longing. Old Father Time walked about the company shaking a staff with coloured baubles. Course after course was carried to the table. The scent of spices – nutmeg, cinnamon, cloves, anise, and ginger – ran through the Hall. Isabel only picked at her food whilst Ailenor ate voraciously.

The Christmas subtlety was served, carried straight to the King's table by the smiling cook himself. In honour of Richard's planned Crusade, the marchpane confection was a gigantic ship coated with sugar. A tiny, brightly coloured crusader flag flew from the mast and miniature soldiers paraded along the deck.

Henry's food taster, a young man dressed in livery bearing his silver tasting spoon and a tiny golden goblet, stepped out from his position behind the King's chair and waited as Ailenor's husband broke off a tiny sliver of the ship's sides and handed it to him. A heartbeat later, Henry nodded to Richard and said, 'You must have the cross or any other piece that pleases you. Choose.'

As Richard lifted his eating knife from the board and chopped off the sugared flag with the painted cross, there was banging at the

Hall door. A tall figure shoved it open, knocking over the pile of scabbards left by it. He marched up to one of Ailenor's men who was posted close to the door yelling, 'Savoyard dog. Cur. Whelp. Get down. You *will* kneel to me, for I am greater than you, foreign pup.'

The Savoyard pulled a sword from one of the scabbards he was minding. He raised it. There was a shout from one of the barons. 'That's my weapon, dog.'

Ailenor leapt to her feet. Isabel, white as bleached cloth, rose from her chair.

The tall figure was none other than Gilbert Marshal, his sword at the throat of the Savoyard.

Richard's knife dropped onto the cloth amongst a scattering of disintegrating bits of marchpane. He whipped a short blade from his belt. Ailenor drew her jewelled dagger from her girdle.

'Stop them,' she demanded, clutching her weapon and turning to Henry. 'He will kill my cousin if you do not. If you don't prevent this, I shall.'

'Gilbert!' Isabel shouted to her brother in a clear voice. 'You dishonour us.'

Ignoring Isabel, Gilbert hurled words towards Henry. 'You refused me an invitation to your feast because I am a Marshal. I'll remind Your Grace I'm the Marshal of England.' There was a brief pause, followed by murmuring from the barons seated at the trestles. Gilbert shouted, 'I have come to claim my lands, those you took from my brother. You grant our lands to foreign interlopers, friends of the she-wolf you call your queen. My eldest brother, William, is dead. My second brother, Richard, is dead too. The Marshal lands are mine by right.' He pointed his sword again at the Savoyard. 'Next time you head for a privy, you thieving cur, you won't reach it.' The Savoyard's face was white as the table linen. His leggings were stained with urine.

Henry puffed out with anger, shouted back, 'Your brother Richard was my enemy. You remaining Marshals hold my sister's dower.' He raised his hand. 'Guards, take them both. Put them in irons. I shall deal with them later. There'll be no brawling at my feast.'

Ailenor watched aghast as Earl Richard dismounted from the dais. Her hand flew to her mouth. He had called her a she-wolf. He'd insulted her. It would be murder now. Richard weaved his way through the gaping crowd, waving his sword at his old friend, Earl Gilbert. Henry called out, 'Put up your weapon, brother.' Richard hesitated for a moment but with a dramatic gesture sheathed his sword. He hurried over to the children who were wide-eyed with terror as they clung to their nurses, burying their heads in the women's mantles. Richard appeared to calm the women.

'Remove them,' Henry shouted to his guards who had already drawn their swords. 'Both of them.'

Guards rushed forward from walls and doorways and quickly surrounded the brawling noblemen, disarming them. Several dragged Gilbert who was kicking and screaming abuse. Others seized the Savoyard and pulled him by his tunic tails through the rushes. Richard returned to the table and stiffly sat down, his arms folded as he stared at Gilbert.

Actors and musicians drew back as the guards removed the men from the Hall. Ailenor felt her heart race. She put away her dagger and sank back into her chair. These grim, backwater, old-fashioned, lacklustre English lords would not have her people removed from court. None would call her a she-wolf. The Savoyard administrators were useful to Henry. Her Provencal courtiers brightened a dull court with new ideas, troubadours and French fashions.

Henry must make an example of Gilbert Marshal. Was Marshal behind the Woodstock plot, not Richard after all? If so, he must pay the ultimate price.

Isabel, shocked and tearful, moved around the table and fell onto her knees before Henry. 'I beg you, my King, spare Earl Gilbert, my brother.'

Henry raised her to her feet. He sounded more composed. 'It is Christmas. He is foolish. You may attend him.' Henry's tone was mild considering the fracas that had frightened the court and ruined the Christmas feast.

Ailenor shook her head, but, ignoring her, Henry continued, 'A night in the cells will temper Marshal's anger.' Henry turned to Richard. 'Go to the idiot with your wife. Earl Gilbert is banished forthwith to the north. This is my final word.'

Ailenor complained, 'He attacked my followers. He insulted me. He should be punished.'

'And I shall punish him. He likes to joust. I am banning jousts forthwith. The Church disapproves of them. I dislike them. Earls and barons will not gather in any of my courtyards bearing arms. Neither Gilbert Marshal, nor any others.' Henry crossed himself and raising his hand signalled to the musicians to play. 'We shall resume Christ's feast.'

'Not enough,' Ailenor said under her breath. She refused to speak to Henry for what was left of the feast. Avoiding the merrymaking that followed, she pleaded exhaustion and, clicking her fingers at Willelma and her other ladies, she swept from the Hall.

Henry did not pass another night with her that Christmastide. The atmosphere between them grew strained.

Gilbert, Ailenor heard on Saint Stephen's Day, had not only been banished from court. He must pay a fine to Ailenor's smarting cousin. The same cousin demanded Earl Gilbert's head to be set on a spike by London Bridge. She stormed into Henry's chamber.

'I want the Marshal's head. He is a traitor.'

Henry told her, no. She flounced out but not before saying in a chilly voice, 'Marshal will destroy us. Do something about him.'

Relations between them remained frost-like for another week, until Henry remarked on New Year's Day, 'Richard will insist that Gilbert Marshal takes the cross.' Her head swivelled on its long neck as she turned to stare at Henry. He would be out of the way, but the Crusade would not leave England for several years yet. Taking a vow to crusade was only the first stage in the whole enterprise. Still, she looked forward to seeing Gilbert Marshal wearing a cross on his breast, occupied with recruitment.

After a week's absence, Henry visited Ailenor's chamber.

'You have found a fair solution.' She took Henry's hand, determined to keep peace with him. The quarrel had marred Christmas. Everyone saw how they were estranged. There were whispers and speculations. Willelma reported these. Lady Mary had overheard maids saying the King was angry with his queen. It must not continue. This was not good for the prince she carried in her womb. Women had miscarriages for less annoyance. She must discover an equilibrium with Henry. She said, 'They will both be gone from court for some time.' She patted Henry's hand, knowing he disliked quarrels with her as much as she did with him.

'And now, you shall concentrate filling our nursery with children.' Henry offered her a dish of sweetmeats and she lifted one to her mouth and allowed her sharp teeth to bite into it.

'I pray every day for a safe delivery.'

Henry's face brightened. 'London is unhealthy for children. Renovations at Windsor are nearing completion – new chapel, new Hall, chambers for you and for me. I shall design a nursery for our family.'

The quarrel was over. Her ladies preened in Henry's presence, lowered their eyes but, she noted, smiled their approval.

Once the Epiphany Feast was over, the larger court was sent away until Eastertide. Ailenor and Henry began to pass long winter afternoons together. She regained her good temper. Soon it was as if the quarrel had never happened. As they sat by the fire in her chamber one January evening, Henry held up building designs and scrutinised them. He tugged at his sandy-coloured pointy beard and nodded. Ailenor glanced over at him and remarked, 'Who is working on the altar embroideries and the offertory veil for the chapel at Windsor?' She fingered the embroidery she was working, enjoying her talent, pleased at her progress since Rosalind had instructed her and her ladies in the mysteries of working with gold and silver threads. Gold flower hearts gleamed on the border of a coverlet for her baby's cradle. A little green dragon embellished with gold graced the middle ground.

Henry sat the rolls of parchment aside. He looked at her curiously and said, 'Adam de Basing has a team of embroiderers working for me.' He bent over her work and studied Ailenor's neat stitches. 'That is a very fine embroidery. I like the dragon's golden eyes. I see Rosalind Fitzwilliam has been instructing you well. That's accomplished work.'

'She is an accomplished and patient teacher. I have only given her embroiderers secular work. They embellish gowns, cushion coverings, bedcovers, and tapestries for my chambers. I asked them to make a hanging for Nell and Simon's wedding gift.' She grinned. 'Simon on his charger with his colours on his shield. It is very romantic, with a background of roses. He looks like Sir Launcelot of the Cart.'

Henry smiled wryly. 'As long as he is not seeking a crown and stays far away from my Queen.'

'He has his own princess now. He is happy. They are in love.' She thought for a moment, her mind returning to buildings and furnishings. 'Henry, we must choose a country home for our family as well as Windsor.'

'Say where, and it is yours, my love.'

She thought for a moment. 'Marlborough.' Her countenance innocent. 'Was it once in the Marshal family's estates?'

'Not any longer; it was disputed after Nell's widowhood. I'm taking complete charge of Marlborough. You shall have it, Ailenor. I have other estates in mind for Nell.'

Ailenor folded her hands. 'Thank you, my lord.' She had executed her just revenge on Earl Gilbert. Marlborough was one estate he could never claim.

Adam de Basing, the name floated about in the recesses of her memory, was Henry's grocer. His son was to be betrothed to Rosalind. Rosalind had said she was not of a mind to marry anyone but, rather, to have her own workshop.

'At Westminster,' Ailenor had said on the day she offered Rosalind the opportunity to set up the Westminster embroidery workshop. 'But don't think you will never marry. The heart can be difficult to ignore if possessed by a love so great you cannot deny it. All the best legends say so.'

Rosalind had looked away. Something mysterious in her embroiderer's demeanour made Ailenor wonder if indeed the girl's heart had already been claimed. By Lent they would return to the City and she would find another commission for Rosalind, whom she was beginning to like more and more. It must be an important embroidery, a religious work perhaps for the new chapels Henry was building.

Chapter Nine

Rosalind
March 1239

Boats ploughed through the river, creating splashing sounds, as Rosalind was ferried from Westminster into the City. The Queen, resident in the Tower, wished to discuss a new commission so Rosalind asked two accomplished embroiderers to accompany her.

'The wall-hanging for Kenilworth is almost completed. We are ready to take on this commission. You, Martha and Jennet, are my most competent embroiderers.' She frowned at Jennet who was still young and very wide-eyed but deserved a chance – after all, she was only two years older than her apprentice. 'When we meet with Queen Ailenor, you will listen, not speak.'

'Yes, Mistress,' they said, Martha serious, and Jennet in a babbling tone.

'Good, follow me. We mustn't be late.'

As they approached the Tower, the shouting of men and the clang of hammers resounded across the river, drowning out the lapping of water and the banging of boats knocking against each other. Their wherry drew close to the passenger wharf. Helped by the boatman and Tower guards they stepped over the watery channel onto the dock. Glancing upwards, Rosalind was astonished to see how far the building of towers and the new curtain walls had progressed. New outer walls were rising. One new corner tower was already halfway to completion.

She noted the builders' wharf held an enormous flat-bottomed boat from which a crane was unloading white stone. The master mason was directing operations, pointing to where the new stone was to be placed. Horses dragged carts loaded with rubble up to the outer wall.

They picked their way around carts, snorting horses, and yelling men and took a path that sailed up the slope through the chaos of building works. Several masons and apprentices turned to stare at them as they passed by the masons' lodge that was smack up against the walls. Jennet simpered and allowed her hood to fall back, revealing corn-coloured plaits dipping below her white cap.

'Good day to you, Mistress,' one bold young man called to Jennet, his spade raised.

Rosalind primly answered for them all. 'Good day to you.'

Jennet pouted and smiled. Martha, a widow with more than thirty years, glowered. Rosalind turned to Jennet and waved her hand towards a second path.

'Don't you see the King on his way to inspect their work? Look ahead and bow that saucy head of yours!'

Jennet had the wit to lower her head. The King, surrounded by a group of foreign-looking nobles, was fast approaching. His master-builder, waving a sextant and a rod, was hurrying up the parallel pathway towards the new building to greet him.

Rosalind snapped, 'Come along now. The Queen said she would see us before Nones.' She peered up at the chilly blue sky where the sun had reached its zenith. They were late. She chivvied her women through the gateway towards the Queen's apartments. Jennet stopped at the threshold and Rosalind gently prodded the girl forward. 'Don't be nervous.' Their silent guard followed.

Queen Ailenor was specific. The new commission was to be a hanging for the Queen's chambers at Windsor. She had ordered an artist, a Provençal monk, to design it. Rosalind let out a surprised gasp as she studied the drawings. Queen Ailenor had requested a hanging showing Christ's Nativity with two midwives attending the Virgin Birth.

Seeing Rosalind's puzzled countenance, Queen Ailenor said, 'The midwives testify to Mary's virginity. This is what we learned in Provence. *Bien!*' She pointed at the stars. 'These can be couched in silver threads, a sky filled with little glittering stars, but there has to be one golden large star. Oh, and roses, white roses on the borders.'

'Your Grace, is there a reason for your choice of a golden star?'

'It represents my husband's star in ascendancy.'

'The roses?'

'Roses bloomed in Bethlehem when Christ was born. As you know, I am partial to roses.' The Queen smiled.

'But the midwives, Your Grace, they'll will be frowned upon. The Church here believes that the Virgin, herself, delivered the Christ child. Our Lady gave birth alone.'

'Is that so, Rosalind? Our beliefs in Provence are clearly more flexible.'

Rosalind could not find an argument to counter this nor did she dare gainsay the Queen.

'I see. Where do you intend to hang it, Your Grace?'

'In my chamber at Windsor. I don't think the English bishops will be invading my apartments. Midwives it will be.'

'As you will, Your Grace, and with a golden star and roses. We must keep this work secret.'

'That is for you to decide but I want it executed as I describe.' Ailenor folded her hands over her bulging stomach.

Rosalind glanced over at Jennet and Martha, who curtsied and nodded.

Rosalind knew there were no midwives present in the stable at Bethlehem. To include them allied the Virgin with earthly women. Earthly women lacked purity. 'Perhaps the midwives could be nuns who are virgins.'

'*Bien.* Nuns indeed. Why not?'

'We shall work hard on it, Your Grace.' Rosalind knew it could not be completed by the summer when the Queen would give birth. It would be an impossible task.

'It's for my chamber at Windsor, not Westminster, and I expect it ready for when we move there after Christmastide. You may go, Rosalind. I shall send the artist to the workshop this week.'

'Your Grace, as you wish.'

They were dismissed. Rosalind hoped this embroidery would not bring condemnation on her work from the Church or the King. She thought for a moment of how her papa always said he had rescued her mother and grandmother from the Cathar Inquisition in Toulouse. Her mother was not a Cathar, but Rosalind's grandfather had been. She shuddered. She could not afford to be associated with free-thinking Cathars and nor must the Queen.

As they returned to the waiting wherry, she said to her embroiderers, 'If you speak of this embroidery, I cannot keep you in my employ.'

'Yes, Mistress Rosalind, we understand.'

She tried not to worry.

A flock of gulls screeched along the river, too adventurous and somewhat too far inland. Rosalind settled in the boat and never spoke again until they reached Westminster. The difficulty with Queen Ailenor was that she would not be gainsaid. Once set on an idea she had to see it executed. They needed the money they earned. The Master of the Wardrobe, who dealt with expenses, denied the Queen nothing and he had instructions presumably from the King who adored his queen. The whole of London knew this. Yet the burghers grumbled about Queen Ailenor, complaining she was extravagant. Rosalind loved the Queen. She had saved Rosalind from Jonathan de Basing and for this Rosalind was grateful.

As they walked towards the workshop, Martha remarked, 'All those stars and the figures too. It can't be completed for at least a year, Mistress. It is very detailed. It won't be ready for the birth.'

'The Queen said Christmastide or thereafter. Still, it is a larger embroidery and will take all our time to have it ready within three-quarters of a year.'

Jennet wasn't listening. Her eyes had strayed again, this time across the courtyard. 'Jennet,' Rosalind said crossly, 'what are you doing?'

A group of squires were gathered around a practice quatrain. One stood out. The design on his tabard was familiar, since she had just last week embroidered it onto Earl Simon's shield for the gift that was to go to Kenilworth. As if sensing her watching, the squire spun around, waving a blunted sword ready to strike the practice ball. He threw down his sword, spoke to his companions and sprinted over to them.

'Go ahead,' she said to the women. 'I have business here.'

Their guard looked doubtful.

'Go on,' she said. 'I do know Master Thomas. We've met before many times.'

The squire had reached the group of women. He looked straight at Rosalind. The others looked away.

'Come along, you.' Martha pulled the gaping Jennet away.

The guard followed Martha and Jennet, though he threw a look of concern over his shoulder.

Thomas laughed. 'Mistress Rosalind, what a pleasure. I had hoped to see you. We have just returned to Westminster.'

'Yes. Master Thomas, you've have not been at court for nearly a year now.' She stared at the crest on his tabard.

'I have been with Earl Simon in Rome. We are back recruiting for Earl Richard's crusade. I think my uncle hopes that I shall be sent on the crusade and killed. He will claim my lands.'

'Your uncle! You have lands?'

'And a manor house. My family are vassals of Earl Simon. My uncle is my guardian.' Thomas shook his head. 'He doesn't care for me.' Thomas kicked a clump of muddy earth.

'Who are your noble people?' Rosalind's tone was curious. She looked up and held his eyes. They were the blue of cornflowers in the field. Although he had escorted her to the palace before Earl Simon set out for Rome, he'd never spoken of his kin.

'I am Thomas Beaumont, not knighted yet, so just plain Beaumont, a distant relative of Earl Simon. One day I shall be a knight.'

She shrugged. 'Are you, indeed?' She could not help feeling that Thomas had been deceptive by not revealing before whom he really was. She shrugged. 'I'm not sure that I am a suitable person for you to speak with as an *equal* any more, Thomas Beaumont,' she said archly.

'I think you are, Mistress Rosalind. I hope now that I am back at court you will see more of me.' He lowered his voice. 'You are fairer than ever, if I may be so bold.' He reached out to touch her face. She jumped back as if a cat had scratched her.

He reached out again and with one finger lifted her chin.

'Your father is one of the wealthiest guildsmen in London and I am but an impoverished squire. It is you who should consider me lesser.'

She felt disappointed tears gather behind her eyes. 'Not so. You will be betrothed into your own class no matter how poor you claim you are. Your uncle will find you a noble heiress.'

'I shall choose my own bride, thank you, Mistress Rosalind. My uncle will not decide for me. He is only interested in lands to add to his own.'

'I have my workshop to consider.'

'Not for ever.' He spoke with a serious note.

'The workshop is my purpose.' She thought for a moment, softening, and said, 'Perhaps one day I shall want children and a home of my own. If so, I shall choose my own husband.'

'Is that so? Well then, I must return to the sport.' He caught her arm and said in an almost whisper, 'Wait for me to come back to woo you. Wait until I return from the new crusade.'

'Godspeed, Master Thomas,' she said shaking him off. 'Women cannot be wooed so easily.' She longed with all her being to make him the promise, but she could not. She could not risk disappointment. Instead she said, 'Bring me back Ottoman silk from Jerusalem? Bring me back the tree of life embroidered onto it and perhaps I shall be here waiting.'

'Your wish, sweet Rosalind, is my pleasure. Good-day, my lady.' With a backward wave, he was gone, loping towards the entrance to the stable block. She sighed as her eyes followed his golden head. He was of the knightly class. She was a burgher's daughter.

For days following the visit to the Tower Jennet gossiped to anyone willing to listen to her descriptions of the Queen's green samite gown with its trailing sleeves and her Grace's fruitful bearing for she had glowed with happiness. Jennet told everyone how the Queen had offered them sweetmeats from a silver dish and a cup of ale whilst they discussed the new embroidery. Thankfully, Rosalind thought, Jennet was silent on the content of the embroidery. Rosalind locked the worrying design in a chest until the cartoons could be drawn on linen by Queen Ailenor's artist. She called Jennet into her presence and looked sternly at her youngest employee. 'You know you are not to discuss this design with the others, only that it is to be a hanging depicting the Nativity for the Queen's chamber at Windsor.'

'Yes, Mistress Rosalind, I know that I shall lose my place in the Queen's workshop if I speak of it.'

'Good; that is the way of it. No loose talking to builders or craftsmen. Or squires.'

Rosalind blushed, realising just what she had said, and swiftly sent Jennet on her way.

Chapter Ten

Spring 1239

In May, Ailenor's ladies closed the shutters against the spring sunshine and hung cloth over them. The hangings shifted in a breeze drifting through a solitary opened window. Despite predictions that a woman entering seclusion in the four weeks before birthing should be kept warm and a fire burning night and day in the hearth, Ailenor insisted on the opened window. 'Silk cloth of the softest blue must be hung over the other two.' Her tone was firm. Willelma tut-tutted but patiently had sought out the requested blue, an expensive colour, only used in England for a hundred years.

'Ah, *bien*!' Ailenor said as the blue hangings were hung. 'How can light be harmful to a woman about to give birth?'

Despite her ladies' protests, no one had a sensible answer and rays of calming sunlight filtered into the chamber through her one unshuttered casement.

On the day she entered her seclusion, Henry presented her with gifts to help ease her travail – a silver and gilt belt blessed by the Archbishop. 'It is Our Lady's girdle. It was in my widowed mother Isabella's possession. When she ran away from England, stole my sister Joan's betrothed, Hugh of Lusignan, and married him, Archbishop Edmund insisted this stayed in our keeping. Now it is for you, my love.'

Ailenor gazed on the faded belt. 'But Joan was Queen of Scotland.'

'We found her a better bridegroom, one who would help us unite our countries in peace. Alexander was a fine choice at the time.'

Henry knelt before her at the door to her chamber and tearfully wished her well. She would not see any man until after their child was born. They would, he said, love their child, prince or princess. 'After all,' Henry said, 'Your own mother has borne four beautiful princesses.' He seemed to preen. 'Two are married to the greatest kings in Europe. A royal girl child, like Joan, or Isabella, my sister who was married to the Emperor, or even Nell,' – he frowned – 'wed to Earl Simon, is a valuable asset to any royal dynasty.'

Ailenor sighed, thinking of a girl-child's fate. Too soon, girls were stolen away by the dynastic marriage market.

Once Henry bade her farewell, she shook off her irritation at his parting words. Everything, her future position as queen, her position with the barons, and Henry's love, all depended on her successful delivery of a healthy child.

Candles were lit in her chamber, casting their glow upon the image of winter painted on the wall above her fire place. He was gazing at her, clad in a flowing silvery cloak and in possession of an equally long white beard. She stared back at the strange ghostly figure. 'He has such sad looks,' she said, turning to Willelma. 'I suppose he possesses wisdom.'

She turned from the image and lost herself in thought. It was summer, not winter. She had no desire to look upon winter. In England winter seemed to last for ever. It was as well she enjoyed great spitting fires, atmospheric services held by candlelight, and the many entertainments that crowded their winter evenings. She was becoming used to the weather and May, her favourite month too, was green and gentle. Waking from her reverie she clapped her hands and turned to her ladies who had gathered with Willelma by the fireplace. She announced, 'Poetry. Tonight I want to hear something appropriate, a poem the Lord and his Holy Mother must approve.' She closed her eyes and considered for a moment. Opening them again, she said, 'Lady Mary, fetch the Songs of David from my book closet. We shall read after my rest.' She yawned dramatically. 'I shall sleep for a bit.'

She lay down on her coverlet. Lady Willelma drew her bed curtains closed and immediately she drifted into a pleasant doze.

Later, as the bells rang for Vespers, she awkwardly rose from the bed. Lady Willelma helped her to her resting couch by the fire whist Lady Mary scuttled off to fetch the volume Ailenor had demanded earlier. 'I shall use this time well,' Ailenor said. She settled down, feeling content. Lady Sybil read to her from David's thirty-third poem.

That those do lying vanities regard, I have abhorred
But as for me, my confidence is fixed upon the Lord

She must try not to allow vanity to distract her from piety. But it was difficult. Beauty was to glorify God. Beauty was also a monarch's right, as a king or queen was God's anointed ambassador. She could not deny beauty, but what about vanity; that was another thing altogether. She must try harder to deny vanity.

Servants arrived with supper, walking diffidently into her chamber, unfolding a linen cloth on which they laid out dishes that were delicately flavoured. The women ate seated in a circle by the empty hearth. The air was warm. A fire would be ridiculous.

As she dozed into sleep that night, a last thought flitted into her mind. If only her mother, Countess Beatrice, could come and visit England. She would be so proud of her daughter. At such times a woman longed for her mother. She would write a letter to the Countess. No, there would be so much more to say after her child was born.

'My first-born will be a prince,' she said into her pillow. 'A prince for the realm.'

Chapter Eleven

Rosalind
June 1239

Church bells rang. The sky shone blue as Our Lady's robes, as if declaring its own happiness at the birth of an heir for England. Trumpets proclaimed the birth of a new prince for the realm. The birth of a prince heralded a public holiday. Rosalind took an early wherry from Westminster to the City. When she stepped from the crowded boat onto the wharf at St Paul's, she had to thread her way through streets packed with hawkers selling everything from pies to ribbons; noisy apprentices; goodwives excitedly chattering about the new prince; darkly clad priests rushing to services of thanks for the boy child in the hundred churches throughout the City. City merchants paraded, ticked out in their best garb, and dancers and jugglers and City criers blowing horns thronged the lanes leading from the riverbank.

Papa and Dame Mildred hurried to greet her when she entered the Hall at Paternoster Row.

'You've arrived in time for breakfast. How long will you stay this time?' Papa drew her to the table and demanded a place set for her with a wooden platter, eating knife, spoon, and a napkin. He ordered Cook to provide an enormous breakfast of eggs, cold meats, curds, freshly baked bread, cheese, and dishes of strawberries laced with thick cream to be served to the whole household including their apprentices, embroiderers and assistant tailors, to celebrate the royal birth.

'A day or two,' she said, reaching for a boiled egg. A servant poured her a cup of buttermilk. 'The City is wild at the news of the Prince.'

'Queen Ailenor is in favour again. No talk of a she-wolf today.'

Rosalind frowned. She knew there were city merchants who called Ailenor a she-wolf foreign queen. There was no love for the French in London, and although she was a Provencal they still called her French.

'There's to be a feast at the Tailor Hall. Will you join us?' Papa was saying.

'Yes, I'd love to come. Thanks for including me.' There was no Embroiderers' Guild in the City. As member of the Tailors' Guild, her father held office and was highly respected amongst other City tailors. Since she embroidered the Queen's gowns with gold and silver embroidery, pearls and semi-precious stones, she hoped she would be respected also.

He pushed back his platter and said, 'I've sent a golden plate to the palace as a gift for the new prince. The Guild will present a golden bowl set with precious stones.' He laughed. 'King Henry will send his messengers for the gifts today. He's keen to take our wealth.'

'I hope the King thanks you all,' Rosalind remarked, cynicism creeping into her words. Only the very best presents would be considered worthy for a prince of the realm. She had observed how King Henry could be dissatisfied with gifts. In fact, she had once overheard him complaining to Queen Ailenor that his nobles did not give him enough presents. He demanded pure gold of the highest quality and rolls of fabrics such as Italian silk from the London burghers. If a gift was not valuable enough, he would return it and ask for a replacement.

She had sent a purse to the Queen stitched with a cinq-foil design on green velvet that morning and had lovingly placed a silver spoon inside, one she had spent her hard-earned coin on. It was sent to Queen Ailenor herself and not to the King. She even waited in an anteroom until the liveried page she entrusted it to assured her he had placed it in Lady Willelma's hands as requested.

The Westminster embroidery workshop was busy. The day of celebration was welcome to her embroiderers who returned to their families to enjoy their day off. Rosalind had carefully padlocked the long low hall-like building before she set out for Paternoster Lane. They had set up the work for the new tapestry. The ground would be of the finest blue woollen cloth on which her embroiderers would stitch stars, flowers, and vine tendrils. This was her most important commission to date and the largest. It was unfortunate she had to deal with Adam de Basing, who had purchased the backing fabric and blue ground for the tapestry. He was too curious for comfort.

Once she came into Adam de Basing's orbit, he bustled daily through her workshop, his unpleasant son panting at his heels, nosing into whatever work her embroiderers did. Fortunately, Jennet was wary of Jonathan and never flickered her eyelids his way, not once. She sat at her embroidery, serious as a nun, when the de Basings walked into their workshop. Jennet's eyes remained lowered.

Smiling at the memory of Jennet's prim behaviour, Rosalind unpacked the few belongings she'd brought with her. The attic room was always kept available for her, though recently her father spoke of moving to a larger house. Alfred was more successful than ever since Rosalind had become Queen Ailenor's embroideress. Queen Ailenor's Savoyards flocked to him like peacocks in a courtly garden, always in need of new surcoats and tunics.

Rosalind laid out an overdress of fine blue linen with sleeves stitched with celandines and pansies. It was a favourite gown. She'd seen at breakfast how her stepmother glowed with her first pregnancy. Papa seemed proud, hopeful of a son to train up one day to inherit his trade. If he still clung to the notion she would be betrothed to Jonathan de Basing, he never voiced it. She thought of Thomas Beaumont as she plaited ribbons into her hair, wondering if he was in the City with Earl Simon and Lady Eleanor who were lodging in the Bishop's new palace on the Strand.

Their paths had not crossed since the meeting in March. Thomas had departed with Earl Simon to Kenilworth. She was sure the castle lay close to his uncle's manor and let out a pained sigh. He'd asked her to wait for him but the crusade could be delayed for years. He might never return. Tears pricked the back of her eyes. With blue ribbons hanging loose from her fair hair, she stared out at the sparrows lined up on the roof of the gable opposite. They were free to arc up into the heavens when they so wished. Thomas was not free. He was in service to a great earl. She gulped. His uncle would expect him to marry a knight's daughter.

That evening, streets were as busy as they were on Midsummer's Day. Everyone spoke with affection of their love for the King, Queen, and Prince, who was to be called Edward for the King's favourite saint. Hawkers screeched through the narrow alleyways where the second storeys of houses tilted forward, almost touching. Lanterns hung ready to be lit as soon as dusk fell. Pasties and sweetmeats were renamed for the Prince. She heard calls of 'Prince Edward's crown!', 'Saint Edward's coffins', referring to the pastry cases, and 'Prince Edward's cradle' or the more exotically named 'Jewels in the Crown' for the various dried apricots, dates, and currants for sale on grocers' trays.

Dancers pointed their toes and stepped out lightly in chain-like formations, twisting along narrow streets holding hands and inviting passers-by to join them; stages were erected for plays; embroidered cloths hung from windows; jugglers juggled. Fountains flowed wine, and passing them on the way to the guildhall, Rosalind noted raucous apprentices imbibing freely. She was relieved when Gruff, their servant, parted the crowds with a heavy stick from which flew a pennant with the tailors' badge and led them through crowded, noisy streets to the Tailors' Hall.

Inside the high, raftered hall, she spoke with many old friends, happy to see her. Women admired her new gown, her soft leather boots, and the yellow and blue ribbons entwined through her plaited hair. They congratulated her on Prince Edward's birth as if the Queen's child were her own child. Scanning the Hall, she was relieved to see Jonathan de Basing was not present, though she spotted his parents seated close to two City aldermen not far from her. Adam de Basing acknowledged her with a courteous nod. She nodded back and quickly looked away.

Papa swept his napkin from his shoulder and dabbed at his mouth. 'They still hope for a betrothal, you know. De Basing says he visits your workshop. He says you surround yourself with women so Johnny does not even have the opportunity to speak to you. What does he expect? The women are your embroiderers and you must mind them.'

Rosalind glanced at Mistress de Basing, whose mouth was steadily pulsating like a fish's mouth and ugly it was too. 'I *am* surrounded by women. Decent women. Quiet women. My women are not like her.' She indicated the grocer's wife with a sour look.

'Won't you reconsider, my child? You can always give up the workshop. There are other embroiderers there to manage it for the Queen. At seventeen, 'tis time you were wed.'

Rosalind glared at her Papa. 'I am happy as I am.' She attended to the lampreys on her platter but their deliciousness was marred for her. She pushed the platter away.

Alfred ran on, 'The Queen is a mother. Do you not wish this for yourself? Mothering is the state God intended for women.'

'The Queen is generous. I cannot let her down, Papa. Besides, I like working for her.'

Mildred placed her hand over Rosalind's. 'You may change your mind, you know.'

So she was on Papa's side now. 'I shall not. Excuse me,' Rosalind said crossly. 'I need the privy.'

She pushed her way through the tables. How dare her father speak of that alliance again and how could Dame Mildred agree with him? Adam de Basing could source anything – cloth, sugar, spices. He would not source her. She would never unite their families.

Hurrying along a narrow corridor that led out of the great Hall's back entrance, incandescent with anger, she found herself in the yard amongst the privies and the stable. She leaned her head into her arms against the stable wall. A body barrelled into her. Before she could twist around, she felt herself dragged behind the row of stinking wooden huts. Her gown pulled up as she was roughly spun around and shoved against the outside wall.

'Thought it was you,' a hoarse voice was hissing into her ear. 'No women to guard you now. Do not shout out or I shall –'

Winded, she gasped, too terrified to scream. Jonathan de Basing held her pinned to the wall with his enormous, beefy arm, his hand reaching up the skirt of her gown.

'Let me go.' Finding her voice, she shouted, 'Let me go, you monster!' She pushed at him but he was too solid and she could not push past him, no matter how hard she shoved.

'Shut up!' He penned her more tightly against the wall.

'Get off me.'

Lanterns threw a glimmering yellow light over the wall. Someone must hear her but Jonathan slapped a large hand over her mouth. She bit hard. He dropped it, howling with pain.

'You have no business waylaying me,' she shouted.

'Oh, but I do, you little bitch,' he said, pushing his face into hers. His breath stank of soured ale. 'My father wants us wed. Wed we'll be. You are mine, fair Rosalind, witch as you are.' He tried to press his mouth onto hers.

She twisted her face away. 'Do not call me witch, you foul creature.' She shoved again, to no avail. The solid door that was Jonathan held. He laughed. His sweat smelled foul. She began to tremble.

'What a scared little bird you are. It's nice. You'll see. You'll be wanting more soon enough.'

Holding her so tightly her arm throbbed, he began loosening his breeches, pulling them down with one free hand. She screamed again. Her heart raced like the rapids that surged below the City Bridge. Her legs weakened, her knees collapsing.

A shadow appeared around the side of the privy. What if Jonathan had a companion? They would both dishonour her. Johnny was tearing at her gown, trying to lift it. She saw his swollen member. 'Bastard, bastard,' she shouted and pushed. He thrust forwards. The approaching figure grew larger. She was going to die here this night. Smack! Her eyes closed. She felt herself slithering down the wall. She opened her eyes and tried to stand but found her legs unable to move. Jonathan was sprawled on the ground clutching his head. She looked up at her rescuer. Thomas, his kind, concerned face was looking into hers. She couldn't speak. He reached out and helped her to her feet and gently brushed down her dress.

'He didn't?' Thomas said in a gentle voice.

'Thomas, thank God, if you hadn't come he would . . . he'd have ruined me.'

'Bastard son of a bastard father.' Thomas kicked Jonathan in the groin. Jonathan groaned. Thomas did not hesitate. He pulled Jonathan up and punched him over and over.

'Don't kill him,' she pleaded. 'His father is powerful. He's the King's grocer.'

'Come away from here. Come with me, Rosalind, I'll return you to your father,' Thomas said putting an arm about her. 'I know who that scum is. He's often at the Tower with his father.' He spat at Jonathan, who was trying to get up after the last punch caught his stomach. 'Take that.' A gobbet of spit ran down Jonathan's face. 'I know what you were about to do. Your father will hear of this.'

'She tempted me,' the merchant's son whined, trying to wipe off the spittle.

'Liar and a devil's son. You attacked her.' He kicked Jonathan again. The grocer's son shrieked. Thomas laughed. 'Who will be believed, you, scum? Most likely they'll believe an Earl's squire. Stay away from her.' He took Rosalind's arm.

'Thomas, take me home. I can't go back to the feast,' she said. 'Our servant is waiting outside at the front. He can tell Papa I'm returning home and he can see us through the streets. I can't be seen with you alone. It would invite talk.'

'True enough.'

Thomas guided her to where the servant was patiently seated on a bench with a mug of ale on his knee. She told him she had been attacked by Jonathan de Basing and wished to return to Paternoster Lane. She indicated Thomas. 'This is Earl Simon of Leicester's squire, Thomas. He saved my honour. I shall tell Papa later. For now tell Papa I am unwell.' Gruff threw back his ale, nodded and lumbered into the Hall.

They waited in the torchlight until Gruff returned. 'He's not pleased but I said you were unwell, Mistress Rosalind.' Pointing to Thomas, he lowered his tone. 'I never said about him.'

'Let us be off,' Thomas said quickly. 'Rosalind, I'll walk with you.'

With a nod, Gruff held up his lantern. Thomas kept a wary eye out for Jonathan in case he returned with companions to pursue them. She was relieved they had Gruff leading them through the City streets. He was as strong as a siege machine.

Gruff walked ahead with his staff that proudly bore the Tailors' badge held high. Thomas explained to her how he had been sent with other squires and heralds to fetch the Guild's gifts for the new Prince. 'I saw you go out to the privies, and I observed him follow you. I never saw you return so I went to see what had happened. St Thomas's holy toes, thankfully I did.'

'The other squires and the gift? Should you not return with them?'

'I shall catch them up. The gifts from the city guilds are to be kept at the Bishop's house tonight. Earl Simon is there.'

'Jonathan will seek revenge.'

'Tomorrow, I shall visit Jonathan's father, and I won't be going alone. I shall have a guard.'

'Don't go there; you will only make it worse.'

'I should challenge them, you know.'

'The de Basings are too powerful. He will say he was in a fight. He'll say I tempted him. He'll make the story stick. He'll find a sham witness.'

Thomas shook his head. 'Send for me if there is trouble.'

She nodded.

They reached the tall house. Gruff opened the gate to allow them to pass into the courtyard.

'A fine home,' Thomas remarked. 'You live well, Rosalind.'

'It's my childhood abode, but Papa is married now and he's considering a bigger house. My stepmother is with child.'

'You are safe here in Paternoster Lane and you shall be at

Westminster too. Rosalind, I heard what Jonathan de Basing said about marriage. Don't allow them to force you into that family. Promise me you will wait for me.'

Her hand was on the door latch. 'I won't be marrying anyone if Mistress de Basing speaks ill of me after this, but if I do, you are he.'

'Wait for me,' he repeated.

'I don't know what the future holds except that I will not marry Jonathan de Basing.'

'I can hope.'

'You may hope?' she murmured. His response was to take her hand, turn it over and kiss it.

'I shall wait for *you*, my love,' he said.

Opening the door, she slid into the house. If only she *could* hope. Her hand tingled where Thomas had kissed it. Her heart soared high as she recognised her love, flying into the night, like the swallows that crossed the summer skies.

'So who is this gallant knight who rescued you from that oaf? Mildred and Rosalind were in the small herb garden behind the house gathering angelica for a cordial. Later they would add honey and vinegar to it. The days were growing hotter and Papa found the aromatic flavour of the drink refreshing. 'I can make candied pieces with these stalks,' Mildred said as she placed a plant into her basket. 'You can take some back with you.' She ran a kerchief over her forehead. 'So, do you like him?' She popped an angelica leaf into her mouth and began to chew it. Her eyes were twinkling.

Rosalind felt herself blush. She glanced around to make sure the cook was nowhere about or any of the apprentices. She would have to tell them sometime and they must understand she would never, ever marry into the De Basing family. They could still persist. Her papa could weaken and give into them. She shuddered to think of what Jonathan had tried to do to her.

'Let me tell you why I like Thomas – and he's not a knight. He's a squire.'

They sank down onto the garden bench and Rosalind did her

best to explain her feelings, their mutual feelings. She found Mildred a good listener.

'You must speak to Alfred and soon,' was all Mildred said but when she laid her hand over Rosalind's, Rosalind was sure she had an ally in her stepmother.

'Rosalind, he's a knight's son,' Alfred shook his head. 'Trade weds trade. Noblemen wed noble women.'

'But he asked me, Papa.'

'His guardian would never permit such a union.'

Mildred said, 'Sweetheart, never will you wed Jonathan de Basing after what has happened, but you are comely and there will be many others of your own class. They'll be queuing up to be betrothed to you.'

Rosalind shook her head. 'I shall marry Thomas or find my own way in life,' she said stubbornly.

'I hope, Rosalind, you will change your mind on this matter,' Alfred said, frowning.

'Excuse me, for I need to rest,' she replied with simplicity, knowing she would never change her mind.

Chapter Twelve

August 1239

'You have given birth to a warrior. He is a very long baby, a long-shanks. And he has a powerful cry,' Sybil had remarked after Edward's birth. Well, thought Ailenor, it would take a warrior to control the difficult English barons and earls. This birth had been easy. Edward had slipped from her and into the world with a strong cry, but she must breed more children. Edward would be surrounded with devoted royal siblings.

On the ninth day of August, Ailenor prepared for her churching. She could not enter the world again until she was cleansed and purified by prayer. Domina Willelma and Margaret Biset laced her into her cloth of gold gown. They plaited her midnight hair into filigreed crispinettes and placed a narrow jewelled crown over it to hold her veil in place. Edward was swaddled so tightly only his small face appeared peeping above his gown. She took him from his rocking woman and kissed her son's downy head.

The purification ceremony was to take place in the Abbey, only a step away. Ailenor worried constantly about her infant son. Who knew what childhood dangers lurked in hidden corners to threaten a baby's well-being? No harm could possibly befall Edward on this short walk. A huge number of noble ladies attended her; she did not know how many – so many that she hoped she did not have to greet each by name.

She was aware the greatest nobles in the land were watching as she entered through the Abbey's west door. Followed by her ladies, she approached St Edward's Shrine. Archbishop Edmund waited to bless her at the high altar before the shrine. A paean of Lauds floated through the nave. She had wanted Nell to hold baby Edward during the long ceremony that would follow but Nell had not arrived by the time she had reached the Abbey Church. Her eyes searched for Nell and Simon amongst the gathering of nobility. She could not see her anywhere. The de Montforts were lodging at the Bishop of London's palace outside the City gates. They would not have to negotiate crowded City streets to reach Westminster.

'Where is the Countess of Leicester?' she said, turning to Joan of Flanders who walked beside her. Countess Joan was visiting the English court with another of Ailenor's uncles, Thomas of Savoy, who was now married to Joan. As the new Count of Flanders, Joan's husband sought alliance with England and had arrived at the court to do homage to Henry. Ailenor liked him least of her mother's Savoyard brothers. She suspected Countess Joan disliked her, but she could not fathom why. Perhaps it was because the de Montforts enjoyed Henry's favour, and it was rumoured Joan had once wanted to marry Earl Simon herself. Today, as a countess of high rank, ruler of Flanders in her own right, and because she was Ailenor's aunt by marriage, Joan would walk close to Ailenor.

'I have not seen her,' Countess Joan said with nonchalance. Through the luminous silk of her veil, Ailenor noticed her shrug and her haughty upturned nose.

She dislikes Nell, Ailenor realised, recognising a potential enemy in Countess Joan. She turned to Sybil Gifford who had been her midwife and said, 'Hold Edward. He is happy in your arms.' Joan gasped her displeasure.

Ignoring the woman, Ailenor stepped towards the five hundred tapers that burned at the shrine of St Edward. Bowing her head as she passed, she proceeded towards Archbishop Edmund who stood waiting beside the altar. Prayers were said over her until finally her purification ceremony ended. Its end was accompanied by beatific glory and song. As she left the altar, the noble ladies gathered behind her, their expensive gowns gleaming with gold and silver embroidery. She proudly reclaimed Edward and carried him back through the Nave, her veil drawn back to reveal her face. She was purified. Yet, although she glanced from right to left, nowhere could she see Simon or Nell.

She was joyful as she floated out of the great doors into the August sunlight outside the Abbey doors where she was greeted by Henry. He would know what had happened to Nell and Simon.

'Where is Nell? Has she not come? And Earl Simon, where is he?'

'Not now, my love. Later.' Henry kissed his son's head. He took Edward into his own arms. Accompanied by the greatest nobles and ladies of the land, he walked with her, carrying their son to her apartment where she would rest before joining the purification feast.

Since Edward's birth, Henry had made her brief visits. Hand in hand they had walked in the quiet garden below her apartment, admiring summer roses and breathing the scent of wild flowers. Henry was more attentive than ever, sending her gifts, many of which were presents from the guildsmen of London. Some, he remarked, he had returned to the burghers, asking for more expensive presents for his son. Ailenor shook her head when he told her this. It was ungrateful, she said. It must not happen every time they had a child.

Her ladies sat beside her at the feast. Henry sat with his noblemen on an adjacent table. Simon was not amongst them, Nell was still nowhere in evidence. She tried to ask the women seated about her but her questions were met with shaken heads and tight lips as if no one knew anything – or claimed not to know anything. Countess Joan was placed further along the High Table. She felt sure the Countess knew something. Ailenor puzzled at this odd conundrum all through the procession of courses for her feast.

Nell had visited her after Edward's birth with Hal, her first child, to see the baby Prince, his cousin. Hal was out of swaddling and, at eight months old, he was beginning to crawl. They planned visits to Odiham where the de Montforts hoped to spend the autumn season. Simon would be recruiting and planning the crusade. She and Henry would hunt in the woodland close by and spend joyful autumn evenings in the castle where they had first consummated their love for each other.

Later, when Ailenor and Henry were settled in their private chambers and Edward was with his wet nurse in the nursery, she asked again, 'Where are Nell and Earl Simon? No one will tell me. My question was met with a sour face from Joan of Flanders. Why?'

Henry's face darkened. 'My sister and the Earl are no longer fitting company for you.'

'She is jealous,' Ailenor said.

'Of whom. Of Nell or of you?' Henry frowned and his left eye lid lowered.

She dropped the tiny silver rattle she'd been holding. It clattered onto the floor tiles. 'Have you gone mad, Henry? Explain this nonsense.' She folded her arms and raised her head determined to remain calm. 'I have no idea. Not fitting company?' she repeated so quietly she could hardly hear her own voice. 'Why?'

Henry shook his head. His face had turned stony, his eyes darkening to the startling blue of a stormy sea, his eyelid drooping as it did when he was furious. Ailenor waited patiently.

'Earl Simon put my name forward to the Pope as surety for a loan to pay for the negation of Nell's vow and forgiveness for their wedding. I never knew. He never consulted me. Forgiveness, indeed. He claimed she was pregnant, the reason I saw them wed, the wedding to avoid scandal. He deflowered her, I believed, but, Ailenor, as we all know, no baby remains eleven months in the womb.'

She opened her mouth to defend Nell and Simon.

He said, 'No, wait for the rest. Simon had to pay the Pope for Nell's vow to be rescinded and their marriage recognised. Paying God is expensive. The Pope's accountants sold Simon's debt to your Uncle Thomas. They thought Thomas would have a better chance of extracting the debt money from me than from Earl Simon.' Henry paused for breath. He pursed his mouth and spat out the amount. 'Two thousand marks.'

She remembered that when Nell had come to see her, Joan of Flanders had excused herself and had swept past Lady Eleanor, and

122

out of her chambers. She had been followed by her own large entourage of ladies. Ailenor wondered at this at the time but was so pleased to see Nell she had not asked Joan of Flanders the cause. Joan of Flanders was an unpleasant and jealous woman, not worth a second royal thought.

Henry's face reddened, his left eyelid drooping further as he spat uncharitable words at her. He poured himself a goblet of wine. 'Earl Simon has been living in the Bishop's comfortable palace at my expense. Never once, not once, all summer has he mentioned I was surety for his debt.'

'You gave more to pay Richard off last year,' Ailenor reasoned. 'Does it really matter? Has Uncle Thomas been whispering evil in your ear whilst I was in my birthing chamber? And you, Henry, you have listened to that uncharitable toad.'

Henry reddened further. She saw his temper rising and said quickly, 'Of course it does matter. My Uncle Thomas is right. Simon must pay the debt.'

'Nell can kick her heels at Odiham. Simon will be put on trial, as your uncle and his countess demand. I'll send guards in the morning to turn him out of the Bishop's Palace. They dared to show up at the Abbey today. I sent them away.' Henry threw the rest of his wine into the fireplace where it hissed on the glowing logs. 'This Malmsey is an apology for wine.' He bellowed at a page. 'Bring me good Gascon wine.' He stared at Ailenor. 'I'll remind you, your other uncle, William, has never supported my sister's marriage.'

She drew a deep breath. For Nell's sake she must try to change Henry's mind. She must remain calm.

She took another breath. 'Put Simon on trial for what? We all have debts. Earl Simon is a loyal knight. He's devout, as fervent as yourself. He'll be off on the crusade soon.' She lowered her voice. 'In time, Earl Simon will pay the debt. I'll speak to my uncle. Of course, Simon must pay. His lands can be surety. It is not a serious enough matter to go to trial.'

'His lands come from the Crown! I own all.' Henry let out a roar that made her sit straight up. 'Where will Simon find the means to crusade?' He yelled, 'I am confiscating his lands. In the morning he'll be arrested and put in the Tower. My sister and their child can retire to Odiham. As for Simon, he won't get as far as Chelsea.'

'You've not thought this through,' she said as she blinked away tears. 'Give pause for thought.'

The Gascon wine arrived. Henry was about to drink himself senseless. He threw back the first full goblet at once and demanded his cup be recharged. Gulping down the next cup, he sank into his huge carved chair. She might as well not be present. She could not reason with him when he was like this.

Her eyes brimming with tears, she said, 'My lord, I must rest.'

He never glanced up as she left the chamber calling for Domina Willelma to attend her at once. She would warn them before it was too late and Simon was carried off in chains. Shuddering at the thought, she wiped away her tears and contrived a plan.

When Willelma followed her into her chamber she sent all her other ladies to their rest, closed the door and bolted it. 'Willelma, I have a task for you. I must write something which you will deliver.'

Willelma shook her head. 'I heard the King. Others will have heard him too. I suspect your intention is to save the Earl; it's unwise.'

'Just think of their baby without a father. Think of Nell. Henry will regret it if he puts Earl Simon on trial. He, himself, is in debt to his earls and barons. I think they might side with Earl Simon. Just think if Chester, Ferrers, Hereford, Warwick, and Warenne side with Simon. Remember the nobility's Great Charter. The barons are dangerous if roused.'

Willelma nodded. 'You are right. I shall take your letter to him, but it's a dangerous thing to warn them. No one must know you did this.'

'Not as dangerous as what might happen if I don't.'

Ailenor frowned and chewed at the top of her quill. What would happen if Henry discovered what she had done? Her ship was sailing from Queenshythe to Calais in the morning. Nell and Simon and little Hal must be on it. She wrote the message, folded the paper, and sealed it with her rose seal which she used for private communications. As she waited for the soft wax to set, she called for a page she could trust. He was a quiet, pleasant French lad who was devoted to her, listened to her requests with a grave face and soft puppy eyes.

She said, 'Accompany my lady Willelma to the Bishop of Winchester's palace. She has a message for Lady Eleanor. Deliver my lady safely there and back. Tell no one, absolutely no one where you went tonight.' She pressed a purse into his hand. 'For the wherry. The rest is for sending you out into the night.'

'I'll guard Lady Willelma with my life. We won't be seen.' He bowed low.

'Good. I am trusting you.' Ailenor said.

He seemed to glow in the candlelight, having been entrusted with Queen's business. Turning to the waiting Willelma, Ailenor said, 'Take the garden path. Tell Nell to destroy this. No reply.' She pressed the little folded letter into Willelma's hand.

After the page and lady slid through the side door into her garden, Ailenor fell to her knees. Clutching her beaded rosary, she begged God to keep Nell and Simon safe.

Chapter Thirteen

Nell

Nell paced the floor, her footsteps echoing as the soles of her shoes clicked on the floor tiles. How could Henry be of so changeable a nature? How could he send them away from the Queen's churching? They were Edward's godparents. Her heart pounded with fear. Henry had shamed her in front of the court that morning, saying she and Simon had deceived him and he should never have agreed to their marriage. He'd called Simon debtor, liar, and a cheat. She remembered with pain how Joan of Flanders looked down at them disdainfully; how her husband, Thomas of Savoy, had been contemptuous towards them.

'You owe me, Earl Simon,' he had shouted as they stood outside the Abbey waiting for the Queen's party to arrive. Thomas of Flanders turned his back on them.

'I owe you nothing. My debt is to the Pope,' Simon said.

Thomas turned back, glared and said in a loud voice, 'His Holiness has sold me that debt. You said the King would back the debt. He didn't even know of it.'

Henry stepped forward, waved his hand at Simon. 'Get out, Simon. Leave.'

Although she knew nothing of this debt, she had tried to intervene. 'Henry, I shall pay any debt we owe with my dower money.'

'What dower? You have none, Nell. The Marshals have set your dower lands against your first husband's debts. Seems you have a habit of marrying expensive and defaulting husbands, sister.'

'I had no choice whom I married when at nine years old I was sent to Pembroke.'

Henry glared at her. She had never seen him so furious. 'You are not welcome here.'

Count Thomas said, 'Earl Simon should forfeit his lands.'

There was no choice. They left. Their sumpter carts were packed for the return to Kenilworth Castle with all haste. All plans to travel to Odiham were delayed. A letter had arrived from the Palace that afternoon confirming they were no longer welcome.

'We must be gone from here by dawn. I must protect Kenilworth and I must repay the debt.' Simon's head was in his hands. 'Henry will recall us,' he said, though doubt was creeping into his voice. 'I'll sell off lands and repay the debt.'

'You should have told me, Simon.' Nell stopped pacing and came to stand by Simon's chair. 'It will not be enough. Henry feels you take advantage. He thinks we are ungrateful. Joan of Flanders has her husband in leading reins. She is behind this.'

'I'm sorry, Nell. I just did not want to upset you.'

Nell hated to see Simon defeated. She threw her arms around him. 'We have each other and we have Hal.'

Simon looked up. 'Nell, I was arrogant. The money must be paid . . . a written apology made. Henry cannot remain angry.'

She heard the clang of the knocker on the entrance door. 'What now?' she sighed. 'Is he planning to turn us out in the middle of the night?'

The knocking persisted. Their whole household knew that they were disgraced and no one moved towards the door. That rankled Nell.

'Go, Thomas. Open the door,' she said to Simon's squire. 'I shall be behind you.'

Thomas drew open the door and stood aside. He turned and looked at Nell. 'It's Lady Willelma, the Queen's domina.'

'Willelma!' Nell said on seeing who slipped inside the opened door. 'Why you?'

'Ailenor sent me. Here.' She thrust the Queen's letter into Nell's hand. 'No reply is needed. It's a warning and you must heed it . . . do so by daybreak. Burn the letter when you've read its contents. Let me see you destroy it before I leave this Hall. My servant waits outside.'

Nell broke Ailenor's seal, read the note, and passed it to Simon. She could feel blood drain from her face. 'We must heed it,' she whispered. 'The Queen says we are in grave danger. She has a ship that can take us to France.'

After he had read it Simon said, 'Thank you, Lady Willelma. Tell the Queen it shall be done at once. Do you need escort back to Westminster?' His usually ruddy complexion was ashen.

Willelma said, her voice urgent, 'The wherry is waiting and I have an escort. Ailenor has thought of everything. She says to give you this purse for immediate needs.' She placed a leather purse into Simon's hand. 'Godspeed, Earl Simon. My mistress loves you well to put herself in danger like this. She will work hard for your return.'

Simon inclined his head. 'Thank her and for the purse. We are in her debt.'

Simon left instructions for their sumpter carts to leave for Odiham Castle rather than Kenilworth. Nell assented, saying, 'Henry will be more interested in Kenilworth and its lands than any of my manors. He'll assume we're travelling towards Warwickshire.'

She hurried to rouse Hal's nurse.

They were able to take a craft belonging to the Bishop along the river, fortunately escaping the rapids that surged under the bridge before the tide turned. As dawn broke, they were being rowed towards Queenshythe and Ailenor's ship. As well as Ailenor's purse, Simon carried a bag of gold and smaller coins. 'We shall be safe at Montfort-Amaury,' he reassured Nell. 'We've enough coin here to keep us for a time. Soon enough, Henry will relent. You'll see.'

'I pray it's so. At least it's safer than Kenilworth. I can't understand why Henry is so angry. It's as if he was looking for an opportunity to punish us.' She looked back at the City which was bathed in a rosy light. When would she see it again? 'I don't know if I can ever forgive my brother his ill-will.'

'I am not sure either.' Simon's face was stony.

Nell held Hal close in her arms the whole way along the river, darkness creeping around them; the splashes of oars in water echoed louder than they normally should. They were accompanied by only a maid, Hal's wet nurse, and Thomas, Simon's squire. The Queen's ship was to sail to Calais. From there they would purchase horses from a dealer known to Simon and a sumpter cart for their few possessions, the baby, his nurse, and their maid.

Thomas agreed to drive the cart disguised as a peasant. Although their destination would be Montfort-Amaury, near Paris, Amaury, Simon's elder brother was in the Holy Land. Simon said his brother's wife, Beatrix, would welcome them cordially

'My family will protect us. It's what families are for,' Simon reassured Nell. 'Linen and horses can be replaced. Heads cannot.'

Henry had sorely disappointed them.

Nell said, hope creeping into her voice, 'I have long wanted to meet your family. I am sure Beatrix will be kind.'

'You will be introduced to many kind people in France. You'll meet Queen Marguerite of France and King Louis too. My family are high in their esteem. Amaury was Constable of France before he went crusading.'

'What if Henry takes my castle of Odiham?'

'It's protected by law. The debt is mine. Those who were my enemies last year will be my friends again. Once the excitement of a new prince is over, the barons will question Henry's extravagance, his building plans, his relic-collecting, all at great cost – their own. The Pope's men are out and about in England gathering money from England's abbeys for the Vatican, never mind the Crusade. Henry is funding the Queen's relatives and this makes him vulnerable. He will want me back in time.'

Simon was more often right than wrong. She drew her furred

mantle around her sleeping child because the dawn was chill. Nell's body felt as if it were made of heavier bones than she possessed. Withdrawing into her thoughts, she wondered how the Queen's sister, the Queen of France, would greet them when they visited Paris. In time, she would remember this night as an adventure and not a disaster.

The Lion of Provence was easy to locate. It bore a queen's crown on its figurehead. Royal flags flew from the masts. For several years, Queen Ailenor had commissioned the vessel to carry fashionable gowns and expensive fabrics from France, as well as the variety of delicacies she had enjoyed during her pregnancy such as frogs' legs in aspic, French walnuts, almonds, and bags of lavender from Provence to refresh the royal linens and to sweeten her garderobes.

The ship would sail to Calais with English wool from Queen Ailenor's own estates. Simon was to pose as a wool merchant, Master Harcourt, travelling to Paris with his wife, child, and servants, on account of a death in the family.

The plank was lowered. Simon, wearing a nondescript tunic, his squire equally plain, and the three wimpled women, one carrying a sleeping child, boarded the ship without incident. The little group had made it just in time. The weather was calm but Nell remembered nothing of the crossing because once the captain gave the women his small cabin, she lay down on a pallet and fell into a deep sleep.

Chapter Fourteen

Ailenor
December 1239

'Your Grace, the embroideress is waiting below. She's upset.' Lady Mary burst into Edward's nursery chamber.

'Why is she upset?' Ailenor sighed. There had been no repercussions following her part in Earl Simon's departure for France. Even so, summer and autumn passed uncomfortably. Henry took possession of Kenilworth and refused to discuss his sister or her husband.

The week that began December had been particularly demanding. Henry, who always enjoyed extravagant feasts, had complained there had not been enough dishes provided for the November Feast of Saint Edward. He had run out of money that summer because of his building projects and, in addition, to pay off Thomas of Flanders he had had to borrow from the Jews. Ailenor was growing tired of appeasing her difficult husband.

She handed Edward back to his cradle-rocker and swept down the twisting staircase that led from the baby's nursery to her ante-chamber. Ailenor liked Rosalind so much, she had recently wondered about granting her a minor position in her retinue of ladies.

Rosalind stood by the door to the antechamber. She was in a state. Her eyes were swollen and her whole demeanour showed pain. Even though she was distressed, she made a deep curtsey to Ailenor. Ailenor wondered if the grocer's son had been plaguing her. She had heard he accompanied his father to the embroidery workshop.

'Bring us honeyed wine and cakes,' Ailenor said to Lady Mary as she ushered Rosalind inside the chamber. Lady Mary rushed off to fetch a jug of hippocras and cakes from the kitchens. Ailenor drew the embroideress to the warmth of the fireplace. 'Rosalind, take a deep breath. Sit on the stool. We shall make ourselves comfortable and you shall explain.'

When Rosalind sat on a stool opposite, Ailenor took her chair and leaned forward.

'Tell me all. What has happened?'

'Madam, it's a break in,' the girl said, gulping tears. Drawing breath, she continued, 'Our silks are ruined. Threads are dirtied. Embroidery frames broken. The Nativity hanging for Windsor, so nearly completed, and to be ready by Christmas, has been cut into pieces.'

'You have a gown of mine to embroider. Is it ruined too?'

Rosalind shook her head. 'No, that is intact. It is only the Nativity embroidery and our threads and needles.'

'It seems the hanging was the purpose for the attack. Was *anything* stolen?'

Rosalind shook her head.

Lady Mary bustled back with a pitcher, two cups, and a plate of honey cakes. Ailenor considered as she poured the wine. 'You have had a shock, Rosalind. Drink first and after you are warm, you'll take me to see the damage.'

Rosalind lifted her cup, new tears filling her eyes, and drank as bidden.

'Fetch me a mantle,' Ailenor said to Lady Mary. 'I shall see this for myself.'

The Queen, a group of her ladies, and Rosalind followed a wide candlelit passage that led to Westminster's hammer-beamed hall. Guards stood to attention as they passed into the courtyard. A wintery chill sliced through Ailenor despite her warm mantle. Followed by Rosalind and Mary, she hurried through the groups of knights practising their sword-fighting. A band of Benedictines crossing over the outer courtyard towards the Abbey Church bowed low as she passed. Angry thoughts filled her head. Had someone dared to destroy the embroidery because they saw it contained the midwives? If so, what narrow-minded people would attempt such a crime in the Queen's workshop? When she discovered the culprits, she would have them boiled to death in a vat of embroidery dye.

The workshop door lay open. Ailenor inspected the broken padlock. Inside, the frightened group of embroiderers were endeavouring to salvage fragments of fabric. The new embroidery was in ruins, chopped into pieces and polluted beyond repair by red dye the shade of blood which had been tossed over it. Ailenor drew a deep breath and turned to Willelma.

'Fetch my Master of the Wardrobe. Tell him to bring me the Palace Sergeant. Go. Find out which guards were on duty here last night.' She turned to Rosalind. 'Save what you can, Rosalind. It is heartbreaking but you can start again. This time you must move the work to Windsor. Assess the damage and make out a new order for fabrics and silks. Your family supplies us with gold and silver silks but who supplied the fabric?' She drew breath. 'Is it Master de Basing?'

'Yes, Your Grace, the King's Grocer, Master de Basing purchased the backing cloth, silk and linen both.'

'Well then, Rosalind, he'll source new fabrics and when you have them you will start afresh. Master de Basing will gain profit out of this night's destruction, assuming he is quick to purchase all you need.' Hearing footsteps approaching, she looked out of the doorway. 'Ah, here is Master Gatesden.'

The Wardrobe Keeper expressed horror at the damage. He spoke in a gentle tone to the embroiderers, reassuring them that none of this was their fault. 'Look,' he said stroking his thick black beard. 'All is not lost.' He pointed to the Queen's new gown of russet brocade decorated with borders of flowers and tendrils in silver and gold thread. 'The devils have not even stolen those pearl buttons. It seems they were intent on destruction, not theft.' He pointed to a clothing pole with a cape trimmed in fur and a basket of silk kerchiefs. 'And those too,' he added. 'They are all unspoiled.'

When the sergeant arrived, Ailenor chose this moment to take her leave. Master Gatesden would treat with him. 'Rosalind,' she said gathering her cloak up. 'Come to me on Monday, and we shall discuss the future.' She smiled a thin smile. 'I wonder if someone disliked Christ's midwives.' She glanced around the workshop. She addressed the sergeant-at-arms. 'Until we move to Windsor, there must be a guard on the workshop, day and night. Do you understand, Sergeant? Find out who was on duty last evening.'

Ailenor examined some markings she'd noticed on the cutting bench. They were not the usual marks associated with the cutting of fabric. She had seen the like carved into church door frames in Provençal villages. Surely the embroiderers had not made these? These were carved in wood as protection from witchcraft. She addressed the embroiderers, 'Scrape that table down ready for your move to Windsor. Stain it with walnut dye.' She decided not to remark on what she'd noticed.

To Ailenor's relief, after his initial fury when he discovered Simon had fled to France, Henry grew distracted by petty household economies, his new designs for Westminster Abbey, and the building works still in progress at Windsor. He began to speak in a more kindly manner about Earl Simon. It was as if he had never threatened to put the Earl on trial. Ailenor shook her head and smiled to herself.

A few days after she discovered the crime in her workshop, Ailenor decided she must tell Henry about the destruction of her new hanging, but Henry was busy looking at a letter. It could wait until he had finished. Henry tossed the letter he was reading at her and burst out, 'The scoundrel has written at last. He promises to pay the debt.' Henry's laugh was cynical. 'I have set aside his lands in lieu of what I paid Thomas of Flanders . . . for now, until the debt is paid in full. Montfort also has sheep on his lands. He told me so himself. It's a lucrative occupation these days. English wool sells well abroad.'

'Simon won't like it,' Ailenor said, a little abstracted as she read Simon's curt letter. He was not begging to return but, rather, had offered the produce from his lands in England towards payment of his debt. 'He sounds penitent,' she said in an abstracted manner, still thinking about what to do about the workshop. There had been no arrests yet and she wondered if she should move the embroiderers to a safer place. Windsor perhaps. 'Simon doesn't ask to return to England,' she said.

'He's in Paris. I doubt Louis will dream of lending him money. It will be a while before Simon pays up in full. The bailiffs up in Kenilworth will be busy for some time.' He gave a satisfied grin.

She handed Henry back the letter. 'I think you should pardon Earl Simon; bring him home.'

He wrinkled his brow and frowned at her. 'You may be right. I'll see.'

'If you don't, Louis of France might call on his services. Simon is your best knight.'

'Good luck to him with the French.' Henry looked petulant as he took back the letter. Moodily he tossed it on the fire, where the sealing wax dripped red and smelled pungent.

This letter was proof Simon was intent on paying the debt and Henry had destroyed it. She shook her head. 'I hope Nell meets my sister in Paris and tells her all about Edward.' She looked fondly down at Edward who slept peacefully in his cradle. A bevy of rockers and maidservants sat on benches far away by the door, out of hearing range. Standing, Ailenor called one over.

'The King and I shall walk in the garden. Rock Prince Edward's cradle.'

The girl made a curtsey and took her place by the cradle. A moment later she was swaying it gently back and forwards with her foot. Henry at once appeared calmer as if he, too, was being gently rocked. Ailenor peered down at her sleeping son and felt drowned with love for him.

'I shall send for Earl Simon and I shall forgive him,' Henry announced, his mood of a sudden jovial.

'So you should. Earl Simon is better as an ally than enemy,' she said, turning around. Deciding to leave it at that, since the girl rocking Edward's cradle was no doubt all ears, she said, 'Come, Henry, the wind is down and I want to show you the last roses. Let me tell

135

you what happened. There was a terrible incident in my embroidery workshop two days ago.'

'Oh, really?' he said.

'Yes and I think the workshop should move to Windsor with us.' She took his arm and they climbed down the private stairway that led to the gardens.

Although they searched far and wide, the guards responsible for the workshop's security that night had vanished. Troops crossed the City, searching every inn and church where they might seek sanctuary, but their families had not seen them for weeks. Spies were posted at the end of the lanes where they lived. They saw nothing.

Rumours claimed the guards were seen paddling across the night sky in a basket, on their way to Jerusalem to atone for their negligence. Others said they were seen galloping on dragons out of the City gates, heading for Wales where they would join one of the warring Welsh princes. Of course, Ailenor speculated, they have been paid by an enemy and promised a safe escape route out of the City. Without suspects, motivation for the destruction remained undiscovered.

On Monday, Ailenor welcomed Rosalind into her chamber. She sat on a cushioned chair at an oaken desk that slightly sloped, and indicated a stool opposite for Rosalind. Winter peered out from his wall above the fire place where logs blazed. Ailenor folded her hands and studied the embroideress.

'You must be ready to move to Windsor in the New Year,' Ailenor said, opening the conversation gently. She raised an eyebrow. 'You will have a temporary workshop there. I shall pay your stepmother generously for her golden and silver threads. I have ordered pearls for embellishment on the new tapestry.'

The girl seemed relieved. She clasped her hands in her lap and her eyes were bright and enthusiastic again. She leaned forward. 'Your Grace, do you really mean it? We are to remove all to the castle at Windsor?'

'Yes, for now. I think it safer and the apartments there have been redecorated. It's well away from evil odours.' She did not add 'evil doers' but she thought it. 'We consider the castle a healthier home for Edward.'

Rosalind's head was nodding like a puppet on a miniature stage. 'So be it. My stepmother will be pleased to provide thread again.'

'Windsor is a distance from the City. Everyone can go home for the major feast days and the Easter period, or stay, as they wish.'

'My embroiderers will have a comfortable dormitory and I my own chamber?' Rosalind tentatively asked.

'You shall all be comfortable. The embroiderers will be paid extra because of the inconvenience.'

'They will be relieved by your generosity, Your Grace,' Rosalind said.

Ailenor tapped a finger on her desk. 'I have another suggestion I want you to consider. After the new embroidery is completed, would you consider becoming my personal embroideress, remaining with me wherever I travel?'

'But I am already that, Your Grace.'

'I think you misunderstand. I want you to be part of my personal retinue. We shall make you welcome. You'll travel when I travel. You'll see places you will never see if you remain at Windsor.' She smiled. 'I would not prevent you from marrying if you wished. After all, as one of my court, you may meet a courtier and have the opportunity to marry well.'

'May I think about this,' Rosalind said, smiling back. 'May I remain with my embroiderers until the new embroidery is underway? I need to see it started again.'

'I have been thinking about that too. Why don't we make the embroidery one depicting the Virgin's Birth, rather than the Nativity. The midwives won't be so controversial if present at the Virgin's birth. Perhaps that was why someone destroyed it.'

'If your monk can draw it again for us, my artist will transfer the drawing onto a new background. Shall we have a moon and stars again and this time spring flowers such as celandines and pansies and primroses?'

'And white roses.' Ailenor loved roses. She must have a few roses in the borders of the new embroidery.

'May I order the linen and silk through my father's workshop this time? He will give us a good price.'

'Of course, Rosalind. The King has been speaking of economies. Talk to Master Gatesden.' Ailenor thought for a moment. 'Purchase what you need.'

'Thank you, Your Grace.'

After Rosalind had departed, Ailenor thought about the proposal to bypass the King's grocer. She disliked Adam de Basing, whom she was sure cheated Henry. There was no reason why a queen should not buy fabric from her own tailors, cloth merchants or grocers. *Rosalind* wanted her father to provide the fabrics, but why? Master Alfred had more business than he could manage. He worked for Earl Richard and of late for many of her own Savoyard retainers. Could Rosalind be suspicious of the King's grocer? Even so, as days passed and the Christmas season passed and with plans to remove to Windsor after the festival, Ailenor forgot about Adam de Basing. She had one child in the cradle. Her courses had returned with regularity. It was time to make a second child for the royal nursery.

Chapter Fifteen

Spring 1240

Ailenor conceived again by Christmas and in February the royal family moved to Windsor. Henry said she could choose who was to hold all the important offices. Windsor was to be her own personal kingdom and she revelled in this. Her first thought was to keep Master Gatesden as Wardrobe Master overseeing all areas of her domestic life. But there was a new man called John Mansel who interested her. She knew him to be astute and loyal. A position as an administrator managing her accounts would suit him.

By the time she moved, her chamber at Windsor was freshly painted and the walls newly panelled.

'Look at this,' Henry said, pointing to the largest window as they walked through her apartments. 'The Tree of Jesse is painted in the glass, and the windows open and shut too.'

She opened and shut them using a catch to push them out one by one. Well-stocked gardens lay below. It was a perfect bower. 'How clever.' She turned to Henry. 'I shall have my lying-in here in my new bedchamber.' From the garden, the scent of spring herbs, rosemary and thyme, floated up on a spring breeze. She breathed in the scent and sighed with pleasure. 'Thank you, Henry.'

Henry still delighted in pleasing her. Nothing must upset their harmonious life. She was fortunate in her husband. Instinctively she touched the brocade covering her growing belly. 'I am so happy, Henry. It is all perfection.'

He said, with a huge smile widening his face, 'I am too, my love. Westminster will have a new abbey to house Edward Confessor's shrine. Your new chapel will be dedicated to Saint Edward, and when we are in residence we shall make sure that one hundred and fifty poor are fed from our kitchen daily.'

Ailenor pressed his hands into her own. 'God has blessed us and in turn, we must bless the poor of Windsor. You remind me to be humble and grateful for all that is given us.'

He kissed her on the mouth. 'And you inspire me, my beautiful Queen. You are as pure and as devout as the Virgin herself.'

She held his pale eyes with her own dark eyes. 'Henry, I am God's earthly queen. I care for his people of England as do you, and I take that responsibility most seriously.'

'Of course, my love.' She saw how his countenance doted on her.

Sad news arrived from Viterbo in Italy. It concerned Bishop William, who had returned to the Italian state to guard his lands.

And now her beloved uncle would never return. He had been poisoned by enemies.

Henry, who had comforted her for days after this terrible news, returned to the City. He reluctantly took leave of her, promising to organise mourning in William's honour.

'Come,' she said sadly to Willelma and Mary, after Henry rode off with a large number of knights. 'I cannot stay inside. The walls of my chambers seep sorrow for my uncle. Fetch a basket and we shall collect herbs.'

This loss felt as if it had shattered her heart into a thousand pieces. Yet, it would not do for a queen to show weakness. She reined in her emotions. Despite all of Uncle William's faults, including his objection to Nell's hasty wedding, she loved him dearly. She walked calmly down the outside staircase and hurried through a low door into her herb garden. When she was a child and Uncle William had visited her family from Savoy they always sent him home with a satchel full of lavender and thyme. She bit back tears at the memory. He liked the scent of herbs. Often as they walked amongst herbal beds, he would pinch lavender between finger and thumb and raise it to his nostrils. Amongst flowers and herbs, she could grieve in solitude and peace.

As she gathered rosemary, so reminiscent of sorrow, to place about her bed-chamber, she wondered what poison had caused her uncle's death. Who had concocted the poison, and would he or she be found out? Gently touching the herb's sharp needles with a finger, she lifted it to her nose, inhaled its sharp scent, and shuddered. She must take extra care to select people with care for her new household, especially the servants employed in their kitchens. Tears filled her eyes. Uncle William had accompanied her all the way from Provence during the wettest winter she remembered. He had been her faithful advisor during the first years of her marriage; not only her chief counsellor, but Henry's. Uncle William had been a father to them both.

She paused by a hazel tree where a clump of forget-me-nots grew. Gathering a posy of these fragile flowers, she determined to keep the flowers in his memory. They would dry between two sheets of parchment. She would never forget Uncle William, never as long as she drew breath. Who would be Bishop of Winchester now her favourite uncle was gone? Uncle Peter might come to England, or Uncle Boniface. Winchester might suit Boniface who was already a bishop without a see. Her tears flowed and dropped into her posy. Uncle William would not return to England – ever.

She felt Willelma at her elbow. 'Let me take those flowers, Ailenor. I shall place them in a silver chalice for your chapel – to comfort your prayer.' Willelma curtsied and, posy in her hand, fled the garden. Carrying her basket filled with rosemary, Ailenor returned through the low door and mounted the staircase to her chambers. She would never forget her beloved uncle as long as she drew breath.

Chapter Sixteen

Rosalind
Easter 1240

Rosalind returned to her father's workshop for Holy Week. She slowly recovered from the loss of the embroidery by keeping busy on its replacement as well as the move to Windsor Castle. She was puzzled by the witch marks carved into their cutting table, looking like ancient runes. Rosalind wondered if the de Basings were behind the destruction in her workshop. After all, Jonathan de Basing had called her a witch on the night of the guild feast. Were witch marks cut into her work bench to suggest she was a witch?

On Palm Sunday her eye followed guildsmen wandering about the crowd outside St Paul's dressed up as the Old Testament prophets Elijah, Moses, and Joshua, and the Easter procession of merchants, craftsmen, and clergy that followed the prophets. The de Basings walked behind a bishop. She looked away and back. Papa and his journeyman stepped behind them. After the guild feast, when she told Papa about Jonathan's attack, he said furiously that Jonathan de Basing would never darken his door.

When Rosalind confided to Dame Mildred in the stillroom of the Paternoster Lane house about her suspicions of the de Basings's involvement in the attack on her workshop, her stepmother had crossed herself and said, 'Never speak of this. It would be your word against his. Adam de Basing is powerful. Best it's forgotten until there is evidence of their involvement.'

Rosalind shook her head. 'I told you what Jonathan attempted on my person, and now it's my workshop.'

'You *think* he was responsible for the attack on your workshop. You can't be certain.'

'Jonathan almost deflowered me. He was violent.'

'Yes, we understand that. De Basing has been terse with your Papa ever since. Jonathan, for his part, claims you tempted him. He says you are a witch who called upon a knight from Hell to knock him senseless that night.'

'That knight was Thomas Beaumont, Earl Simon's squire. Thomas can attest to that.'

'We told them Earl Simon's squire saved you.'

'What did they say?'

'Jonathan shrugged and claimed that you bewitched the squire as well.'

'What a lie.' She folded her arms and looked Mildred straight in the eye. 'One day I am going to marry Thomas Beaumont, you'll see.'

Mildred had taken her hands, drawn her close and gently said, 'Sweeting, I want your happiness but that young squire is well above your station in life.'

'We'll see.' She'd shrugged. 'Besides, I may join the Queen's court. What will my station be then?' She raised her brows in defiance.

Mildred said, 'I hope it is so and that your association with Queen Ailenor helps you discover true happiness.'

'Papa was pleased to provide us with the new cloth.'

'Yes, but Adam de Basing won't like it,' Mildred replied. It was during this conversation that she dropped an interesting snippet of information. 'Did you know that the de Basings have announced the betrothal of Jonathan to Marigold Musgrave? That'll be a strong alliance, Rosalind. King Henry's grocer's son and the Bishop of London's grocer's daughter.'

Rosalind nearly dropped a jug of ale on Mildred's feet. 'I know Hubert Musgrave is the Bishop's grocer. Good luck to poor Marigold and good riddance to Jonathan.'

She would wait for Thomas. Earl Simon had been forgiven and

permitted to return to England and was preparing for the Crusade, which had been long delayed. It was often the way with a crusade, delay after delay and then the year arrived and the crusaders were on their way. At long last it was to be May and once they set off for Jerusalem this spring, she might not see Thomas again for years.

She wiped a tear from her eye but reasoned as they watched the Easter procession, if she accepted the Queen's new offer, there would be safety for her as one of Queen Ailenor's ladies. Perhaps, too, the Queen would, one day, set out on a crusade with the King. If she stayed at court with Queen Ailenor, she might go too.

Rosalind picked up one of the tiny woven crosses strewn in the churchyard by the processing tradesmen. She let it rest in her hand. It was intricately woven, a lovely Easter token.

Mildred reached over and touched the little cross. 'We must light an Easter candle for Earl Richard. He is grieving for his wife. Lady Isabel was a good customer. Alfred said that you used to embroider her mantles when you were a slip of a girl.'

Lady Isabel had taken ill with jaundice before the birth of her last child. Neither mother or child survived. Earl Richard, Mildred informed her, was so heart-broken his grief rumbled St Michel's Mont far distant in Cornwall; his sorrow had flown on the wind all the way from Wallingford Castle. Dame Mildred may never have heard how Earl Richard had strayed from his marriage and Rosalind who had heard the gossip at Westminster would not speak of it. Let her think well of Richard. Relationships were complicated. She suspected Earl Richard regretted that he had not loved Lady Isabel enough, or that in his own way the Earl *had* loved Lady Isabel deeply. Perhaps his Crusade would be a form of atonement.

Rosalind said, 'It *has* been a terrible year. Queen Ailenor once said that my mother was an angel in Heaven watching me embroider. I hope Lady Isabel is an angel in Heaven watching over Earl Richard on his crusade and watching over their little Harry. I saw them last year at Westminster. She adored her boy.' She murmured a short Pater Noster over the little straw cross.

★

Eastertide was over. The Queen's guard had arrived. Rosalind packed her small oaken chest and descended the rickety staircase from her attic room to bid Papa and Mildred farewell. She kissed baby Edwin's head, sad to leave the quiet sanctuary of her old home and her family. This was to be another new beginning as the Queen's lady.

The street of burghers' wives appeared by their gates to watch her depart. Rosalind swept along Paternoster Lane, her head high, with her lion- and gold-liveried escort helping her to avoid offal, carrying her chest for her. They began to wind their way through narrow streets to the river where the royal barge waited to whisk her back to Windsor, a journey that would take the greater part of the day.

As they approached St Paul's Church, she heard a trumpet sounding. A host of banners were flying against a blue spring sky. A multitude of huge red crosses on a white linen background jostled in the breeze. Fork-shaped pennants displaying various coats of arms were fluttering amongst the red dragons of England. She could hear cheers and cries of 'Path to Heaven', 'Jerusalem, Jerusalem,' and 'Destruction to the infidel' as they fell resounding from the ancient churchyard.

She stopped. The guards urged her on.

'I won't be more than a moment.' The escort set her chest down, wiping sweat from their brows with their sleeves while she edged through a crowd into the churchyard.

On a platform, Earls Simon and Richard stood shoulder to shoulder clad in full chain mail, wearing white flowing sleeveless gowns with large red crosses stitched onto them. A host of knights, Templars, and priests surrounded them, as did their squires. The crowd of citizens pushing closer were working themselves up into a frenzy as the call to take the cross grew louder. It was delivered by Earl Richard himself. A restless squall gusted through a host of tangled pennants flying above the Crusaders but even so his voice carried over the wind.

As her skirt blew up and she caught at it, she scanned the cheering throng until she saw Thomas. She elbowed forward, ignoring complaints. He loosened himself from the gathering of knights and squires and pushed his way towards her. 'Rosalind, my love, I never dared hope to see you today.'

She stared at his white tabard, at the blood red cross that almost covered it, at the bright passion in his blue eyes, wondering if it was for her or the cross. 'Are you recruiting?' she said simply.

'We leave for France within the month. Delay after delay to raise funds and men, and then Lady Isabel's death. Years of preparation – we are going at last.' His eyes blazed like stars.

She caught his arm. 'Don't go! No, go, I mean, but please, please come back safely.' Tears sprang into her eyes blurring her vision. He could not change his mind, had he so wished. A squire always followed his knight. Thomas was enraptured at the thought of seeing Jerusalem. He was determined to fight heathens and she must wait for him. She slipped a cross on a silver chain over her head and pressed it into his hand. 'Take it. This cross belonged to my mother. Think of me sometimes.'

'Always,' he said. 'Every day until I return to you.' He stared down at the silver cross. 'My father died on crusade and my mother soon after of a broken heart but, my love, I shall return.' He slid the cross and chain into his purse. 'And, when I do, I shall return it to you, and silken threads.'

'God bless you, my Thomas.' She could not even imagine it: Jerusalem, the centre of the world. 'How many knights have you raised?'

'Forty-odd this week, and not enough.'

One of the warrior priests cried out, 'Kneel. Let us pray for God's guidance.'

'Go, go, go,' she said, her voice anguished, a lump rising in her throat. 'Go with God's grace and my heart in your keeping.' She embraced him and turned away. Her escort was patiently waiting for her by the gate.

Chapter Seventeen

August 1240

Ailenor trod the garden paths, Rosalind walking alongside reporting how the embroidery was progressing.

'They are about to begin on the roses already,' Rosalind said. 'The four embroiderers working on it are determined to finish soon as they can.'

'Are they content with the new arrangement?'

'The chamber is huge and they are happy to be close to the embroidery at night, to watch over it.'

'And your chamber. Is it comfortable? Sybil Gifford says it's little more than a nun's cell.'

'It suits me well, Madam.'

'When the hanging is completed we shall move the embroiderers back to the workshop at Westminster but you will remain with us, yes?'

'Thank you. I am pleased to stay with you, Your Grace. Martha will supervise the embroidery workshop. Her apprenticeship ended last year.' Ailenor noted Rosalind's shining eyes and wondered if the girl had personal reasons to be at court, the attentions of a young courtier perhaps. She was surprised at the ease of persuasion. Rosalind had loved the workshop. Perhaps the break-in had frightened her more that she admitted.

'Even so, it will always be your workshop. When we travel, you will share a chamber with my junior ladies, do you understand?'

'Thank you. I do, Your Grace'

'We shall speak again very soon.'

Rosalind curtsied and hurried away back through the garden to the workshop inside the castle. Ailenor watched her speed through the hollyhocks and beds of herbs until she vanished through the arched door into the castle keep. She would still embroider. Rosalind would certainly embroider roses and stitch pearls on the sleeves and train of her churching gown. She touched her stomach. *A daughter this time. I am sure of it.*

Ailenor passed her seclusion in Windsor much as she had done at Westminster. Because Simon and Richard had departed for the crusades, she requested a copy of a map of the world for her chamber so she could see the strange lands through which they were travelling. There was a painting of the great world on the wall of the King's chamber at Westminster. She stared at it for ages, reading aloud the mysterious places it contained until Henry would call her away. When a copy arrived in her own chambers she was delighted because now she could examine it for as long as she wished.

'Look,' she said to Willelma after they'd unrolled the scroll and laid it out on a table. 'There is Jason's golden fleece by that sea.'

'They call it the Black Sea, Madam.'

She peered more closely at the map and squinted. 'Is that the Minotaur of the Greeks close by Noah's Ark? Look there.' She traced the three continents shown on the map, Europe, Africa, and Asia. Her finger stopped at the very edge of Europe where the map led to Asia, where she could see the city of Constantinople and the Black Sea.

Her ladies gathered around. 'And Jerusalem is right in the centre of all, as it should be,' Ailenor said, looking up with wonder in her voice. 'I wonder, has Earl Richard reached the sea yet.' She pointed to a blue patch on the map that stretched from Spain to the Holy Land. He set off in May so –' Ailenor counted on her fingers, 'if he left Paris in July, he should be in Provence by now. I sent letters with him for my mother and sisters. He promised to write before he sailed from Marseilles.'

148

'He will carry news of your lying-in to Paris?' Sybil Gifford, who once again would be her chief midwife, said.

Ailenor was thoughtful for a moment. Marguerite had recently given birth to a daughter. A miracle indeed. She often wrote to Ailenor about how the White Queen wished her ill. Queen Blanche persistently separated the royal couple. She was a dominating, bitter woman who wanted the marriage annulled so she could choose a grander princess for him. Ailenor confided in her ladies that if she were Marguerite, she would find every way possible to make that scheming woman's life miserable.

'Difficult,' Lady Mary said. 'Her only hope is if the White Queen takes ill.'

'Just to allow Louis and his queen to sleep in the same bed long enough for her to conceive,' good-natured Sybil Gifford said.

'If only she would disappear into a convent,' sighed Ailenor as she folded Marguerite's sad letter. It did not make her feel better for her beloved sister that she was about to give birth to a second child.

Henry's mother, Isabella of Lusignan, hated Queen Blanche with a vengeance. Isabella had been a beautiful queen. Since she had wed Count Hugh de Lusignan, she had been regarded by Blanche as a lesser queen, an ex-queen, and a disgrace for abandoning her own children by King John. Isabella, Henry loyally insisted, was his mother, too, and as the mother of a king, she should never, ever have to kneel to Blanche. They were equal in rank. It was unfortunate, he said, that John lost Poitou to France and his mother and Hugh owed Louis fealty.

'I'll get Poitou back one of these days,' Henry would say.

Ailenor looked away when Henry had such outbursts and changed the conversation. She did not want war with her sister. It would separate them for ever. Henry, Ailenor often tried to remind herself, after these tirades about his mother's treatment by Queen Blanche, may be changeable but he *was* a great king, greater than Louis. She, Ailenor, would make sure that everyone knew it. She would never create misery in a daughter-in-law's life. Edward would grow up in a loving

149

family and when the time came, she would welcome Edward's bride, whoever she was, into it.

When Rosalind showed Ailenor a pair of new sleeve bands covered with little pearls and silver embroidery, Ailenor gave them a quick approving glance and drew her to the map. The girl stared at it with wonderment in her eyes. Ailenor watched Rosalind's delight and fear as she peered down on Jerusalem.

'Madam, the Holy City is as distant as Heaven. So many dangers, shipwrecks, and monsters lurk between here and there.' She pointed to the monsters painted in the sea, the storms and giant fish.

'They are not all real, Rosalind. Some are just stories.'

She was sure she saw anxiety cross Rosalind's countenance.

'Do you have family on crusade?' she asked. The girl was a puzzle. Sometimes she seemed older and wiser than her years and at others she was childlike. Rosalind thought the Gorgon with her tangled, snake hair to be real and that the monsters peering from the sea could overturn a vessel and gobble a sailor up for supper.

'I have a friend who is on the earls' crusade,' Rosalind replied with diffidence. 'Earl Simon's squire has gone with him. He has been a good friend to me since the day you were crowned, Your Grace.'

'Ah, his name is . . .?'

'Thomas Beaumont.'

Ailenor found a smile hover about her lips. So Rosalind was in love. It may even be the reason she had so easily accepted a position at court. 'I am sure he will return safely to us. When we write to Earl Simon, I shall ask about him for you.'

'Thank you, Your Grace.'

'And I shall add the squire to my prayers.'

'I pray for his safety every day,' Rosalind said, her voice a whisper.

Ailenor lifted the intricately decorated sleeves she would wear at her churching. 'Rosalind, how can I thank you? This embroidery work is without price.'

When the girl smiled she was beautiful. Her eyes shone like the sky on a clear day, her mouth widened, and her head lifted as if she was about to sing praise to Heaven. 'I am happy to serve you, your Grace. That is thanks enough,' she said.

'And we are happy to have you with us.'

Ailenor's first daughter was born on a sunny September day. Henry stood by her bed whilst her women set about attending to the child, rubbing salt on her small limbs, placing a drop of wine in her mouth, and wrapping her gently in swaddling before laying her in a new wooden cradle carved with celandines, pansies, and roses.

Henry kissed his wife and gave up his thanks to God as he knelt by her bedside.

'We shall call her Margaret for your sister,' he said, looking up from his prayer.

She smiled at him. 'Perhaps you had hoped for another boy.'

'We *have* a boy. And, God willing, there will be others. This daughter is every bit as beautiful as her mother. *Très belle, cherie.* I love her as I do you. Now rest. You must get strong again.'

Ailenor closed her eyes, glad to sleep, after Henry was swept from the chamber by Sybil Gifford. 'The Queen simply needs rest. She is young and she is strong but she is exhausted. It was a difficult birth, Your Grace. God be praised for she has borne you a beautiful princess.'

'I shall, indeed, recover and have more children,' Ailenor whispered as she drifted into a pleasant sleep.

Days passed pleasantly until she was churched in the beautiful gown embellished by the embroideress who was enthusiastically accepted by her company of ladies, for they were for ever asking her to embroider this sleeve or that.

Ailenor could not resist spending hours with both her tiny daughter and little Edward, who toddled around on a pair of very long legs. She insisted the children were brought to her apartment daily. As Edward played, watched over by his nurse, Ailenor rested, longing for him to grow into a little boy. 'And you, little Meg,' she would say to her baby daughter, 'one day, you will marry a king just like your mama, but not for many years yet. I want to keep you close for as long as I can.'

Ailenor received letters from Nell, who now had two boys of her own and who had passed a pleasant month following the birth of her second son, little Simon, at Isabella's castle in Lusignan. She had met her half-brothers and sisters at last. She wrote how they every bit as beautiful as her mother and as charming as Count Hugh, their father.

Ailenor read Nell's words to Henry. She hesitated as she read, *My mother is unhappy. Queen Blanche hates her.*

Henry looked thunderous. 'One day I shall reclaim the lands my father lost to France, all of Normandy and Poitou. My mother will never have to bend her knee to that dowager. Never, do you hear, Ailenor. I care not if your sister is Queen of France. Those lands are our children's inheritance.'

Ailenor shuddered. She loved her sister. What if Henry, despite a peace brokered by his advisors, was now threatening war with France? All their best knights were crusading.

She lifted up Nell's letter and looking at it remarked, 'Nell is accompanying Simon to Southern Italy.' Dropping the letter onto her lap, she gasped, 'She will be there already. Simon will have reached the Holy Land by now.'

'And Richard, who rarely writes home.' Henry pouted, narrowed his eyes, one settling into a squint, and he looked petulant. 'How I wish I was leading an army too.'

'No, you do not, Henry. You have a kingdom to rule, the Confessor's tomb and a new abbey to finish building. God will be pleased with his new church. It is enough and it is costly.'

'We'll see, Ailenor. One day I may wish to see Jerusalem. I may not be satisfied with knights' tales and looking at a map all my life.'

She gave him a serene smile that hid her concern. Henry was not made for crusading. She prayed a silent prayer to Saint Bridget: 'Please protect him. Turn him from this foolish notion.'

'What is that you are saying, Ailenor?' Henry asked. 'Your lips are moving.'

'I hope that Simon and Richard return safely, a small prayer on their behalf,' she said, reddening as she spoke the half-truth. She found being secretive difficult but sometimes it was for the best. On such occasions, Ailenor kept her true feelings hidden deeply within her breast.

Chapter Eighteen

1240 – 1241

By the calends of November 1240, Ailenor had fully recovered from the birth of Baby Margaret. Edward would stumble around her solar where he played with little wooden knights in an alcove he had made his own retreat. Baby Margaret slept in her cradle close to her mother's chair. She was a peaceful child who had smiled already. Margaret promised great beauty. Ailenor and Henry were besotted. Her heart sang when she looked down on the baby and even more so when Henry visited them at Windsor. On those occasions they were an intimate family just like her own family had been when she was growing up.

She sat by a blazing fire, a cup of hippocras by her elbow, reading more letters Henry had brought her from Westminster. On this occasion one was from Earl Richard. She set Richard's aside. The second was more mysterious. She studied it closely before reading, her eyes scanning the neat precise script. 'Mon Dieu, it's from Uncle Peter,' she exclaimed to the room, empty of sound excepting the fire's hiss. She read her uncle's words aloud to herself. 'He promises to be in England by Christmas – a month off – and intends bringing a wife, small daughter, and their own attendants.' Had Henry invited him? She looked around the chamber. Where was Henry? They were to enjoy a private supper. His bath was taking a very long time.

Henry arrived comfortably clad in a loose robe. He dropped a kiss on her head and took the chair opposite hers. She thrust Uncle Peter's letter at him.

'Read it,' she said. 'Uncle Peter. He's on his way to us with a retinue in tow. Did you invite him, Henry?'

'Yes, I have invited him. He was not asked to bring his retinue with him. My economies . . .'

'Too late for that. He'll be here in time for Christmas.'

'Best time of year.' Henry's frown turned to a grin as he handed her Uncle Peter's letter. 'We must make this a special Christmas. Westminster or Winchester this year?'

'Westminster, but the New Year at Windsor.' She stopped as she opened Richard's letter from Sicily. Henry opened a volume of poetry and muttered as he read them to himself.

After a while, she glanced up. 'This one you'll have read but listen to what Richard says of Marguerite and Sancha. *"Your elder sister is in good health. I was entertained with great pomp in Paris. The whole court rode out to meet me. Sadly the Count of Toulouse is making many troubles for the Queen's father. Raymond of Toulouse seeks Marseilles and Provence and he seeks a bride. He has been offered the Queen's sister to end the tension between Toulouse and Provence. Sancha is very beautiful. She is young, sweet, and timid and I fear she will be horrified at this destiny . . ."'* Ailenor read on in silence. A moment later, she glanced up again. 'What! *Non! Non! Non!* Toulouse! Henry, this marriage must not happen.'

'What can I do?'

'She must marry your brother. Make it happen. It'll ensure Richard's loyalty to us.' She studied the letter and looked up, smiling this time. 'He's utterly besotted with my sister.'

'It may be too late. Anyway, Richard grieves for Isabel.' His smile was sarcastic. 'Without doubt, he is busy whoring too. I hear that Eastern women are very beautiful.'

Ailenor laid the letters aside. 'As well *you* were not on the Crusade.' Her tone was cool.

'You, my Ailenor, are the only beauty I love or need.'

'May it ever be so,' Ailenor said firmly. 'Write to Richard. Suggest he attends my family in Provence again. Suggest he woo Sancha.'

She put a finger on Uncle Peter's letter again. 'If I recollect correctly, Uncle Peter is an excellent negotiator. If there is a betrothal already with the Count of Toulouse' – she shuddered as she thought of how aged and toad-like Raymond of Toulouse was reputed to be – 'it can be broken if words are placed in the right ears.'

Henry shook his head but by his pleased smile she knew he would pursue this. After all, he had himself broken off a betrothal to the hideous Joan of Flanders in order to marry her, his beloved wife.

It had been years since Ailenor had seen Uncle Peter, who had long lived in Savoy, Italy, and in Switzerland. He had visited her father's castle at Les Baux and brought them all gifts – Italian glass goblets, a carpet from Spain, and silver bracelets set with amethysts for her and Marguerite. She remembered him tall, dark, and elegant with smiling brown eyes.

He arrived with his wife, Agnes of Faucigny, and their baby daughter, another Beatrice, in time for the Christmas festivities. Henry liked him just as he had liked Uncle William. Uncle Peter was a good listener and considered his words carefully before he spoke. He was judicious. He made himself amenable to Henry's barons and earls and Ailenor was pleased when Henry granted him the Honour of Richmond and the manor of Boston as an inducement to remain in England as the King's advisor. He knighted the charming Peter on New Year's Day.

Uncle Peter was such good company that Ailenor enjoyed her best Christmas since she first came to England. Agnes was thoughtful and she, too, considered her words carefully before she joined any conversation. When Ailenor confided that she had learned to speak English, though not well, Agnes smiled through her green eyes and said that she must learn English too. She clearly wanted to please. Ailenor liked her and always invited little Beatrice to share their company, which pleased this newly discovered aunt.

'My Uncle Peter is much pleasanter than my Uncle Thomas. I hope they never visit us again, ever,' she confided to Agnes, not caring if Joan of Flanders ever heard those words repeated.

'Oh,' Agnes said and lifted a belt, a gift Ailenor had given her before her attack on her Uncle Thomas of Flanders. She peered at the golden flowers embroidered on it. 'The embroidery is beautiful, the seed pearls exquisite. It is such a valuable present, Ailenor.'

'Embroidered by my own hand.' Ailenor clapped her hands. 'You absolutely must meet my embroideress, Rosalind. She has taught us the precious gold and silver embroidery you see on our gowns and in our chapels. After Christmas, before you ride north to see Castle Richmond, we are to spend a week at Windsor. The embroideress is with her family this Christmas but she'll return to court by New Year's Day. I'll ask her to teach you some of her stitches.' Joan of Flanders and her husband were forgotten.

'I would like that very much.' Agnes glanced over at Ailenor's sparrow-hawk sitting on his perch by the window. 'Do you hunt, Ailenor?'

'Not since Margaret was born. I used to ride out with Ness on my wrist.' Ailenor stroked the hawk. 'She may look calm enough now. Send her into the air and she is vicious with her prey as the lion prowling his cage in Henry's zoo.'

'I have much to look forward to . . . though perhaps not the lion. Ailenor, I'll miss you when we leave for Richmond.'

'I hope you are not hidden away for long in the north. I'd like to see you at court. As our children grow older, Beatrice will be happy in the nursery with Edward and Margaret. I intend to have my daughter educated and Beatrice is so happy here.'

Agnes folded her hands in her lap. 'Thank you.'

Ailenor reached out, unfolded Agnes's pleated hands, and held them. Little Beatrice, playing with a kitten by the hearth, glanced over at them then resumed her game.

'You and Peter must be with us often. Henry needs trustworthy advisors.' She lowered her voice. 'His barons can be difficult and penny-pinching.'

As the year turned, the royal household moved to Windsor. Ailenor took great pride in showing Agnes the embroidery workshop. During

157

January, Agnes mastered the basic couch stitches needed to produce fine work in gold and silver. Ailenor consulted with Rosalind. She ordered valuable gold and silver thread and velvet cloth for Agnes to take north.

'We have an embroideress whom we can spare, Countess Agnes, if you would like her company.' Rosalind looked with uncertainty at Ailenor for permission. 'Is it possible, Your Grace?'

'Of course,' Ailenor found herself agreeing. 'Can she speak French?'

'I was thinking of Jennet. Her father would be honoured for his daughter to be employed as a personal embroideress to Lady Agnes. He has so many daughters and sons, it would be a relief if Jennet were settled. We have enough embroiderers here. She has just completed her apprenticeship. Jennet is young and good-natured. She is lively and speaks French and English both. I think she will agree.'

'In that case, I shall treat Jennet as if she were one of my own *demoiselles*. She shall be paid well.'

Rosalind turned to Ailenor. 'Your Grace, we have almost completed the embroidery.'

Ailenor said, excitement creeping into her voice, 'When will it be ready?'

'By Eastertide.'

After Rosalind returned to the workshop, Agnes remarked, 'Rosalind is lovely, sweet and clever and very pretty. I wonder how long it will be before a knight claims her.'

'There is one such, I fear, a young squire. He is in the Holy Land. Let us hope, however, she remains with me for some time yet. I value her company as well as her talent.'

On a windy March day Countess Agnes, Uncle Peter, and their daughter, accompanied by Jennet and the large retinue that had accompanied them to England, set out on the long journey north to Richmond, brightly coloured pennants gusting as they went before them. Ailenor shed a few emotional tears, for she enjoyed Agnes's company. Now Agnes had left her, as had Nell.

She was not sorrowful for long. Soon another uncle visited

England. Unlike Uncle Peter, Ailenor's Uncle Boniface was trained for the Church though he had not yet been granted a bishopric. Within weeks of Boniface's arrival Henry had offered the Savoyard Winchester. Although it was Henry's right to appoint bishops with the Pope's approval, the Winchester clergy objected. Henry insisted. However, Uncle Boniface diplomatically departed and did not return to England that year. Ailenor had her doubts about his qualities. Handsome Boniface was too worldly for a bishop, or how she felt a bishop ought to behave, but Henry was taken with Boniface's charm. He would not hear a bad word against him.

'We'll get him back,' he said. 'He will be my bishop.'

Ailenor kept her silence on the matter.

Apple and pear trees sprouted buds and in the garden below Ailenor's chamber there was new growth amongst the herbal beds. Henry bustled into her ante-chamber just as Ailenor was about to suggest they all walk amongst the trees. He told her to take off her cloak and chased away her ladies. Once the chamber was theirs alone and they sat by the fire sharing ginger cakes and wine, Henry proceeded to tell her his news. He had appointed Uncle Boniface as the new Archbishop of Canterbury. The archbishopric had been vacant since Archbishop Edmund's death the previous year.

'That will tempt him back to England. Winchester has not, clearly.'

She almost choked on her wine. If Uncle Boniface was an unsuitable choice for Winchester, Canterbury was madness. 'I don't think . . .'

'Edmund Rich is dead a year. I need someone I can trust. Edmund was a saint. He was my friend,' Henry interrupted. 'I need friends in high positions in the Church.'

She had never liked Archbishop Edmund but Henry considered it his royal right to choose the new archbishop and he would do so.

Henry continued his argument. 'It will take care of the Winchester problem. Negotiations have travelled between Rome, Westminster, and Canterbury. The Pope agrees.'

Ailenor considered this. She put her embroidery aside and closed her eyes as she thought. Her own uncle as an archbishop, the most senior position a churchman could achieve in England. Perhaps the rumours about Boniface's excesses were untrue. It would be best to agree and she might benefit after all, though she was unsure about this. Uncle Boniface was never going to be a popular choice as archbishop, never with Henry's earls and barons and never with the clergy. Yet there was no point in arguing this. Henry was not going to listen.

After a short silence she said, 'If the Pope agrees, Uncle Boniface must accept such a prestigious position. For Canterbury, he will return. At least, my uncle will change the Church in England. He is . . . well, he is reforming, I have heard say.'

'If you say so, my dear.'

'I do.'

'Boniface is still in Rome. There will be resistance in Canterbury, of course.' Henry said. 'I intend to make the monks there see sense and I have a hunch that they will yield without a whimper. It leaves Winchester open, of course, but since I take its revenue, Winchester can be left as it is, without a bishop, for a while.'

She drummed her fingers gently on the arm of her chair. 'And our throne will be guarded by Uncle Peter and Uncle Boniface. Safe for Edward.' She leaned towards Henry and lowered her voice in case the wall panelling possessed ears, 'My uncles will keep the barons and clergy in check. They will make sure there's tax for the Crown, not to line the barons' pockets.' Ailenor had convinced herself but in her heart she still knew Uncle Boniface could bring them trouble.

Henry's brow furrowed into creases. 'We owe Rome taxes. It's a wretched thing. Ever since my father's day.' For a moment Henry looked fearful. She reached out to him and patted his arm. He shook his head. 'If we don't pay the taxes we owe Rome there will be an Interdict again. Churches will close. There will be no burials or christenings, no marriages either. The people will rebel. We need a strong clergy and uncomplaining barons. That tax must be paid.' His face reddened with fury as he added, 'Simon was another complainer. He has more debts than ever now he is on crusade.'

'Henry, you are wrong about Simon. He is loyal, even now. I miss

160

Nell. I hear Emperor Frederick has granted her a palace by the sea in Italy. It is a sadness to me that you quarrelled with Simon. We need Earl Simon as much as we need our uncles. He is family too, after all.'

'He seduced my sister and I allowed him back.' Henry furrowed his brow again. How like a child Henry could be, yet she knew she could reason with him.

She tried again. 'But not into your heart. You have never been close again. You know that Simon can keep the barons in check.'

Henry crossed his legs. He lifted a poker and prodded at a log sending sparks up into the vast chimney. 'Many dislike him. Ah well, Richard will return soon. The pair of them have freed the French prisoners. Your Earl is putting order into Jerusalem, I hear.'

'Simon is not my Earl. He is yours.'

'We shall see about that when the Crusaders return.'

She poured them both wine and lifting her cup said, 'Richard and Sancha. We must make sure of it. A betrothal. You must write to Father.'

'I have done so, but no reply as yet. I shall offer to pay her dowry to my brother and suggest Countess Beatrice must accompany Sancha to England.'

'What if Richard is not interested?'

'I shall make it worth his while. He won't decline.' Henry laid down his cup. His mood brightened, his voice turning from serious to gay. 'Ailenor, by the way, have you decided which ladies will accompany us to Shrewsbury and Chester?'

'Only my favourites.' She was thinking about bringing three with her on their summer progress that year. She touched the golden flowers on her robe. They would sit in summer gardens, embroider, and enjoy verse, and Rosalind must be one of those who accompanied her.

They had welcomed Rosalind into their company. Willelma and Mary taught her the art of being a courtier, how she must walk and sit, eat and speak. They ensured her daily lessons were light-hearted and funny. Rosalind learned how to raise her head high and look down her nose if displeased. She learned how to politely give orders to servants. Soon she was dabbing her mouth daintily with her napkin and holding her eating knife with style and knew to only eat little morsels at a time. Ailenor smiled to see how her new lady had progressed within a very short time.

The new embroidery was ready at last. There was only the matter of hanging it in her bedchamber. Ailenor inspected the embroidery, fingering the couched threads, studying the nun midwives, smiling down on the face that belonged to St Anne.

'St Anne has a beautiful face; serene,' she remarked as she trailed her fingers over the embroidery. 'And the midwives . . .' Ailenor stood back for a moment before considering them. 'One resembles Margaret Biset and the other Sybil Gifford. They will be delighted.' Ailenor traced the gleaming gold embroidery that decorated the hems of the midwives' gowns. She peered closely at St Anne's face. Anne's eyes were dark like her own and her hair, whilst tucked under a fragile silken veil, appeared shadowy. Minute pearls edged Saint Anne's oval face.

'Just a little in your own image, Madam,' Rosalind said. 'I hope God does not object.'

'I hope not either.' Ailenor started. 'Though an archbishop might.' She smiled, thinking, *but not if he's my uncle.* 'I think baby Mary looks like my little Margaret.' She stared at the baby nestled in St Anne's arms. Her eyes were blue as the background sky. Ailenor's eyes lit on the glittering stars and the silken roses that created the piece's borders and exhaled, making a small sound of pleasure. Turning to Rosalind she exclaimed, 'By my Lady's halo, it is beautiful.'

Rosalind accepted a new court gown with trailing sleeves and matching bliaut bordered with seed pearls as a reward, and anticipating the summer court Ailenor presented Rosalind with two new linen gowns for everyday wear.

'You look as well-dressed as Willelma and Margaret,' Ailenor said when Rosalind presented herself in one of the new gowns. 'Pink suits you. I shall send you crispinettes for your hair.' She touched Rosalind's chin. 'Chin bands and short veils are more fashionable than those plain linen caps you wear. We shall make a swan of you yet.' When she spoke to Rosalind like this, years fell away. She smiled as she recollected the day they sat together in her window seat watching the river. She never regretted this friendship and could trust Rosalind's loyalty.

Rosalind sank into a deep curtsey. 'May I say farewell to my family?'

Ailenor took her hands. 'Of course you may. We'll set out shortly after the Pentecost feast.' She let the girl's hands drop again and clasped her own to her chest. 'I love summer. There will be hunting and walks and I hope the sun shines every day.'

'I can't hunt!' All the formality had fallen away. They were those girls again.

'You will learn, Rosalind.'

'I don't know how to be a queen's lady,' she said. 'Most of the time here I am employed with embroidery. But to attend you with only two others . . .'

'Rosalind, we have servants and maids to attend us. As for the rest, we shall teach you. Would you like to have lessons on the lute? And the harp? We value your talent with the needle. We can keep you occupied but I want you to have fun too. Besides, you can read and that is a great thing for a lady to master.'

Rosalind looked abashed. 'I want to learn all these things. I am very happy here with you but I've never been further than Windsor. I don't know what lies beyond.'

'Discovering what is out there in England's forests, rivers, villages, and fields will be a great adventure in which I hope you take joy, for it is a good thing for a woman to know what lies beyond her home.' Ailenor clapped her hands. 'Let us start now. Bring me my lute, Mary, for I am, myself, going to show Rosalind how to make just a few notes.'

Laughing, Ailenor, who delighted to instruct, bade Rosalind sit on a stool. She was sure the girl would learn quickly because she had heard her sing as they embroidered. Rosalind was quick and curious and that endeared her to Ailenor.

Ailenor wanted everyone else to share her happiness. Two uncles in England, two healthy babies in her nursery, the possibility that her sister might come to England with her mother, a summer adventure ahead with three ladies whose company she enjoyed, and a generous if stubborn husband whom she loved. But, above all, she loved being a great queen who was, she imagined, loved by all.

Henry intended moving along the border with Wales.

Ailenor knew it was important to visit the Welsh borderlands since there was a dispute to settle. Two princes vied for control of North Wales and one, Dafydd, had imprisoned the other, Gruffydd. Henry had ordered Dafydd to release his half-brother Gruffydd from captivity in a Welsh castle. Dafydd wrote to Henry, *Wales can never be at peace if Gruffydd is released.*

Gruffydd however considered himself his father's rightful heir, as he was the older of the two brothers, but the succession of the eldest son was not common in Wales as in England, even though the Normans had tried to impose it on the conquered northern territory of Gwynedd. Henry considered himself Dafydd's overlord, and when there was unrest in Wales it spilled over into the Borders.

Just before the summer progress set out from Windsor, Prince Gruffydd sent word to Henry that if Henry would free him, he would take over Dafydd's lands and pay Henry two hundred marks a year. The English barons would take varying sides. Folding his letter, Henry said, 'I have no choice but to go to Chester and meet with the Marcher lords and, Ailenor . . .' He pursed his lips. 'And I'll raise an army to march on the Welsh if we must.'

Ailenor wondered if Henry was wise thinking this was to his advantage. Gruffydd would do homage to Henry for his lands and he promised to subdue parts of Wales the Normans had never reached. There could be advantages if Gruffydd supported the English Crown, and more if he paid for the privilege. Henry gathered an army at Gloucester and Ailenor and Henry rode along the border towards Shrewsbury.

*

'Another letter from Wales,' Henry said as they sat at the long table talking in the refectory of Shrewsbury Abbey. His mouth began to work in anger. He threw the letter with its dragon seal and fluttering red ribbons onto the table. The seal already opened, cracked into quarters. He lifted it and neatly tried to put the parts together again.

'What is happening now?' Ailenor sighed. The Abbey at Shrewsbury was comfortable, the gardens pleasant, but she longed for Marlborough. If only Henry were free of this Welsh problem.

Henry recovered his temper. In a quieter voice he said, 'Dafydd refuses to come to our council in Chester. It'll be war yet. You'll remain here until it's over. You ladies can . . . well, do whatever you do . . . embroider.'

Ailenor inclined her head. Hopefully this would be resolved peacefully. She worried for Henry. He was trained as a knight but he was not a warrior like Earl Simon.

'I am sure Dafydd is determined to free North Wales from our control. I cannot trust him. We'll support Gruffydd.' Henry said as he folded the letter.

'Will Dafydd free Gruffydd? Are you supporting the most honourable prince? Do you really want Dafydd as your enemy?'

'I want a peaceful outcome.'

She leaned her arms on the table. Welsh politics were complicated. She had never fully understood the complications, though the Welsh princes had frequently intermarried with English nobility. Henry's illegitimate half-sister Joanna had been married to the powerful Llewelyn and Dafydd was Joanna's son, which made Henry Dafydd's uncle and Ailenor his aunt by marriage.

The sun slid through the refectory's painted glass windows, creating lozenges of coloured light. She studied them. How peaceful it was. She released a deeply troubled sigh and thought how sad it would be if this conflict led to battle. How beautiful these borderlands were with their wealthy towns, peaceful abbeys, and glittering rivers filled with jumping trout. War – she shuddered at the thought.

'Dafydd might ride against you. War is costly.' Caution filled her voice.

Henry shook his head. 'There has been a drought in Gwynedd this year. He cannot ride against me. His army would die of thirst. I prefer peace to war. My nephew *will* come and there'll be a treaty.'

Ailenor relaxed. She glanced out through another, unglazed, window into the garden to where Rosalind and her two other ladies were gathering posies of late spring flowers for their bedchambers. Her little dog bounded after them. She would remain in this peaceful abbey and pray for a solution to Henry's problem with the two Welsh brothers.

Henry rode to Chester, leaving Ailenor in the pleasant, airy abbey. He returned, to her surprise, after only a few days, galloping into the abbey courtyard late at night accompanied by a blaze of torchlight, the snorting of horses and the clanking of armour. Henry clattered up the outside staircase. She was at the entrance to her bedchamber within a heartbeat.

'Get me ale and meat. I am famished and thirsty as Hell.' He was breathless. 'Send your lady.' He indicated Rosalind. 'We shall dine privately tonight. I have news.'

Once they had settled in their ante-chamber, one of the best rooms provided by the Abbot, clean and well-furnished, its low table laden with a selection of dishes from a well-appointed kitchen, Henry told Ailenor that Dafydd had joined his council at Chester. He agreed to release Gruffydd and other hostages he had held into the King's care. 'But,' he added, 'he insists Gruffydd is to be incarcerated in London, in the Tower. He insists he is the only King.'

'In London?' Ailenor said, laying down her jewelled eating knife. 'His own brother in the Tower. Why?'

'My nephew claims his brother is exceedingly dangerous. I agreed to take charge of Gruffydd as long as Dafydd does homage to me for Wales. The barons along the Welsh borders are content with this outcome. See, my love, I have triumphed without bloodshed and avoided war. To show God thanks, I have ordered the poor of Chester to receive alms for a year.' He leaned over and took Ailenor's hand. 'Would you like to go hunting before we return to London?'

She thought for a moment. 'I would enjoy that, Henry.' At last she could look forward to the rest of the summer with pleasure and with Henry by her side.

Henry talked about how they would hunt, feast and dance in the castle at Marlborough. 'We shall pass a month in the Savernake forest. I promised you a country residence and I've made improvements at the castle.' He kissed her nose, tickling her with his beard. 'And, I want to see if the refurbished chambers are pleasing to you.'

She pulled him to her, into a deep embrace. A delightful summer of pleasure awaited her. 'I can't wait.' She felt like a young girl all over.

As summer starlight slanted in through the shutters that evening, Ailenor and Henry entwined their bodies amongst ruffled sheets on the Abbot of Shrewsbury's feathered bed. Moments later, they were moaning with delight in each other until they rolled over exhausted, sated by lovemaking, glistening with sweat.

Exhausted by his ride from Chester to Shrewsbury, Henry slept, and Ailenor, not at all tired, raised herself on one elbow and gazed down on his face. She loved him. She truly loved Henry as her king and as her husband. Theirs was a union of body and mind. How fortunate she was, that all those years past, Henry of England had sent to Provence for her. She loved her life and now the summer lay before them. Perhaps God would bless them with a third baby for the royal nursery. She turned on her side and drifted into sleep thinking of a new embroidery stitch Rosalind had taught them that morning.

Chapter Nineteen

Rosalind
Marlborough, 1241

The castle keep at Marlborough rose above the small sleepy town. A host of buildings including a buttery, a still room, laundry, and an enormous stable block scattered themselves about the bailey. Ailenor's apartments were newly painted with scenes from the legends of Arthur and Edward Confessor's life. The first days passed with unpacking and settling in. Ailenor explored the gardens with her three ladies. They feasted on venison, salmon from the Severn brought to Marlborough by fishermen, and fruit pies, often eating supper in the garden.

The morning of the Savernake hunt arrived. Rosalind had never ridden a horse other than the aging mare her father had kept for her use. When she saw the palfrey the Queen's groom had chosen for her to ride, she began stumbling over her words. 'I can . . . can't.'

'Nonsense,' Willelma hissed into her ear. 'You can. I shall ride my mare behind you.'

Lady Mary, serene as ever said, 'If I can ride, you can. The sumpter cart follows with refreshments. Just say that your horse refused to canter and stay with the cart.'

'Canter!' Rosalind was terrified at the thought. 'I have never ridden at more than a trot. Our horse generally proceeds at a walk. I cannot . . .'

'It's as well the Queen is delayed this morning. Get up on that mare and a squire will walk you around the yard.' Willelma waved at a group of squires who had led the King's chestnut destrier, Confessor, out into the castle yard. 'Come here. Can one of you walk the Queen's lady around the yard? She is frightened of new horses.'

Two squires came at a run. Moments later, white-faced, Rosalind found herself lifted up onto the side saddle, was shown how to catch the pommel with her knee, and, gripping the mane, was walked around the yard.

'My lady, take these.' One of the pair handed her the horse's reins, beautifully studded with gems and glinting silver. 'We are going to go at a trot,' he said. 'This horse is called Mirabelle. She is gentle. Are you ready?'

Rosalind nodded. My lady, she thought as, her confidence gathered, she bounced up and down on the trotting horse He called me 'my lady'. Would he, if he knew I was a merchant's daughter? She held the jewelled reins and sat tall, feeling noble, her initial fear dissipated. The palfrey responded to her light tug left as she tapped its withers lightly with her boot.

'I see the Queen and King coming,' called Lady Willelma across the yard. 'Hurry. You seem to have mastered the creature.'

Rosalind, breathless from her trot, slid down from the palfrey's back. One of the squires moved away, but the other held her palfrey's reins and bowed as the King and Queen passed. She, who had been constantly and patiently tutored in etiquette by Lady Mary and Lady Willelma, sank into a deep curtsey. As she rose, the young squire looked at her in a contemplative manner as if trying to place her. A moment later he said in French, '*Merde*, I know who you are – Rosalind, daughter to Alfred Fitzwilliam, the tailor. You are the embroideress.'

'I am.' She held her head up proudly, though she felt her face flush with embarrassment as he had reminded her of her origins. 'You are?' she ventured.

'Alain Froissart.' He studied her. In turn she stared back. His hair was brown, fashionably styled under at his neck and around his eyes. These were grey, hard, and cold as slate. He had a slight curl to his lip which she did not like either.

'I wish you good hunting, Mistress –'

'I'm a Queen's Lady.'

He laughed, his mouth shaping into a snarl. 'Lady Rosalind, huh! I heard . . .oh never mind . . . a rumour.'

'What did you hear?'

'Something told me by that grocer, Master Basing's son.'

'You know him?'

'I'm a King's squire. Of course I know who comes to speak with the King. Master Basing is often at Westminster with Jonathan.'

She stiffened. Her heart thumped slowly. What, by the cross, had Jonathan de Basing said? It would be nothing good.

As if reading her thought the squire said with a sly look in his cold eyes, 'For a start, he said Rosalind the embroideress is a one for enchantment.'

'I am not. He lied.'

His finely trimmed eyebrows rose. 'He said your mother was a Cathar and a witch. My father dealt with Cathars in France. He and old Count Simon wiped those sorcerers, witches and heretics out of Toulouse. Walled them up if they didn't confess, burned them if they did.' He leaned over her and hissed, 'Put thousands to the sword, women, children, old and young. God's own righteous work.'

'My mother was not a Cathar, nor was she a witch. She was Norman and certainly not a heretic.'

'Are you sure? I am only repeating what I heard.' He opened his hands and dropped the palfrey's reins. For a moment they dipped to the ground between them.

'Help the lady up,' he called over to the other squires who had helped the King and Queen onto their mounts and were waiting to follow them out of the castle gateway onto the raised drawbridge.

A heartbeat later, another squire was helping her onto her mare as Alain Froissart looked on speculatively. She detected a malicious glint in his eyes. He turned away and hurried off to join the King's squires. She was glad to get away from him. Had her mother only pretended to be Norman? What if her father had lied? He had always said her mother was not raised as the Cathars were, to be damned as a heretic believing that God was as evil as the Devil and the Devil as

170

good as God. She controlled a shudder and walked Mirabelle over to the Queen's other ladies. She believed her father. This was a foul slander. These uncomfortable thoughts tormented her as she rode behind Lady Willelma, and as the company stopped now and then to send falcons and hawks coursing along sunlit forest streams.

By the time the sun reached its zenith, they had reached a spacious glade with a scattering of ancient oaks and a stand of beeches. The Queen moved into their midst. 'My turn now,' she said.

The King replied indulgently. 'Let her take her flight. I see wood pigeons up there.' He pointed vaguely into the air.

The Queen tossed back her veil and sent off her sparrow-hawk. It flew high into the trees until it was etched dark against the sky. Ailenor clapped with delight. Then it swooped lower again. Its prey came tumbling down below a beech tree. Delighted, Ailenor slid off her mare and, veil flying behind her, ran to see what the hawk had caught.

'A wood pigeon,' she shouted as the King's squires raced forward.

'Don't touch it, Your Grace. She could turn on you,' Alain Froissart said, as he had reached her first. Instinctively, not wanting to draw attention to herself, Rosalind remembered to gently ease back on the reins. She was relieved when Mirabelle responded and she could draw the palfrey into the shelter of a sprawling oak.

Ailenor didn't listen to the squire. She held up her gloved hand and reached down for the wood pigeon.

'No,' Henry shouted and cantered back to his wife. 'Do not!' It was too late. The hawk lashed out at Ailenor, inflicting a tear in her sleeve. Froissart captured the hawk, but a second later it snapped its tether and soared away, swooping above the company into the air, the dogs racing and barking in frenzied pursuit. The sparrow-hawk rose up into the canopy and circled again in and out of the trees. It vanished.

Blood was seeping through Ailenor's sleeve. She laughed and said, 'It's only a scratch.'

Henry peered at it. 'Not a scratch. It's deep.'

Willelma and Mary dismounted their palfreys and hurried to Ailenor, the aging Willelma slower than Mary. Rosalind tried to dismount but her mare would not be still. It turned in circles with Rosalind trying to control it. The King examined the wound, trying to staunch the blood flow himself with a cloth. Bells rang out, resounding through the trees. Nonce already. 'We shall continue to the Friary. I want the cut looked at by their herbalist.' Henry held onto the Queen's arm and peered down at the blood seeping into her sleeve, concern creasing his face and his eye drooping badly. He looked up again and said to the squire, 'Help the Queen onto her palfrey, lad.'

The King called for the hunt to stop and for the hawk to be captured and destroyed.

'You, you, and you, turn about.' He pointed to half the company crowded into the glade. 'Return to the castle. The rest, come with me. I know the Friars.' He looked at the two squires who were bagging the catch. 'Leave that and find the wretched bird. Alain, go with them.'

The sumpter cart turned back. Rosalind's mare was calm at last but she was not sure what she was supposed to do now that Lady Mary and Lady Willelma were riding ahead with the King and Queen and a small band of nobles. In the chaos she'd been forgotten. She assumed she was meant to ride with them too and egged the mare on to follow Domina Willelma and Lady Mary. Mirabelle obeyed but the riders were trotting so fast she couldn't keep up. There were trees everywhere and now she was frightened a branch would leap out like a serpent and catch her. She reined Mirabelle to a walk. By the time she reached a fork in the trees she couldn't see them. She could hear the distant jingle of bells and the clatter of hoofs. But which way had they gone?

For a few moments she rode along the left track until beech trees seemed to close in on her. Soon the trail vanished. She would have to turn back and take the other fork. By now the forest had become so dense with holly, brambles and strangely shaped coppiced trees she made a decision. She dragged her leg around and over the pommel and awkwardly slid off Mirabelle's back. It was best to lead the horse. At first, her legs felt wobbly but she wasn't afraid of the palfrey anymore. It was the shadows amongst the trees that scared her witless. She couldn't hear the royal party at all, nor could she hear the Friary bell because it had stopped ringing.

Moments later, retracing her way, she discovered the second path and took it. She had not been leading Mirabelle for long when she came to a stream. Her palfrey bent her neck and began to drink. Rosalind waited for Mirabelle to quench her thirst, wondering if this was the correct path to the abbey as the trees seemed so gnarled and ancient, when of a sudden something swooped out of the tall trees. Fast as a small siege missile, a stone hurled, the sparrow-hawk dropped onto her arm. She remained standing very still. The bird's broken strap trailed down to the forest floor, its leather pleats unravelling. She knew she must not terrify the creature. Mirabelle raised her long neck from the water and gave the hawk a wary look.

' 'Tis fine, Mirabelle,' Rosalind spoke softly. 'The hawk knows me.' She turned to the sparrow-hawk, no longer afraid of it. Touching the velvety brown creature, she said, 'You do, don't you?'

The sparrow-hawk surveyed her through tiny jet-black beady eyes. She softly stroked its head and took hold of the creature's jesses with her other hand. If she returned the hawk to Queen Ailenor they would kill it, a cruel fate for such an intelligent, beautiful creature.

Voices travelled along the trackway. Horses trotting through the woodland! Anxious as they came closer, their hoofs scudding the earth, she glanced towards the pathway, wondering should she release the bird.

'There it is.' A horse came bursting through the trees, its rider shouting gleefully.

'What, by the cross!' called the second rider, waving a net from a pole.

Petrified, frozen by fear, Rosalind remained still. Mirabelle raised her head and whinnied at the approaching horses as if in protest. A moment later, three squires had surrounded her. Alain Froissart and another leapt off their mounts and tossed their poles on the ground.

Rosalind tried to hold onto the sparrow-hawk. Finding her voice, she spoke gently to it. 'Don't be afraid, I won't let them hurt you.'

'By all that's holy, she is a witch indeed. What is this, crooning to that beast of a hawk,' snarled Alain Froissart, who led the pack. 'I believe she commanded the hawk so it scratched our Queen. She has called her creature back to her.'

'What are you doing here, girl? Why are you not with the Queen at the Friary?' his companion demanded.

'I lost my way. They were riding so fast. The hawk knows me. When I am in the Queen's chamber I feed her titbits. She's not my creature. She's a sparrow hawk that's frightened. Come no closer.'

'A likely story.' Alain pointed at Rosalind. 'What witchery is this?' he hissed through his teeth. 'Low blood always outs.'

'Who is she? You know her?' said the second youth. The third just looked down at her haughtily from his mount.

'The palace embroideress. I've heard she deals in the dark arts. Embroiders forbidden things, secrets I hear. Claims she's afraid of horses.'

Rosalind backed away as the three squires came closer, one turning his horse's head in a threatening manner. Focused on the bird, he raised his net. The hawk spread her wings and began to flap them wildly as if to take off in flight.

'I said, don't frighten her.'

Alain laughed. Rosalind stepped closer to the stream. She turned her back on the squires and let go the hawk's jesses.

'Fly to safety,' she commanded.

As the hawk rose up, dived down and flew up again, Mirabelle galloped off along the track.

'The horse is frightened of her,' said the mounted squire, laughing.

'Enchantress,' Alain spat at Rosalind. 'You'll come with us back to the castle and explain yourself. Get up behind Simon there.' He reached up and prodded Simon in the back with his net. 'Eric, help me get the girl up. I'll catch the palfrey. You stay with Simon.'

Before Rosalind could protest, she was seized roughly from behind by two pairs of hands, lifted off the ground and placed behind Simon.

'Hold onto him and none of your spells either, if you wish to live that is.' Alain spat on the ground and hurried off in pursuit of the palfrey. Moments later he returned, leading Mirabelle back by her expensive, jewel-studded reins.

Rosalind said, 'I can ride her now.'

'I think not, my lady,' replied Alain.

'The Queen will have much to say to you for this,' Rosalind protested. Tears sprang up and threatened to spill. She blinked them back. Queen Ailenor would not countenance this treatment.

'We have much to say to the Queen,' Alain said. After that there was no further speech as they rode towards Marlborough, no noise apart from the rustling forest, horses' snorts and the metal of their hoofs striking the packed earth.

Some days earlier, a newcomer to the summer court, a Dominican friar named Alphonse, had arrived. He was hunched over, black-cloaked and white-gowned, and flapped his way through the castle Hall, swooping forward like a buzzard. The friar had blown into Westminster some months previously from Languedoc where the Black Friars had dealt with the heretics, calling them sorcerers. It was their remit to root out heresy wherever they could discover it. This one had walked west to attach himself to their court at Marlborough.

To Ailenor's irritation, the Friar, a malevolent presence, drew her devout husband into his dark company. He dampened her gaiety from the moment he appeared in their Hall. She had felt him frowning when, some days previously, she suggested taking parts for a play about the unfortunate lovers, Tristan and Iseult and, in particular on the day she'd decided to put the question *was it a women's right to keep her own property after marriage* to discussion in the garden one afternoon. Henry, on the other hand, liked the Friars' consideration for the poor and refused to turn the obsessive away. She disliked the way he moved now, as if he had an evil purpose in mind. She was sure it concerned her embroideress.

Within a day of the hunt, talk had spread throughout the castle suggesting that her embroideress had bewitched her sparrow-hawk.

Rosalind returned from the hunt accompanied by three of Henry's squires badly shaken. At the time, Ailenor, whose wound was of little account to her, felt grave concern for Rosalind as she would for all of her ladies.

She ordered a posset for the girl and asked Willelma to watch over her. Yet, it was odd, because since the incident, Rosalind had not broken her fast nor had she left her chamber. Ailenor did not know what to do to persuade her to eat and speak. She wondered if Rosalind had heard the gossip. Something, she said gravely to Willelma, must be done to allay the cruel rumours that were whispered amongst the castle servants. She suspected Friar Alphonse was involved.

So when Friar Alphonse reached the dais that morning, Ailenor stared angrily at him, at his hooked nose, piercing blue eyes and long sallow face and felt disgust. Her eyes fell on his jewelled ring and fine woollen cloak. He did not look impoverished. Nor did he strike her as humble. He stared back at her before bowing low, his countenance immoveable.

He jerked up his head and said, 'Your Graces, may I speak privately about a matter concerning the embroiderer, Rosalind?'

Ailenor rose without speaking and raised her hand to her ladies to follow her. Henry lifted one of his hands to stay Alain Froissart as his squire began to moved forward, ready to follow his master. Opening a door, Ailenor, the King, her ladies and the Friar entered the sunlit chamber behind the Hall.

Henry took his velvet-covered chair, arranged his mantle to flow gracefully over the sides, and only then did he acknowledge the Friar who hovered by the window. 'Explain why you have disturbed our dinner.'

'The hunt.' The Friar was hesitating. Henry raised his brow. Ailenor was seated calmly on her chair but now she, too, looked quizzically at Friar Alphonse, though she, forewarned by gossip, had an inkling of his business.

'What about it?' Henry folded his hands and studied the friar.

'The Queen's hawk was enchanted by that girl. I heard her mother belonged to the sects, the heretics in France, Sire. As you know . . .'

'I know of the story you bring me. It's the talk of the court, thanks to loose tongues and speculation. Pah, it's not proven her mother was a heretic. If it were, it does not make the Queen's lady a sorceress. She attends service daily with the Queen and her ladies.'

'That may be so. Such creatures are sly. I wish to question her. Cathars deny the sacrament . . .'

'These are false accusations. Her mother was French and is long dead. Her father has remarried,' Ailenor interjected. 'I know my ladies' history. You do not need to question her or me as to whom I chose as my attendants, Friar.'

'If she is innocent she will pass my questioning.'

Henry opened his hands. If she was innocent it would out, he said, though he had no doubt of her innocence.

He finished by saying, to Ailenor's horror, 'I shall consider this matter. Thank you for bringing it to our attention. That will be all for now. You may leave us.'

Ailenor turned to Henry after the Friar gathered his cloak about him and left the chamber. 'They cannot accuse her. This is nonsense.'

A plate of wafers sat between them untouched. Henry reached over and poured cups of crimson wine.

'Ailenor, let me worry about the girl.'

Ailenor sat her wine cup on the table. It tasted sour. She glanced over at the window seat where her ladies sat with downcast eyes sewing. Lady Margaret seemed tense. Ailenor considered the empty perch beside the window.

'Henry, my hawk was not bewitched.'

'Where is your lady now?'

'Rosalind is resting. Your squires frightened her. All this talk of Cathars, witchcraft, and sorcery.' She leaned towards Henry. 'No wonder she is distressed. How could you agree to Alphonse's questions? It will destroy her. I don't want her accused of anything. Alain Froissart's head is full of the Inquisition, and all from his father. For some peculiar reason, he has spread untruths about Rosalind and spoken to Alphonse. Question your squire, my lord.'

177

'Maybe so. But, do remember, heretics don't adhere to the teachings of the Church. They believe in an evil God.'

'And a good God in Heaven. Nor do Jews adhere to our faith. You are happy enough to borrow money from Jews.' She could not resist this stab at Henry, though she too borrowed from the Jews.

'I simply confiscate their wealth. That is different.' Henry's lower lid was drooping and that was a warning sign. He was not getting away with this attack on her lady.

'You should banish the Jews from the Kingdom, if they really do offend you.'

Sand sifted through the glass clock on the table. Henry lifted her arm and studied her bandaged arm. 'This occurred.'

'It is healing. The monks applied comfrey and honey.'

'Maybe so; perhaps the girl meant no ill.' Henry's anger had reduced but not entirely dissipated. He would treat with her now.

'Rosalind was on her horse and nowhere near the hawk when it happened.'

'But if her mother was a Cathar and a sorceress, or whatever the squire claims, it's possible the girl inherited traits. Her embroidery is too perfect. Maybe it's bewitched.'

'Don't be ridiculous, Henry. How can embroidery contain spells? I will not have her questioned.'

Henry rose and sighed. 'My dear, I hope you are right. As she's your lady, I shall leave you to decide what to do. If you cannot find a solution, this talk will touch you too. If that happens I shall have to let Friar Alphonse question her . . . and you.'

'That will not be necessary.'

'You could ask the nuns to examine her for witch marks. Otherwise . . .'

'What? What are you suggesting?' For a moment Ailenor recollected the witch marks carved into the bench in the workshop and had to repress a shiver.

Henry continued, 'Alphonse knows all about these heretics. You do not. You, Ailenor, must not be tainted with heresy. Many could whisper you are. They don't like foreigners at court. Your people. Queen's men . . . whom they call *our* Savoyards.'

'I shall speak with her, Henry, but remember that you are a king. A king cannot be ruled by his subjects. You are appointed by God to rule, not by your subjects.'

'Ah, lesson observed. You have a week to get that girl away from here back to her people, Ailenor.'

Henry hurried from the chamber angry-faced, slamming the door closed. Ailenor's ladies looked startled, their sewing dropping onto the floor tiles. She waited for a few moments listening to him stomping into the Hall. After his steps faded, she turned to Willelma's shocked face. 'You cannot believe this nonsense.'

'I do not, but others will.'

Lady Mary said, 'Rosalind will not eat nor drink.'

'I can't subject her to questioning. I cannot.'

'If she is willing,' Lady Mary said quietly, 'it would be safer for her to enter a convent. The sooner she disappears from court, the safer she will be, and, in time, she'll be forgotten. Talk will fade.'

'Where do you suggest?'

'The Convent of St Helena. Are not the nuns of St Helena stitching a bishop's cope? They are a small convent and open-minded, respected Benedictines. They teach embroidery. Rosalind will prove herself a true Christian if she joins them. She must not return to her father. Tales will follow her there.'

'Bring me parchment and pen, Willelma. And my writing desk. She may not need to take vows. They can use her skills. Who knows, she may enjoy Church embroidery. I'll miss her, for I've found her company pleasant.' Ailenor paced thinking quickly. 'With a fast messenger and an inducement, a gift of a relic, we can send her to the nuns within the week, assuming she agrees.'

As Willelma hurried to find both writing desk and ink, Ailenor said to Lady Mary. 'Walk with Rosalind in the garden. We have a solution, tell her, but she must eat before we explain it. Speak to none, no maids, nor to any of the servants. For now, Rosalind must remain secluded.'

'She is too frightened to not remain hidden.'

'Poor girl,' Ailenor said, taking up her pen. 'We must get her away. We must.' Ailenor bit her lip as she wrote. She should never have brought Rosalind away from the other embroiderers, but then, she rationalised, this evil could have attached itself to her anywhere and at least with her close she could offer protection. Could the de Basings be behind it all?

A response from Prioress Elizabeth arrived by messenger. The Queen summoned Rosalind to her antechamber. She asked her embroideress to be seated on a cushioned bench by her own chair. Rosalind was thin and her appearance neglected; her eyes were red from weeping and her face pinched and pale. Her fine linen gown hung loose looking as dejected as Rosalind herself.

'Rosalind, how are you? Not well, I suspect.'

Rosalind clasped her hands together. 'Your Grace, it's untrue, all of it. I don't know why it has happened, why anyone could or would accuse me of witchcraft? I am confused. I am frightened. I don't know what will become of me.' She twisted her hands, anxiously rubbing at her gown.

Ailenor said quietly, 'I am so very sorry for it. This misery should never touch one such as you. But I have to ask. Did you enchant my hawk?'

'The squire lied. I'm no witch, Your Grace.'

Ailenor, by now, thoroughly disliked Henry's squire. The week had been painful for her. She had publicly attended every Mass, three times daily like Henry, praying for calm and for the Madonna's guidance. Braving Friar Alphonse's scrutiny, she insisted that likewise Rosalind attended Mass accompanied by Lady Mary and two loyal maidservants. She observed the extent of Rosalind's unhappiness for herself and promised herself that once Rosalind was safe, she'd persuade Henry to send Squire Alain to one of their Border barons for the rest of his training, to the de Bohuns. They would not be easy on him. They were harsh men.

'I believe you, Rosalind,' she said aloud. 'However, there's cruel talk. Unfortunately, talk can become fact whether true or not. I cannot risk gossip at court claiming I have an enchantress in my service.' She leaned forward. Her tone earnest, she added, 'And I want you to be safe from Friar Alphonse. You know whom I mean?'

Rosalind's blue eyes flashed anger for a heartbeat. 'The Black Friar who seeks out heretics. I have seen him staring at me at every service I attend. I know he wants to interrogate me but I have nothing to say. I'm truly a good Christian . . . what is to be my fate, Your Grace?' she asked quietly. 'I would like to return to my father.'

'No, not yet. You should stay away from your father's workshop too. People are easily suspicious. They look for witchcraft in the innocent. They accuse with injustice, and they attack the Jews, too, on the slightest suspicion. Stories easily become exaggerated. They claim the Jews eat Christian babies.' Ailenor glanced at Willelma who nodded. She said in as gentle a tone as she could manage, 'Rosalind, you must be sent away. In time this talk will die away, Lady Willelma thinks . . .' Ailenor drew breath. 'If you willingly enter a convent. If you stay away from prying eyes . . .'

'But my family . . . Your Grace?'

'I believe you are no enchantress, but many won't. So . . .' Ailenor paused and lifted the Prioress's letter from the table.

'How will Papa know what has happened?'

'A moment, please . . . let me explain.' Ailenor drew breath. 'I have received an invitation from a small convent, one you shouldn't refuse.'

'You wish me to become a novice?'

'The Convent of St Helena will take you as an embroideress. They have an important commission from the Bishop of London. They need your help.' Ailenor leaned closer and took Rosalind's hands. They were icy cold. The girl was so frightened. 'For your safety, Rosalind. In time you'll return to us. I'll send Lady Mary to speak with your family and explain.'

Rosalind looked crestfallen. 'My workshop?'

'It will continue. Shall we say that you are working on Church embroidery? I ask this because I value your work and because the nuns are kindly and will care for you and because I am their patron and yours.'

Lady Willelma added, 'We would say you have chosen to spend time in the convent. It would proclaim your innocence. You are joining the sisters who are embroidering a new cope for the Bishop of London. We shall say you may be considering vows . . . if we are questioned further.'

Lady Mary looked at Rosalind with sad grey eyes. 'I shall pray for you, my dear,' she said. 'Every day.'

Rosalind nodded. She recognised the seriousness of her position. 'I have no choice.'

Ailenor inclined her head. 'It is for the best.'

Rosalind finally said sadly, 'I shall accept your offer. Clearly I must.'

Ailenor noted what an effort it had taken for her to agree and it saddened her. Before Rosalind changed her mind, she patted the girl's arm and said, 'You'll depart in the morning. I hope that when all is settled again you will return.' She added, 'Please, Rosalind, rise above these accusations. Try to accept this decision is made to keep you safe.'

On the long journey to London, Rosalind sat miserably inside the canvas covered wagon stamped with gold and red royal lions. Her journey would end at St Helena's Convent by Bishopsgate, Lady Margaret's at the Queen's apartments in White Tower. Branches were blowing about, tossed by a summer's gale, when after two days of travel, they reached London. The wagon rattled into the city gates and over cobbles, splashing through puddles accompanied by the clanking of wooden pails, squawking hens scurrying for shelter, and pigs snorting through sodden discarded bits of food. Lepers desperately rang clappers, monks in gowns and hawkers hurried about their daily business in the rain. London was the same. Nothing felt different except her new situation, one which she must for now accept.

Rosalind's mood matched the stormy weather raging beyond the convent walls. She felt damp, bedraggled, and dispirited. Once inside the Hall where a fire burned, she could hear the storm seeking entry at every shutter, blowing its damp breath on the hearth.

Words repeatedly echoed through Rosalind's head, beating like a mummer's drum, 'For your own safety.' She had done nothing wrong. How would Thomas ever find her in this chill place inhabited by eight nuns? Rosalind stared at the tall prioress who greeted her with her mouth turned up into a smile. She might be kindly. A few words were exchanged. Lady Mary apparently knew Prioress Elizabeth well.

She took Rosalind's hands in her own and kissed her on her cheeks. 'All will be well and if I may, I shall visit you here.'

A lump in Rosalind's throat prevented speech. The Prioress bade Lady Mary goodbye, lifted Rosalind's baggage, and guided her from the Hall along a passageway to a small chamber hardly larger than a cupboard. On the cot lay two simple novice habits and two wimples, a leather belt, and a long woollen cloth with a head opening that was called a scapula. It was poor exchange for the elegant gowns she must set aside.

'You shall wear these garments here and we shall look after your gowns for now.' She paused. 'Rosalind, I am afraid we must cut your hair. It is our rule to keep all earthly temptations out of our house.'

Rosalind glanced over her shoulder for Lady Mary's calm reassurance but she had slipped away. A nun appeared at her shoulder with cutting shears. Rosalind drew back and looked for a door through which to escape, but where could she go? Her father's business would suffer if she ever returned to the house by St Paul's and she would be tainted with the suspicion of witchcraft – if Jonathan de Basing had any influence.

'My dear,' the Abbess spoke in a voice so musical her tone was like that of the nightingale's song. 'We are fortunate to have you with us. Whilst you remain here, will you join us embroidering a cope for the Bishop of the City? We need your opinion.'

'Is my opinion worth anything?' Rosalind was so sad her heart was breaking.

'Without doubt. You are one of the best embroiderers in England, I hear.'

'I am not so experienced with Church embroidery.'

'We are privileged to have you.'

At last Rosalind weakly smiled. 'Then I am happy to help. I have known the skills of embroidery since I could hold a needle.'

The nun with the scissors spread a linen cloth by Rosalind's feet. Another sister brought a stool for Rosalind to sit upon. 'I promise you, Sister Blanche will not cut your hair above your shoulders. When you leave us it will grow again. Will you allow her to cut it?'

Rosalind felt she had no alternative. 'Yes, but it saddens me so much.' Tears spilled from her eyes as her silvery hair dropped to the floor. A trap felt tightly shut on her life from the moment she had walked through the Convent door.

Chapter Twenty

Autumn tumbled in with wind rattling at doors and tree branches scratching at windows like cursed souls demanding entry to the palace. Candles were lit early. Light glowed from cressets placed in wall niches. Corridors grew shadowy early in the evening. Ailenor took an hour's leisure with Henry in her bedchamber whilst their children slept through the storm in their nursery above. She lifted a tiny shirt she was sewing for Edward and unpicked a rogue stitch.

Ailenor slowly drew her thread through the fabric. She was grateful to Rosalind for teaching her such fine work and she missed her. It had been a dreadful and frightening incident. When she had summoned Rosalind's father to the Tower to explain his marriage to Rosalind's mother, she had felt uncomfortable when his misery at the accusations against her caused him to appear outraged. His first wife, he'd explained, hailed from a Cathar family. On her marriage to him, she denied heretical beliefs and renounced her family. She had made a difficult choice but she had chosen him. He wiped a tear from his eye.

Ailenor, moved by his story, leaned forward and assured him that she would protect Rosalind, safe in St Helena's Convent, where she working on a cope for the Bishop of London. Rosalind was doing God's work. He should be proud of her.

'May I visit her, Your Grace?'

'The nuns are strict and you would only be permitted to speak with her through a grille.'

'I understand. How long –'

'Friar Alphonse, her accuser, will be returning to Spain very soon. The squire who threatened Rosalind is far off in the Borderlands. Rosalind can return to court in time.'

'Your Grace, I would rather have Rosalind at home. My wife would too.'

'We should let Rosalind decide. The nuns, I have heard, are delighted to have her instruction. They like her quiet presence. She is one of the best embroiderers in the land, you know,' Ailenor said. Lady Mary nodded. 'The accusations were nonsense, but people talk. I have heard that the grocer's son Jonathan wished her ill. Is this true do you think? It is better that she is safe.'

Alfred said thoughtfully, 'The De Basing lad has married. He should be content. I should never have wished him on my daughter.'

Ailenor frowned. 'But the grocer's son wanted to marry Rosalind, did he not?'

Alfred nodded again. 'She refused him.'

'That explains his spite. She prefers another?'

'She likes a squire who is on Crusade with Earl Simon. His name is Thomas.'

'Earl Simon will return any day soon. And then we shall see. Thomas could be a good match. He will inherit his father's lands. She would join the knightly class.'

The tailor shook his head. 'I would be honoured if she did but I fear she is overly hopeful. Still, I pray daily for my daughter's happiness.'

'Stranger things have happened, Master Alfred. It is not unknown for a young man of noble heritage to be betrothed to a master craftsman's daughter, particularly when that family is wealthy.'

Once the embroideress had gone to dwell in St Helena's, Henry never spoke of her again. For her part, Ailenor considered she had managed the situation well. It was a small price to pay for the crystal reliquary containing a piece of the true cross she had donated to St Helena's in return for Rosalind's keeping, her clothing and food.

She wondered if one day she could help Rosalind and Thomas – it would be a fine match for the embroideress; that is, if the young squire returned safely from Jerusalem.

Henry stretched his stockinged feet towards the fire, unfolded a creased letter from Isabella, his mother, and read it again. Ailenor swallowed a sigh. Since they had returned to Windsor from Marlborough, Henry had been obsessed by thoughts of war with France. He glanced over at her. 'I'll regain the territories my father lost,' he declared, scanning the letter.

If only he would return to his building designs.

'What if I *could* win back all my French possessions? France is already greedy for Poitou. Gascony will be next. Toulouse, too, could be captured. The French always wanted Toulouse.'

'I don't like the idea of war with Louis.' Without looking up, she made another stitch. 'My sister . . .'

'I can't ignore my mother's pleas for help. She was a Queen of England. She is insulted by Spanish Blanche . . . you know she is . . . she writes for men and arms and I must grant them to her.' He slapped his free hand on the parchment, scattering fragments of red wax from the broken seal over his blue damask gown. 'Louis has appointed Alphonse, his brother, as Governor of Poitou. That is Lusignan territory. Besides, Richard is Governor of Poitou, or he should be.'

'My sister is Queen of France. Besides it's unwise and costly.' She lifted her eyes to his but did not reach out to sweep the wax slivers from his gown. 'The new shrine to St Edward. Pure gold is expensive. You are building all the time. The shrine, the Abbey Church, Windsor, Marlborough. It's all costly. We cannot go to war just because Louis has appointed his brother as governor of Poitou.'

Henry thrust Isabella's letter at her. 'When did you care about expense?' He jabbed a jewelled finger at her rich brocade gown. 'Read it. They went to Poitiers to offer fealty to Alphonse last Christmastide. Blanche ignored her. She kept my mother, a queen herself, waiting for three long days!' He stared at her. 'Three days and my mother has been a Queen. Pah!' Henry shook his head. 'When my mother was granted admission to their presence, Louis and Blanche sat together on their raised chairs. Neither rose to greet her. Nor did they speak, and before you ask, Ailenor, Marguerite was not present, just Louis and his mother.'

Ailenor read the passage aloud – '*I expressed my loyalty. Louis nodded. Blanche spoke not a word but looked down on me coldly. I departed without complaint but returned with Hugh later so he could make his oath. Hugh was treated with a winter's chill as he proceeded to dispute Alphonse Capet's right to Poitou. It is Richard's entitlement to govern Poitou. And where is he now? We climbed on our mounts and departed* – It is rude, I grant you, Henry, but Richard, as your mother implies, has never showed any interest in governing Poitou. The territory is ceded to the French.'

'Read on,' Henry muttered with a scowl.

She studied the letter again and looked up saying, 'It has developed further, I see, "*Hugh has met with the Gascon barons at Pons and with Raymond of Toulouse.*" So Count Raymond of Toulouse is concerned about France too.' She returned to the letter. 'They ask for your support.'

'I intend to give it. My territories in Gascony are at stake.' He paused. 'Our son's future.'

Once he spoke of Edward, she saw his point. One day Gascony would be Edward's inheritance, with all the trade in wine it possessed. 'But Richard – what will he think?'

'Richard is expected home any day now. I shall ask for his support. And I shall ask the council too.'

Ailenor thrust the letter back at him. 'I cannot advise you. You must do as you think best.'

She picked up her sewing again wondering if she should write to Marguerite. No, her first loyalty was to Henry and to their children. She lifted her eyes to the new embroidery that hung over her great bed. Henry, who was so conservative about faith and who would have had her embroiderer questioned about her faith, had never commented on the midwives hovering about St Anne's bed. Talk about Rosalind *had* died down, as Lady Willelma had predicted. Henry, neurotic at the thought of heresy, would ally himself with Raymond of Toulouse who had shown clemency to Cathar heretics.

'You pacified Wales. Perhaps the Council will recognise your ability and grant us a war to protect Poitou and Gascony.'

Henry consigned Isabel's letter to a jewelled casket he kept for his own personal correspondence. Locking the little box, he tucked his key into a belt purse he wore under his surcoat. 'They must,' he muttered.

She had soothed him with mention of Wales. He was smiling and stroking his beard. 'How shall we welcome Richard home?'

'I wonder if Richard visited Sancha on his return. We must send Uncle Peter to Provence to negotiate her release from the marriage contract with Raymond of Toulouse.'

'We shall have to convince my brother first. I think we'll ride down to Dover to meet Richard on his return. He'll have a crusader's welcome home. London made festive. Streets cleaned up. Tapestries hung from windows. Tableaux everywhere. By St Edward's shroud, the city merchants shall welcome our brother home with a magnificent feast. It won't cost us anything. If Richard is flattered and feted, he'll agree to anything, especially marriage to a beautiful woman.'

Ailenor stood and swept the bits of wax away that clung to her gown. 'A magnificent homecoming. If anyone can persuade the Council to grant you money, Richard can. He spent so much of his own treasure on his Crusade, they owe him loyalty. They owe us all much since we rule in the service of Christ to keep their lands safe and protect the kingdom from England's enemies.' She felt a glow of pleasure in her heart as she did every time she considered the rightness of her queenly state. 'We'll make Richard's return glorious, that of a humble knight who has fought to protect Christendom. After all, he freed prisoners and has beheld Jerusalem with his own eyes.' Henry looked petulant. He would like to see Jerusalem. 'A homecoming all shall remember,' she swiftly said.

'I doubt the City guildsmen would consider my brother humble.'

'When your brother marries Sancha, the people of England will see a devout couple and they will love them both.' She folded her hands. Her voice determined, she repeated, 'Send Uncle Peter to

Provence. Make him our diplomat. Bind Provence to us.' And Richard, she thought to herself.

They welcomed Richard in Portsmouth and escorted him, surrounded by nobles bearing banners with embroidered crosses, to Winchester. The royal party was greeted with garlands of greenery and cheers. Ailenor affectionately remembered her procession from Canterbury to London after her marriage nearly six years earlier.

At length they crossed the bridge into the City. 'See how they greet you, brother.' Henry reined in his stallion as he, Ailenor, and Richard rode through the streets at the head of a glittering caval-cade. Londoners had donned their best clothing and there was not a beggar, pig, or hen to impede the royal passage from the Tower to Westminster.

'Good to be home.' Richard smiled broadly. He had entered the City wearing his crusader cross with pride, his head high, and his Arab stallion as white as wintery clouds that skittered through a blue sky. He grinned. 'Lingering in Provence was as delightful as visiting a perfumed garden filled with roses and lavender; those gleaming castles and an enchanting court that loves song and dance.'

They waved at the crowd with enthusiasm. Ailenor smiled to herself. Provence had welcomed Richard. This boded well for San-cha's future. Richard would love Sancha. She was young and lovely – and her sister. How could he not?

It was a joyful day. Groups of traders and merchants cried out 'For God and the Holy Cross' and 'Richard and Henry' and 'Welcome home, God's warriors, peace be with you.'

The cheering grew louder. After the procession reached the great conduit that provided water for that part of London, it quietened and Ailenor was able to speak again.

'Is my father well, my mother in good health? Did you speak with my sisters?'

'Your sister Sancha is as enchanting as the moon and calm as the cloister. Her nature is as pure as that of the Holy Virgin herself. If she were free, I would press my suit. They are all well.'

Ailenor turned to Richard, her mouth widening into a large smile. 'Sancha may yet be free. Uncle Peter can be persuasive. If you agree, we can send him to my father as our ambassador. Who would not wish to be a princess of England?'

'She is the most beautiful damsel in Europe . . . apart from her sister, that is.'

'You flatter me, Earl Richard. It is not necessary.' She glanced towards the gate. Henry, riding a little ahead, had not overheard their conversation. He was distracted by a tableaux. Edward Confessor knelt before him and on either side of the Confessor, in the shadow of the gate, stood an angel and a devil. The angel darted forward but the devil skulked malevolently by the wall.

'Bless you, Earl Richard,' the saintly figure of Edward Confessor said solemnly as they reached the gate. Throwing a vial of holy water at Henry, the angel added, 'God's blessing on Your Graces.'

As they rode under the gate tower, a shower of white rose petals descended from arrow slits above. It was as if they moved though a scented snowstorm. Ailenor brushed the flowers from her sleeves.

Richard rode alongside Henry. Ailenor smiled to herself as Henry beamed at them both and turning to his brother said, 'Ah, Richard, you must see my shrine to the Confessor. Finished at last. Pure gold and wondrous to behold.'

'Costly, I imagine.'

'Nothing is ever too costly for our Lord and his saints. Crusades are expensive. Yours in the Holy Land, mine in our kingdom – God's kingdom. I shall soon have masons building a new abbey for Westminster. Though we shall need all our gold if we are to save Gascony and protect Poitou.'

Richard lowered his voice. Straining to hear, Ailenor stilled her jangling reins. 'You are determined to break the French treaty, Henry. Is this wise?'

'You are nominally Governor of Poitou. The White Queen has insulted our mother again.'

'But a war. Is it worth it?'

'Our mother is. I intend calling the Council in January when the

191

barons come to my Christmas crowning. It'll remind them who is appointed by our Lord to rule the kingdom. Will you grant me your support?'

'What knights do we still have? Gilbert Marshal was slain at a tournament. I thought you banned tournaments.'

'Oh, I had. Served Marshal right. He was always disobedient.'

'And Walter is the Marshal heir now.' Richard laughed. 'If he dies there are only girls left in that family. Great heiresses, huh?'

'Aye, that's true. Valuable heiresses the lot of them. You should know. You married one. Walter is even more difficult than Gilbert. He'll wait for his earldom.' Henry turned to the cheering crowd, nodded, and waved at a band of monks who stood by their riverside monastery gates calling out blessings.

Red crosses fluttered in the breeze against the grey walls of Westminster as they approached. Ailenor fell to thinking about Poitou. Henry was right. It was a gamble, but if the people were happy with them now they would be ecstatic if they recovered lost Poitou. This thought made her think of Richard's son who was in their nursery with Lord Edward. Looking across Henry to Richard she said, 'Henry and Edward cannot wait to see you – Margaret, of course, is a baby.'

'Healthy, I hope.'

'They all are.'

She noted how Richard's eyes looked moist. Isabel had lost children, several babies that lived only a short time, but, of course, he could have a family with Sancha who was young. Richard shook his head. 'Thank you for your care of Harry. He needs brothers and sisters.' There was a break in his voice.

Ailenor wondered if Richard had missed Isabel in death as he had not in her lifetime. They must all look forward, not back. Isabel's death was a great sorrow, but it was a sorrow that was God's will.

Isabel of Cornwall's death was not the only death that touched them during those years. Just as barons and earls rode in for the Christmas feast two months later, Henry received news that his sister, another

192

Isabel, had died in childbirth. He raged to Ailenor when the messenger from Sicily arrived with the terrible news. This time, she did not know how to calm his anger. Henry, who had been neglected by his run-away mother, craved family and loved his sisters.

'Emperor Frederick never loved her,' he said, wringing his hands and weeping. 'The ungodly heathen kept a harem as the sultans do. Richard says he cared more for Arab dancing girls than our own sister.'

'Calm,' Ailenor said, entwining her hands around his neck to comfort him, repressing a shiver. She was pregnant again herself and although she was pleased, childbirth was dangerous. 'It is not unusual for a woman to die giving birth; it's not Frederick's fault, no matter how strange he is.'

'God was displeased,' Henry shook her away. 'God took *her* instead of Frederick.' In a flash of temper, he swept his hand over a low table, scattering chessmen laid out on a chess board. The thump of carved bishops and pawns dropping to the tiled floor disturbed Edward. He ran to his mother and buried his head in her gown.

'Papa angry,' he whimpered into her skirts. He balled his tiny fists as he let go handfuls of silk, looked up red-faced and shouted, his face as red as his father's, 'I shall kill the bad man who made Papa angry.'

She forced a smile. 'He is an Emperor who lives far away over the seas. Aunt Isabel took ill and died, sweeting,' she whispered. 'Papa is angry because he loved her. He will have thousands of candles lit in the chapel to honour her memory. Later, you, he, and I shall pray for Aunt Isabel's soul. But now you need to visit your pony.' Ailenor called for Edward's nurse. 'Take him. The King and I wish to be alone.'

Edward was persuaded away. Sinking back in his chair, Henry said with bitterness, 'The Emperor never permitted Richard to see our sister on his return to Sicily. He claimed she had already withdrawn from court. That was August. It is now December and she is gone from us.'

'Shall I order the candles lit in her memory?' Ailenor said after a while.

A silence followed until Henry said, 'Mansel will see to that. There has to be a feast in her honour . . . for a thousand of the City's poor, more than a thousand if they can be found.'

'There are always poor in need of sustenance,' she said in a placatory tone.

Another expense when they wanted money granted for a war. At least the impoverished would benefit from poor Isabel's death. 'Where do you wish this feast to be held?'

'Here, in the Hall at Westminster.' He smiled a sad smile. It was as if his temper had never shown itself that day. The thought of planning a feast to remember his sister mollified his anger. Henry became as subdued as the little dog that had curled up under her chair, where it had slunk at his first outburst of anger.

'I shall find our clerk at once,' she said. 'It shall be done. Your sister will be honoured before the nobles and our people.'

As she swept from the painted chamber to seek out John Mansel in his office behind the Great Hall, she thought how although Henry hardly knew this sister, he was broken-hearted. Now two Isabels were gone to Heaven and the third lived in a state of outrage in Poitou, determined to drag them, unready as they were, into war with France.

If only Nell and Simon would return to court. Simon, such a great warrior and a knight with integrity, would give Henry sound advice about war with France. She exhaled a long breath. According to Richard, Simon had been offered the governorship of Jerusalem where he imposed peace and order. He had declined the honour and was now resting in Italy with Nell. There was no knowing if they would ever return to England, not with huge debts and confiscated lands. Simon might chose to dwell in France indefinitely. Ailenor turned into another corridor. Simon de Montfort would become a formidable enemy if he fought for Louis in the coming conflict. As Ailenor knocked on the door of her clerk's closet, she felt herself alone and fearful for the future. Candles for Isabel. One day there might be candles lit for her. Childbirth was dangerous. And war terrifying, no matter how justified it was.

★

Poor were fed daily in honour of a princess they had never known. Candles glowed for Princess Isabel's memory beside the new shrine to Edward Confessor. The usual period of fasting that led to Christmas followed. Earls and barons gathered at Westminster.

As Christmas approached, the court became merry again. Henry wooed his barons with exotic foods from the day they all rode into his courtyards. Ailenor watched with concern for expense as he ordered salmon and sauces laced with cream for the fasting period leading up to Christ's Day. Herring, green fish, haddock, and eel pies graced his table, accompanied by fresh-water fish from his ponds. There was no shortage of rice imported from Italy, almonds from Spain, and sugar-coated fruits.

Christmas revels, dancing, and music edged their way into court festivities as the fasting period ended. Henry provided a more luxurious feast than usual on Christmas Day and paid for it from his own coffers. He played chess with his barons and rode out with them through the woods around Westminster. They, though Ailenor doubted their sincerity, admired his golden, jewelled shrine to St Edward that now dominated the Abbey's Nave.

In January when the Council met, the barons changed their tone. Ailenor knew they would not want to provide from their coffers for a war in Poitou. They were reconciled to the loss of their ancestral lands. They would not take their knights and villeins away from lands that needed planting in March and reaping in August. Rather, they wished to look to what they cared about in England, the kingdom they now considered their native land.

Despite these sentiments, Henry optimistically remained hopeful until Walter Marshal declared, 'Sire, we have heard rumours from Poitou that Hugh de Lusignan is not to be trusted. He changes alliance as quickly as a rotten apple sheds it skin. It's imprudent to side with him. He will betray us.' Assents of agreement raced through the Council.

Henry shouted so all could hear, 'I should never have brought Walter Marshal back to court. He is a bad influence. He's worse than his brother Gilbert. Worse than that other traitor who once challenged my authority, Richard Marshal, Gilbert's older brother, long since gone to his maker.'

It was Richard of Cornwall who recounted the story to Ailenor. 'Your uncle Peter calmed it all down. Ailenor,' he reported, 'the majority of the barons, and it's not just Walter Marshal, have refused to finance a war requested by our mother and her husband.'

'How did it end?' she asked fearing total disaster. The barons would quote rights to their own freedom of opinion, contained in the Great Charter of King John's reign.

Richard drew breath, his face darkening. 'Henry told them they must think further on the matter, insisting Gascony is threatened. They said, "Our merchants say that if there is a war with France and a French King ever comes to London again, they will all be ruined. There is peace now with France and peace equals prosperity. They will not spend their hard-earned groats on a war against France." Groats indeed. They possess more silver than I.'

Ailenor snorted at this. 'That, I doubt.'

He glared at her. 'They say if we don't contest Poitou, Louis will leave Gascony alone. And for all his fine words and haranguing, Henry could not persuade them otherwise. Our Council insists we cannot afford a war.'

'And you, do you support Hugh and Isabella? Do you support Henry, Richard?'

Richard looked away. 'I fear I must. She is our mother and Count Hugh our stepfather.'

A month passed and the Council met again. They said that since their King had in his treasury a sizeable income from the empty see of Canterbury since Edmund Rich had died, he could well afford to equip an army without taxing London. Henry was collecting funds from the see until the Pope approved a successor as archbishop. They would not grant funds, but neither would they oppose the war if Henry could afford to equip his own army to protect Gascony. Again, they voiced distrust of Hugh de Lusignan.

Henry invited those knights he considered loyal to him to a private supper. 'We shall make ready an army once the weather improves. When we win back territory, they will be only too glad to back us. We depart after Easter,' he said.

'Let us hope that you are right.' Richard laid down his eating knife and turned to Uncle Peter who sat across from him. 'And when do you leave us for Provence?'

'Ah, a pleasanter subject. I wondered if you would ask. Agnes will accompany me. We intend visiting Savoy and then my Lady Agnes's lands before we visit Provence. We leave as soon as I put all in order in Yorkshire.'

Ailenor said, 'Do not wait too long. I would not like to hear that Sancha was married before you reach my father's kingdom.' Richard nodded with enthusiasm. She continued, 'Time is short, Uncle Peter.' Smiling at Henry she said, 'Perhaps tonight it is appropriate to announce our news.' She took Henry's hand in her own. He nodded and for the first time that afternoon beamed around the Painted Chamber.

'My lords, the Queen is with child once again.'

'He will be born in Bordeaux.' She wore her most gracious smile as she contemplated each lord seated at their table. It was, as ever, her triumph when she was about to produce a child for England.

'Or a princess,' Richard said.

'Girls are always welcome,' remarked Henry. 'I myself had three, nay four, sisters because Joanna, wed to Llewelyn of Wales, was always owned as my sister even though my father was not yet wed to my mother when Joanna was born. Her mother was only his mistress, but my father loved Joanna and honoured her, God rest her soul.'

'Girls bring marriage alliances,' remarked Uncle Peter.

'They are expensive too,' Richard said pointedly, possibly aware that Sancha would bring no dowry. He turned a worried face to Ailenor, 'Is it wise that you cross the seas? It's safer for you here.'

Ailenor had wavered but decided it was prudent she accompany her husband to Bordeaux. 'I have my ladies to watch over me.'

Henry squeezed her hand. 'And, after all, we'll be returning before next Christmastide, my mother's honour restored, the French running for cover in Paris and Gascony safe for our son.'

'I see the cooks have made us a subtlety,' Ailenor said, changing the conversation, pointing to where a group of cooks stood in the doorway waiting for a signal for them to move forwards to the table.

'Come, come, show us your magnificence,' Henry called to them.

It was an apt subtlety, a small fleet of ships bearing red crosses on their sails settled on a blue sea with sugared waves, so well executed that Ailenor was reluctant for it to be broken. Henry, as usual, invited Richard to select the first piece.

'Another crusading fleet,' he said, sweeping his hand back through his dark hair, before breaking off a mast. 'Let us pray for another success.'

After the ships and their sails were shared around the company, Ailenor looked down on a shipwreck and could not repress a shiver. France was the more powerful and larger nation.

Chapter Twenty-one

Bordeaux, 1242

Ailenor made her way along the deck of the King's vessel, *The Royal Lion*, her ladies and Henry following her, occasionally glancing towards the fleet that trailed the foamy wake of their lead ship. Pennants of England flew proudly in a gentle breeze below a sky the shade of eggshells. The sea was unruffled. It boded well for a safe crossing.

Ailenor lifted her face towards the freshness of the breeze. Although she knew she ought to be resting, she felt exhilarated by the sea's slow roll. After all, she could rest for weeks once they reached Bordeaux, whilst Henry led his knights forth to reclaim his father's lost lands.

Flags fluttered from the other ships, gold and silver embroidery glinting, red, yellow, blue—a bright rainbow of colour. She admired the glorious pageantry presented by their knights who made an impressive showing for England – their chain mail covered with embroidered surcoats, their mantles of silk and velvet emblazoned with golden lions. Many knights remained at home—malcontents who would not share in the spoils—it came as a surprise when at the last minute Walter Marshal joined the venture. She smiled to herself as she spotted the Marshal red lion rising proudly on green and yellow silk cloth, flying above the ship he commanded. Marshal simply wanted his Earldom of Pembroke confirmed, she thought with cynicism.

'Look!' She pointed towards another vessel. 'Henry, I can see

Richard.' Passion filling her voice, she declared fiercely, 'If I were not so heavy with child, I would take up arms and ride with you.'

Henry placed his arm under her elbow as the ship gave an unexpected heave. 'War is not like it is depicted in books of romance, my love. I am not King Arthur. Richard is no Launcelot of the Cart. War is messy, violent, and cruel and I wish with all my heart it was not necessary.' He gathered her into the crook of his arm. His next words were a repetition of his usual refrain since she had announced her intention to sail to Bordeaux with them. 'You, my Ailenor, should be in your bower at Windsor resting.'

She shook her head. 'It is right we show the people of Gascony we remember them. Our child will be born in Bordeaux.' She regarded him coolly and added, 'You will lead us to victory. You will recover Poitou for our crown. And after that, Normandy.'

'Let us pray it will be so.' Henry lifted his arm and waved to his brother who bowed low in acknowledgement, the breeze whipping his cloak into a golden cloud as he rose. A sailor shouted, 'Land ahead.'

Ailenor twisted her head around to see the coast rise from the sea to greet them. Before long she would be resident in the mysterious *Palais des Ombres*, Palace of Shadows. She had not seen it since her wedding journey six years before. It had seemed to her youthful eyes a beautiful, mysterious castle, even in deep mid-winter.

After a poignant night at Royan, sadly passed because of her imminent parting from Henry, Ailenor's travelling chests were carefully loaded onto sumpter wagons. With her clerk, John Mansel, leading her household, she prepared to travel on to Bordeaux and her haunted castle. Henry and his knights would ride north to Saintes on the border with Poitou. She eased herself into soft velvet cushions within a carriage led by two strong black horses, protected by a strong escort as Henry pushed his head through the gap in the carriage curtains and kissed her. 'Send for me when our child arrives. If I can come to you, my love, I shall.' He gave her his blessing and a gold ring set with a huge ruby he slipped from his finger. 'God be with you and keep you safe. I shall write often.'

'I'll miss you.'

'Godspeed, Ailenor.'

She dropped the curtain on Henry and his glittering column of knights, mercenaries and the loyal earls who were ready to march where he led. He planned to establish his camp at Saintes, from where scouts were instructed to ride out and find the French.

Ailenor gave Henry's ring to Willelma for safekeeping. She would add it to her cross and beads, and the precious belt belonging to the Virgin, which they carried in her birthing coffer. She would wear both as she gave birth. Touching the crucifix that hung about her neck she murmured, 'God bless you, my Henry, and bring you home safe and victorious.'

Two weeks passed as Ailenor and her household settled into the castle. As May gave way to June's colourful profusion of early summer flowers, a messenger riding a grey jennet clattered into the courtyard of the Palais des Ombres. He carried two letters in his satchel. One was for the seneschal of Gascony who dwelled in the castle. The other, a letter with Henry's lion seal attached to dangling silk ribbons, was for Ailenor. Since neither messenger nor seneschal had permission to enter the Queen's darkened apartments, and since she could not leave her birthing chamber, the seneschal slid Ailenor's letter through a screen slat to Domina Willelma.

Ailenor sat in the window seat with her feet raised on a faded, tasselled velvet stool, watching beech trees waving branches over the placid curving river. No gracious steps led down from this apartment to a secluded garden as in Windsor. 'It's airless,' she complained, wiping glittering beads of sweat from her brow. 'No, don't hang dark curtains about my chamber. I won't have it.'

Protesting, her ladies obeyed because Ailenor insisted on sunlight and shade whenever she desired either. The Palais des Ombres was, she considered, a disappointment, not as she had recollected it – decorated with tapestries and with comforting fires blazing in huge fireplaces. The large castle within Bordeaux's ancient town walls had been sadly neglected, lacking the luxury to which she had become accustomed.

It was fortunate she had brought her own bed linen and cushions with her as well as the precious embroidery depicting St Anne's
Travail. She stared at the hanging, imagining she saw messages of
perseverance and hope concealed within its golden stitches. If she
turned to the right, she could enjoy its profusion of glittering stars,
roses, and bulging-eyed figures. Remembering the saint's labour, she
would gather strength for her own. She glanced down at her belly
which spilled over the cushions. It could not be long until she was
released and feel sunshine on her face.

She broke the seal on Henry's letter. Lady Mary came over, knelt,
dipped her fingers into a bowl containing a soothing balm and massaged her swollen legs with oil of roses, pressing gently on her puffed
up ankles. She softly read Henry's letter aloud.

'. . .We have marched to Pons, where our Gascon barons have convened
with mercenaries and arms. Earl Simon has joined our venture. Nell is with
child again. The child will not be birthed this side of Christmastide but my
sister is exhausted. Her two boys are with her as well as their nurses and a
small household. Our mother joined us in Saintes. She is as beautiful as I
remembered her. We have captured castles on the approach to Pons. Louis
sent a request for peace demanding those castles returned him – L'Aurus, Le
Poitou, part of L'Auvergne, and, in addition, suzerainety of La Marche with
Alphonse governing all this territory instead of Hugh de Lusignan. No, no, no.
The title Comte de Poitou belongs to my mother's eldest son by Count Hugh,
not to the Capets. My mother rages against France daily. Count Hugh is now
sending her from Saintes into Angouleme for her own safety. We advance to
Tonnay-Charente from Pons without further delay. May God protect you and
the child in your womb.'

Henry was not returning to Bordeaux yet. She stiffened her
resolve to be patient and wiped away a tear with the edge of her veil.
It was good news that Earl Simon had returned and was forgiven.
She would see Nell.

Ailenor gave birth to another girl, whom she called Beatrice for
her mother, but this joy was marred when she heard how Nell was
trapped in Saintes. A messenger arrived at the Palais des Ombres

with reports of fighting near a place called Taillebourg, not far from Saintes.

Ailenor greeted him in an antechamber. 'There was a battle at Taillebourg in July. The King himself directed the use of pontoon bridges. The bridge at Taillebourg is narrow.' He expressed the confined width with his hands. 'It restricted the passage of our forces. After losses of life from fire and drowning, Earl Richard crossed the bridge carrying a pilgrim staff. He entered Louis's camp and announced that if they could have a truce, the King's army would withdraw.'

'That was courageous of Earl Richard,' she remarked, fear creeping into her voice. She sank onto a stool. 'My husband, the King, where is he?'

'The King is safe. Earl Richard saved lives and prevented hostage-taking. Earl Richard persuaded the King to pull back into the Saintonge, but we were too near Saintes should Louis give pursuit. Earl Simon rode to rescue his wife and children.' He paused and drew breath. Ailenor's hand flew to her heart.

'Nell,' she whispered. 'Nell is in danger for her life.'

The messenger continued, 'I can report Earl Simon rescued his family just in time. A large French army was riding towards Saintes, King Louis at its head. And siege weapons and fire. We moved south. The French took the castle of Frontignac. We moved forward into Gascony.' He shook his head and fell onto his knees. 'I fear the French are determined to lay siege to Saintes, Your Grace.' The lad added, 'But the King is resting at Blaye. He has a bout of dysentery, nothing to worry about, your Grace. He has sent me to you with this news.' He leaned forward and she discerned fear in his eyes. 'The King says he will come to you very soon. It is not over yet. "Tell the Queen she is safe in Bordeaux," the King said.' The lad looked up with tears in his eyes. 'But, your Grace, I fear we have lost Poitou.'

'Is Earl Simon riding to Blaye or Bordeaux?'

'Bordeaux. His squire fought bravely at Saintes. He is injured. He'll be cared for in a monastery where they have stopped to rest.'

'What is the squire's name?' she asked.

'Thomas. His injuries are grave but it is hopeful he will recover. He is brave. Earl Simon loves him as a son and will not leave his squire until he is assured he will live.'

'I shall pray for Thomas and for the people of Saintes, for them all.' She felt tears slide down her cheeks. When would she see Henry again? How long before Henry could see his daughter? It had not been an easy time for her either. She had endured a long difficult birth and she had been churched without him present.

She sent the lad to the kitchens and called for Willelma and Mary. 'We must prepare for Earl Simon and Lady Nell's arrival. They will be here within a week.'

When she was alone, she wept for Henry, for Thomas whom her embroideress loved; she wept for Earl Simon and Nell and, finally, for the disastrous campaign that had not brought them glory but, rather, loss.

Ailenor had advance warning of Simon's crossing the two rivers that flowed close to the city from a scout who rode ahead. She ordered an apartment readied for her guests, chambers for their maids and the children with their nurses. In the event, no servants rode with Simon and Nell, none at all. Simon had sent them back to France. Nell was accompanied by one lady and two nurses. Ailenor made the travellers welcome and ordered her household steward to oversee accommodation for their small company of knights.

She requested supper to be set out in her antechamber for Nell and Simon and his squires.

'Where's the King?' Simon asked as he slid into his chair between Ailenor and Nell.

'Henry, Richard, and their troops are at Blaye. He has not yet entered Bordeaux.' She bit her lip as she said, 'Henry apparently is ill.'

'Wounded?'

'No, Earl Simon, he was not. Henry suffers dysentery.'

'What, our King too.' Simon guffawed and lifted a chicken leg to his mouth. Dropping it on his plate, he pulled the napkin from his shoulder and waving it like a flag said, 'He's not alone in that. Louis

204

and half his camp have dysentery.' He dropped the chicken leg. 'Two kings with dysentery. Well, well, Saintes has escaped siege because of it. The villages between Taillebourg and Saintes knew the French were on the way and poisoned many of their wells.' Ailenor could not help smiling. 'I hope Henry did not drink foul water.' Simon's gleaming dark eyes turned serious.

'Perhaps, but Henry is, I hear,' she said, 'recovering.'

Nell, beautiful gracious Nell, with vivid eyes, even features, and luxurious plaits which fell onto the crimson gown Ailenor had given her to wear, turned to Ailenor and said, 'We must make peace with the French. This is a hopeless war. It gets worse every day it continues. Hugh de Lusignan, the lords who were aligned with him, and even my mother herself, whose cause we were supporting, have deserted the cause, *their* cause.'

Ailenor gasped, shocked by this news. 'What? You are saying your mother's husband has played us false?' she said. 'But he asked us to come. I don't understand!'

'Traitors, the lot of them. Nell is right.' Simon said with a shrug of his shoulders. 'I shall ride out to Henry in Blaye tomorrow and find out if we are seeking peace.' He drained his cup and signalled to a page to refill it. 'It's the only way forward, the only way to protect Gascony too.'

Ailenor heard disappointment in her voice as she slowly said, 'Yes, without peace, Gascony will be threatened. But we can't leave now, even if we want to.'

'That, Ailenor, is asking much of those knights who would like to see their families by Christmastide,' Simon remarked.

'I suppose their families can come to us here.'

'At whose expense?' Simon was curt.

Ailenor said she had no idea. Leaning over Simon she said to Nell, trying desperately to create a lull in this terrible conversation, 'Would you like to see Beatrice? She sleeps nearly all the time; she's a peaceful baby.'

'Go and visit our new niece,' Simon said to his wife. 'I need to see to my men.'

Ailenor, feeling on safer ground talking about children than discussing knights who hungered for home and families, led Nell from the chamber up a wide staircase to the floor above.

Simon, Richard and Henry rode back from Blaye. Henry, fully recovered, was in good spirits. He embraced Ailenor. On seeing baby Beatrice, he wept. He greeted Nell warmly, making much of her small sons. He remarked that she looked well despite her ordeal in Saintes. Ailenor, glad to have her family around her again, declared they must have a feast to celebrate their reunion.

'Celebrate what?' Henry said when he was alone with Ailenor and his new baby daughter, now almost two months old. 'Simon will only stay if I excuse his debts and return Kenilworth to him. That is not worth celebrating. As for Richard, he has demanded Gascony for himself. I have agreed he can govern the province. It has brought naught but trouble -'

'What?' Ailenor broke in. 'No, Henry, Richard cannot have Gascony. It belongs to Edward, along with the castles in England you gave me before we sailed in May. Remember those too. You gave those lands to me in case something happens to you.'

Henry bowed his head. 'I promised Richard Gascony in return for his courage at Taillebourg. He walked over the bridge carrying a pilgrim staff with crossbows pointing at him. Had it not been for him, I might not be here now.' He shuddered.

'Simon's debts, Henry. You say you are paying those off. This war has cost you a fortune. You must un-promise Gascony to Richard. Think of the wine trade profits, the taxes you'll relinquish.' Ailenor thought for a moment whilst Henry stared down at his baby daughter. 'Stop concentrating on Beatrice for a moment,' she snapped. 'Here is what you can do. Provide Sancha with a dowry and pay Richard off, but whatever you do, he cannot have Gascony.'

Henry glanced up from his daughter's cradle. His eyes were determined. 'We shall see. Let us first have peace.' He called for a rocker for Beatrice's cradle. Drawing Ailenor to the window and sitting her in the window seat, he said, 'How would you like to spend the winter here in Gascony, maybe at Blaye? It's a pleasant castle. You have not seen Gascony yet. Not properly as Queen.'

'I miss Edward and Margaret. I expected to see them at Christmas. They've not met their new sister yet.'

'We'll send for them.'

It was no use quarrelling when Henry was determined to get his way. 'Is that wise?' she asked, attempting an appeal to his common sense. 'It'll be winter soon. Edward is your heir. He mustn't take a chill.'

'If you want Gascony for Edward, the sooner he comes the better. It will please Gascony's nobles. All the children should be here with us. If Simon and Nell stay too, their children will have their cousins for company. Gascony would see us as a united family.' He lifted her hand. 'We shouldn't worry about Raymond of Toulouse either. When Count Hugh betrayed us and joined with Louis, the Southern League against France fell apart. Count Raymond will now have to accept Louis as his King, and with him Louis's Dominican inquisitors. It'll be uncomfortable for him because Louis won't suffer heretics in Toulouse.'

The reference to heretics reminded her of Rosalind. Whilst Ailenor did not really care about heretics, she *did* care about the embroideress who had been in her service. A full year had passed since the accusation against her was made in Marlborough. If Ailenor was to spend a winter in Gascony, she must have winter gowns. If the children came to Bordeaux, Rosalind could accompany the party. Besides the sombre castle needed tapestries and embroideries, new bed curtains and cushions.

She affectionately placed her hands on Henry's shoulders. 'Uncle Peter has written from Provence. He will bring Sancha to us as soon as her betrothal to Raymond is annulled and she has permission to marry Richard.'

Henry embraced her. 'Good news, indeed.' He turned away and scratched his head. 'The Pope will seek favours from us in return for support over Richard's marriage. He'll want the best positions in the Church for his people. He'll try and take Canterbury from us for one of his own relatives.'

'Not if Uncle Boniface comes to England and takes up the position you offered him,' she said to his back. It was the first time in months she had mentioned Uncle Boniface.

'I'll lose the income from Canterbury. It has suited me that Boniface is taking his time to come to us.' He reminded her that a see without an archbishop or bishop meant its revenue fell to the royal purse.

She shook her head. 'But you need loyal men in high positions to counteract the stubbornness of your Council.'

He spun around. She noticed how thin and light-footed he had become. 'There can never be another Barons' War as happened during my father's time. Bishops must remain true to us. You are right. A loyal archbishop. Boniface must be placed in Canterbury without delay.'

'And we shall send for Edward and Margaret.' Ailenor smiled as she said this.

She excused herself, leaving Henry with his baby daughter and her nurses. As she hurried down the stairway intending to summon the master cook to her chamber to discuss menus for a feast to honour Nell and Simon, she determined to bring Rosalind to court. She would command the best tailors in Bordeaux to the palace. Perhaps it would be pleasanter in Gascony after all than returning to England. They'd avoid listening to complaints concerning her uncles from bitter barons and clergy and criticism over the disastrous Gascon campaign. Her father would never have permitted his authority to be questioned but, as she reminded herself, Henry was not her father. England was not Provence.

Ailenor and Nell purchased fabrics from the City's drapers and planned new gowns. Henry, Simon, and Richard opened peace negotiations with Louis. Riders rode north and returned with news that an army with siege weapons was indeed moving towards Saintes. Louis's army was recovering from the illness caused by poisoned wells and he had increased its size with mercenaries and troops commanded by the traitor Hugh de Lusignan. How could Count Hugh betray them? Not a

208

word arrived from Isabella, who had returned to Angouleme. Ailenor pondered this. Where did Isabella's loyalty lie? Ailenor considered it wise to remain silent on the subject of Henry's mother and half-siblings. It was an uncomfortable subject with him.

'I'll ride to Poitiers with Simon,' Richard announced firmly some days later at supper which they held privately each evening in her panelled antechamber, so they could discuss strategy without the danger of spies lurking behind every arras. 'I'll return with a promise of peace. We'll insist that as part of it, the French do not attack Saintes.' He frowned. 'But you must accept reasonable terms, Henry.'

Henry grunted his response. 'I have no choice. Louis will be after Gascony and Gascony is my son's territory.'

'What?' Richard said. 'Gascony is mine. You promised.'

Henry studied Richard through his drooping eyelid. 'How about you have a dowry for Sancha from me, and your territory in Cornwall increased in size.'

Richard raised an eyebrow, and clearly recognising defeat, said, 'You had best make this marriage worth it, Henry.'

Ailenor smiled to herself. She had won this battle with Henry. Now she must make sure that Uncle Boniface came to Canterbury. She would write to him herself.

As they were sewing in the spacious room she had made her bower, Ailenor remarked to Nell, 'I am pleased Richard and Simon are seeking peace but it sits hard with Henry because it means he's admitting defeat. If it had not been for Hugh of Lusignan's betrayal he would have had a chance to recover lost territories.'

Nell knotted a thread. 'London's burghers would never finance a prolonged war with the French. They don't want French merchants in the City again. You are too young to remember the last time they came but I remember it. The French occupied London and much of England. Don't you see, Simon and Richard must stop this war before it grows impossible to prevent it escalating?' She studied the piece of embroidery Ailenor was working on. 'You have learned the art of

English embroidery,' she said with admiration in her voice. 'Whatever happened to Rosalind? I remember her at Westminster teaching your ladies. She has taught you well.'

Ailenor recounted what had occurred at Marlborough the previous year. 'Rosalind is not a heretic but a rumour was circulated by a rejected suitor who desired revenge. I hope it's forgotten now. She has withdrawn to a nunnery to work on a cope for the Bishop of London and if it's ready, there's no need for her to remain in St Helena's.' She lifted her sewing again, a coverlet for baby Beatrice. Making a delicate stitch, she remarked, trying to keep her tone nonchalant, 'Henry says we shall stay on in Gascony so we'll send for the children. I'll see if Rosalind is willing to return to me.'

'And if she is not?' Nell gave Ailenor a firm look. 'Simon might disapprove of heretics, as did his father. but *I* believe the Cathars to have been cruelly dealt with. Do you think Rosalind wants to return to court where she could be regarded with suspicion?'

'She might prefer to become a nun, I suppose.' Ailenor considered her stitching. She looked up her work abandoned on her lap. 'Nell, Rosalind refused the suitor because she is in love with a squire. He's attached to Earl Simon. That might persuade her. She's in no danger here and my ladies like her.'

'Simon has three squires. What is the squire's name?'

'Thomas.'

'Thomas is courageous. He was injured at Saintes protecting peasants. We left him in the monastery at Etauliers. In fact, I sent for a report a week ago. He's recovered enough to sit in the garden. Perhaps it'll make him happy to see Rosalind.'

'A romance between a squire with lands and a City embroideress?' Ailenor creased her forehead. 'You know, Rosalind's father is wealthy, but he is not of the nobility. I wonder if the squire's family might object. What do you think, Nell?'

'The world is changing. The merchants are rising in importance, especially in London. It could be a good connection for Thomas – no father or mother, his uncle will try to marry him to an aged cousin old enough to be his great-aunt and his uncle is connected to the

Marshals. That clan have more than enough lands of their own. They still owe me dower castles.'

'We shall try to bring Thomas and Rosalind together here, rather than in England.' Ailenor stabbed her needle into a pincushion. 'I shall petition for the return of all that the Marshals have stolen from you.' She appealed, 'Stay with me here in Bordeaux this winter too, Nell. Please say you will.'

Nell placed her needlework on a bench. 'It's up to Simon. If he agrees, I am happy to remain, though I do so miss Odiham.'

'It will be pleasanter to see Odiham again in the summer. Let us pray that Richard and Simon bring us peace with France,' she said. 'I dislike being estranged from Marguerite because of this war. Since it began, my sister hasn't written. I imagine the White Queen has forbidden it.'

When Nell raised her violet eyes, Ailenor noticed tears glistening in them. 'It is a matter of great sorrow when siblings are estranged.' Was Nell thinking about Henry? The quarrel between Henry and Simon brought her divided loyalties. It had, without doubt, been difficult for her.

'Families should be united,' Nell said.

'They should, but it's not always possible.' Ailenor's thoughts returning to peace, she remarked, 'I wonder if the French have pulled back from Saintes?'

'I fear for Lord Hubert, the Seneschal, and for Lady Ida.'

'I never knew them but I shall pray for their safety.' Ailenor fingered the rosary beads that hung from her belt. 'Nell, why don't we go into the chapel now and pray for peace.'

Nell nodded and packed away her threads and linen.

'And for love between siblings too.'

'And friendship.' Nell reached out and touched Ailenor's hand.

In that moment, Ailenor felt gratified for all who heartened her life. Family was a precious gift.

Later that week, coloured light darted in from the Nativity window patterning the cathedral floor as a bishop shuffled towards the High

Altar clad in a glittering cope studded with sapphires and emeralds. For a moment there was quiet. Clouds of sweet-smelling incense from censors drifted about the worshippers, around the rich burghers of Bordeaux who were expensively clad in velvets and silks. As of one, their heads swivelled around to see Ailenor sweep through the Nave followed by her retinue.

With a whisper of silken gown, Ailenor slipped into place beside Nell and Hal. She tapped Nell's arm to get her attention and whispered, 'Word came late last night. The French won't resume hostilities. A treaty will follow if we observe the truce and Henry gives up his idea of attacking Poitou. Our prayers are answered, Nell. Lady Ida and her lord are safe. The French are removing their siege weapons from Saintes.'

'Thank God,' Nell said. She looked past her to a statue of the Virgin, one that was painted blue and gold and Ailenor heard her friend murmur her thanks. 'Thank you, my Lady Mary.' Nell leaned down to her little son and said, 'Papa is on his way back to us.'

'Is the war over?' he whispered back, clutching at her cloak.

'Let go my clothing, Hal. Remember where you are,' Nell said gently. Hal's tiny hand let go of his mother's mantle. 'And soon your cousin Edward will be here.'

'Who is he?'

Ailenor whispered to Hal, 'Your royal cousin.'

All the children would come together in Bordeaux. This was a day for celebration. War was cruel. It was better it was over. As she watched the choir chant, Ailenor determined never to call any of her children for Henry's mother, never. There would be no Isabellas in their family and certainly no sons named Hugh.

Now that their pact to support a war was broken, other Poitevin lords also capitulated to France. There was nothing to be done. Hugh and Isabella had broken Henry's trust in them. They survived, whilst many English had died for their cause. Hugh had defected to France to recognise Louis once again as his overlord to whom the couple would do homage.

Ailenor bowed her head to God and prayed Gascony would be

safe. God would protect their dynasty. He would not, could not, favour the Capets for long because God must have a plan for England. Henry's and her children were the future. Their girls would make marriages . . . great alliances for England. One day, Edward would need a territory to rule.

As the precentor led the choir in praise, Ailenor considered a happier future. Richard's wedding would be a diversion for the people of London. Her thoughts drifted to Simon and Nell. If Simon desired Kenilworth returned to him, he would remain in Gascony until the treaty with France was signed. They all could return to England together. She glanced sideways at Nell's veiled head. Her rich brown hair under a veil was almost as dark as her own. They were as sisters again. How grateful she was for this. As Nonce ended, Ailenor stood and stepped with a light bearing through the cathedral nave.

Long anxious faces greeted her as she exited through the West door. For a moment she, Nell and Harry waited on the cathedral steps whilst their ladies and guard swiftly drew up behind them. Ailenor turned to her steward and pointed to the purse hanging from his belt. He opened it. Servants distributed alms amongst the expectant poor by the entrance. Ailenor signalled to her herald to sound his trumpet and the people fell silent. In a clear, confident voice she announced, 'There will be peace with France. God protect our King.'

For a moment it seemed as if they doubted her words, until a man amongst the gathering below the cathedral steps shouted out, 'God bless the King.' The people, their people of Bordeaux, joined in, cheered and shouted, 'God bless King Henry. God bless our Queen.'

Ailenor clasped Nell's hand and lifted it high. They were a family united, destined to continue a great dynasty. If England sometimes forgot it, Gascony would not.

She noted a gleam of admiration in Nell's eyes. 'You think quickly, Ailenor,' Nell said in a quiet voice.

It would be a pleasant winter if they made improvements to the shadowy palace. Tapestries must be purchased, others mended, heavier curtains hung. Redecoration must commence in time for

Christmas. Whilst these improvements were carried out, they would spend a few months at Blaye.

Rosalind must oversee the purchase of new tapestries and the restoration of older ones, so that week Ailenor wrote to her friend Abbess Elizabeth of St Helena's, requesting Rosalind travel to Bordeaux with the children and their servants. There were no Dominicans amongst their priests in Gascony, none of which she was aware, to threaten her friend.

That evening, Ailenor wrote to Walter Gray, the Archbishop of York, who had charge of England during their absence, demanding that the royal children come to Bordeaux.

Chapter Twenty-two

Rosalind
Autumn 1242

Rosalind was seated under a mulberry tree in the peaceful garden of St Helena's Convent sorting threads. The Bishop of London's new cope was almost ready. It had taken the nuns a whole year to complete most of the embroidery. There were still two borders to embroider. The Bishop wanted to choose the final details decorating the hem's border and that day Rosalind would take the extravagant garment to his palace.

At noon, accompanied by Sister Beatrice, she would travel through London's streets in one of the episcopal wagons. It would be the first time in months she had left the convent and she could hardly contain her excitement at the thought of this adventure. Life as a novice nun was not her destiny. She desired the world of men and women and thought about Thomas whom she missed every day on awakening and at night as she fell asleep on her narrow cot. Little news entered the sleepy convent. Papa and Mildred knew nothing about Earl Simon's squire but on one of their visits from behind the latticed screen that separated her from her visitors, she heard how Earl Richard had returned from the Crusade. Had Earl Simon returned? Papa did not know. He had heard nothing of Earl Simon or his squire. Richard of Cornwall was to be married again, this time to the Queen's sister.

'Rosalind, Rosalind, there you are!' Sister Anne came rushing through the herbal plots, her habit flapping about her legs. Rosalind glanced upwards. It was a lovely day; the azure sky she glimpsed above the high walls was cloudless.

'Have they come for us already?' she called. 'If so, they're early.'

'No, no. It's not the Bishop's carriage, not yet. You have a letter with a royal seal and ribbons. Prioress Elizabeth said I was to bring it to you at once.'

'A letter for me?' Rosalind dropped her sewing into her lap. 'It must be another note from one of the Queen's ladies. As she stood up, her threads fell from her apron onto the dusty path. 'Holy Madeline,' she gasped. 'They'll get dirty.'

'I'll pick those up. You read your letter.' Sister Anne thrust the small folded missive into her hand. 'Oh, and Prioress Elizabeth says she will see you after Vespers, after you see the Bishop.'

The nun bent down and collected the threads into her apron as Rosalind turned over her letter. Its seal was broken. Prioress Elizabeth had read it first. She grimaced annoyance. The Prioress would always read her private letters. A tangle of ribbons hung like withered scarlet stems from cracked wax. With shaking hands, Rosalind sank down on the shaded bench and began to read, thinking it was as well her father had insisted she had learned her letters. Rosalind's eyes widened as she glanced at the signature. It was from the Queen herself, not from Lady Mary at all.

Rosalind, we request your presence in Bordeaux. Your services are required to oversee the mending and hanging of our palace embroideries. You will travel on the Griffin, my personal ship, with our children. Arrangements will be made for your journey forthwith.

Ailenor the Queen

It was, in short, a summons. She stared at the small folded letter. All those scarlet ribbons on such a small document containing such a brief message. No reference to her year's exile from the court. No mention of her work on Bishop Fulk's cope at St Helena's; nothing of the workshop at the palace of Westminster which she had been compelled to abandon when she had joined Queen Ailenor's court. Not a word about her supposedly Cathar mother or her hard-working

216

father. It was simply a royal command, one that must be heeded. A shudder grasped her at the memory of the King's part in her banishment and as she wondered if the Dominican friar was still with King Henry, her heart turned over with fear.

Beyond the Priory walls, bells echoed throughout the City. She folded the letter and glanced up to see one of the novices hurry towards her carrying a dark cloak over her arm. 'The Bishop's men are here for you,' she said breathlessly. 'Hurry. They are loading the carriage. Sister Beatrice is waiting for you in the workroom.'

Rosalind tucked the letter into the belt purse that hung beside her scissors and her knotted measuring tape.

'Don't get gobbled up by Nero,' Sister Anne called after her from where she was now seated in a pool of sunshine drawing a stitch through the embroidery Rosalind had started. Nero was the enormous black hunting dog that accompanied Bishop Fulk on his visits to the nunnery.

Rosalind called back over her shoulder, 'Not a chance of it.'

The journey across the City took an age and the hourly bells rang in a cacophony again before they arrived at the palace. Carts, animals, and people jammed up the thoroughfares. It was a scene she had once enjoyed and Rosalind thrust her head through the curtains to watch. The streets were lively in contrast to the sleepy convent. She missed them.

The Bishop kept them waiting on a cushioned bench outside his chamber as he examined the precious cope with his band of acolytes. Sister Beatrice, who had helped in the infirmary that morning as well as overseeing the careful packing of the cope, closed her eyes, leaned back against the wall and began to snore softly. Rosalind wandered along the corridor until she reached a curtained off annex at the end. Hearing voices seep out from behind the curtain, she could not resist putting her ear to its folds. The loud whispering beyond this arras sounded anxious and secretive.

'What is the delay?' a voice exclaimed. His accent was French. She peered through a slit in the curtain. Two men holding the conversation had their backs to her. One, she noted, was wearing a priest's robe. The other, the one with the French accent, was dressed in a long, blue gown. The embroidery on the hem caught her eye. It displayed glittering serpents with jewelled eyes. This man was wealthy to possess such embellishment on his gown. Her eye followed the gown upwards to the back of his head. A hat with fur trim was perched on shoulder-length grey hair. The pair shifted their positions so she drew back and allowed the folds of the curtain to come together again. She laid her ear to the folds.

'As soon as possible.'

'Saint Augustine's bones, who knows when that will be.'

'The Church tires of the King's profligate ways,' the priest was saying. 'Bishops resent how the Queen's relatives are placed in positions of power. Henry is bankrupting the kingdom. Poitou is lost.' The voice lowered but Rosalind leaned further into the curtain to hear what was said next. 'Why not ensure the King never returns to England? You have contacts in Bordeaux. No one knows who you are, a wine merchant, one of many.' There was a chortle. 'Best Gascon wine, fit for a king's table.'

'Priest, I cannot be part of that. I'll lose my business . . . my life. *Merde*! Take my wine for the Bishop. Forget this nonsense.' A moment later he said, 'How much? How much for a King's life? Tell me that.'

A silence followed. The priest never answered.

'Well?' the merchant said.

Rosalind's heart beat quickly. She cast a glance along the corridor. Sister Beatrice still had her eyes closed, but she must return soon.

The priest spoke at last. 'My contact would pay you a thousand pounds.'

Rosalind heard the merchant's gasp, 'So much for a king's life.'

'You would benefit. Edward is a small boy. Richard, an astute prince, would rule. He'd guide the prince. So, an accident . . . an unfortunate cup of wine. And before you ask, Earl Richard knows nothing of this. I repeat, the Council is losing patience with the

King's games in Poitou; the Church tires of Henry's interference in Church affairs. We tire of Rome's taxes. An arrow gone amiss, an assassin's dagger, a fall from a horse, a glass of poisoned wine.'

Although voices continued, they grew fainter. The two men had moved away through another arras into another corridor in this palace of corridors. Rosalind felt blood drain from her face. Clutching her gown, she stumbled back along the corridor. The enormity of the conversation she had overheard struck her deeply, as if an arrow was striking into her own heart. Regaining the bench, she sank down with a thump. Sister Beatrice's eyes shot open. Before the nun could speak a word, the door into Bishop Fulk's chamber opened.

'The Bishop will see you now.' The servant, a monk, hovered in the opened doorway. Sister Beatrice stood up shaking her habit, awkward and stiff. Rosalind rose shakily to her feet. Beatrice was looking quizzically at her. 'Are you well, Rosalind?' she muttered.

'Yes.' Rosalind said, even though she felt as if she had swallowed a snake and it was curling around her insides, squeezing breath from her.

Bishop Fulk expressed his appreciation of their work. 'Magnificent,' he said. 'St Thomas and St Hilary in particular – most noteworthy. Indeed, indeed.' He pointed to the silver-gilt thread and coloured silks gracing the images of saints. 'The crucifixion on the cope's back will gleam its message as I face the altar. Yes, indeed, indeed you have worked hard. Your priory will be well rewarded.'

'Thank you, my Lord Bishop,' whispered Rosalind, hardly able to speak, wondering if he was in truth the King's enemy. 'Prioress Elizabeth will be pleased to hear that,' she managed to say.

'Now, now, as to the rest.' The Bishop moved slowly along the table on which the cope was displayed. He traced a ringed finger along the edges of the cope. 'I would like a border of roses intertwined with a star and cross pattern along all of these hems and around the neckline also. Yes, roses, silken and embroidered. Indeed, indeed.' He sniffed through his long nose. Rosalind took a pace backwards. 'Can the embroidery be . . .' the Bishop turned from the cope to face her. 'completed by Eastertide?'

'Without doubt, my lord.' She regained her courage and studied him, his smooth face, proud long nose and hooded eyes. Did his eyes conceal secrets?

As they left the palace, Rosalind knew she must confide in Prioress Elizabeth. The Prioress was Queen Ailenor's friend. The King could be in great danger.

Prioress Elizabeth inhaled and exhaled slowly. She spread her hands on her desk. 'This could be nothing but then it could be something. Either way, it is too serious a matter to trust to a messenger. You will be in Bordeaux, yourself, as quickly as any messenger can reach the Queen. You *will* go to Bordeaux, won't you, Rosalind? You will accept the Queen's summons?'

'Yes, Prioress, I must.' Even before she had overheard whispers in the Bishop's Palace, Rosalind had decided to return to Queen Ailenor and discover what had happened to Thomas.

Prioress Elizabeth's long hands shifted to meet under her chin, her elbows leaning on the sloping desk. 'I'll write what you have heard and you shall take her my message. No doubt this is one of many plots against King Henry. Nothing may ensue, but no risk can be taken either, none at all. Trust no one, Rosalind. Speak not one word of this to anyone travelling on the *Griffin*. Earl Richard has been on the Crusade for several years. I suspect Templars may be behind this. Henry borrows persistently from their coffers but has he ever returned the loans? I think it unlikely.'

Rosalind nodded. 'Prioress, I shall not share this with anyone. Do you think Earl Richard *could* be involved?'

'Earl Richard is an honourable knight and good brother to the King. He does not hide behind plots. He fought on Crusade and he has freed French knights from the Infidel's clutches. He has been with King Henry since. This hails from elsewhere. As I have said, Templars.' She lowered her voice as if the statues placed in wall niches could listen and carry tales. 'Bishop Fulk was not King Henry's preferred choice when Bishop Roger Niger died. He is close to Walter Marshal though, in truth, I do not suspect Earl Walter either. Queen Ailenor has recently helped him regain his inheritance and he is in

Gascony with the King. Nor may the Bishop be part of this. I cannot think who your blue-gowned would-be plotter can possibly be.'

'I shall be cautious, Mother.'

Prioress Elizabeth shuffled papers on her desk, sat erect and said firmly, 'I am thinking of your own safety, my child. Walls, curtains, and screens have ears so be careful whom you trust.'

A moment's quiet was broken by the Prioress's little bird, a linnet, chirruping in its cage. For an intake of breath, Rosalind was reminded of the peace and purpose she discovered here in a nunnery, of the quiet friendships she had made. She would soon face the Queen's busy and bustling court again, which thrilled her, though what she had overheard that day was unsettling. It made her both excited and afraid. Staring down at her dark gown and white apron, she said, 'Must I wear this novice's habit in Gascony?'

'No, my child, we shall return your gowns to you, and if they need altering, we shall alter them.' She seemed lost in thought for a moment before saying, 'My child, I shall provide you with a new one. Tomorrow, go to your father's workplace, bid him farewell and he will see it is made. I think blue might be your colour. Tell him to spare no cost and to line the garment with squirrel fur. Winter approaches. It must be ready within a few days.'

'Thank you, Prioress.'

Prioress Elizabeth rose from her stool, circled her sloping desk and embraced Rosalind. 'My child. It is you I must thank. Remember, there will always be a home for you at St Helena's should you need one. May God bless you and protect your new journey.' She removed the coif from Rosalind's hair and touched the knot on the back of the girl's head. 'I see your locks have grown in brighter than ever. I had hoped your place would always be with us, but . . .' she sighed, 'apparently God has other plans for you.'

'It may be so, Mother,' Rosalind said. Her heart leapt for joy. For a moment she closed her eyes and tried to summon up an image of Thomas, whom she had not seen for two long years. She could sense him close, in her heart.

He was alive and he was waiting for her.

Chapter Twenty-three

1242 – 1243

Ailenor broke her fast on bread and honey. On hearing the clatter of horses in the courtyard, she pushed her cup of small beer aside. Her bread fell into her napkin as she leapt to her feet. Throwing open wooden shutters, she peered from the window. Henry was riding into the bailey with his earls, barons and their retainers. Roger Bigod, Will Longespee, and Walter Marshal, plus Earls Richard and Simon, were all impatiently jangling reins, and she was sure they were glowering as they stilled their prancing mounts. Simon and Richard dismounted first. They marched off, crunching dry leaves as they led their horses towards the stables. Henry climbed down from his horse. She noted his thunderous countenance and her stomach churned. Had the truce negotiations failed after all?

When Henry was in such a mood it was best to wait until he came to her. She returned to her breakfast but the bread and honey she usually loved stuck in her throat. She pushed it away and hurried to the nursery to seek distraction with Beatrice. All morning she patiently waited, wondering what had passed. From what she had observed below, it felt like a quarrel. The hour turned twice as cathedral bells clanged over the city followed by a cacophony of carillons from Bordeaux's churches. The dinner hour was approaching when Henry burst into her chamber red-faced, his garments untidy. He dismissed her ladies with a scowl and sank into a chair clasping its arms so hard his knuckles were as pale as soured milk.

Ailenor knelt in front of him. 'My lord, what is amiss? Is it the peace?'

Henry's left eyelid closed making him sinister in appearance as well as angry. 'There will be a peace of sorts,' he grunted at her. 'It's Montfort. By Christ's holy bones, he'll pay for his words.'

'What has he done now?'

'The knave compared me to the mad King of France, the idiot they call Charles the Simple, the one who was locked away centuries ago. I suggested we make another attempt to save Poitou whilst the French were laid low and those who are not ill are riding south to subjugate Toulouse.' He threw his arms up with the high drama of a player about to speak something of great import. His next words horrified her. 'What a great opportunity for us to get back our stolen castles.'

Ailenor's eyes widened with horror. It would be madness to extend the war against the Poitou knights who have gone over to the French. How could Henry contemplate endangering the peace treaty?

Henry rambled on, clearly more concerned by Simon's blunt words than the importance of the treaty. 'Montfort said I should be secured behind bars as strong as those on the windows of Windsor Castle. I have, he says, led a failed campaign; it was a waste of men and money. Mere Earl as he is, he yelled at me, Ailenor. He accused me, saying I had followed a Poitevin traitor in whom I placed my trust foolishly. He shouted insubservient words in front of all my knights. He cried out, "Gascony is endangered by your ineptitude."'

They could lose Simon. For a moment she simply stared at Henry's furious face. At last she said, 'Simon is furious at Hugh's defection. He spoke out of turn, Henry, but trying to take back those castles from the French is foolhardy. You have neither men nor money for weapons.' She drew breath. 'What of the Treaty?'

'For now we have a truce, one that will be in Louis's interests. He gains and I lose.' Henry sank his head into his hands. 'It will take months to negotiate the peace terms. Louis is still ill, almost to death, with dysentery. It is an excellent opportunity to outmanoeuvre him and get a better treaty.' He raised his arms and cupped his hands around his head. 'My Earls, those remaining, are planning to return to their lands in England.'

This was not good news. 'What if Simon goes over to France? He's your best general. Have you thought of this? Although he has spoken wildly, Simon is an asset.'

'If he turns to Louis, he will never get his lands back.'

Ailenor said firmly, 'We must safeguard Edward's inheritance. And there's the wine trade. Don't endanger it with a war you are not sure we'll win. Focus on Gascony, Henry, not Poitou, nor Normandy.'

'Richard is uncompromising and difficult. He and Simon are in accord. I retrieved Gascony from him, despite my promise, but at a cost.'

'Once Richard and Sancha are wed, Richard will forget Gascony,' she said. 'Give him money and land in England. That should make him content.'

Henry gave her a sardonic smile. 'I *have* granted him lands in lieu of Gascony and I shall grant the dowry also.'

'Good. The proxy wedding took place in Tarascon but Mama has written that they can't travel through France until peace is confirmed. They could be seized as hostages. We need peace, Henry.'

Henry looked up at her. 'Richard wishes to return to England.' He let go a long sigh.

'Good. He can prepare for his wedding. London loves him and they like weddings. They're a distraction.' She folded her hands in her lap. 'I have news, my love.' She lowered her voice a decibel so it was soft and loving. 'I've sent for our children. God willing, they'll arrive soon. So, you see, you cannot go off attacking castles in Poitou.'

Henry reached for her hands. 'You are a joy in a time of great darkness, war, and mistrust. Let the dust settle on the Poitou campaign as wine pours into England from Gascony.' Petulance crept into his tone as he added, 'It's an ignoble truce but it'll protect Gascony for Edward. Besides, I've heard the Solers and Columbines, the great families, wine families, are quarrelling again down in Gascony's southern parts. I shall send a troupe of knights deep into Gascony to tame them and collect tax. Montfort can lead them. That will keep him occupied. And if Simon apologises and conducts himself well, he can have his English lands returned to him.'

Ailenor moved onto his lap and he encircled her waist with his arms. 'We shall make this cold palace comfortable,' she said. 'Tapestries, embroideries – they all need mending.' She pointed at the damaged, fraying tapestry covering the table. 'That, for instance, and my bed curtains. All are damaged. The embroideress, Rosalind, is coming too with the children. I've asked the convent to release her.'

He raised an eyebrow. 'Did that girl not take vows? I want no taint on our court. No heretical connections.'

'She *did* spend a year studying scripture and prayer as well as embroidering Bishop Fulk's cope. The Prioress reports well of her. There's no taint there. Besides, that Dominican priest is far away in Castile.'

'I suppose the girl may return to you.' The angry miasma that had clouded his mood lifted. 'You can have your palace improvements. We'll retire to Blaye with the children for a time.' He looked at her with admiration. 'Let's attend Vespers together this afternoon. I've had enough of my petulant knights for now. Their men can eat what they can forage from the kitchens. We'll dine privately.' He smiled, his quarrel with Simon tucked away, though Ailenor knew better. It could reappear when least expected, when Simon crossed Henry again. 'This winter, we shall be a family and make another child.' Henry drew her deeper into his embrace. She thought to herself, she was certainly not adverse to that. Two girls now. She needed another boy.

Earl Richard left Gascony on the *Griffin* with a group of nobles who wanted to pass Christmastide with their families. It was the same vessel that carried the royal children to Bordeaux. As they departed for England, the weather was as unpredictable as Henry's moods, changing from calm to unsettled with winds cursing the coast. Anxious to be away, the earls refused to wait for a storm to blow itself out but without his earls and knights, Henry could not renew the campaign. Ailenor did not regret their departure.

A week before, Henry had parted with Simon and she with Nell.

'You plan to remain here?' Henry said coolly to Earl Simon. 'You are not abandoning me too?' Simon had grudgingly apologised to Henry for his anger and Henry equally grudgingly had accepted his apology.

'I gave you my allegiance, my King,' Simon said quietly. 'You have my loyalty. As we have agreed, you will need help taming the wine merchants.'

Henry had muttered something unintelligible under his breath. Simon raised a bushy black eyebrow, apparently not in the least disconcerted. Ailenor exchanged a nervous glance with Nell. The atmosphere between Henry and Simon remained as tense as an over-tight lute string. Neither woman spoke.

'Nell and the children and I will leave for the south,' Simon said, breaking the unease. 'We'll return as soon as disputes are settled and as much tax as can be seized is collected.'

Henry nodded. 'Then go with my blessing, Simon, but take care not to alienate the Gascons.' Henry sounded sincere in this last part at least.

'Our baggage is packed and now, my liege, if you will excuse us we have the children to organise.'

'Go, go in peace, Earl Simon.' Henry drew Nell forward and kissed his sister, but to Simon he gave only a nod.

Ailenor welcomed Rosalind into the palace hall. The girl looked fresh-faced whilst the nurses accompanying their children were green about the gills and unsteady on their feet.

Ailenor blinked away tears as she took Rosalind's hands in her own. 'My dearest Rosalind, we are pleased to have you with us again. But let us talk after you have rested. Lady Willelma will introduce you to embroiderers from the town who will be employed under your tutelage. Lady Margery will conduct you to your chamber.'

As Rosalind drew a small package from her furred mantle, Ailenor noted the girl's new gown, and noted the cloak's deep red squirrel lining as it fell back. 'Your Grace, Prioress Elizabeth has given me a letter for you. It relates to something I overheard in Bishop Fulk's palace in

London.' The embroideress held the missive forward. Ailenor stared down at the seal. When her eyes returned to Rosalind, she thought the girl looked fearful. What was so important it frightened her? Glancing across the Hall she saw Henry holding Margaret in his arms and Edward clutching his gown and in that moment she longed to be with them too. This correspondence must wait awhile. She had not seen her children for months. They had priority.

She handed Willelma the letter. 'Willelma, take this for me. I shall read it later. The King is waiting for us to settle our children in the nursery.' Addressing Rosalind again, she said, 'Thank you. Supper will be served in the ladies' bower tonight. I shall come to bid you all goodnight.' She called Lady Margery St John forward from her ladies, a junior lady who had joined her damsels before they had sailed to Gascony. Ailenor turned away as a servant lifted Rosalind's baggage and Lady Margery ushered the girl towards the staircase.

Simon and Nell had left Bordeaux accompanied by their children, their nurses, squires, and a troupe of horsemen on the previous Wednesday. As they said farewell, Ailenor had noted a golden head amongst Earl Simon's retainers and creased her brow. Thomas, the squire whom she had hoped would be reunited with Rosalind, was apparently recovered enough from his weakness to ride south with Earl Simon. For a heartbeat, she regretted that it could be weeks before Rosalind was reunited with her squire. Nell had not communicated to him Rosalind's imminent arrival at court and Ailenor had assumed incorrectly that the young man remained in the monastery where he was recovering from his wounds. Nell and Simon would not return to court for months.

Later that day, Ailenor read the letter from Prioress Elizabeth. It caused her concern though as the Prioress pointed out, there were always plots, but it was wise to be wary. It was as well Henry was in the courtyard showing Edward a bow and clutch of arrows. She glanced up and caught St Anne staring down at her from her chamber wall. She was sure the saint was frowning. 'What would *you* do?'

she whispered into the stillness but St Anne had resumed her usual beatific expression, albeit her silken-rimmed almond eyes were staring at her. She tapped her fingers on the arm of her chair. Templars indeed. Was such a plot far-fetched? Precautions must be taken, the Bishop of London's palace closely watched, Templars observed, and new food tasters employed. Every jug of wine must be sampled before Henry drank it. Ailenor had her own contacts in London, within certain groups of the clergy, thanks to Uncle Peter's connections. The Templars' Hall and their church must be placed under scrutiny. Thinking of such dangers she called John Mansel to her closet, then sent for Rosalind.

Rosalind's hands were shaking as she curtsied. The girl was wearing the beautiful pink court dress that she had received as a gift from Ailenor a year before. As usual, a neat linen coif covered her hair. Ailenor praised her appearance and bade Rosalind sit with her. She poured them both small cups of sweet honeyed wine. John Mansel sat discreetly behind a screen to observe the interview. It was his idea since Ailenor did not want to intimidate Rosalind with his presence.

'The wafers are fresh from the kitchen.' She proffered the plate and watched as Rosalind visibly relaxed on a stool by the fire and bit into a wafer.

Ailenor sank back into a pile of silken cushions and began with casual conversation. 'I believe that Lady Willelma has shown you over the palace. Do you think you can oversee the embroidery work here? It's not too overwhelming?'

'With the help I am promised by Lady Willelma, the work will take a few months to complete. I suggest we make you a complete new set of bed curtains.' She smiled. 'My father can't make them this time but we'll find someone who can.'

'Good.' Ailenor lifted the jug and refilled their cups. She lifted the letter from the side table. 'This letter you bring me carries a warning. It says you overheard treasonable words when you visited the Bishop's palace. Can you tell me what exactly you overheard?'

Rosalind recounted the incident. She added, 'Your Grace, it may mean little or, possibly, it is very serious. Prioress Elizabeth said you needed to know.'

'Indeed, she is right. You did not see these two men's faces?'

Rosalind shook her head. 'They had their backs to me. There was an arras.'

Ailenor was pensive. She said, 'We cannot identify anyone in particular, but we *can* be vigilant, especially of the clergy, and in particular of the English bishops. Bishop Fulk is not our friend, Rosalind. He may not be at fault or even knowledgeable about this, though the merchant was either negotiating a wine sale or delivering it. Yes?' Rosalind nodded. 'It suggests the monk at least works for Bishop Fulk. His palace is a nest filled with vermin. I'll have it watched.' She leaned forward. 'The King and I shall retire to Blaye for a few months with a small court and a large guard. Keep your eyes and ears open. Note who comes and goes. Let my clerk, John Mansel, know if your hear anything suspicious.' She frowned. 'There are always plots against the King. Generally we root them out. I shall leave John Mansel, Lady Margery, and Lady Mary with you. Both my ladies can be trusted. You must not speak of this to anyone else and Lady Mary will know what to do if you are suspicious of anyone or recognise either of those two men, as will my clerk.'

'Thank you, Your Grace. I know Master John. I am happy to report to him.'

Ailenor smiled. 'It is truly good to have you here, Rosalind. Are you happy with your bedchamber?' It would be foolish to mention the squire so she did not.

'Very.'

'Come with me now. I have a gift for you.' She called for her ladies. John Mansel could see himself out.

Lady Mary and Domina Willelma gliding behind, Ailenor led Rosalind down a private staircase to the courtyard and across it into the stables. She pointed to a stall where a brown and white palfrey was munching hay. 'She is for you. Lady Mary and the squires will take you riding. Besides, you must get out and about the town seeking out new fabrics.'

'For me?' Rosalind's eyes widened. 'What is her name?'

Ailenor had no idea of the palfrey's name. She shook her head.

'Luna,' the groom said. 'She answers to Luna.'

'Moon. She's beautiful. Thank you, Your Grace.'

'A fitting reward for a service given.'

Rosalind's face filled with joy and Ailenor's heart warmed to see her eyes shine. After sending Rosalind away, she crossed the court-yard to John Mansel's office in the great hall. They must inform Henry there could be a plot to poison him and relate their suspicions without involving Rosalind. Ailenor did not want to draw Henry's attention to her. John Mansel could have had such information from anywhere.

Chapter Twenty-four

1243

New tasters were employed for the royal court in Bordeaux. Henry dismissed all talk of a Templar plot as foolish. He had more important things on his mind. Despite the threat of poison, he still dipped his hand greedily into plates of marchpane and Ailenor found herself whipping the little dishes containing sweetmeats away. She banished marchpane from their chambers unless she saw it tasted first. Henry was not permitted the Gascon wine he adored unless his wine jug was rigorously sampled before he quaffed it down.

He raised his hands in frustration. 'I cannot live freely in my own castle. Send those wretched tasters away.'

'Just think of the poisoning of Roman senators or Greek princes. Let us give this regime another month, my dear. Make sure there's no danger.'

Henry stumped off, saying he was dining with the Bishop of Bordeaux at his palace and he'd not drink anything the Bishop didn't, but he'd drink plenty.

Peace was signed between England and France in March, promising a new five-year truce between them. After Christmastide, Ailenor received a messenger from Nell who had given birth in the south. Her third child was another son.

They call their towns bastides. *They are fortified. We are safe. The communes are cooperating with Simon. He is collecting tax into coffers to send*

231

north as soon as roads are open. There have been heavy snowfalls which makes the land silent and soft as if covered with a furred mantle. When the sun shines it is silver. Our lodgings in Pau are more than satisfactory. The castle is as beautiful as those of legend, with rich hangings, turrets, and views towards the mountains. I was most comfortable here during my laying-in. We have named this son Amaury. Harry and Simon have met their brother and are delighted with him . . .

'I hope they return to us soon,' Ailenor confided to Henry as she folded away her letter.

Henry looked down his long nose. His praise was almost begrudging. 'He has assiduously managed those warring merchants. He extracted tax from them all.'

'You should reward Simon, Henry,' she said with just a little caution in her tone, because although Henry seemed pleased with Simon, one could not trust Henry's moods.

'I am purchasing some of his debts in lieu of payment. He still owes money to your Uncle Thomas in Flanders. He can have Kenilworth back.'

'Henry and Nell can return to England at last.' Ailenor patted the little dog by her feet, a descendant of the dog, Beau, she'd brought to England years before. She smiled to herself and whispered to her dog, 'Well, Snip, it looks like I shall have Nell's company after all, as well as my mother and sister once they arrive for Sancha's wedding.'

In the spring, Earl Simon and his family returned to Bordeaux. Earl Simon rented a merchant's house in the town rather than taking up residence in the newly decorated palace. He said he was better placed to control the warring merchants if he dwelled amongst them. Ailenor thought to herself, Pah! An excuse! He's avoiding Henry. That's the nub of it.

She first encountered Earl Simon's squire in the rediscovered garden behind Palais des Ombres. It was weeded and planted with herbal beds. New pathways were freshly laid. Gardeners created rose arbours. She had ordered banks and benches carefully placed amongst hedging so her ladies could take their rest there. As Nell admired these innovations, Ailenor noted how Simon's squire who attended Nell stared at Rosalind who was walking with her attendants, and although the girl discreetly lowered her head, she raised it to occasionally glance over at the squire. Ailenor's heart beat faster. The pair were in love. They longed for each other's company. This much was obvious. She watched Thomas from the edge of her vision.

As they lingered by a mulberry tree, the squire excused himself with a bow and crossed the broad pathway to Rosalind. He fell onto one knee and said some words Ailenor could not make out, but the girl was crying. He then rose and took Rosalind's hand. When her party began to walk into an adjoining cherry orchard, stepping one by one through a latch gate, the couple fell back. Ailenor glanced over her shoulder. The couple walked as far as they dared behind her ladies. Rosalind was smiling, her tears vanquished like a sudden summer storm.

The tiny court meandered back into the garden. As their company broke up into smaller groups near a statue of St Francis, Ailenor noted how Thomas drew Rosalind to one of the new stone benches. For a moment the pair held hands. She held her breath. Rosalind stood, smiled down on the youth, and rejoined Ailenor's ladies, slipping into place beside Lady Margery. She saw Lady Mary squeeze Rosalind's hand and turning to listen to Nell enthuse over her three olive trees that grew beside the garden walls, she found she was smiling too.

To Ailenor's delight, romance flitted about the palace halls, colourful, light, and darting. It filled the dim corridors with laughter and secret assignations. She laughed at how love chased the couple through the corridors of Palais des Ombres, spreading into the gardens and through the courtyards. For the first time in years, she wrote a romantic poem in which Thomas was one of Launcelot's knights and Rosalind attached to Queen Guinevere's train. She would present it to the couple on their wedding day.

Ailenor praised Rosalind's desire to marry Thomas. 'They are meant for each other, don't you think, Nell,' she would say. 'We must make the wedding happen without delay. Speak to Simon, dear Nell. After all, we supported your marriage, a love match.'

'Look at the trouble that followed.'

'It was worth it.'

'It was. It is,' Nell said. 'I shall do my best.'

Nell persuaded Earl Simon to assent to his squire's wedding. Ailenor worked on Henry and in a jovial mood her king bequeathed his blessing on the union. He approved the squire's knighthood. Earl Simon wrote to Thomas's uncle, promising to knight Thomas for his valour at Saintes. Ailenor read the letter before it was sent out from John Mansel's closet.

Simon wrote *My squire, Thomas Beaumont, forthwith is to take possession of his inheritance.*

Simon received a terse letter back from Thomas's uncle. Nell brought the letter to Ailenor who took the letter to Henry.

The uncle was disgruntled. He claimed reimbursement for Thomas's broken betrothal with another party. With reluctance he wished the couple well since Thomas was of an age to take possession of his lands.

'They must wed at once,' she said to Henry as she waved the letter in his face. 'We shall pay Thomas's uncle for the broken betrothal from our own coffers. More expense but it cannot be avoided.'

Henry grumbled, 'You would have me pay a dowry to Richard for Sancha and bear the expense for that wedding. Now you want me to find money for a squire's wedding to an embroideress with dubious ancestry and a Cathar mother.'

'A queen may petition her king and this queen has rarely done so. This embroideress is my friend and my lady and no Cathar, as you know well.' Ailenor knew how to be persuasive. She entwined her arms about Henry's neck, drew him to her bed and whispered into his ear. 'It's not the same. It's less expense. It's a squire and a maiden, not a prince and princess.'

Henry, lying on her coverlet fully clothed, complained, 'My Council will not like all this money we spend on your family and servants.'

She knelt and tugged off his leather shoes. 'They will not complain if we provide another son, my love,' she said knowingly and, kneeling by him, stroked him into arousal.

By morning Henry agreed to pay for the broken betrothal and for the squire's wedding.

Thomas and Rosalind married in the Queen's chapel in June, the blue skies filled with midsummer birdsong. Nell elected to attend Rosalind. Simon stood in for her father. The Queen's ladies were present. King Henry appeared later at the bridal feast dressed elegantly in a fine green satin gown studded with gems. Ailenor took his hand, 'Look at how joyful they are. Be happy for the happiness of others, my love.' Henry smiled back. He enjoyed a festivity, the pageantry, the gorgeous clothing, and most of all the many dishes for a feast provided from his kitchens.

Chapter Twenty-five

Nell
1243

Nell poked around the herb beds in the garden of their rented townhouse. It was not as grand as Ailenor's palace garden but she loved it, the scent of basil, of rosemary, and thyme, and miniature pink roses climbing a trellis by the wall. She could almost be in England. Hal was at the palace that day playing at sword fights with his cousin Edward. Young Simon was learning to sit his own pony, trusted to a groom's care in the meadow beyond the palace courtyard. Baby Amaury was dozing in his cradle, a serene child, perhaps destined for the Church, she thought as she looked down on his fat little face with love.

By the time Simon joined her just before Vespers, all was quiet except for birdsong and the humming of bees. Simon was particularly vigilant of a particular merchant whom the Queen's clerk, John Mansel, had asked him to watch. Apparently, Rosalind had alerted Master Mansel's suspicions to the merchant's presence in the City after her wedding to Thomas. Simon needed a detailed description of the man.

'You've asked Rosalind to speak to me today, as we agreed?' he said as he sank down onto the roundel bench surrounding a mulberry tree opposite her own. Baby Amaury slept on, oblivious to his parents.

'I said a quarter before the Vespers hour.' Nell glanced towards the still room door where Rosalind had been squeezing lemons for a cooling drink using a recipe her father's cook used and Nell enjoyed.

The girl was emerging with a jug covered with cloth on a tray and three beakers.

The garden was the perfect place for them both to speak with Rosalind who, after a week with Thomas, had only returned briefly to Ailenor's service. Beatrice and Sancha of Provence were due in Bordeaux and would be accompanied by a huge retinue. Ailenor had suggested Rosalind should live with her husband. If her services were needed as a queen's lady at court, Ailenor would send for her.

'Rosalind, sit down beside me,' Nell said when Rosalind arrived in the garden, apologising for her tardiness. She took the wooden tray, poured their drinks, handed a beaker to Simon and one to Rosalind. Taking a sip from her own beaker, she said, 'Sit, Rosalind. Earl Simon only wants you to describe the merchant you thought you saw at the Bishop of London's palace and at your wedding feast.'

Rosalind sat on the edge of the bench, looking uncomfortable and thoughtful; her blue eyes were troubled. Perhaps, Nell thought, she should have kept Simon away and questioned Rosalind herself. Simon could be so intimidating with his dark eyes, his black hair, his height, and most of all his reputation as a hard man. She, herself laughed at that because with Nell Simon was as soft as newly churned butter.

Nell gestured to Simon. 'I just want to tell Earl Simon what you saw at your wedding feast. Earl Simon knows all the Bordeaux wine merchants and wants to get to the bottom of this. You know John Mansel, Rosalind?'

'Yes, Lady Eleanor, I do. I told him about the merchant I saw on my wedding night and before in the Bishop of London's palace.'

Simon leaned over. 'There's no need to be nervous, Rosalind, but if you could describe him to me I would be grateful.'

Rosalind thought for a moment before saying, 'Well, he's not easy to describe. It was the gown that caught my eye. The hall was crowded for my wedding feast. Thomas was laughing and he threw an arm around me. I said I saw the man I'd seen in London. I pointed him out to Thomas. It was his gown. It was silk and embroidered with a border of serpents. He was also tall like the man in London, but I couldn't see his face then, because I was listening by the arras.

237

He had his back to me.' Rosalind frowned. 'Thomas just said, "As well it is just a gown you noticed, wife of mine. He's one of the Soler merchants." He chucked me under the chin. "I expect he has been about the palace. The Solers are one of the most prominent families in Bordeaux. In fact, my lord's house belongs to them."

'"No, it's not here, I saw him." I said to Thomas. "It was in London. That time I told you about, what I overheard in Bishop Fulk's palace. It is him." I said, "Look, Thomas, look down at the deep border around the hem of his gown. The serpents!"

'So Thomas looked more closely. "He's a Bordeaux merchant. That's all. If he is the man you think you saw in the Bishop's palace, I can assure you he's not plotting now. He won't risk his trade . . . or his neck."

'I said, "Prioress Elizabeth thought the cleric he spoke with was associated with the Templars." Thomas said I should tell Master Mansel.

'So, my lady, I thought to myself, could there be two such gowns? I couldn't fathom it at all, so I told John Mansel the very next day. Is he plotting against the King, my lady?'

Nell looked at Simon who smiled and said, 'I know not, Lady Rosalind, but I shall discover it if he is. I have business tomorrow with the Columbines. If he is a Soler, I shall find out and question him. The Solers and Columbines are competing wine merchants and they won't want any part in plots, or plots, let us say, involving Templars. Lady Rosalind, you have been helpful. Are you comfortable sharing the rooms above the stable with Thomas? I can move you into the manor house.'

'Thank you. We have all we need.'

Nell thought, as she watched Rosalind hurry back to her stable abode, how happy they were. How will Ailenor do without her when we return to England? She's a treasure.

Nell was in the still room with a heap of lavender for drying when Simon unexpectedly arrived into her domain. He plonked down on the bench and wiped his forehead with a cloth.

'What brings you here?' Nell said, surprised.

'Those wretched merchants, Nell.' He sniffed. 'Smells like a linen chest in here.'

She hung a bushy stem from a line. 'Well tell me, since you intend to anyway.'

He stretched his legs out, contemplated his boots for a moment and began to recount his conversation with one of the Columbine merchants. 'I was looking into the description Rosalind gave us of that merchant with the serpent trimmed gown.'

She sank down onto a stool by the long plank table, piles of lavender in front of her.

'The first Columbine I spoke with identified the man who had been delivering wine to the palace for the wedding. Mind you, I almost gagged as I entered his cellars to inspect the wine – more intense than this.' Simon waved around at the hanging lavender. She frowned. 'And access the tax he owes. Later, over a cup of wine his tongue loosened. "Soler wine." He complained, "Time the King favoured my wine."'

'"The King will try to be fair. Your wine will have its time," I said back to him. He was also quick to identify a wine merchant who might be defaulting on tax. And he fits the description.' Simon laughed. 'I've found my man, a Soler, as I thought he might be.'

'You must question him. Tell Master Mansel of your discovery.'

'I intend to. I doubt he will have anything to do with the Templars, though you never know. I've met him before, I suspect, since he provides wine for the Bishop of London. I'll seek him out later today.'

Simon confided to Nell, as she was folding sheets in their bedchamber, that he could find no evidence that the merchant was plotting against the King. 'His name is Master Abelard and our dear Master Abelard was clear that he could not recollect any cleric proposition-ing him to commit treason.' Simon creased his brow. 'I think he was lying on that score. He looked uncomfortable, though he said he would swear to this on Holy Relics in the Cathedral in front of wit-nesses. He claimed no wine business with the London Templars

239

either. I asked him if he knew the King's grocer, Adam de Basing, and he said "If I do, what of it?"'

'Did you ask him if he knew the son?' Nell placed a folded sheet inside a cupboard.

Simon sat down on their bed. 'Oh yes, he does, but the De Basings, unpleasant as they are, are loyal to Henry.' He let out a laugh. 'And, they are certainly not monkish.'

He paused for a moment.

'I shall speak to Ailenor, warn her. As long as Henry has all his food tasted and his wine sampled . . .'

Nell spun around. 'Still . . . can you trust any bishop these days? With no bishop in Winchester Henry has collected revenue from both Winchester and Canterbury. Henry still wants Boniface as Archbishop of Canterbury. The clergy are angry.' She shook her head and folded two more pillowcases. 'Henry always insists he is right. I hope they are not all plotting against him.' For a heartbeat she considered. Simon might be forthright and impatient with Henry, but *he* was loyal, though he had good reason to be disloyal.

Simon shrugged. 'Unlikely any of them are, in truth. But there's no sensible order. No Pope in Rome either, Nell. Not since the old Pope died, though they say Innocent will be confirmed as Pope this year . . . so *he* must arbitrate between the King and the Church.' He frowned at her. 'Your grandfather, old Henry, did not learn that lesson either. Remember Becket. It's nothing new.'

He came to stand by the cupboard where she was now stacking swaddling and feminine items, slipping sachets of lavender amongst them. 'Boniface as Archbishop won't please the English bishops. Henry doesn't like or trust Bishop Fulk of London. He infuriates the old baronial families. It all bodes ill. Henry wants new men administrating the exchequer so he gets what money he wants for his pageants, his friends, building projects, and his hopeless wars.' Simon gave a deep sigh. 'The barons always had their own men controlling the Crown's purse. They don't like Henry's clerks from Savoy.'

'Why,' Nell said, turning from the cupboard to face him, 'why does he upset the barons and bishops? Henry never thinks of consequences.' She lifted a sprig of lavender to her nostrils and inhaled the scent.

'He's not as foolish as you think. The Savoyard clerks are efficient and they are manipulated by him. But Henry is careless with money. It will come to a bad end one day. There's little control of his spending. Pageants and weddings, he adores them all. Dreams of recovering lost lands . . .'

'What's to be done?'

'Enough said for now. I'll report my conversation with the wine merchant. Master Abelard will be watched closely.' He grasped her hands. He looked exhausted, his eyes shot through with red. She raised her hand and sweeping back his dark mane, rose onto tiptoes and kissed his forehead. How she still loved him. 'We'll keep out of Henry's disputes,' he said into her hair. 'Once we return home, we'll stay away from court and enjoy our boys, our lands, and our castle of Kenilworth. That is what will be done.'

Drawing back, Nell looked into his eyes. 'When can we leave?'

'Henry wants to return to England in September.'

She nestled her head against his chest. 'Our goods will be at Kenilworth before us, waiting for us to return.' She sighed. 'So many beautiful tapestries and fabrics, and they all tell the story of my longing for your return from the Crusade,' she said. She shook her head. 'Though if they had been lost, I would not have minded at all. How I long for home. So many lost years.'

Simon smiled down at her. 'They soften our lives, but you speak truth. They are only things. I long for Kenilworth too. Two of our children have never seen it. How the years fly by us like dragons in stories racing through the skies. The sense of time passing is lost.' He frowned, 'We must attend Richard's wedding and that's in November.'

Nell tucked the sprig of lavender into her bodice. 'That's true enough, so why don't we spend the winter at Odiham? It is closer to London. Besides, Henry owes me my lands, those the Marshals took.'

'He paid my debts and confirmed me as Earl of Leicester. I have Kenilworth, you Odiham. Isn't it enough?'

'But we need lands for our children.'

'Perhaps. We can only hope he is in a jovial mood for Richard's wedding. Then he might listen to you.'

They docked at Portsmouth and rode to Winchester. Nell dreaded the welcome they might receive in England after the disastrous Poitou campaign. Her anxiety was unfounded. The streets of Winchester were lined with flags and banners belonging to the barons who had gathered to welcome Henry home. No one dared condemn the King and Simon was cynical. 'He is blaming his barons for sending him to war in the first place.' A guffaw escaped his mouth. 'Probably believes it too. Like John the father, we have Henry, the son. Henry is playing them all off against each other whilst appearing pious and angelic. You'll see, Nell, he'll demand a magnificent wedding and it'll cost the kingdom a fortune.'

'Richard will have eased a way for him.'

'Henry has to take responsibility for his own foolhardy decisions,' Simon said.

'But our stepfather and mother asked for Henry's help in Poitou in good faith.'

'Good faith, my bollocks. Nell, you cannot say that. Count Hugh switched sides taking his own supporters with him when it went wrong last year.'

She held her reins tightly. 'At least England is at peace. There are crops in the fields. The people will forgive Henry because a good harvest is what matters most. A short rest, Simon, in Winchester, no more,' she insisted. 'Odiham is waiting for us. Think of the hunting in the park.'

'Worry not. I've sent word ahead. All will be ready for our return to Odiham.'

Nell glanced over her shoulder to the wagon that carried her boys and their nurses. Young Simon and Hal were excitedly climbing out. Her eyes strayed sideways to the golden-headed squire seated on a dark jennet and the pretty girl who rode beside him on a dun-coloured palfrey. Both were laughing and glancing at each other.

Love-struck, she thought, remembering how five years ago she felt the same about Simon, and how she still felt.

The rest of their small household trailed into the bailey of Winchester Castle, including their falconer who rode beside a large cage with their hooded birds perched on a cart. It rattled through the gate and along the courtyard's cobbles; its precious load three goshawks and a falcon. They would soon be home and hunting in Odiham's woodland.

Sancha and Richard's wedding was held on the twenty-third day of November. It was the most magnificent wedding Nell had ever seen. Thirty thousand dishes had been prepared for the wedding feast. Three thousand guests were seated at the fabulous gathering.

Nell considered Sancha gentle, sweet, kind, and beautiful, and fearful of the duty expected of her as Richard's wife. Sancha was overshadowed by her mother. A powerful personality and cultured beyond compare, Countess Beatrice proudly walked about the wedding guests in a ruby silk robe which Henry had ordered made into gorgeous gowns for Ailenor, Beatrice, and Sancha. Somehow, Sancha managed to appear regal, if not entirely confident, on her wedding day and Nell hoped Richard would treat her with consideration. *He always marries beautiful women, but this girl is simple in comparison to Isabel Marshal, by far she's too unworldly for him. Sancha of Provence is a child whereas Isabel was the daughter of the greatest knight England ever knew.*

They attended the Christmas Feast Richard held at Wallingford. After New Year, Henry led Nell and Simon into his private chamber. Countess Beatrice, Ailenor, and Sancha sat by the fire fingering embroidery in their laps. They were invited to sip cups of Henry's best Gascon wine and eat wafers. A liveried servant stoked the fire and another stood close to the King's shoulder. He dismissed them both and addressed Simon.

'They have tasted this wine. It's not poisoned. *Your* merchant was banished from my kingdom, both Gascony and England, exiled. His trade has been confiscated as you requested and I am granting his business to the Columbines.' Henry threw another log onto the fire.

'Nor are the wafers poisonous.' He offered Simon and Ailenor the silver plate laden with crisp wafers.

Simon said. 'Not my merchant, Sire. Still, he was suspicious. It might be sensible for Mansel to watch the Bishop.'

'He will, indeed, indeed,' Henry mumbled, his mouth full of wafer. 'Be sure the Bishop will be watched.'

Nell nodded and Ailenor said, 'Amen to that incident, I hope.'

For a time after that, they talked of non-consequential matters – the Christmas gleemen; the procession of dishes at the Christmas Feast; the Yule Log that burned endlessly, and the subtlety, a great castle with marchpane turrets; the magnificence of Richard's hospitality.

As the afternoon darkened, more candles were lit. After calling for supper to be served, Henry turned to Nell, 'I know, dearest sister, you are returning to Kenilworth tomorrow. As a New Year's gift, I am reimbursing you for the rest of those lands the Marshals neglected to give you, your dower.'

In disbelief, Nell thanked him. Henry had confiscated Marshal lands which he considered did not belong to the clan.

Henry turned his attention to Simon. 'We hope that all previous bad feeling between us is gone, Earl Simon.' There was lightness in the way Henry waved his long jewelled fingers towards the windows. 'As dissipated as the mist out there. We intend granting you five hundred marks as a gift. I pardon the final thousand pounds of your debt.'

'My King.' Simon leaned his great frame forward, knelt on the floor straw, and kissed Henry's hand. 'You are most generous. Thank you. The mist has dissolved.'

For now, thought Nell, lowering her head to conceal the cynicism in her eyes.

Countess Beatrice bowed her head discreetly over her embroidery. Nell did not miss the fact that as Henry made promises Beatrice was smiling like a contented cat that had supped cream. Were Ailenor and her mother behind Henry's generosity, a clever plan because this way Simon would never join the discontented barons and bishops once life was business as usual.

Nell narrowed her eyes and bit into another wafer. What favours might Countess Beatrice be demanding from Henry for her own family? She studied Sancha who sat demurely beside her mother but, as usual, never seemed to speak for herself, her large eyes looking to Beatrice and Ailenor for approval. Poor lovely Sancha was a sacrifice. But then, when one considered it, they were all pawns in this cruel game of kings and queens.

Chapter Twenty-six

Ailenor
Spring 1245

For several years freezing winters turned into gentle springs, hot summers, and damp autumns. Spring again and Ailenor curled up in the window seat of her chamber in Windsor Castle enjoying the March sunshine. She had been in England nine years and had reached the great age of twenty-two. She considered herself not only a queen but almost, though not quite, a matron. Her nursery was filled with children's happy voices. She was content, though the year after Sancha's wedding to Richard she had miscarried. Sadly, Sancha too had endured a miscarriage. Therefore, Ailenor was joyful when she conceived again but saddened when her beloved sister suffered a second loss.

Edmund, the new royal baby, smiled at her from his cradle. He closed, opened, and closed his blue eyes again and slept. Ailenor lifted her Breviary from a cushion and gazed at the page appropriate for the day, March 25th. The exquisite illuminations always stole her breath away. She studied a gilded miniature containing a drawing of *The Annunciation*. Lady Mary and the angel Gabriel were placed before a snowy white castle surrounded by spring flowers – anemones, primroses, and garden pinks. Angels peering from the foliage decorating each corner of the page spread their wings; others lifted up trumpets in tiny hands just like baby Edmund's.

Turning the page slowly, Ailenor read aloud the prayer known as *The Little Office*. Could Breviaries like this one be written in English rather than scribed in Latin? If so, all women wealthy enough to own these little books could read the prayers they contained. She squinted at the pretty script. Her daughters must be as well educated as her sons, just as *her* father had taught his own daughters to read and to write, to speak French as fluently as the Provençal dialect, and to understand Latin.

Two sons and two daughters; she was as happy as the tabby cat that purred by her fireplace.

Henry, too, was delighted with their family. There will be more, she promised herself, safe in the knowledge their throne's future was secure. Gascony was for Edward when he came of age, where he could learn to rule. They must seek a suitable inheritance for Edmund too, perhaps another kingdom or betrothal to a great princess.

She ran her hand along her slim figure. I never thicken after childbirth, she considered. I'm still attractive. Henry loves me. It's time for me to conceive again.

Shortly after Vespers, Henry swept into her antechamber. One look at his face told her all. Her heart beat faster. He was in a passion over something. What now? We've had months of harmony. He tossed his velvet mantle over a settle and waved her ladies away. His face, usually pallid, was fiery-red; his eyes glittered like icicles.

'Archbishop Edmund's mantle. What did you do with it after Edmund's christening?'

'In the Abbey,' she faltered. She had not wanted the fusty relic near her birthing chamber and had sent it away.

Henry glowered. She waited for him to speak again, her patience stretched, her hands gracefully folded in her lap.

Without raising his eyes he grunted, 'Boniface is siding with the Pope over the election of Paselewe to the bishopric of Chichester. Says my man is ignorant of scripture and Latin, not good enough to be chosen as bishop! I should never have appointed Boniface to Canterbury.'

The words slipped from her mouth. 'My uncle has a point perhaps.'

Although she knew the candidate for Chichester was no scholar, she would do better to humour Henry, and not side with Boniface, well, not obviously anyway. Her uncle had turned out to be a better archbishop than she'd expected. He was pleasanter than Edmund Rich.

'How dare Boniface support Innocent's selection, an exiled Pope at that. How dare he?' Henry's voice was chill as winter which was worrying because it meant Henry was determined to be stubborn. 'After all I have done for your uncle.' He jabbed a heavily ringed finger in her direction. 'Too worldly to be an archbishop, handsome, and ambitious. He's modernising clergy who don't want his new ways. The bishops are furious.' Henry folded his arms. 'I should never have requested him for Canterbury, following in the footsteps of that good man, Archbishop Edmund. And,' Henry drew breath, 'after all that *I* do for God. Who is more holy, I ask you? Uncle Boniface or myself? Daily I give alms, feeding hundreds of our poor, rebuilding Westminster, presenting God with a beautiful house with high vaults, elegant arches, window traceries, flying buttresses ; no less than a cathedral as good as Amiens, Chartres, Reims.' He put his head into his hands and groaned. 'God's house costs highly and they all resent it, all of those bishops . . . Fulk of London, Grosseteste of Lincoln, Bishop Raleigh . . .' He banged his fist on the knobbly carved arm of his chair, hurting it because he lifted it and groaned. 'I need my man Paselewe within that hornet's nest.' A spray of angry spittle sprayed her gown. She drew back. 'I need Uncle Boniface's support,' he shouted at her. 'See to it.'

Ailenor kept her voice even as she said, 'You are wrong about Uncle Boniface, Henry. There is a letter from him. Allow me to read it to you again.' Before Henry could answer, she was rummaging about the top of a small oak desk. 'Here it is.

'*Please beg the King's pardon . . . there is little I can do on the question of Paselewe as he is not of the Church. He is a lowly clerk. The bishops are of the opinion Paselewe is not versed enough to be Bishop of Chichester . . . Pope Innocent refuses to consider Paselewe as a bishop. Even so, you will have my support as far as I can give it.*'

'As far as he can give it is not good enough,' Henry said with petulance. As Ailenor glanced up at Henry she could see the storm was passing. If she was quick, she could make use of his temporary calm.

She opened her arms, the letter hanging from her hand. 'Henry, you are right when you say Paselewe is far, far better at collecting money than any tax collector we have in our own service. Why don't we use him that way, not as a bishop but working for us? If we insist on raising a clerk to a bishopric we shall make enemies.' She tapped a finger against her forehead, causing the parchment she held in her hand to crackle. 'I think I have a solution.'

'Have *what*?'

'A suggestion.' She modified her language. Henry must think it his own idea. 'I wonder if that other man I heard mentioned for Chichester – what was his name – Wych – would be better. We can keep Paselewe to collect money for us from the Templars and Jews.'

'Yes, the Templars have too much wealth. And they may be involved in plots to destroy the Crown. Paselewe might be useful rooting those out. I did think Paselewe could collect money for us.' He swallowed. 'Perhaps Wych is better for a bishopric, less controversial.'

'Well, Henry, I'm glad that is settled,' she said. She put the offending letter away and set out to distract him. 'How is Westminster progressing? Have you sent masons to France to learn those new designs you talked of?'

Henry smiled at last. He took himself to the door, pushed his head out, and demanded a flagon of wine, the best Gascon wine, and supper to be served. Discovering herself to be hungry, she requested salmon poached and a honey sauce to accompany it.

'Westminster will surpass anything Louis has built, even Sainte-Chappelle,' he said after he sent the order to the kitchens.

When food arrived in golden serving dishes, Henry lifted the gleaming lids and, with approving sounds, sniffed the steam that rose from them. After everything was tasted, he sent the servants away. Once he had placed a white napkin over Ailenor's shoulder and another over his own, he served up the fish, placing a manchet

249

of white bread on her golden dish. 'I am travelling to Wales again,' he announced.

'Why?'

'Trouble on the borders.' He leaned forward. 'I'll starve the ungodly Welsh into submission this time.' He stabbed his bread, leaned back in his chair and called for a page to place another log on the fire. 'We need a new, stronger castle. That'll stop that traitor, Dafydd.' He glanced up, his anger suddenly gone. 'Do you know, Ailenor, that if Dafydd dies childless, I am legally his heir. Remember I told you how his mother Joanna was my half-sister. Pity he's not as sweet as his mother.'

Ailenor sighed. Wales was such a muddle with its warring princes, but since Gascony was for Edward, Wales might be Edmund's one day to govern. Henry had to go to war in Wales.

'When do you travel?'

'Within the week. I am having new armour made.' He tugged at his beard as he did when in thought. 'Why don't you take Edward and the children to Winchester for Eastertide? The change of air will do you good.'

Ailenor spread butter over her bread and on top placed a slice of cheese. 'We could continue to Woodstock to see the new gardens.'

'I'll join you once it's over. A campaign in Wales could last all summer.' He sighed. 'Richard has offered to finance it. He is reminting our coin. That always makes more money.' He looked more cheerful. 'The barons support a war with Wales, but then they would. Many of them own border castles and lands.'

Ailenor raised an eyebrow. 'Whom does the mint advantage most? Richard, no doubt.' She thought of Nell. 'I expect Earl Simon will campaign in Wales. If so, Sancha and Nell could come to Woodstock.' She thought for a moment. 'And Rosalind too, as she is often with Nell. I have missed her since Thomas took up his estate and she has children.'

'You could visit Winchester first, for Easter.'

'And Canterbury to see Uncle Boniface,' she said.

'Remind him of where his loyalty lies.' Henry pushed away his empty plate. 'I have a letter to write to Boniface. So Richard Wych it will be.' He dropped a kiss on her head and hurried off, saying, 'I'll return later.'

Ailenor called for the maids to change her linen sheets, sprinkle lavender water on her pillows, and perfume her nightgown. She sang to herself at the thought of another baby in their nursery. It was time.

Chapter Twenty-seven

Sumpter horses lined up in the yard. Edward and Margaret sat erect in the carriage beside their mother, brimming with impatience to be on their way. It was a soft April day and Ailenor's heart sang with the joy of a journey ahead.

Her cavalcade of wagons, servants, and guards crossed London Bridge, wound their way through Southwark and plunged deep into the gentle Kent countryside. Their first destination was Canterbury where Uncle Boniface was in residence, having that very month returned from the meeting with the exiled Pope in Lyon.

Boniface, tall and smiling, greeted them in the palace courtyard. Soon they were guided to aired and pleasant-smelling chambers, possessing glass in the windows and views of a garden filled with mulberry trees. The children loved Boniface. He made such a fuss of them, especially his new great- nephew, baby Edmund. His eyes were seductively warm as honey, but whilst he possessed a good-natured smile, Ailenor knew that beneath this affable personality lay danger and ruthlessness.

Before she set out from Canterbury to Winchester on the second leg of their progress, she took Edward and Margaret to visit one of the holiest of England's shrines, that of St Thomas Becket who had been murdered on the orders of the children's great-grandfather.

Their party joined a swarm of pilgrims entering the Cathedral. Visitors stood back to allow the Queen's company passage, bowing low in homage as the royal family walked slowly along the Nave. Ailenor smiled graciously. After all, she was an earthly and heavenly queen, blessed by the Virgin Mary, a queen who would always be penitent, humble, kind, and generous of heart. She paused for a moment and whispered to Sir Hugh, Edward's household steward. She ordered alms to be given to the poor of Canterbury. And later, as did the common folk visiting the shrine of St Thomas, Ailenor departed Canterbury with purses full of little metal pilgrim badges to give as tokens to her retinue. Edward and Margaret couldn't wait. As they walked with her from the Cathedral they wore theirs pinned onto their mantles.

Their progress reached Winchester on Palm Sunday.

Once settled into her apartments in the palace, Ailenor began to recount the Easter stories. Margaret and Edward were fascinated. Beatrice, a little young at less than three years old, listened intently, seated on Ailenor's knee staring at the gilded illuminations in her mother's Psalter until her head nodded and her nurse swept her off to bed. Ailenor smiled fondly as Edward picked out all the letters as his mother read from the Psalter, translating the prayers from Latin into the French they spoke at court.

Margaret and Edward always begged her for more stories, but those they most enjoyed most were not Biblical, but rather tales of Arthur and his Court.

'The Grail Castle, please,' Edward pleaded.

'After I read you one more Easter prayer.'

'One day, Mama,' Edward announced, 'I shall have a round table for my knights. It will be painted with gold and silver and sit under a canopy of gilded stars in a blue sky.'

'That's a fine idea, Edward,' she said closing her Psalter. 'I'll tell you one more very short story and then you must go to bed.'

'I shall be one of Edward's court ladies,' Margaret prattled.

Edward studied his sister. 'You talk too much, but I shall consider you. The Grail is the very chalice Christ drank from at the Last Supper. And,' added Edward, 'the lance pierced Christ's side as he hung dying on the Cross.'

'That is so,' Ailenor began and started to describe the Grail Castle to the children. Her description was drawn from her own imaginings and soon she lost herself within her telling. She never forgot that, one day, the wide-eyed little girl with dark curling hair might one day leave her side to live in her own castle just as she had to leave Provence so many years before.

The following Friday, Edward and Margaret watched as priests and monks crawled on their hands and knees towards Christ hanging from the enormous cross in the Cathedral nave. On Saturday the children were permitted to stay up for the midnight Service of Light. Edward was entranced by the procession that walked around the shadowy cathedral followed by the lighting of the Easter Paschal Candle.

'It represents the risen Christ,' Ailenor whispered to the children. This was the Church ceremony she liked most of all. They glanced around and their eyes widened as more and more lights entered the cathedral and church bells slowly pealed. 'It's magical,' she murmured to them.

On Easter Sunday, Ailenor led her children in the festive procession when the sacrament was paraded around the concourse outside the Cathedral. As they entered Winchester's nave, priestly acolytes shook hand bells and sweet incense drifted through its columns of ancient pillars. Ailenor pointed to the tall windows beyond the altar. 'Look, there you can see Christ's story.' Although she swept her hand towards colourful walls on which every space was painted with Biblical stories and the images of saints, she avoided drawing their attention to the Doom painting, with its descending ladders and hideous devils and their imps holding prongs to push sinners into Hell's fires. The thought of being tortured in Hell frightened everyone, even her, the Queen, but surely purgatory would be short for the Virgin's representative on earth.

'Mama, it's beautiful,' Edward gasped.

'Beautiful,' repeated Margaret. 'I want to stay here with God for ever. I want to become a nun.'

'You chatter too much to be a nun,' Edward said.

'You, my sweeting, will be a great queen like your mother. She turned to Edward, 'And for you, the crown of England like your Papa wears for the crowning ceremonies, filled with jewels – emeralds, rubies, sapphires.' She paused. 'You will marry a beautiful princess as in all the histories of the past. She will be an earthly queen as holy as the Queen of Heaven and as gracious.' She felt her children's hands clasp her own tightly and saw how their eyes glowed with awe in the candlelight. One day, they would understand their great destiny.

Margaret pointed to one of the magnificent windows. 'Look, Mama, I see the angels and Baby Jesus. I can see the manger.'

Edward, not to be outdone, gestured to the great cross. 'He should never have been killed. I hate Jews. They did that. When I am king I shall destroy them all.'

'It was a long time ago, Edward.' Ailenor said. 'Not all Jews are evil. They are good business people. It is not charitable to be vengeful.'

Edward grunted. 'They eat Christian children.'

'Whoever told you that nonsense?'

'A servant. The one with the big teeth and fat belly.'

'The servant's name?'

'Roland.'

Roland must be removed from their service forthwith.

'Look,' Edward exclaimed, 'the Madonna is crowned in that statue. She is a queen like you, Mama.'

'She is almost, but not quite as special, as her Son.' She thought for a moment. 'I shall take you to Beaulieu Abbey one day. It is a great abbey. It will be consecrated next year, we think.'

'And me too?' queried Margaret.

'I shall take you to see Wilton Abbey on our way to Clarendon. We shall spend a night there, my love. Many noblewomen were educated in the Abbey school.' She leaned down. 'And it has a beautiful chapel dedicated to Saint Edith.'

Margaret was mollified by this, and even more so when her mother announced that she would sit beside her mother that afternoon for the Easter feast. 'There will be venison and beef, and marchpane treats

255

and syllabub.' Clasping her hands with pleasure, she said, 'The fasting time is over, my children.'

After Easter, Ailenor's cavalcade set out for Woodstock. She kept the children safe inside the carriage as they travelled through the leafy English countryside. There was always the threat of bandits in the forests. Diseases lurked within towns.

If the road was smooth, they played checkers. Occasionally she relented and allowed them to ride on special saddles that fitted onto the horses adults rode. Every now and then Edward would sit behind Sir Hugh. Riding pacified Edward's protests at being confined to a carriage.

A week later they rode into the palace courtyard at Woodstock and she reminded them, 'After Midsummer you'll return to Windsor but I must wait here until Papa returns from the Welsh wars.' They were so happy being with her, she had to gently prepare them for another parting. 'Lady Sybil and Sir Hugh are your guardians. They'll watch over you when I cannot be with you.'

The children nodded and were soon distracted as they ran about the courtyard, glad to be on their feet again. Ailenor also determined to enjoy the two months they had left before the children would return to London without her. She clapped her hands. 'Let's look at Lady Rosamund's maze and the gardens. Edmund and Beatrice need their naps.' Leaving the nurses to settle the babies, she led them, their eyes wide with expectation, into the gardens.

Nell arrived at Woodstock in time to celebrate the Midsummer holiday with three of her children, a band of servants, and several sumpter horses. By now Nell had four boys. The youngest, Guy, born during the previous year, remained at Kenilworth with his nurses. Each time Ailenor saw the boys they were taller and even more delightfully mischievous. Amaury was two, Simon five, and Hal had passed his sixth birthday. They were much loved by Margaret and Edward.

Rosalind accompanied them. Ailenor had not seen her for a year though occasionally they exchanged letters. The workshop at

Westminster thrived and Ailenor still referred to it as Rosalind's workshop. She noted how Rosalind remained slim; how her eyes sparkled and her skin glowed with life. Now Lady Rosalind, she wore fashionable netted crispinettes on her golden hair, which was plaited in coils around her ears rather than hanging in the single long plait she had worn in the past. The embroideress now had tiny children of her own, both boys, one a baby.

'Rosalind!' Ailenor opened her arms in greeting. 'Come and join us, you are welcome.' Rosalind curtsied gracefully. Ailenor raised her up and turning to her maids called for basins of rose water, towels, and refreshments for all her guests.

'The Countess mentioned you would like some gowns embellished.' Rosalind smiled, showing her pretty, even teeth. 'I am happy to embroider whilst we are here, Your Grace.'

'I brought you here for your company, not to work for me.' Ailenor glanced around. 'Here is Lady Mary and Domina Willelma to welcome you. They will show you your chamber.'

Rosalind was surrounded by Ailenor's ladies. Ailenor didn't mind at all when they ushered the embroideress into the Hall, fussing around her and chattering as if Rosalind were queen bee of their hive rather than herself.

Ailenor turned to Nell. 'I am so, so pleased to see you, my dear friend. Sancha was supposed to come for Midsummer but she is ill.' She lowered her voice. 'My sister didn't say it in her letter but she might be with child. I am hopeful.'

Nell held Ailenor's hands. 'Try not to worry. Sancha is delicate. I hope Richard takes care of her.' Accepting a proffered basin and towel from a maid, she added, 'Our children bring us joy. I've not seen Edmund yet.'

'Come and you shall.' Ailenor looked over at how Edward and Margaret and toddling Beatrice were surrounded by Nell's boys. 'They are so delighted with each other's company. If only time could stop and they never had to face the world. If only they could be little all their lives.'

Nell dried her hands and face. 'Let us hope that since they

cannot, our world is kind to them all and that they stand by each other.' She smiled down at Margaret and Beatrice who were both swirling about, skirts flying around small legs. 'I am praying that next time we, too, have a little girl.'

'Girls are company but alas too soon we bid them farewell. We hope for an alliance with Scotland.' Ailenor smiled, shaking off the melancholy sentiment. 'Come, Nell, no sadness. Let's enjoy wafers and mead together in my solar. It's a warm day but the windows open onto a garden, and I want to hear all your news from Kenilworth.'

Soon, the bedchambers in the palace were filled to overflowing with Nell's ladies and Ailenor's ladies sharing two spacious chambers. For two days Nell and Ailenor discussed children and complained about the war in Wales. As they walked together in the gardens, they relaxed in each other's company. They wore their hair loose, simple gowns of silk and linen with gauzy sleeves, fine linen stockings, and light slippers.

Despite Ailenor's protests, Rosalind settled down to embroidering and when she promised to take an order back with her to trim a valuable velvet over-gown with gold thread and jewels, Ailenor said, 'Allow me to make you a gift of a green velvet robe. I have many similar.' Ailenor knew that even her oldest gowns would look beautiful on Rosalind. Nothing must ever be discarded or wasted. All would be handed on or cut down for the children or given as a gift to one of her ladies and allowed new life.

On Midsummer's Eve, Ailenor awoke to a cloudless sky of azure blue. Courtyard cobbles had been scrubbed. Benches were placed in a horseshoe because the children were to see a Midsummer play. Afterwards they would enjoy a feast outdoors.

The colourful troupe in a tall cart trailed in through the palace gates banging tambourines, one carrying a rebec, another playing a clarion, two in glittering flowing robes clashing cymbals, and one in a parti-coloured tunic of red and yellow beating a pair of nakers. An actor wearing a stag's horns led the actors' cart, blowing loudly on a bagpipe. Ailenor hurried forwards and welcomed the players. In a state of anticipation the children crowded onto the front benches. Their ladies squeezed in behind. Soon there was standing room only, but nobody minded.

Once they were settled the actors, who had retreated into the changing room on the lower floor of their two-storey wagon, appeared on the stage which was the cart's upper floor. What emerged was not a religious play, as Ailenor had expected, but a play drawn from the story of King Arthur. Cymbals clashed, the audience hushed as the boy-king Arthur pulled a sword from a life-like stone and the wizard-druid Merlin declared him England's king. Three young player-knights wearing chain mail shirts appeared on the stage to herald the young King Arthur. They were dressed as crusaders, wearing white cloaks with red crosses. One by one they announced their names to be Galahad, Perceval, and Bors. They pointed to a round table filled with knights that was depicted on a cloth hanging behind the actors. The king, who was of a sudden mysteriously grown up – he had donned a beard – spoke to the three pretend knights, giving them their quest.

They trotted off on hobby horses to seek the Holy Grail in Jerusalem, their armour clanking. The children laughed as the actors disappearing behind a curtain caught their swords in its folds, causing it to fall. Their eyes grew round as the same curtain was replaced with a forest of painted trees.

Sir Galahad wandered onto the stage looking confused. He had lost his way. An old lady with a wavering finger directed him towards a castle painted on the forested hanging. He was met by a lovely lady who promised to help him if only he would follow her onward to the highest adventure ever a knight saw. A gilded make-shift ship on wheels rattled onto the stage. Perceval and Bors waved from its deck, eliciting delighted cries from the audience on the benches. Galahad gazed up at his two companions. The old lady informed Sir Galahad she was Sir Perceval's sister. She warned him not to enter this ship unless he was without sin. Galahad declared he would be glad to die if he was discovered to be tainted and thus unworthy. He joined company with the other knights. On board the ship, which was crowded and looked as if it could collapse, Galahad fumbled about until he discovered a sword and crown. In turn, they all tried to hold the sword but neither Bors nor Perceval could grip it though they struggled and struggled as Galahad watched. The ship shook. Hal called out, 'Bring Arthur back. He can do it.' And then he added, 'My Papa can. He is without sin.'

'He's not here and really, Hal, be quiet,' Nell said crossly.

Edward turned to Hal. 'My Papa can beat yours any day. He is totally without sin. He is building a new cathedral for God.'

'Mine was a crusader,' Hal hissed back. 'Crusaders have seen Jerusalem.'

'Hush, children,' Ailenor said with an elegant finger pressed onto her lips. 'Neither of your fathers are here, so let us see if Sir Galahad can take the sword up.'

And a moment later, Galahad achieved the feat and held up the sword. He led the knights from the rocking ship which was carefully pushed behind the forested curtain. The sword was a magical sword. Following Sir Galahad, the knights approached a second castle painted behind them and slayed devil-like enemies of God who climbed up a ladder from the ground onto the stage. Margaret closed her eyes. Beatrice clung to Ailenor's gown. But soon all the devils were vanquished and chased down the ladder. They fled into the changing area.

Another lady appeared. She was ill and told the valiant knights she needed a dish of blood from a noble maiden's arm to cure her illness. Edward whispered, 'Mama. You could offer your blood.'

'No, I could not. Just watch, Edward.'

That was the moment Ailenor's day changed. The noise of cantering hoofs penetrated the air. Trumpets sounding outside the courtyard walls competed with the actors' cymbals and trumpets. Horses were neighing and snorting in the distance. Ailenor could hear male voices. This was not the stuff of stories. A moment later the courtyard was filled with pennants, riders, and knights dismounting. Henry was helped down from his mount by a squire. She ran to greet him expecting joy on his countenance. His face was cheerless. She glanced back towards the stage.

The play abruptly stopped. Actors fell to their knees. Her court gasped and the children stood together in a huddle.

'Ailenor, I must speak to you privately,' Henry said. His voice was gentle but seeing his face so sad, her heart seemed to stop beating.

'Are we about to be attacked?' She could think of no other reason for his unexpected appearance.

'No,' he said. His knights were dismounting. The smell of horse and sweat cut through that of actor's paint and the apple blossom that decorated the courtyard.

Ailenor turned to her ladies and said firmly, 'There is to be no more today. The servants will lay out our feast.' She pointed to where kitchen help, who were already covering trestles with cloth and beginning to place cups and goblets on them, had fallen to their knees. She signalled to them to rise and continue. Touching Henry's hand and saying, 'A moment, please.' She hurried forward to the actors and said, 'It was a fine play. Join the feast. Our steward will grant you places. Perhaps the children could look more closely at your costumes?' Her eyes searched out Nell, whose face showed the confusion she herself felt. 'Nell, look after the children. Henry and I must speak privately. I fear bad news.'

'Papa,' Edward exclaimed, breaking from the group of children and running to Henry. 'You're back.'

'Not now, Edward,' Henry said in a voice that was sobering. 'Look after your sisters. I must speak with your mother first.'

The actor who played King Arthur knelt down to the children, 'My Lord Edward, would you like to come to our dressing room and see our swords?' Ailenor gratefully nodded.

Nell ushered the children to the cart where the actors with great reverence allowed the older children to try on masks and hold blunted daggers and swords. The knights silently took their horses to the second courtyard away from the actors' cart.

'Come, Henry,' Ailenor said, once all seemed calm again. She led him through a gate into the orchard. 'We are private here. Now tell me what this is all about.'

Henry's face slowly turned ashen as he told her her father had

261

died. It had taken a whole month for the news to reach Henry on the Welsh borders. As he held her in his arms, he promised her that no expense would be spared on Count Raymond's behalf. They would return to London and services would be held in every Church for his soul. Alms would be distributed to the poor. There would be a period of mourning. His beloved father-in-law, Raymond Beranger, was surely already by God's side.

This news broke her heart. She passed hours on her knees in candle-light before the altar in the small Lady Chapel adjoining her apartment. Only Lady Willelma and Lady Mary served her. It was Henry, Nell, and Rosalind who saw life carried on as before in the palace.

When Ailenor returned to the world she was composed but her heart remained heavy. Nell returned to Kenilworth a few days later. Woodstock fell quiet as Ailenor made ready to remove to Westminster where Sancha and Richard would join them in solemn mourning. Wales, Henry assured her, had been brought under control. It was not necessary for him to return to the borders. It was a small consolation for the loss of her father but she was glad of Henry's consideration of her feelings and she loved him all the more for it.

During October, as leaves swirled golden from the trees lining the riverbank, Ailenor and Sancha received a long worrying letter from their mother. Their sister, Beatrice, was to be their father's heiress. She inherited all. Provence would be Beatrice's dowry. Ailenor read the letter, feeling as unsettled as the swirling autumn leaves outside in the courtyard. *It may come to you as unexpected*, their mother wrote, *but Provence cannot be divided, nor can the province belong to France or England. Beatrice will be its new countess as she is our only daughter unwed.* Ailenor felt resentful.

'At least France doesn't have it,' Henry said, with a satisfied smile after he read Countess Beatrice's letter.

'That depends on who marries Beatrice, doesn't it?' Ailenor replied.

'Are there any French princes available?' Sancha remarked.

'There's Charles of Anjou. He's the White Queen's youngest,' Ailenor said.

Henry scowled. 'Well, we have none to offer. Not Edward. He's too young and he's destined for greater than a princess of Provence.'

Ailenor, feathers ruffled at this foolish remark, retorted, 'Princesses of Provence are valuable princesses, as you well know, Henry, but in any case no child can wed his aunt.'

She was pleased to note how Henry looked suitably chastened, his face red and his shoulders slumping. He opened his hands, palms turned upwards. 'Of course, of course, my beloved Ailenor.'

Chapter Twenty-eight

Winter 1246

Snow blew in from the east covering England with its white softness. Ailenor and Sancha retired to Windsor to be with Ailenor's children. Sancha confided tearfully that her pregnancy of the previous summer had not lasted longer than three months.

'It took me a long time to get pregnant with Edward,' Ailenor said, trying to comfort her sister. 'And now I have four healthy children. You have much time to conceive.'

'Richard is away, either involved with the new royal mints or in Cornwall or Wales. I don't see my husband enough to get with child.'

'Travel with him.'

'I prefer to remain at home and watch the new abbey at Hailles grow. It eases my constant anxiety. I seek peace.' She glanced out of the window at the drifting snow and her tears fell.

Ailenor placed her hand over her sister's. 'In that case, Richard must seek peace too. He has a beautiful, sweet wife.'

As Sancha clung to her, she held her unhappy, weeping sister.

Two days later a letter arrived for Ailenor, the second she had received from her mother since Papa's death. She called Sancha to the hearth, ordered wine to be poured and cakes served. Looking up from the letter into Sancha's patient eyes, she said, 'How can I tell Henry this news. Beatrice is married to Charles of Anjou, Louis's brother, and Charles, is, by all accounts, utterly indulged, totally spoiled, and not very nice.'

Sancha's mouth opened and closed like a beautiful bird's beak. 'What else does our mother say?'

Ailenor studied the letter again. Sancha bit into a cake, the crumbs falling carelessly onto her rose-coloured velvet gown.

'Charles will provide protection, she says, by which she means France's protection. Raymond of Toulouse has been pursuing her too.'

'That old goat. I can understand her fear. Well,' Sancha said through another dainty mouthful of cake, 'France is quick to the field. She has inherited our homeland, all of it. And she's only thirteen.'

'Our dear, loving Mother has betrayed us. Let me read on . . .' Ailenor studied her mother's letter. She looked up. 'Here is the real reason this has happened. King James of Aragon brought an army up to Aix to claim Beatrice for his son. Huh, another greedy toad.' She started to shake with laughter at the absurdity of it all. 'What a catch our sister has been. Emperor Frederick, too, wanted her for Conrad, his son. He has sent a fleet for her.'

Sancha lifted her goblet and swallowed a large amount of Malmsey before saying, 'What did Mother do about that?'

'She ordered all her ports to refuse his landing. She placed Beatrice under the Pope's protection and whipped our sister off to Lyon . . . accompanied by Uncle Peter, no less. The Pope sent for the White Queen and Charles of Anjou, having decided that Beatrice ought to wed Charles for her safety. In return, King Louis will protect the Pope from the Great Serpent, as he calls Emperor Frederick. Because . . . oh, no . . . Frederick moved a land army to Lyon once he heard that Beatrice was there. He's determined!' Ailenor reached for her goblet. 'Oh, listen on, they sought refuge in the monastery at Cluny. They are safe.' She crossed herself. 'Praise God. Charles and Uncle Peter fetched Beatrice themselves to Cluny with an armed troop. It's done. They were married in January.' She threw the missive down. 'Henry will have much to say about this marriage.'

'I wonder what Richard will think of it all.'

Ailenor smiled. 'Not a lot, I imagine. Henry suspected something like this would happen, which is why he sent Uncle Peter to them. He thinks we can control castles in Savoy in return for further marriages between Savoyard heiresses and English heirs so it's not so bad. We shall have at least one of our cousins here married to Edmund de Lacy or John de Warenne.'

'Why?' asked Sancha, looking mystified.

'Sancha, don't you see it?' Lovely, cultured Sancha was slow to understand political manoeuvres. 'Because, sister, Henry can control the Alpine passes and decide whether or not to allow Emperor Frederick through to attack France or the Pope or both.'

'Would he really do that, let Emperor Frederick attack the Pope?'

'Probably not, as he would bring France's wrath down on us, but he *could* if ever Louis attacked Gascony.'

That month, Alice de Saluzzo, Amadeus of Savoy's granddaughter, journeyed to England with Uncle Peter, to marry Edmund de Lacy, a handsome flaxen-headed youth of only seventeen years who was heir to Lincoln. Uncle Peter and Henry were manipulating English interests in Savoy as well as furthering Savoyard interests in England. Ailenor was pleased more cousins were coming to England, though she recognised how the English barons seethed as this match was made. Clearly they worried other foreign marriages would follow.

Not long after Uncle Peter arrived in England with Alice de Saluzzo, Ailenor and Henry received sad news. Isabella, Henry's mother, died at Fontevraud Abbey. Henry grieved for her deeply, spending hours on his knees in his private chapel, ordering alms distributed and candles lit day and night in her memory. At the end of her life, Isabella had dwelled in a small cell hidden within the abbey for her own protection. She was accused of organising an attempted poisoning of Louis in Paris and had barely escaped to the abbey with her life.

The embroidery workshop at Westminster was busy day and night working on new garments for Alice de Saluzzo and her train. The expectation of a wedding in the family lifted Henry's spirits after his mother's sorrowful death. A relic he had purchased from Constantinople, a vial believed to contain drops of Christ's precious blood, made him forget his mother's death for a time, though he blamed

Spanish Blanche, the French Queen-mother, for it. His mother was innocent of the poisoning. She would not have endangered her immortal soul by committing such a wicked deed. Ailenor was not so sure.

The wedding ceremony was held within the Cathedral of Lincoln on a sun-blessed day in May.

'Did she?' Sancha said to Ailenor as the sisters snatched a few moments in the de Lacy castle's garden before the banquet was served. 'I mean, did Isabella really arrange to have Louis poisoned? They say she bribed his cooks.'

Ailenor drew Sancha towards the rose hedging, carefully eying Henry, his head bent in conversation with Robert Grosseteste, Bishop of Lincoln, and Earl Simon, the Bishop's dear friend. She lowered her voice. 'I don't want to think Isabella responsible for such a terrible act. Henry denies it, but perhaps she did. It would not surprise me.'

'Richard said the King's cooks confessed. They were boiled alive.'

Ailenor shuddered despite the warmth of the afternoon. 'I heard that story too. Henry says it is speculation, but King Louis has been unlucky. During the war against him in Gascony villagers poisoned wells and when his men drank the water they suffered dysentery. Louis was ill then, too, for weeks.'

'I do remember hearing that story. We were frightened to travel from Provence to Gascony. Villagers might have taken against us and poisoned me too.' She shuddered.

'Nonsense. They all love a wedding. You were not pillaging their lands.'

Ailenor led Sancha back to the company. She studied the bride and her young husband. Alice was gowned in blue satin embroidered with golden thread, the embroidery work completed in the Westminster workshop. It pleased her that the de Lacys had gathered around them the most elegant court in Christendom. 'I suspect Henry might arrange marriages for his own siblings, now Isabella is dead,' she said.

'Then,' said Sancha. 'I am glad we shall have our own cousins married well before he favours the Lusignans.'

Richard would have remarked on this possibility, of course. After all, the Lusignan stepbrothers and sisters were his half-siblings too. Ailenor glanced down at Sancha's burgundy gown. Could her sister be with child?

'I know what you are thinking, Ailenor,' Sancha said quickly. 'As I told you, he's always away.' She glanced over at her husband who was congratulating the bride.

Ailenor took her hand. 'Soon, I hope.'

Sancha removed her hand and changing the subject said, 'Is it true that Earl Simon is to return to Gascony?'

'Yes, as Gascony's governor. He is the only one who can manage the warring nobles there. There are so many disputes,' said Ailenor. She sighed. 'I'll miss Nell when they depart.'

A month later the court visited Beaulieu Abbey for the abbey's consecration ceremony. On the day of the abbey's consecration, Edward collapsed, pale as a beached codfish. He was attended by the abbey's infirmarer and made comfortable in the guesthouse close to the infirmary

For two days Edward lay in a fever. Ailenor was afraid they would lose her beautiful son. She could not leave him. Henry though could not stay. The successful Welsh campaign of the previous year had that winter turned into a shameful disaster when the Welsh prince Llewelyn decided to attack the border castles again. Henry had to return to Wales.

The young princely brothers had united. The Welsh were advancing.

Although Ailenor wanted to stay with Edward until he made a full recovery, the Abbot was not accommodating. The Cistercians did not permit women in their abbey. She determined to remain by her child's side until he recovered and Henry, due to set out for Wales, agreed. After Candlemas, they'd heard of Dafydd's death. Owen and Llewelyn, Gruffydd's sons and Dafydd's nephews, were now joint rulers in Wales. They were harassing Henry's new castle of Deganwy in revenge for the sacking of the Cistercian Abbey of Aberconwy during the previous summer.

On the day the court was to retire to Winchester, Ailenor, Henry and their retainers gathered by the abbey gate ready to depart. Ailenor said firmly that she was staying with Edward. The Abbot wailed to Ailenor, 'Your Grace, you cannot be accommodated here. It is against our Cistercian Rule. No woman stays in this abbey. We shall care for Prince Edward. He has taken a chill and has a raw throat. Our infirmary has remedies for both. Return to Winchester with the King and Earl Richard.'

Ailenor stiffened, set her shoulders, and looked the Abbot in the eye. 'You will bend your rules for your future King. I and my Lady Willelma will take up residence within the abbey precinct to nurse Lord Edward. The rest of the court will return to Winchester. Let this be my final word on the matter. Have a guest room prepared for myself and my lady close to Lord Edward's chamber.'

The Abbot appealed to Henry, 'Why cannot the tutor stay to look after the boy? He is his guardian after all.' He stopped short of suggesting that Henry, himself, took responsibility for Edward.

Henry's forehead creased. 'Lord Abbot, your abbey has been received by God. My father endowed it, as shall I. There is no care such as a mother's care for her child. The Queen will remain with her lady to attend her. This is my demand. Heed it. It is as God would wish.'

He pointed to the Abbot's large manor house on the opposite side of the river. 'My guards shall lodge there, as will members of Lord Edward's household, but the Queen remains within the abbey walls, close to the infirmary, with our son. That is my final word on the matter.'

With impatience, the King swept his cloak over his arm. Ailenor noted his eyelid drooping. Henry was near to losing his temper with the Abbot. She stepped between them. 'My husband, the King, has urgent matters in Wales to which he must attend and I . . . I am returning to my son's bedside.'

Stiffly, she withdrew from the silent group by the abbey gateway.

The Cistercians signed with hands and expressions. With the exception of the Abbot, who only spoke on rare occasions, there was no conversation spoken. Ailenor walked sedately through an archway, past groups of monks with fluttering hands, and entered the cloisters with Lady Willelma hurrying after her. Not a word was spoken until they reached the abbey's guesthouse. She was aware of shuffling, of bees humming, of the breeze catching at foliage, and of Edward's coughing. She had done the right thing.

Henry came to say goodbye to them before his departure. He was brief. Out of respect for the abbey's silence, he lowered his voice. 'He's agreed to your stay and is readying a chamber for you. Guard our son well.'

'You would consider,' she confided to Willelma when Henry had gone, 'that after two days of Beaulieu Abbey having been overrun by noisy courtiers, the Abbot would be relieved that the court no longer invaded his palace or occupied his Hall and bedchambers, eating fish from his ponds and mutton provided by his sheep.'

'Well, he's agreed, if with reluctance,' Willelma said.

'Thank God for that.'

Ailenor well knew her responsibility. Henry trusted her to bring Edward to full recovery and she would. When Willelma relieved her watch, Ailenor hurried through the shady cloisters to the great church where she found a chapel dedicated to Lady Mary. 'You, at least, are permitted ground here,' she murmured to the stone figure.

Falling onto her knees before the Madonna, she prayed for her son's recovery. Using her amber beads, she counted off Pater Nosters.

A week passed during which Edward sometimes lapsed back into fever, too weak to speak coherently. The Abbey's apothecary wanted to bleed the Prince, but Ailenor insisted that blood-letting would weaken her son further and forbade it.

Willelma comforted her. 'God is watching over him. His saint smiles upon him. Lord Edward will recover. Look how the warmed wine with poppy, honey, aloe saffron, balsam, and cloves helps him sleep and soothes his cough. His fever is gone.'

Ailenor gave her friend a fragile smile. 'Whilst the herbalist is without doubt in possession of good sense, make sure you know precisely what he has put into his unguents and potions.'

She leaned over Edward and discovered his breathing to be easier. He was cooler. She left him with Willelma and entered the Abbey chapel to thank the Lady Mary. Edward was sleeping peacefully, thanks to the herbalist's soothing paulinum.

Edward's tutor came to visit Edward later that day hoping he was well enough to travel to Winchester. He diligently crossed the bridge daily from the Abbot's manor to the Abbey guesthouse to visit his charge.

After he had glanced at the sleeping prince, Ailenor drew him out into the cloisters and said in a low voice, 'Edward is still too weak to be moved.'

Monks walking to Vespers avoided them, taking a longer route than they normally chose. None came to her to ask how the Prince was today. 'You'd think they would care,' she said.

They watched the monks enter the chapel and the Abbot flying after them.

The tutor shook his head and smiled a cynical smile. 'He's late for his prayers.' After they'd all disappeared through the chapel door, he laid out his mantle on a stone bench for Ailenor to sit upon. 'Tell me, your Grace, can Lord Edward eat? He's still pale as a root in the ground.'

'Sips of broth only. Not much else. Goat's milk with honey today.'

'Try mashed mutton and ask for possets of hyssop and juniper. My mother swore by such remedies.' He thought for a moment and added, 'Your Grace, are you keeping up your own strength?'

'The Abbot sends us fine dishes but I lack hunger.'

'You must eat for your child's sake and for your own. Take air in the garden? The weather is fine, not too hot and not too chill. There's a gentle breeze today to lift your spirits. Summer is here with all its pleasant scents.'

'I shall think on it.' She knew she would enjoy the herbal garden but would the silent monks condone her presence there or avoid her as they did if she entered the cloisters? Would hands flutter with outrage that she had disturbed their peace?

Another week crawled by. By its end, Edward was able to sit up propped with pillows. She had listened to the tutor's advice and took Edward into the sweetly scented herb garden every day. In the pleasant garden, she read to him from her psalter and pointed out flowers that grew amongst the herbs. Three weeks after she entered Beaulieu Abbey, Edward was recovered. Relieved beyond words, she sent a monk to fetch the tutor from the Abbot's residence. They could travel at last.

When her carriage and escort arrived, the Abbot said, 'Your Grace, Lord Edward is fortunate to have such a mother. The Lady Mary could not have watched over our Lord as well as you have your son. God be praised.' Even though his words were kindly she knew he was relieved they were taking her recovered son away because she and her lady would leave too.

'Lord Abbot, remember there is no love like a mother's love and nothing heals as well as a mother's prayer.' The Abbot's face was inscrutable, his smile insincere. Well, thought Ailenor, he did not like being told this, even by his Queen.

She hurried them, Willelma, Edward, and his tutor, into the royal wagon that was curtained and painted vividly with the lions of England. Her only words were, 'Time we were on our way.'

Last to enter the comfortable cushioned carriage, she inclined her head to the Abbot and pleased to leave Beaulieu at last, Ailenor did not look back once at the silent, bowing monks.

Chapter Twenty-nine

Summer 1249

Wales settled down. Henry returned to his building projects. Ailenor pored over designs for a pleasure garden she was designing for Clarendon Palace which Henry had granted to her as a new residence.

She was lost in thought when Henry burst into the closet where she was working. At once she swept her plans to one side and glanced up. Henry was red-faced and irritable. What was it this time?

'What's the matter? Come, tell me outside,' she said in a quiet voice as if she were speaking to a miserable child. Snatching up her cloak she suggested they walked in the gardens below. He nodded without a word and followed her down the outer staircase.

They strolled along the perimeter of the new Hall, admiring its silver-grey patterned windows. During the previous winter, Henry had ordered a major refurbishment at Clarendon especially for her to use as a residence second to Windsor. As well as a new hall, Ailenor enjoyed a newly decorated chapel, three chambers, and an enormous wardrobe chamber, as well as a two-storey privy chamber adjacent to her spacious private apartments. After approving plans for the garden Henry said, his eye twitching and anxiety creeping into his voice, 'I shall have to return to Westminster, Ailenor. There's trouble in Gascony. The Solers and Columbines draw family connections into disputes . . . Again!' He buried his head in his hands and sank onto a stone bench. 'I need money. And I want Earl Simon to crack down on these rebels and in Bordeaux. He's not agreeing.' Unsurprised, she raised an eyebrow. Henry was so ungrateful for Simon's help. Henry raged on, his face redder and redder. 'They are fighting in the town. It must stop. They are destroying trade, destroying Gascony!'

'Insist that Simon goes there and stops it,' she said calmly, sinking down beside him, dabbing at her forehead with her veil. It was a hot day and she could do without Henry's tantrums. The veil fluttered around her plait as her hand flew to her mouth. She had remembered that which Henry had forgotten. 'Simon and Nell have taken the Cross. That's the reason he hesitates. They plan to join King Louis's Crusade.'

'What!' He turned to face her. 'You must persuade Nell that Simon goes to Gascony.' As Henry became more insistent, she moved along the bench to avoid his spittle. 'Edward's inheritance, remember! Write to them. Hunting at Windsor this September. That's it. Simon enjoys hunting and you can work on Nell's cooperation. I'm counting on you, Ailenor. We shall make their stay persuasive.' He reached for Ailenor and took hold of her arm, pressing hard. There would be a bruise. 'Simon enjoys feasting too. We'll discuss Gascony with them.'

She gently removed his hand. 'It would be pleasant to have Nell's company. She can bring her boys. Edward and Hal can hunt together. Did you know, your son butchered a stag yesterday . . . out in the forest? He's ten years old! Hal's only a year older and I believe he's keen on the hunt.'

'I have heard.' Henry shook his curling locks. She smiled. Her husband, a handsome healthy man still in his prime, was not a great huntsman. However, Edward, well, he was already tall, long-legged, and strong, Longshanks they called him with affection. She was sure he would be an impressive king one day, though not for decades yet. 'And Nell?' Henry added, his voice, already insistent, rising a few notes. 'You'll write to her?'

'Of course. I won't mention crusading.' She fingered her plait and gave him a firm look. 'This means, Henry, you need to fund Simon if he agrees to govern Gascony, provide him with troops if he has to besiege their castles.'

'He will have a commission to keep order there. I want him in Gascony and Bordeaux for seven years.'

'Seven years is a very long stretch. Henry, be careful. Simon is much loved by Louis. Never forget he is French.'

'If he values his English properties and if he loves my sister, he knows where his fealty lies.' Henry rose abruptly, saying, 'I leave for Westminster tomorrow. Write to Nell today.' He swept off, his curling hair, grey sprinkling the brown, dancing on his collar. At least, she posited, he was in a better mood than when he'd interrupted her earlier. She would write the letter this afternoon. The pleasure garden must wait.

'I'll only go to Gascony if assured I can finish the job I set out to do,' Simon insisted as he cantered alongside Henry. Ailenor riding behind with Nell nudged her mare forward into a faster canter and said, 'I believe you will have complete control.'

Henry said, 'You will manage the province's revenues. I can grant you a thousand sovereigns and fifty knights a year for service. You'll be reimbursed for anything you spend on castles and fortifications. The tenure would run for seven years. You will make decisions for me and you'll be Viceroy in complete control of Gascony.'

Simon drew a deep breath. Ailenor held her reins tightly and her breath. She noted that Nell smiled her approval. Nell had not wanted to go on the French Crusade. It was Simon's idea. He had been successful in the Holy Land years before and he was much loved there. Nell confided to Ailenor that it would be a harsh place to take their children. She would miss them if parted from her boys. At last Simon exhaled.

'Yes,' he said, 'what do you think, Nell? Shall we accept? Gascony is not so far away and we can return to Kenilworth from time to time. We'll send the older boys to Lincoln for their education.'

'Aye, it is for the best,' Nell said.

Henry looked joyful. Ailenor said, 'I've planned a feast for tonight for Michaelmas. Now this is agreed, Nell, you must tell me how Rosalind fares? Do you think she would accompany you to

275

Bordeaux? I imagine Thomas, now he's a knight, will accompany Simon.'

'I'd like to have her company.' Nell said.

Simon and Nell sailed to Gascony in October and returned in December. That year, Christmas was held in Winchester. Henry was pleased with Simon. Ailenor was even more pleased to pass relaxed, pleasurable hours with Nell and Rosalind in her bower at Winchester Castle, knowing that Edward's inheritance was safe in Earl Simon's care.

She drew them to her embroidery frame and shooed her women away to work on Christmastide favours. When they were settled with their work baskets opened, she asked about Gascony. 'So how did you find Bordeaux? How was the shadowy palace, Nell? Rosalind, did you enjoy meeting the embroideresses you knew from all those years ago?'

'So many questions, Ailenor,' Nell said as she took the stool nearest the window to get the best light. 'What lovely work,' she exclaimed. Rosalind agreed and approved the design. Ailenor smiled widely, enjoying their approval. Ailenor and her ladies were working on an intricate hanging for her chapel depicting the miracle of loaves and fishes. She may be a queen but she was also a woman who loved to create beautiful things. Nell threaded her needle and pulled a silver thread through a fish's gill. 'So many fishes to stitch and so much silver. It will take many Christmases to finish. You answer first, Rosalind. Gascony? What do you think?' The way Nell said it implied the Palais des Ombres in Bordeaux was not an easy place to be these days.

Rosalind snipped a silken length from a long string of gold thread. She threaded her own needle before replying, 'I did, Your Grace. I met them all. They are seven years older now, of course, and many have babies and husbands. They thrive, though in truth, they are all frightened by the disputes between the Soler and Columbine families. Husbands belong to these families but, Your Grace, the women do try to rise above the disputes which often are over family castles, land, and vineyards.' She looked earnest. 'They avoid the quarrels but it's hard if a member of one family is killed by one of the other. When that happens the atmosphere in the city is revengeful and the women are not permitted to speak to each other. If their lords are enemies, they are at odds.'

Rosalind smiled. 'However, when they all came for a celebration at the palace, dining on cakes and wine, quarrels were forgotten and it was as if they united over embroidery.'

Ailenor fiddled with her needle. Rosalind leaned across and threaded it for her, a gentle gesture that touched the Queen.

Resuming her work, Rosalind said, 'Thomas accompanied Earl Simon into the countryside where barons are waylaying travellers. He locked some of them up. Thomas says they deserved it.' She smiled. 'They didn't get out for Christmas without paying ransoms.'

'Yes,' Nell added. 'Ailenor, he is ruthless. Simon wants permission to crush all your other enemies in the province when we return to Gascony.'

'I thought terms were such that Simon has total control. Surely, Henry trusts him,' Ailenor said, making a dainty stitch into her fish. She smiled. 'Let's give these fish popping eyes.' She found she was giggling like a girl. 'Black thread, Rosalind, for the eyes.'

How pleasant it was to be in the company of women again, these women whom she loved. She found herself blinking back tears, 'You will both go back there too soon. That saddens me. As for me, I shall have to entertain Henry's half-brothers from Poitou. They are coming for an Eastertide visit.'

'All of them?' Nell said.

'No, just Aymer and Geoffrey and Guy.' She lowered her tone so her ladies across the large room could not hear her. 'They are loud and arrogant, just like Gilbert Marshal used to be, God rest his soul. Last year, when they visited us, they sought quarrels. I pray that they never come here indefinitely.' She shuddered at the memory of how Guy had tried to challenge Richard de Clare to a tournament and Henry forbade it, not out of concern for Richard de Clare, but for his half-brother, Guy, because he was not as able a horseman. 'I hear that the older one, William, is the worst of those nephews.' She grimaced. 'I hope he never comes to us.'

'They might all descend upon Henry's court one day. Their father has joined Louis's Crusade,' Nell said as she pulled a length of black thread from a spool. 'We shall have to keep William of Lusignan busy fighting for Simon. If he doesn't fight for Gascony they'll lose their castles. The White Queen is regent now Louis is gone on Crusade. She has long had her eye on Lusignan castles in Poitou.' Nell had set her face with a determined look.

This was news to Ailenor. 'But Simon extended the peace with France in November. You even went to Paris to catch Louis before he departed for Marseilles. Would Blanche dare penalise Henry's brothers?'

'She has a way of taking property on very slight pretexts. And, after all, Poitou is not Gascony. The Lusignans do homage to France.'

'I suppose,' Ailenor said pensively. 'Henry thinks by entertaining his half-brothers, he is keeping them loyal to him. I wish they were less unruly and selfish. They manipulate Henry.'

'We shall endeavour to keep them out of England,' Nell said. She glanced towards the bench close to the fire where Ailenor's ladies were busy making pomanders. 'Something smells good. There's the scent of oranges and cloves.' She breathed deeply. 'How I love Christmastide.'

But Ailenor could not let the conversation leave those detestable brothers. She said with anger, 'At least we can celebrate this one without those awful brothers playacting here, upsetting our children with their swearing, imbibing too much, and making crude jokes.' She knew in her heart one day they would come, stay for ever, and steal away her husband's affection. He adored them. He never had a proper mother so Isabella's second family was important to him. Ailenor lived in dread of them disturbing her peace.

Nell said, 'They are my half-brothers too. My mother is their mother. Even so, I feel nothing for them.'

'As well you don't, Nell. They are trouble.'

Spring arrived. The Lusignans came and went. Ailenor was glad to see them sail away. They had imposed themselves on the court for several months and their presence felt as if they were an invading army rather than three arrogant coltish youths.

After the brothers returned to Poitou, Ailenor travelled to Clarendon with her whole family including their nurses and a bevy of ladies. Clarendon was filled with activity, happy voices and pleasure. The weather was hot with endless blue skies so day after day she donned a sunhat and wore airy light silk gowns. She held courts of love, rode across meadows surrounding the castle, and enjoyed her children's company. Edward was ten years old. He loved to ride out with the squires, jump hedgerows and hunt with his falcon, Wolf, proudly perched on his wrist.

'It's not going well in Gascony,' Henry said in a complaining tone as they sat in the pleasure garden at Clarendon. 'An uprising has burst out again in Bordeaux city. It's spread into the countryside.'

She closed her eyes. This was not good. 'What has happened?' she asked without opening them.

'Gaston de Bearn, your own cousin, has attacked lands he claims on the border with Navarre and Gascony. The nobles are resisting to protect their castles. He is behaving like a brigand, waylaying clergy and nobles and causing terror by besieging them. Simon, after a successful ambush, has had him taken. My dear, he's sending him to us here in Clarendon for judgement.'

'You must deal with him firmly. He may be my cousin but he's not liked by my family. I remember my mother saying he was destined to be a brigand one day.' She pursed her lips. 'Though I expect he'll come here all charm, begging forgiveness.'

'Simon wants me to disinherit him. I can't do that, Ailenor. It would make it worse. He has supporters.'

Ailenor shrugged. 'It does seem extreme to disinherit him. He needs a firm warning.' She was pregnant again and, happy, was prepared to be generous-hearted, even towards this Gascon rogue.

When he appeared at their court, Henry and Ailenor both found the handsome, dark-eyed, witty Gaston charming. They enjoyed his tales of adventure. They listened to his complaints about Earl Simon. He was given a freshly painted chamber in the old palace, servants to attend his every need, and a horse to use whilst their guest or prisoner; Ailenor could not decide which. He made himself popular with Lord Edward, whom he taught to skin rabbits and to sword-fight with skill. As Lammas approached with her cousin flattering her, attending to her fluttering ladies, flirting with them all and making himself indispensable, Ailenor's shrewd guard weakened further. She was saddened when Henry sent him home without even one charge laid before him. In September, a furious letter came from Earl Simon. Henry was storing up future trouble by releasing Gaston de Bearn.

Chapter Thirty

1249 – 1250

Nell did not come for Christmas. The season passed quietly, or would have, if Henry's dreadful half-brothers had not arrived in England to disturb Ailenor's peace. The year turned and Simon wrote to Henry asking for money: *marauding bands of knights from Southern Gascony, led by Gaston de Bearn, are once again looking to increase their lands by war. He has not kept the peace.*

'They plan,' Henry said to Ailenor as he stared at Simon's letter, 'to strike in large bands to burn, pillage, plunder and hold citizens to ransom. Simon wants to take even harsher measures with them.' Henry thrust out his chest and laughed. 'There are complaints about Simon's ferocity.' Henry closed the letter. 'He brings this state of affairs on himself. He wants to strengthen castles. What *is* he doing with all the coin I sent him to manage affairs for us? I'm sending accountants to check up on him.'

Ailenor closed her eyes. 'I know about all this. You told Simon to be ruthless. We were duped by my cousin Gaston and his honeyed words. Nell is with child again.' She sighed and opened her eyes. 'Simon is apparently harsh with her too these days.'

'Nell is not on his side?' Henry's eyes widened.

'Is this about sides, Henry? Really? Anyway, this is different. Simon likes the Franciscans and has taken one of them on as his confessor. Nell has upset the Franciscan clergy by being outspoken to her husband, by wearing gold, pearls, and costly gowns. I doubt though she would be overly jewelled whilst carrying a child.'

Henry laughed. 'Some women over-reach themselves. They should support their husbands. She could sell her jewels and help her husband out of his financial difficulty and he should tame the bullying knights he speaks of with treaty, not attack.'

Ailenor found her hand touching her jewelled hair net. 'That's not fair, Henry. Nell says he has borrowed from Italian bankers. You promised to pay Simon for his troops and defences.'

'I hope I'm not surety for his loan this time.' Henry's tone was as brittle as the tree branches scratching the window panes outside their chamber. 'There's another matter, Ailenor.'

She felt her eyes narrowing. It would be the Lusignan brothers again. They were still at court. Ailenor could not decide which was worse – Gascon youngbloods or the Lusignan brothers. Hugh, their father, had accompanied King Louis on Crusade and it had gone badly. News had come that Louis faced defeat and Hugh de Lusignan had died in his campaign. The boys were orphaned. Since January, Henry had been more indulgent towards them than ever. 'Well?' she asked.

Henry beamed a wide grin. 'I intend taking the Cross, in Westminster in front of the Archbishop on the sixth day of this month. I will give myself four years to plan it, by which time I shall have Church funds gathered in our coffers.'

'What?' she gasped. 'Jesu, Henry, Louis's Crusade has been a disaster. My sister is there with a little baby recently born in Egypt. Louis is in retreat. You want to take the Cross and become embroiled in all this? God will be happy with the new abbey at Westminster.'

'God wants his holy city returned to us.' He shrugged. 'Louis will recover. He captured Damietta after all, the most important city in the Principalities.'

'He was routed at Mansoura. So many deaths and carnage and beheadings. Englishmen died as well as French knights. Your uncle Longespee died. Hugh Lusignan is dead. By Saint Bridget's veil, what else can happen?'

'The rout is only a setback.' he insisted. 'God is on Louis's side. And the Church will pay.'

Ailenor secretly wondered if Henry taking the Cross was another way to extract money from the clergy. She dropped her arguments, became resigned, and doubted he would ever set out. She had other battles to fight and win.

What Ailenor dreaded came about. The Lusignans had come for Christmastide and never left. Worse, the Bishop of Winchester, who had replaced Ailenor's Uncle Boniface when he was appointed to Canterbury as Archbishop, had died. Now Winchester was vacant again, Henry saw an opportunity to further family interests, this time using the Lusignan brothers. He appointed Aymer of Valence, his half-brother, to the See. Aymer de Valence was not even thirty years old.

'He's ignorant,' Ailenor protested to Henry, hissing at him through her teeth whilst still kneeling after prayers in their chapel in Windsor Castle. 'Uncle Boniface won't like it, nor will the monks of Winchester.'

'You said similar about your Uncle Boniface once and just look how successful he has been as Archbishop of Canterbury.'

'It's different,' she retorted. 'He, at least, was cultured when he came to us. The Winchester monks will never agree to Aymer. Uncle Boniface met Aymer at Christmas and he was shocked by his ignorance of scripture.'

'I recollect a time when you said Boniface was lacking scripture.' Henry threw the sentiment at her. She gave him a furious glare in return.

The quarrel continued all morning with Ailenor angrily pushing Henry out of her bed, meeting him after breakfast when they finally prayed in their private chapel for guidance over Aymer's appointment.

Henry said at last, 'I shall hold the See and its revenues open until the monks agree to appoint him. They'll do as I request.'

'You are favouring your relatives. It is wrong,' she hissed into his ear.

Henry clasped her hand so hard his knuckles were white as the bones beneath the skin. 'As indeed I have favoured your own relatives.' He pressed harder on her hand.

'From what? Let go, Henry. You are going to break my hand into two.' He loosened her fingers which she shook, looked towards the beautiful coloured window above, turned to him and said, 'My uncles are cultured, educated, and appreciate beauty such as that window up there, filled with scripture and the music a choir has just sung in praise of our Lord. They are polite and sensitive. That is the difference.'

'You would do well, Ailenor, to keep your opinions to yourself as a wife ought and focus on our daughter's forthcoming marriage to Alexander of Scotland.'

Ailenor swept from the chapel, leaving him kneeling in a pool of coloured light. She had not meant for the quarrel to spill over into a holy place but it had.

She could not like Henry's half-brothers. There had been trouble with them. The previous winter, William of Valence, Aymer's older brother, had returned from serving as a knight with Earl Simon. He badly injured an English knight during one of the forbidden tournaments. Henry stoked the barons' resentment by not punishing William and now he would further annoy everyone by appointing Aymer, equally unpleasant, to Winchester.

Temporarily chastened, Ailenor decided she *would* think about Margaret whose marriage to Alexander of Scotland was due to take place in December. She would be aloof when William and Aymer came to court. As for Guy, she utterly detested the spiky fair-headed young man, who had appalling table manners and even worse breath. He over-imbibed. He gossiped. He spat in her presence. How could Henry tolerate them?

Thinking about her daughter's wedding led her to wonder what marriages Henry might consider for William and Guy. What wards were available? There were, of course, the Marshal heiresses. If William was married off to the eldest Marshal girl, he might disappear to Pembroke Castle, a good idea. What strategy might rid her of the rest? She massaged her forehead with two fingers circling them around and around. It was no good. Henry was determined and the hideous Aymer was here to stay.

By May Day, as she'd predicted, Henry had organised a marriage for William of Valence, marrying him to Joan de Munchensi, the granddaughter of William Marshal. Joan's grandmother had been Isobel de Clare, Countess of Pembroke, and this meant Countess Joan was the co-heiress to the Marshal estates.

Satisfied, he said, 'I have Alix and Mary to consider, my half-brother Hugh's daughters. I'll provide for them too.' Ailenor winced when Henry reminded her of his half-nieces. More Lusignan weddings. More trouble. She remembered her father's advice, *Keep friends close but enemies closer*, when Henry said, 'You could use one as a Lady-in-Waiting until I find a suitable match for them. Mary is the younger. She's only nine and for now will remain in Poitou. But Alix is fifteen. She is of marriageable age. I might arrange a match with Gilbert de Clare for her.'

'What? He's a child, only eight, if I remember.' She drew breath. 'Alix may join my ladies,' Ailenor said, because she did not want another quarrel. 'She can join my junior ladies.'

Ailenor and Henry attended the magnificent wedding between the Marshal heiress Joan and his half-nephew William in Pembroke Castle. She was relieved when it was over and she could retreat to Marlborough for a month. She took Alix with her, having found the girl pleasanter than her uncles. Even so, the sooner Alix was wed, the better.

Ailenor thought much about Rosalind whilst she was at Marlborough, recollecting the time so many years before when the embroideress had been disgraced and sent to the Priory of St Helena. It was serendipity when a letter came from Rosalind. It had been delivered to Westminster and Henry, who was embroiled in the usual ongoing discontent to do with Church matters, sent the messenger to Marlborough with Ailenor's correspondence. She walked into the peaceful walled garden to read this rare letter privately.

Thomas is released from Knight's service with Earl Simon. We have returned to our manor of Midway. Who would have thought it? I am, at last, managing our estate. She wrote of her duties but she also said. *I pray every day for a third child . . .* Ailenor folded the letter and tucked it away into a cedar box where she stored all her correspondence. The line *I miss my Westminster workshop* touched her. Rosalind's name was legendary amongst those who worked in the embroidery workshop. She still owned fame as one of London's most accomplished embroiderers. Ailenor interlaced her fingers under her chin. Possibly, Rosalind might consider helping her with Margaret's wedding wardrobe. She would write to her. Yes, it was time to assemble Margaret's coffers in readiness for their journey to York in December.

Chapter Thirty-one

1250 – 1251

Ailenor did not want to lose Margaret to marriage, but Margaret would be a queen, and queens were God's representatives just like kings. Margaret would be dutiful and see how important her wedding was for good relations with Scotland. Ailenor dried her tears and prepared to be firm with her daughter.

The coming Christmas would be a happier occasion than the previous one had been. It had taken months for Ailenor to feel herself again. She had lost a baby a year earlier, just before Christmas. If losing a child had cracked open her heart, it made her even more protective of her living children – Edward, Margaret, Beatrice, and Edmund. Henry reminded her she was still young. They would have more children. She brightened as spring turned to summer. Margaret's forthcoming wedding was a distraction from sorrow and anger at Henry's halfbrothers' sense of self-importance.

That the Lusignan brood, apart from the beautiful dark-haired Alix, were away from court in Pembrokeshire with William and his new wife and, in Bishop Aymer's case, Winchester, improved her relationship with Henry. Even so, she checked her tongue around her husband, smiled at him with serenity and never complained; sound advice from her uncles, Peter and Boniface. There were other ways to get what she desired.

Ailenor ordered new gowns and linens for their daughter and talked with enthusiasm to Margaret about her wedding. Everyone must look extravagantly dressed if they were to impress on the Scots England's superiority. The whole court would travel to York at Christmas. When Nell wrote from Bordeaux promising they, too, would return for Margaret's wedding, Ailenor was delighted. It would not be the same without Nell and Simon.

Margaret remained understandably frightened. This change to her sheltered family life was too much for the child to take in, even though she appeared to others as resilient, self-possessed and understanding of her duty. For months, Margaret had insisted, 'Mama, I don't want to go to a kingdom of strangers. I want us all to stay together.' On those occasions Ailenor was at a loss how to respond and wondered if they had been too close a family. She felt deeply for Margaret's reluctance to become a bride in a strange, wild land but forced herself to reply, 'You are the child of the King and Queen. You shall make peace between our nations. We want this marriage and so must you.'

'I do want peace but I want us to be together for ever,' Margaret complained. 'I liked Wilton Abbey when we visited the nuns there. Mama, I want to be an abbess.'

'No, Margaret, you think that now. You are young.' She made herself look stern. 'Sadly, a princess must grow up. I was so happy with my mother and father of Provence, I wanted to live with them always when I was a little girl, but I came to England to marry your father. I was only two years older than you are now and I came without my parents. You, my sweeting, will travel to your wedding with us all in attendance.' She drew Margaret into her arms, thinking what a little thing she was. She leaned her chin on her daughter's dark head. 'I promise you will come south again to visit often. Edinburgh is not so far distant.' She paused, remembering the father she had never seen again and felt choked by emotion. Composing herself, she added, 'But I could never return to Provence.'

Margaret twisted from her mother's embrace. Ailenor winced as her daughter reminded her, 'Aunt Sancha is here. Grandmother Beatrice has come to England twice.'

'Yes, so you see, Meg, you will see us again soon.'

*

Once they returned to Windsor from Marlborough, Ailenor devoted attention to Margaret and let the other children take second place. Edward found companionship riding with his cousin Harry, Uncle Richard's son who was only a few years older than he. Edward was determined to beat Harry at swordplay and outride him, making Ailenor smile at his exploits. Six-year-old Edmund grew closer to his papa. Henry spoiled him, saw he had his favourite treat of barley sugar, and engaged with Edmund in games of merills which the boy enjoyed. Beatrice trailed around the castle after her older sister, begging scraps of material left over from Margaret's new gowns to stitch little garments for her poppets.

As July passed, Margaret, at last, responded to Ailenor's attentions. She appeared almost happy. By October she seemed to have forgotten their coming parting. Ailenor relaxed as she selected jewels and garments for her daughter's wardrobe.

'Quintises.' Ailenor lifted a length of burgundy quintise. Quintise was an imitation antique silky fabric that was soft and clinging. 'This is what you must wear after the ceremony. Your gown will be edged with gold and pearls and stitched with roses in gold thread.' She thought for a moment. 'Lady Rosalind is in London. Her father is stitching your Uncle Richard's surcoats. Why don't we send for her and ask if she can embroider this one gown with gold thread. She might sew pearls onto the sleeves which will be long, flowing and must have scalloped edges.' She studied Margaret's slim, undeveloped figure. Some of her gowns must be designed to allow her to grow into them. Quintises were perfect. 'So, my love, cloth of gold for your wedding day and quintise for afterwards. How think you, my sweet?'

'I like it well, Mama. I like the way the fabric moves as you move.' She made a small turn, pretending she was holding up the fashionable garment with her hand. She curtsied. 'My Lord Alexander,' she mimicked, 'I am pleased to meet you.' She spun around on her slippered heel to Ailenor. 'Shall I wear it long and trailing or with a jewelled belt?'

'You will wear these garments again and again in varying ways, long and flowing or belted and just touching your ankles. Whatever way you choose, you will look elegant – as a princess soon to be Queen of Scotland must.'

Margaret allowed the material to slip through her fingers. 'It reminds me of how a lady of Rome in ancient times might appear, quaint like the name!'

As they laughed together, for a moment something rattled the window panes startling them. As a shadowy, dark crow tumbled past the glass to the ground, Ailenor felt a presentiment. What if Margaret *was* unhappy in Scotland? What if she were treated badly by the Scottish lords? She picked up the slippery fabric and trailed her hand over its smooth silkiness, seeking comfort. If that happened, Henry must send an army to fetch their precious daughter home.

The royal cavalcade wound its way up the old North Road towards York, Margaret riding on a gentle brown mare between Henry and Ailenor. She was wrapped in a soft but warm woollen travelling cape, and wore comfortable furred gloves and boots. Ailenor and Henry tried to be cheerful but, even so, they could not help sharing sadness at the coming parting. The grandeur of the procession compensated. Along the route the people cheered for them. Ailenor remembered her miserable waterlogged procession from Dover to Canterbury many years before and was glad for Margaret, for the December weather was mild and it did not rain. A hundred knights gleaming with gold and silver, jewels glittering from silk and velvet, accompanied them. It was a stately procession with Henry generously distributing alms as they passed through towns.

Ailenor drew the children around her. In the privacy of the chambers they occupied, in whichever monastery or city, she read stories of Scotland and the North. She discovered tales of giants, fairy folk, magic, and adventure. *The Gododdin* was her favourite and even Edward, his cousin, Harry, and Nell's children, also cousins, joined them to hear it told. This long poem about a battle lasted for days.

Ailenor explained that the Gododdin, a tribe at the time of the Romans, held territories in Northumberland, beyond York, which was their destination. The story originated in Wales but no matter; the location was magically in the north. A force of three hundred warriors assembled from Pictland to drive enemies from Scotland. Their king permitted his warriors a whole year of feasting in Edinburgh before they attacked north Yorkshire. Their heroes fought for glory and to the children's delight, the valiant King Arthur was present at their battles. The book Ailenor read from was one she had commissioned especially for Margaret. She said, 'It was originally written in Welsh but I asked a scribe to translate it into French so you can read it. Tis a gift for you to bring to your new land so they do not think you ignorant of their history.'

'Not if it was written in Wales,' Margaret pertly said. 'I shall treasure it always, Mama. I'll think of you every time I read it.' She touched an illustration of a warrior clad in mail very like her own Papa's best suit of chainmail, the one he had worn to Wales when he recently took homage at Woodstock from the Welsh princes. She peered at the French writing and listened closely as her mother read:

'Gododdin, I make claim on thy behalf
In the presence of the throng boldly in the court
Since the gentle one, the wall of battle, was slain
Since the earth covered Aneurin
Poetry is now parted from the Gododdin.'

'So sad for a kingdom to lose their poetry,' remarked Margaret.

'Poetry is what makes us civilised. That and our love of God. Always remember this, my sweet.'

'Were they Christians?' Edward said, his long legs nonchalantly stretched out towards the blazing monastery fire.

'The poem says they had altars and did penance, but their enemies were heathens.'

'See,' said Edward. He unfolded his legs, stood to his full height and squinting over his mother's shoulder at the text, remarked, 'It says he fed ravens on the rampart of a fortress, *though he was no Arthur.*' He read, 'Amongst the powerful ones in battle, Gwawrddur was a palisade.' He returned to the fire, saying, 'I shall be a leader like this hero, Gwawrddur, or Arthur perhaps, and fight with Uncle Simon in

Gascony. He will make the rebel lords obey me.' Hal, Simon's son, glanced away. Ailenor knew Hal wanted desperately to squire in Gascony with his father.

'We must all fight for Uncle Simon,' said Harry, Richard's boy, looking fiercely from Hal to Edward.

'My husband Alexander will be a warrior too,' Margaret declared fiercely.

'As long as they decide not to do battle with each other.' Ailenor carefully closed the book. 'That would never do.' She turned to Edward. 'I don't want to hear another word of Gascony from *you*. You are still a boy.'

Edward too often talked of fighting and of his territory of Gascony. He admired the older boys, Hal and Harry, who were almost of an age to squire. Ailenor hoped it would not be too soon. Next, Edward would be betrothed. And to whom? She puzzled at this often, now that Margaret was to be wed.

After the wedding ceremony, with a heavy heart Ailenor watched Margaret ride from York. She looked minute as she rode beside little Alexander, but Margaret seemed happy with her husband. She would surely be well and safe. After all, she had Maria de Cantelope, a widow and trusted lady-in-waiting, to watch over her. A long train of sumptuary carts followed her, filled with gowns exquisitely embroidered by Rosalind as well as expensive tapestries, linens and silver tableware.

Ailenor slept well, comforted by the thought that Alexander and Margaret were too young to consummate the wedding. They would have time to get to know each other. Ailenor recollected how impatient she had been, but she and Henry had taken their time. Ailenor studied her husband's countenance with affection and hoped Margaret would come to love Alexander as she did Henry.

After Margaret and Alexander departed for Edinburgh, a storm blew in from the North Sea. Skies darkened. Joy fled. The storm hung about for two long days and nights whilst Ailenor prayed daily for her daughter's safety on her journey north. She remembered the crow that had knocked against the window in Windsor months before and shuddered. The sinister omen had not been forgotten.

The Court continued to celebrate in York. Ailenor sat beside Nell throughout the feasting between Christmas and Epiphany, glad of her sister-in-law's company. They had not seen each other since the Christmas Simon had returned to Gascony to put down the rebellion. It was a rebellion that was proving impossible to quash. Nell said Simon was constantly besieging castles, assiduous in his insistence on oaths of loyalty from the lords he had punished. If they were slow to obey, he imprisoned them and demanded ransoms.

'Do you think perhaps Simon is too uncompromising?' Ailenor said at the Epiphany feast.

'I think he hopes to keep Gascony loyal to Henry. He hasn't enough money to pay his troops and recruit more.' She looked resentful. 'We are in debt again to the Italians because of Gascony.' Nell shrugged. 'Now Hal wants to join his father as a squire.'

'Will he?'

'Not yet. I won't countenance it.'

'Why don't you permit Hal and young Simon to join Edward's court? They can train with him.' It was not the first time Ailenor had made this suggestion. They already had care of Harry, Richard's son by Isabel, who was to begin his training as a squire at Windsor that year. It was safer than being thrown into combat too soon.

Ailenor glanced over at the table where Nell's two older boys sat with Edward and Harry. They were a lively company of boys and bonded as such on the journey to York. She said, 'They are all growing up so fast.'

Nell said, 'My sons are studying with Bishop Grosseteste in Lincoln. They seem content. Perhaps next year they can join Edward's court at Windsor.'

Ailenor lifted a spoonful of lampreys in a lemon sauce. 'I shall pray for you and Simon. There is no better leader than the Earl. He will achieve peace in Gascony.'

'Amen, Ailenor,' Nell said. 'I pray so too.'

Chapter Thirty-two

Rosalind
Gascony, 1252

Rosalind glanced up from the tunic she was embroidering for Nicholas. 'Must you return to Gascony, Thomas? We've been so happy since we came home.' Thomas looked away, clearly unable to face her disappointment. The family were lodging with her father and Dame Mildred at Alfred's new house in St Martin's Lane. She enjoyed its private, south-facing courtyard, and liked to visit the barn-like busy workshop on the far side of it. The merchant house was far grander than the house Rosalind had grown up in, though Papa still retained the creaking old house in Paternoster Lane as a home for his journeyman's family.

Although Alfred was approaching fifty years his eyesight was as keen as ever. Mildred's haberdashery trade was a successful addition to Alfred's tailoring concern, so much so she was able to employ two extra apprentices and several embroiderers of her own. Their two boys had grown quickly, too soon, mused Rosalind looking at her own children. At nine and ten years of age respectively, her half-brothers were already apprenticed to become tailors themselves. One day they would inherit one of the best businesses in the City.

Thomas was at her elbow in the garden adjoining the courtyard behind a large kitchen. He had just come from a meeting with Earl Simon at the Bishop's palace on the river. 'Rosalind, my love, I *have* to go to Gascony again. There's trouble there again. I owe Earl Simon

294

loyalty.' He glanced down at his sleeping daughter, a little girl they called Eleanor in honour of Earl Simon's Nell. 'And fealty.'

She swallowed back tears. She was with child again and more than usually emotional. Biting her lip, she said, 'Let us pray you are back soon.' She would miss Thomas. He was her rock and she could not imagine her life without him.

'Stay here where you have good people to care for you,' he said, taking her hands. 'Until the baby is born.'

She nodded. This time she was not returning to the troubled province. Being with Mildred and Papa was a fair compromise. She loved the City. She enjoyed the bustle and the opportunity to visit the Westminster workshop as she had when she had come to stitch Princess Margaret's wedding trousseau. 'I think I should, if they will have me.'

'Of course they will,' Thomas said. 'Our steward will look after the manor.'

Winter was a quiet time on their estate. In recent years they had enjoyed warm summers and mild winters with rain and sunshine at the right times. Their estate had prospered before whilst they had been in Gascony with Earl Simon. Hopefully, it would continue to yield good harvests with Thomas away from England once again.

Alfred and Mildred were pleased with the arrangement. Their house was spacious, with five bedchambers, and there was room for all of them. By now Papa was an alderman, known and respected in the City. He sat at the top table at Guild feasts held on saints' days, was called upon to judge internal Guild disputes and he donated generously to their parish of St Martin. After Thomas took his leave and crossed the Narrow Sea, Rosalind's days passed pleasantly helping Mildred in the still room, with the haberdashery and embroidering for Alfred's business.

Because Rosalind had been favoured by Queen Ailenor and had proved her innocence of any heretical leanings, no one dared to challenge her again. The grocer, Adam de Basing, and his son had avoided her family since. Even so, Alfred warned her never to go out without the faithful Master Gruff by her side, saying, 'There's unrest in the streets. There's bad feeling rising amongst City traders against King Henry. His daughter's wedding was extravagant. He is now talking about a crusade. All talk. I'll wager he'll spend the money he's collecting on his great abbey at Westminster or pour it into Gascony.'

'Ah, I suppose I must understand how the people feel,' Rosalind said, though in her heart her loyalty to Queen Ailenor had never faded. 'Is it true the King asked the merchants to pay for Princess Margaret's wedding? Surely the traders are wealthy enough. You contributed fabrics, suits for nobility, sourced quintise for Princess Margaret's gowns at your own expense.'

'But, Rosalind, it really was too much. It almost bankrupted us. I could afford it, just. When the grocers, ironmongers, fishmongers, chandlers, and the rest refused a tax levy on top of gifts, King Henry thought up such a nasty revengeful scheme.' He grunted as if in pain. Rosalind reached out to him and caught his arm fearful he might have a seizure. Alfred ignored her and continued his complaint. 'He established a fair at Westminster that went on for a fortnight. If any London shops opened during that period they were fined. Either traders lost two weeks' business or they paid his tax.'

'Did they pay the tax?' she said, knowing it was harsh.

'No, they thought it cheaper to lose business.' Alfred shook his head. 'Ah well, he's a weak king but at least he's a loyal husband and a good father. His son, people hope, will make a better king. Henry won't rule for ever. Even so, the King must take care. Londoners will not put up with his taxes. If there's a prolonged war in Gascony, they won't support it either.' He put his hand over hers. 'If I were you, I'd avoid seeing Queen Ailenor for now. I have gathered from Guild chatter the King is unhappy with Earl Simon. This could become an issue of loyalty for you and Thomas. You helped Queen Ailenor with the Princess's wardrobe. You are with child, and if she does not know you are in the City, she will not send for you.'

Rosalind recognised wisdom in her father's words. Much as she longed to visit the Queen's ladies, some of whom she considered her friends; much as she loved the workshop in the palace courtyard, she resisted the temptation to visit Westminster. She continued to busy herself with Dame Mildred in the buttery making cheeses, in the pleasant still room with herbs, and on embroidery in her solar.

Before she knew it, the new baby quickened. She grew more careful of her diet and although winter was mild, the spring that followed was chill. She kept out of the wind and rain. She remained calm as she baked, stitched, and looked after her children.

A day came when she did leave the house to purchase rennet for cheese-making, taking her two little boys with her for company. The dairy was only a short distance away so there was no need to ask Gruff or one of the maids to accompany her. A mistake, because that was the very day she tumbled into Jonathan de Basing. It was, she realised later, an inevitable event, given they both dwelled in the same section of the City. She tried to push past the merchant's son who over the years had grown larger. His girth looked like an enormous blown-up pig bladder children kicked around. He refused to give her passage and stood, legs akimbo, wide as a church door, blocking the lane. She stared him out and did not retort when he looked greedily at her russet velvet cloak and remarked in his squeaking voice, '*Lady* Rosalind, you are well-wed, I see.' He glanced down at her boys. 'Children, too. So, by St Jerome's balls, you condescend to leave your estates and visit us humble merchants?' He sneered at her two small lads. 'Little lords.' She continued to stare straight at him without losing her temper. His face was pock-marked. Jonathan de Basing certainly had not aged well.

Clutching her sons' hands tightly, she said quietly, 'I have nothing to say to you, Jonathan de Basing. I am about my own business.'

At that, he moved aside and she pulled her boys past him as he called after her, 'De Montfort will come to no good end. I have it on reliable authority. Your knight will die in Gascony with his master.'

She momentarily glanced back, her face furious, and hurried on, the bag containing the rennet swinging from her shoulder. She clutched her two shocked boys' hands tightly in her own and after what seemed an age at last gained the gate of her father's house. Her breath caught as she let go their hands and ordered the children not to move from her side. On her frantic knocking, the gatekeeper slid back his peephole. He hastily opened up. As Rosalind pushed the boys into the courtyard, bells from nearby St Martin's rang out the midday Angelus so loudly her ears tingled. She shook her head when her older boy began to ask who the stranger was.

'No one we want to know. Go and see if Cook has gingerbread for you.'

The little lads ran off gladly. She drew in a long deep breath, glad to be safely inside her father's gates. For a moment she leaned against the wall before entering the dairy. What had Jonathan meant about Earl Simon? She shook her head. If all was amiss, Thomas would send her word soon. In his last letter to her, he said they were besieging Castle Castilian.

After that April afternoon Rosalind made sure she was accompanied by both Jane and Gruff every time they exited their tall wooden gate into St Martin's Lane. Occasionally when she'd see shadows she often wondered if Jonathan watched her and still sought revenge. She prayed daily before the statue to the Virgin in St Martin's that Jonathan de Basing would leave her alone and that Thomas would return to her before the baby was born.

It was past midnight. The knocking on the gate, though not loud, was persistent. It awakened Rosalind because her chamber was to the front of the house, up on the third floor, and she wondered who could demand entry at this time of night, unless they had news? She climbed down from her bed, feeling cumbersome because she was in her seventh month. She opened the shutters and peered into the courtyard. Starlight was not as clear in the City as it was in the country. She could just make out the cloaked figure crossing from the gate towards the house. The cloaked person approached the front door leading into the great hall where they ate and servants slept; by his walk, she realised who it was. She pulled a mantle over her nightgown, and lifting the chamber latch quietly so as not to waken her maid and children sleeping on pallets by the great bed, she climbed down two narrow staircases into the hall. Servants slept in alcoves about the hall. Thankfully, no one stirred as she hurried to the great front door. But Papa was there before her, pulling bolts back just as she reached the porch area.

Thomas fell into the porch through the door. He was wrapped in an enormous cloak and clutched a bundle.

'Thomas,' she said softly. She hugged her husband hard. 'You've returned.'

'Briefly,' he whispered back. Alfred placed a finger to his lips and hurried them both around snoring bodies to the small antechamber behind the hall.

Alfred said, 'Why come by darkness, Thomas? Is aught amiss? No, wait, eat first. There is bread and cheese here already in the cupboard and we've wine too.' He turned to Rosalind. 'Fetch it and he can eat. He looks exhausted.'

Rosalind opened the cupboard and within a few moments had placed bread, cheese, and a tankard of wine before Thomas.

Falling onto the bench, Thomas waved the bread and cheese away and drank deeply from the tankard. Rosalind noticed tears gather in his eyes. 'There are two things you must know,' he said slowly. 'First of all, Nell's little Joanna died in April. Nell is distraught, deeply saddened for she couldn't save her. It was an ague in the child's chest. We rode back from Castilian triumphant, but the little girl was already laid out in the chapel at the Palais des Ombres. Earl Simon ordered a hundred candles lit and prayers said. Lady Nell was inconsolable. After the burial, the palace sank into a deep sorrow. How terrible to lose a child.'

Rosalind's hand flew to her breast as she remembered their own Eleanor, sleeping peacefully above them with her nurse. To mourn a child, a little thing only three years old, was tragic. 'I can only imagine their pain,' she managed to say.

Thomas laid the tankard on the bench beside him. 'That is not all. I am here because the King has recalled Earl Simon to London to answer charges of incompetence. They are treasonable charges. We had to sail immediately. Nell too, and their younger boys.'

'God save them all,' she said. 'How can Henry be so unreasonable?'

'Indeed. Amen to all that,' he said. There was a catch in his voice.

Chapter Thirty-three

Ailenor
Spring 1252

Ailenor could cut the atmosphere in Henry's antechamber with her eating knife. Her mouth opened in astonishment as he swept around, his face flushed and angry.

Henry hissed at her, 'What do you mean, taking it on yourself to appoint your chaplain to Flamstead Church? Women do not make clerical appointments. I warned you before.' He threw a letter at Ailenor. It fell onto the floor tiles. He was angry. 'It's from that insufferable Bishop Grosseteste.'

Her eyes widened in disbelief. 'I am no ordinary woman. I am a queen,' she retorted. It was bad enough he was accusing Earl Simon. Now he sought a new quarrel and it was with her. She exhaled loudly, tired of placating him. 'What is it about this time?' she said wearily as she bent to recover the letter. He scooped it up before she could read it. As he crumpled it in his hand, the vellum seemed to crack.

'How high does the arrogance of woman rise if it is not restrained?' His tone remained superior. He twitched his velvet gown about him and looked at her with menace in his pale eyes, one lid sinking lower than the other. 'Your chaplain leaves Flamstead at once. I've called in the Sheriff of Lincoln to evict him. Whilst we were in York last year, you were plotting with Grosseteste, Simon's dear friend, behind my back.'

'Henry . . . I never plotted with Bishop Grosseteste, nor with Earl

Simon for that matter.' But he was gone with a flurry of robes, in an attitude of high pique.

She sank into a chair, mortified, angry, and hurt, all at the same time.

That afternoon, Henry removed himself from the Tower where they were in residence. His tone was icy when he marched into her chamber and informed her she was not to accompany him to Westminster. She looked at him as if he was a beetle to be trampled into the floor. He glared back. 'You will regret this,' he said, anger seeping from his furred mantle.

She had no choice but to wait until Henry calmed down. Her accommodation in the Tower was pleasanter than her apartment at Westminster. She would be out of Henry's storm by remaining in her Rose Chambers. She watched from her casement as he was rowed up river to Westminster, determined not to mind.

A month later Ailenor received a correspondence from Bishop Grosseteste. She fell onto one of her rose cushions, pulled another close and leaned on it to read that Bishop Grosseteste had placed Flamstead under an interdict because the priest appointed was a Burgundian, another foreigner, Henry's choice. She gasped. Everyone feared an interdict. Parishioners could not marry in the church. They could not bury their dead in the churchyard. Their immortal souls were in danger. In addition, Bishop Grosseteste had excommunicated Henry's appointment. She crumpled the letter. 'Oh no,' she whispered into the air. 'He'll blame me for this. I never thought Henry would object to the Bishop's choice. I was not plotting. It was on one of my estates. And now this problem will go to the Church courts.' She closed her eyes. There was nothing she could do. Henry was at Westminster. The only child she had with her was Beatrice. Edward and Edmund were at Windsor with their tutors. She wanted them all to be together again. She did not want this ridiculous situation.

It didn't help that the weather was miserable and cold and she couldn't walk in the gardens. Her ladies tiptoed around her. They kept Beatrice busy embroidering. A tutor employed for her daughter patiently taught the child to read and write. Alix of Lusignan befriended the little girl and although there was an age difference, they sat together holding hands, watching the multitude of ships on the river as Ailenor had done years before. She smiled to see their friendship, glad Alix was not like her despicable uncles.

Ailenor could bear it no more. Henry had called Simon back from Gascony to face trial for fraud. A young nobleman visiting the Tower told her King Henry was in a grim mood and the Bishop of Bordeaux was ensconced in Westminster Palace whispering ills against the Earl. Gascon noblemen including her cousin, Count Gaston, accompanied the Bishop, who was accusing Earl Simon of terrible things.

'What things?'

'Sacking Castle Castilian is one. I'm not exactly sure about the rest.'

'I intend to find out,' she said.

'The King is angry. He rages about . . .'

'Thank you,' she said with firmness to the nobleman, and sent him to find his betrothed, who was none other than Lady Margery. She summoned Alix to her bedchamber. The girl was indeed so beautiful, eyes a deep violet like Nell's and her grandmother Isabella's. She looked artless but Ailenor decided not to be deceived. Alix may be of a pleasanter demeanour than her uncles but she could also be capable of scheming.

'Keep an eye on Beatrice. I shall be at Westminster for a few days,' she nonetheless said to Alix.

'Yes, Aunt Ailenor,' Alix replied, her bright violet eyes softening to blue like the sky on a gentle summer's day.

Sooner the nobleman she was to marry grew up, the better.

When Alix curtsied and was gone, she turned to Willelma. 'Get me an escort. Pack a coffer of clothing and linens. We are returning to Westminster on the next tide.'

On her arrival at Westminster, she sought Henry out. He was in the painted chamber. He, to her disbelief, was warm towards her, but then Henry was always changeable.

'Ailenor, whilst your presence pleases me, I have a problem. Nell has a problem too. Her husband goes on trial. It will commence in the Abbey refectory in a week's time.'

'What has Simon done to deserve a trial?' She knew his accusations but he would repeat them to her and perhaps hear how absurd they were, spoken to her, Nell's friend and sister-in-law.

'The Archbishop,' Henry indicated the shadows where she saw standing by the arras leading to the chapel, none other than the Bishop of Bordeaux, a long thin man in a heavily embroidered chasuble. He had likely just served Mass to Henry in the very chapel where Henry had witnessed Simon and Nell's marriage.

She quickly realised the Archbishop's presence went some way towards explaining Henry's warm welcome. The Archbishop of Bordeaux stepped forward. She knelt and kissed his ring, as was the custom.

His voice slid over his words like wine trickling from an altar chalice. 'Your Grace, Earl Simon is accused of fraud, mismanagement, and cruelty. The Gascon noblemen he has held to ransom threaten to seek a new lord.'

She pondered this. Lord Edward was their ruler in waiting and Simon their governor.

Henry said before she could remark this fact, 'Earl Simon had my full confidence once, but now Gascony, our son's inheritance, is more troubled than ever. He has had money flowing to him as if it pours never-ending from a sorcerer's vat. Gascony's future peace hangs in the balance. I am trapped with the rogue unless we can undo his seven-year agreement. He will be legally challenged before my barons and earls for mismanagement and fraud and, believe me, there are witnesses.'

She said with firmness, though she felt her hands moist because she was so anxious, 'Henry, simply, this is unwise.' She folded her hands inside her mantle.

'I told you, Ailenor, do not interfere in the business of kings.'

Ailenor bit back a response. The Archbishop said smoothly, 'Dear Lady, I am willing to counsel you should you seek my advice.'

'Thank you, Archbishop, but I must go now and pray to my own saints for guidance. If you will excuse me.'

Ailenor bowed low to the Archbishop and to Henry. Without another word, her head held high, she glided to the door, her rising temper reined under control. She needed to think how she could help Simon and comfort Nell. She would return to the Tower and hope she could be reunited with Nell. Unwilling to linger at Westminster, she simmered with anger at Henry. It was clear to her it was Simon who had been trapped, not her husband. Simon was doing his job, the task Henry begged him to undertake when he'd wished to crusade. Her position was difficult. She could not openly challenge Henry's decisions.

She decided not to linger with Henry after all. On her return to the Tower, she wrote to Uncle Peter in his new palace which he called The Savoy and waited for news. Nell accepted her invitation to stay with her whilst Simon lodged with the Bishop of London in his palace nearer to Westminster. Uncle Peter visited her with his wife, Agnes, who on seeing that Ailenor was distressed over the interdict on Lincoln and the trial at Westminster also decided to lodge with them at the Tower. Ailenor prepared a comfortable apartment for Agnes and her two ladies. Some days later, Nell was rowed down river to lodge with Ailenor in the Queen's apartments.

The three women rediscovered a close bond. When Uncle Peter visited he said, 'I shall argue we stay the course in Gascony. Henry has confirmed the grant of Gascony to Lord Edward but it will be some years before Edward can go there himself as their lord. Earl Simon did try to keep the peace.'

'Will others support Simon too?' Nell asked.

'I believe they will. Only the Gascons stand against him. And I can vouch for the Clergy. Boniface, of course, is on side. The barons, too, support Simon. None of those who fought there in the past underestimate the difficulties Gascony presents.' He drew a long breath. 'Only Henry underestimates them all.'

'My dear foolish husband,' sighed Ailenor. She took Nell's hand. 'All will be well, Nell, you shall see.'

Chapter Thirty-four

Rosalind
Summer 1252

Earl Simon's trial began in the refectory at Westminster. Simon was not arrested but he was rigorously questioned. When he could get away from the Bishop's palace, Thomas sped on foot through the stinking-hot, rumour-filled City with word to his father-in-law's house in St Martin's Lane.

He related the news to Rosalind, whose baby was due to be born. 'Henry is listening to Earl Simon's enemies, to stop them looking elsewhere for a new lord. The gossip at the court is that the Gascons hate Simon so much they are now seeking leadership from Alfonso of Castile, grandson of the second Henry . . .' Rosalind wrinkled her brow. 'Through that Henry's eldest daughter,' Thomas explained. 'The King thinks he must convict Earl Simon to make Gascony safe for Lord Edward. Pah, it's nonsense.' Thomas threw back his ale and shook his head. Looking up at her, he gave her a half-smile. She couldn't smile back. She was too worried for Lady Eleanor, who had been so kind to her, and for the Queen who was estranged from the King. Thomas was saying, 'It may not go well for the King. The English earls and barons have a say. As yet they've not said anything. They'll be our Earl's judges and so far, they are not condemning him.'

She stood heavily to fetch more ale. The evening was a thirsty hot one in late June. 'Once, long ago, those same earls resented Earl

Simon,' she said, placing the jug of ale on the table. 'It's freshly brewed,' she added.

' 'Tis a pleasure to drink English ale again. Gascon wine leaves a sour taste on my palate.' Thomas looked thoughtful. 'Henry is trying to throw the weight of opinion against Simon and by Christos, I pray he doesn't succeed.'

As June slid into July, Rosalind thought about Queen Ailenor every day. Lady Eleanor was with the Queen in the Tower. She wouldn't be there if she was at odds with Her Grace so the Queen's position remained a puzzle. When Rosalind asked, Thomas shook his head. He was sure the Queen disapproved of Henry's actions but she had no influence this time. Rosalind, heavy, uncomfortable, and about to give birth, pushed it all from her mind and took herself to her birthing chamber.

A week later, Thomas returned with another report. He spoke to her from the doorway of her chamber. 'The King has hurled the most vociferous abuse against my lord.' He drew a long slow breath. 'Earl Simon responded with self-restraint, meekness, and magnanimity towards the King. Oh, Rosalind, my lord is treated appallingly and my heart aches to see it.' He drew breath again. She heard him painfully exhale with a sigh. He said, 'Countess Eleanor is with child again. They say she is thirty-eight years old.'

Rosalind raised herself and said to the doorway, 'And the Queen. How is she?'

'I've heard the King is still displeased with his wife. He's changed some of her household staff. He told her never to question his Church appointments.'

'You would think the trial would keep him busy.'

'She sides with her uncle Boniface against the Bishop of Winchester. Boniface placed his man as Prior at St Thomas's Hospital and Aymer objected, saying it was in his jurisdiction. Remember he has a palace just south of the river close to the hospital. Well, anyway, Bishop Aymer roused up a great band of Lusignans including his brother, William of Valence, to attack Archbishop Boniface's man in the Hospital. The Archbishop's own prior had Aymer's man ejected from the position.'

'Don't tell me the King sides with the new Bishop of Winchester instead of Boniface who is an Archbishop?'

'Queen Ailenor is furious. Letters are ferried downriver to her daily. She writes back. The messenger is an old friend of mine. He says the King is petty-minded and ever wants his own way.'

'Poor Earl Simon and poor Queen Ailenor,' Rosalind said and sank back onto her pillows, for she knew not what else to say. They would have to wait. They, as little people in the City, were powerless to help Simon or the Queen. If she was not so heavily pregnant she would go to them. Instead she wrote a letter from her birthing chamber giving her support and sent Gruff with it all the way to the Tower.

'Has Countess Eleanor received my note?' she asked Mildred on his return.

'He gave it to Lady Mary as you requested and waited for a reply.' Mildred handed a folded letter to Rosalind stamped with the Countess's leopard seal. She broke the seal.

All will be well, Praise God. When this is over I shall return to Kenilworth. I wish you well with your birth and hope you will attend me when my time comes too. May the Madonna watch over you and may St Katherine take care of you during your travail. Your friend, Countess Eleanor.

It was a brief note but kind.

Thomas returned after several days' absence and this time as he stood by her chamber door he was smiling.

'The nobles are not swayed by the Gascons. Not at all. In fact, the barons and earls extol my Lord Simon's virtues. They said he has been loyal, energetic and just.'

'Which earls took his side?' asked Alfred.

'For a start, Earl Richard and the Earls Gloucester and Hereford all spoke for Earl Simon. Peter de Montfort also spoke in Earl Simon's favour. Peter of Savoy supports him, which suggests Queen Ailenor does too. And then I heard say that Queen Ailenor insists that Earl Simon must return to Gascony to complete his care of the state since he can bring order there.'

'Thank Christ for that,' said Rosalind. 'Now go away, Thomas. I am going to give birth imminently.'

On the next day when Rosalind felt her birthing pains arrive, Thomas brought her the best of all news. He was not returning to Gascony with Earl Simon, and neither was the Countess. They would all go home very soon. The Countess wished to give birth at Kenilworth.

'You shall see her there, Rosalind. I am to keep an eye on her, to be on call, so to say. We are close by after all.'

It was the best news she had heard since Thomas had set off for Gascony in February.

'What about the Gascons? Are they subdued by the court's verdict?'

'Of course they refuse to accept the verdict. Simon offered to surrender his agreement to act as Seneschal to Gascony in return for compensation and absolute exoneration.'

'And?'

'And, indeed, there is more. Henry said Simon was free to break their agreement because he was a traitor to the Crown. Earl Simon retorted that the King's piety was a sham. Henry raised his voice. He shouted, he never repented any act as much as permitting Earl Simon to enter England to gain land and honours, grow fat and insolent.'

'After that?'

'The King said he will prepare to go to Gascony himself to attend to matters. In the meantime, Earl Simon announced *he* was going back there and would not return to England until the Gascon lords grovelled at the King's feet and the King paid him what he was due.'

Rosalind felt her mouth break into a smile. She felt tears gather behind her eyes. It looked like Simon had won a victory against the King himself and the lords of England were on his side.

Thomas began to laugh. 'There is another thing. I nearly forgot. I ran into that ass, Jonathan de Basing.'

'Where? How?' Would Jonathan de Basing never vanish from their lives?

'He was crossing the courtyard at Westminster and said, "You may have the protection of Earl Simon today, and your lady that of the Queen herself, but I'll warrant if they both fall from favour, I could make your father-in-law's life miserable."

'The bastard bored past me, but I caught his arm. He's got a huge bit of beef on that arm these days, but I'm agile as ever.'

The wretch had threatened Papa! Thomas went on, 'I said to him. "Just you try. My father-in-law has Earl Richard's protection. Master Alfred has no allegiance to Earl Simon but Richard of Cornwall, Lady Eleanor's brother, will have you strung up if you threaten his tailor. So be on your way, you fat, strutting cockerel!" I'll swear he looked green. I placed my hand on my sword. I think he thought the better of challenging me. It's as well we are returning to Leicestershire.'

'As well,' murmured Rosalind. It would not be too soon. Of a sudden, she doubled over. Her labour was coming. 'Ouch', she gasped.

'I said only a few moments, Thomas,' Mildred said. 'Now go and wait downstairs. We'll be *very* occupied here as you can see.'

Ignoring Mildred, Thomas crossed the chamber which was full of linen and basins. He dropped a kiss onto Rosalind's forehead. 'God be with you, my lady. I love you with all my heart.'

'I love thee too,' she struggled to say as she groaned again.

'May I stay?' he asked.

'No, be gone.' Mildred shooed him from the chamber.

Rosalind's chamber was too warm. Her bed was covered with white. A birthing stool appeared.

She looked at it, her brow wrinkling in disgust.

'It will ease the birthing,' said the midwife, who had recently arrived. She was a kindly, competent woman with a neat, clean coif on her head.

'But I never needed one for the others,' Rosalind protested between pains descending and swamping her. She tried to stand. Mildred and her maidservant took her arms, one on either side, and began to walk her around the chamber.

'The bed would not be soiled with blood and waters and it is easier on you. But choose whatever is comfortable,' the midwife said, and set out rose oil with which to massage her belly.

Outside the birthing chamber the household prayed for her safe delivery. Thomas was with Alfred in his office off the Hall. The children were in the kitchen out of earshot, managed by the cook. She lay on the bed again as full labour came upon her. The fires were ready. 'I'll use it,' she gasped, pointing to the stool.

She hardly had time to reach the birthing stool. Jane took one arm again, Mildred the other, and the midwife caught the baby as clutching her eagle stone Rosalind pushed down. She was delivered of a second girl in the fourth hour after midday, just as the church bells rang out for Vespers.

'She is beautiful, like her mother and her sister. Baby Mildred. I wonder if now our family is complete,' Thomas said some hours later when at last he was allowed to see her.

'Only God can tell, but happy I am that we are returning home. Happy we are a family again.' Rosalind looked past Thomas to three children standing with Dame Mildred in the doorway hopeful of seeing their new sister.

Queen Ailenor, after Thomas took a wherry to the Tower to tell them he had a new daughter, sent her a basket of fruits. The fruit had arrived all the way from Gascony. As Rosalind looked at the grapes, pomegranates, and oranges, she thought how fortunate she was to have Queen Ailenor's goodwill. She smelled the oranges.

'We could use the skins to make orange waters.'

'We might,' agreed Mildred.

A day later Countess Eleanor sent her a gift of fabric. Thomas smiled as he said, 'It's silk from Italy. She kept it all these years. I am sorry I was never able to bring you back the gift you said you would marry me for.' He smiled down, and she saw how his honest blue eyes were soft with love. 'My present for you was lost in Saintes all those years ago. It was in my bundle.'

'I had forgotten about that, Thomas,' she said, nestling baby Mildred in her arms. 'Just don't think of going looking for it. At least you tried and as you can see it wasn't necessary, not at all.'

She handed Mildred to him. As he took their infant from her he said, 'I love you with all my heart.'

'And I thee.'

The length of silk fabric that had been wrapped in linen with fennel and lavender still smelled faintly of something stronger. It was a foreign scent. She lifted the precious material a second time to her nose. The scent was frankincense with a hint of muskiness from the East.

She glanced up. 'Thomas, what was the gift you lost?'

'It wasn't fabric. It was –'

At that moment baby Mildred began to cry. Rosalind put her to her breast.

'It was?'

'Simply a skein of gold embroidery silk from Jerusalem.'

Chapter Thirty-five

Autumn 1252

Ailenor knew Henry would not easily forgive her for siding with her uncle Boniface against Bishop Aymer's bullying behaviour at St Thomas's Hospital that autumn and he still suspected her of conniving with Bishop Grosseteste. She moved to Windsor after Earl Simon returned to Gascony. Nell departed for Kenilworth in September. Henry came to Windsor, discovered Ailenor in her privy chamber, and sharply told her to pack her belongings and get herself to Winchester. Dropping their embroidery, her ladies stared open-mouthed at the King.

'Leave us,' she ordered and they raced from the chamber, silver and gold threads glittering on the floor by the frame they abandoned. 'Why?' She turned back to Henry. She could not help the challenge in her voice.

'You are interfering. First you caused an interdict over Flamstead. Fortunately that was lifted before it became serious. Now you've insulted my half-brother Bishop Aymer *and* I've heard how you've actively supported Earl Simon's cause. You and Boniface both went against Aymer, had his choice of appointment for St Thomas's Hospital removed. Boniface called my nephew, the good Bishop, to account. No, Ailenor, you will remove yourself to Winchester and there you will keep to your own apartments and your chapel. Bishop Aymer will hear your confession daily. You will humble yourself to him.' Henry snapped his fingers at her. 'Select three ladies to attend you and two maids only. The rest of them return to their family estates until Christmas.'

She stood, stretching her neck and said in a weary voice, 'You cannot do this, Henry. Our children need me. Beatrice . . .'

'Is well-looked after and away from a malevolent influence. She has Alix for company.'

'I am not a malevolent influence.' Ailenor was aghast, furious. 'And is Alix suitable company for our daughter?'

'Apparently you have thought so since you left Beatrice in her care often during Earl Simon's trial to scheme on his behalf.'

'How do you know? This is a lie.'

'Alix. Who else would tell me?' he said with an edge to his tone, 'I hope a period of prayer and solitude will temper your disloyal spirit. I shall pray for your return to steadfastness.'

Steadfastness. When was she not steadfast? She stiffened her resolve, and her posture. She would not beg. Henry's grandmother Eleanor of Aquitaine had been locked away by the second Henry for years and years because she had supported their sons in their quest for independence. What if Henry grew into his grandfather's wicked boots, did likewise, and controlled Edward's future independence? She would not risk that, no matter how wrong he was, how unfair, stupid and stubborn. Her sojourn at Winchester with the detestable Aymer would not be a lengthy one. She would wait and guard her tongue. Her time would come and, despite all, she would regain his love. Alix of Lusignan would be gone from court as soon as Ailenor could arrange it, and she would do so with pleasure.

'I have a request, Henry,' she said haughtily, keeping her face immobile.

'What is it?' he asked. His impatience was obvious by the way his left eye drooped and his arms folded across his silk-clad chest.

'Alix should be one of my chosen ladies for the months I must pass in prayer and contemplation. Beatrice can either come with her or remain with her siblings.'

Henry looked at her askance, his greying eyebrows lifting. She felt him studying her face closely. She lowered her eyes. 'Granted,' he said after an uncomfortable silence had passed. 'But Beatrice stays here with me.'

'As you wish,' she said. When she lifted her head again, her face remained inscrutable.

Ailenor uncovered the embroidery frame that had been tucked away into an alcove in the bower at Winchester Castle. Alix gasped as she looked upon the unfinished embroidery which gleamed with gold thread and pearls. 'What perfect fish, Aunt Ailenor,' she said as she reached out to touch their popping eyes and drew a finger along the silvered scales.

'It has been wrapped away for two years. Do you like it, Alix?'

'I do. I have always wondered at that miracle of loaves and fishes.' She stared at the serene Christ figure. She leaned towards him, studied the stiff little figure and looking up said, 'He looks like Uncle Henry.'

Ailenor nodded. 'It was not deliberate but yes, a younger Uncle Henry. Would you like to learn how to work this embroidery? I don't think Bishop Aymer can object to such an innocent occupation.'

'I want to learn. Aymer will praise it.'

'If we finish it, you may have it as part of your wedding chest. It can go with you into your new life, for your own chapel.'

'That is generous, Aunt Ailenor. When may we start?'

'Willelma and Mary will sort out our threads and tighten the frame. We can stitch a little this evening if you wish, after Compline if the candles give us enough light. I'll show you the stitches. You'll know some of these already.'

A contrite Ailenor walked to Compline in the Castle Chapel attended by her ladies, Willelma, Mary, and Alix. Aymer would serve the evening Mass. Since she was instructed to remain within the Castle and not go abroad, he must come to her. She smiled to herself since it made hearing their confession an inconvenience for him.

He arrived in his elaborate bishop's litter, gowned in an extravagant chasuble depicting the Tree of Jesse, its gold borders glittering. His magnificent chariot was drawn by a donkey and seeing this spectacle she restrained a desire to laugh. He offered to hear her confession after Compline but instead she suggested he return the next day. Prime would be a more suitable time. Indeed, she needed to relieve her conscience, she said. On the following morning, after confession, they could break their fast together. The castle cook had sourced fresh trout; the bakers promised soft loaves, and she'd heard their quails had laid a great number of eggs that day. It would permit him to pass the rest of the day with Church business. She really did not want to take up too much of his time.

'As you wish, Your Grace,' the handsome Bishop said, his chasuble swaying as he moved, and his voice musical. How could he possess such fine looks, a gentle voice, and yet own unsettling undertones of ruthlessness? He looked at Alix with a fond smile. 'It will be a pleasure to dine with such charming ladies,' he said, his voice smooth as the silk he wore.

'Alix is learning English embroidery. You must see our work. It is for God's adoration, to adorn her chapel once she is married.'

Bishop Aymer gave her an approving nod and said he would be honoured to see how his niece progressed. Ailenor knew she was directing all in a satisfactory manner. She exchanged a sideways glace with Willelma as the Bishop's attention was drawn from the Queen to his own beautiful sister. Ailenor bestowed her gracious smile on the Bishop as he departed.

'Alix, we'll work a small sample first.' Ailenor put together two layers of fabric. The upper layer was of fine pink silk and the bottom was velvet. Willelma threaded two needles, the first with silver-gilt thread which she passed to Alix, the second with fine thread. Ailenor said, 'The fabric you are to lay the silver thread over is woven in satin. It has a silk warp and a cotton weft. Some call it kanzi. It comes from the East, from Persia. You may keep this little piece when completed. Make it into a purse for your belt.'

Alix lifted her threaded needle, her face stiff with concentration.

'The double layer is because you will embellish this with the metal thread on your needle there. Later you might like to add ornaments

315

such as tiny pearls. The silver thread is wrapped thread with metal wrapped around a silk core. Now, watch me.' Ailenor lifted a needle and, taking the practice piece on which she had outlined a simple rose, laid the silk thread onto the material following the curve of the flower. 'Secure this with really tiny split stitches. You can make running stitches with green silk for the leaves and outline them with gold thread. Shade in the flower with more split stitches. Shall we work a section of your rose?'

With total absorption, more than Ailenor had ever before observed in Alix's behaviour, the girl began to embroider. She must not work on the larger embroidery until she had mastered the techniques they used. Ailenor enjoyed teaching Alix and after several days, her niece had completed the rose and leaves. She would stitch it onto another piece of velvet for a belt purse.

'How did you learn this, Aunt Ailenor?'

'I learned it from an embroideress called Rosalind. She dwells in Leicestershire. Once, long ago, she was a court embroideress. There's a workshop in one of Westminster Palace's courtyards, tucked away behind ash trees. I'll take you there one day.'

'I should like that.'

'Now you can work on the fish.'

When Ailenor attended confessions, she wore a simple blue woollen gown without any embellishment and a wimple on her head. She humbly begged God's pardon for gainsaying her husband but she was not entirely contrite. She would try harder to understand why her husband made the choices he made and begged God's forgiveness for any errors of judgement she may have made as his Queen. It was not difficult to slide over the surface of things with Bishop Aymer because he was a superficial man. She emphasised the words 'gentle' in her prayers and confessions. She wished to be 'gentle woman and humble woman', a queen who used her queenship to cherish hospitals, to set an example of devotion amongst women, donate to priories, and intercede when intercession was right. She would not interfere with the King's decisions.

For his part, Bishop Aymer nodded and referred to the humility of Mary whose body inclined towards Christ in statues and images and who received her own crown at His hands. He touched his elaborate cope and said on that first morning, 'You are an important link in the royal lineage. Your role is to be a loyal wife.'

Well, of course, it was, but wasn't she an earthly queen too? She preferred images depicting the coronation of the Virgin, seated beside Christ, rather than those of the Virgin with her head humbly inclined towards Christ. She did not say this to Aymer. She was determined to mend the foolish quarrel but she scorned the notions that every married woman was like an infant; that women were less rational than men, or that women were temptresses. She could pretend for a time to be docile and quiet but she knew in her heart, and she knew Henry knew it too, humility was not in her nature. He had once loved her intelligence. He adored her patronage of the arts and he *would* respect her again.

Aymer remarked one morning as they neared Christmastide, 'These courts you have held, discussing matters of chivalry and romance, posing questions that women should not discuss . . .'

Ailenor stared at him because his eyes were full of bemusement. 'They are harmless, Aymer, as you well know yourself.'

'Well . . . as long as you guide discussions with humility . . . I shall tell the King that you regret any misunderstandings arising from your . . . ahem . . . Courts of Love.'

This was a turning point for Ailenor, this and the wonderful breakfasts and dinners she provided for Aymer and had, herself, begun to enjoy. When Uncle Boniface visited from Canterbury she did her utmost to reconcile them both whilst showing them both the embroidery they had almost completed for Alix's wedding coffers. Alix smiled in a most endearing manner at Uncle Boniface.

'I pray, your Grace, you will officiate at my wedding to Gilbert de Clare,' Alix said and moved her sharp violet eyes to her uncle. 'Dear Uncle Aymer, I pray that you can assist the Archbishop.' She sighed engagingly and clasped her dainty hands together. 'We are a close family.' She reached out one hand to Ailenor. 'I love the Queen dearly. She has been generous and kind to me. She has instructed me in many things.'

'Such as?' Aymer said narrowing his eyes.

'Embroidery, marriage, a lady's responsibilities. We read our Books of Hours together daily. We pray together.'

Boniface said, 'Well, Bishop Aymer, what do you think? Will you assist with the wedding?'

'It will be an honour, Archbishop Boniface.'

Aymer studied the embroidery closely, trailing a long finger over the image of Christ. 'What a treasure this is. I had no idea the Queen was so talented with the needle and you, Alix, have been an excellent pupil. Gilbert de Clare is most fortunate.'

'When he grows up,' Alix said, her tone full of sweetness.

Ailenor was sure she may have turned two of that wretched Lusignan family into her allies, Alix and Aymer both.

She happily prepared for Christmas and wrote a long secret letter to Nell who would soon be delivered of her child. Earl Simon was in Paris with the French King and that was a concern.

My Dearest Nell,

I have been sent by Henry, my Lord King, to Winchester in disgrace. My heart aches because he has separated me from the children. He knows this banishment is painful for me, but at least he has not placed me in Wilton Nunnery, as did Edward Confessor his wife, Edith, when, centuries gone by, she was sent from court, or treated me as that other Eleanor, your grandmother who was banished from court for years. I am told to consider my attitude towards Henry's half-brothers and to correct it. Since I am under Bishop Aymer's supervision, I have no choice but to bend to Henry's will. I shall be conciliatory. I am angry but I am Henry's queen and a queen must behave with decorum. There is no point to our quarrelling; there's no sense in maintaining a foolish situation of King's Men and Queen's Men.

Divided, the great barons perceive weakness within our royal house. They will seek to take advantage. Fortune's Wheel may, one day, turn against us, so I shall be kind in speech to William of Valence at Christmastide, though I am sorry for his wife, for her marriage cannot be an easy one. The man has a cruel and arrogant manner.

I wept, my dearest Nell, when I heard Henry had sent Simon away and has installed a lesser man as Seneschal of Gascony. Simon will be safe in Paris for they respect him there.

Knowing Henry, he will change his mind and beg Simon to return to him.

I send you my doctor whom I trust because I believe you may have need of him. He brings you this letter which you must put to fire when it is read.

Ailenor the Queen.

Henry galloped into Winchester at Christmastide at the head of a large court; all was cordial. The harmony that followed his arrival was accompanied by pleasant crisp weather that allowed them to hunt and walk in the gardens enjoying the winter sunshine.

Ailenor made herself loving towards him. She apologised for any lack of loyalty he had perceived in her actions of that year. Nothing was to be gained for them, the future, their children, and the crown if an uncomfortable division between them continued. She took his hand which he left in hers and when Henry complained about Earl Simon, remarking he was in Paris, she held her tongue and shifted the conversation to Nell instead.

'I hear Nell has been delivered of a healthy girl whom she calls Eleanor for your grandmother.'

'I hope the child has more sense than to grow up quarrelsome,' Henry said, but there was a smile playing about his mouth.

'Oh I am sure of it,' she replied. 'Look, Henry, there's a rose on that bush. It's not been damaged by storms and it thrives even into winter.' She took him over to the rose bush and they studied it together.

'A Christmastide rose, delicate as silk,' she said with reverence in her voice.

319

That night, after supper with their court, Henry took Ailenor's hand and led her into her chamber where a fire crackled and candles glowed, customary cakes and wine had been laid out, and the bed cover drawn back to reveal freshly scented linen. 'Let us mend our differences with a child in the cradle.' Henry was still a handsome man, if often foolish. Fortunately, there were flashes of insight and, after all, he was one of the most gentle and cultured men in his court. No one was perfect. Henry certainly was not, but she loved him well, for his goodness and his faults.

Yet anxiety haunted her, despite the return of her family and harmony between her and Henry. There was no further talk of Henry's crusade. His crusade was to be Gascony. Henry was intent on taking on the Gascon rebels himself.

Chapter Thirty-six

Gascony, 1253

Ailenor kept her silence as Henry made plans to sail for Gascony. He had bought back Simon's command for seven thousand marks. Considering he owed Simon the sovereigns promised yearly for his command of Gascony in the first place, Henry was fortunate Simon agreed. Ailenor did not comment. She was relieved to be created regent in Henry's absence and to accept the responsibility he gave her. He granted her custody of the great seal and she would preside over councils whilst regally seated on his throne-like seat in Westminster Hall.

She took on joint regency with Richard of Cornwall. Before his departure, Henry made a new will granting her the right to rule England, until Edward was of age, if he was killed in Gascony. Her patience and quiet strategy had been rewarded. She had earned his trust by forfeiting her frankness, but she cared deeply for her husband. And she was with child again. Ailenor did not want any more upsets or dramas. When Nell wrote from Odiham that she was joining Simon in Paris as soon as she was ready to cross the Narrow Sea, Ailenor prayed that Henry would not take Odiham away from Nell. He had spitefully confiscated the wealth from Kenilworth, directing it into his own coffers.

Ailenor remained in the palace of Westminster, intending to stay firmly in the centre of government. She sat in council meetings with her head proudly held high, wearing voluminous gowns, and veils flowing from impressively tall hats which made her look as if she possessed great authority. No queen since Queen Matilda of Flanders was as regal as she, nor, she smiled as she considered this, had any queen since the Conqueror's Matilda commanded such respect.

She did not withdraw to the birthing chamber until November. When her ladies fussed around her, she sent them away. When the midwives begged her to rest she ignored them. If her doctor complained, she looked at him imperiously, remarking she was Queen and would decide when she withdrew from court. When she did, she determined to rule from her lying-in apartments in Westminster.

As her time approached she found herself obsessive about ruling, because she knew that once she went into seclusion her grip on power could be diluted. Power was precious, especially for a woman, and she had almost lost it during her quarrel with Henry. It must not slip into the hands of Richard of Cornwall. She was negotiating a betrothal for Lord Edward with a princess of Castile and she did not want that mission to fall into Richard's orbit.

Edward's right to rule the Duchy, if married to Alfonso of Castile's sister, Lenora, would persuade Alfonso to give up the ridiculous Castilian claims to Gascony which he claimed through his grandmother, eldest daughter of the second Henry. Henry had reached the conclusion that an alliance with Castile was the answer to the ongoing Gascon problem. What an excellent betrothal this would be for Edward.

Ailenor expected her negotiators back from Castile very soon and it irked her that for a month she had to push matters of state far to the edges of her mind.

On the 27th November she gave birth to a little girl.

Ailenor looked down on her newborn baby's face and said, 'Her name is Katherine. St Katherine watched over me during my confinement.' She leaned back against her pillows, thinking how perfect the baby was. It was difficult for Ailenor to give Katherine over to her wet nurse. 'Care for her well,' she said to the woman who was to nourish her baby.

Taking the baby from Ailenor, the nurse remarked, 'She is a

beauty, but so quiet, not a whimper.' She looked strangely at Ailenor. 'Why doesn't she cry?' Ailenor could not understand why either.

Ailenor's ladies cosseted her back into robust health. Her children came to Westminster from Windsor for the Christmas period. She received a letter from Margaret in Scotland and then worried because Margaret seemed lonely. She sent gifts north to Edinburgh, fabrics, books, a long letter, and decided after she was churched she should send investigators north to inquire into Margaret's welfare.

The other children celebrated the festivities of Christmastide privately in their mother's apartments whilst the court made merry in Westminster Hall. Richard took Henry's place in the hall but Sancha left her husband's side to dine on Christmas night with Ailenor and the children.

'You should be with your husband, Sancha. We are happy enough here, celebrating quietly.' Ailenor said.

'I have come to London to be with you, Ailenor, and the children.'

Sancha had given birth at last four years earlier but never conceived again. She arrived with her little boy, Edmund, his nurse and a few attendants. Edmund was an engaging dark-haired child. His fourth name day would be celebrated on the day following Christ's Day. Ailenor's children anticipated this birthday as much as Christmas itself. They affectionately called him Ed.

They planned gifts for Ed, secreting them about the royal nursery. Ailenor's own little Edmund persuaded his nurse take him to the kitchens to order a special box of barley sugar, his favourite treat, for his cousin. The cousins scurried about the Queen's apartments as their mothers conversed, playing hide and seek in the palace corridors. Occasionally ten-year-old Beatrice joined them but usually she preferred to sit and pore over a pretty Book of Hours with Alix of Lusignan or to disappear into one of the palace's still rooms. Baby Katherine lay solemnly in her cradle.

'She is beautiful,' said Sancha.

'She is exquisite but I fear she cannot hear us, nor will she speak.'

Tears filled Ailenor's eyes. 'Henry has ordered prayers for her to be said in the great Cathedral in Bordeaux. I fear it won't help. God wishes her silence. Sancha, Katherine does not cry.'

'This could change. She is only a month old.'

Ailenor lifted her baby from her cradle and held her close in her arms. 'I have forbidden them to secure her to a board. Her life could be short and I want her to be happy. I love her so much.'

Alix and Beatrice concocted salves, perfumes and soaps. A maid who was talented in the composition of cosmetics helped them and soon they had created gifts for all the family.

Beatrice presented her aunt with perfume distilled from what she swore were secret ingredients. Sancha exclaimed her delight when she discovered the little vial inside a linen wrapping. She unplugged the wax stopper and delicately held the glass bottle to her nose. 'Ah, lemon and orange and bergamot. This reminds me of my childhood. What a kind thought.'

'Mama,' said Beatrice. 'For you.' She held out a gift, another perfume vial enfolded in soft linen.

Smiling at Sancha, Ailenor unwrapped and unstoppered her gift. She held it to her nostrils and sniffed.

'Guess what I used, Mama.'

'I think you have managed to use my favourite roses and something else. Now what could it be?' She smelled it once again. 'Almond?'

'Yes, Mama.'

Ailenor dabbed it onto her wrists and touched her throat. 'I have gifts for you all as well but they must wait.'

As candles flickered and afternoon snow drifted down through the pale light outside the chamber windows, Ailenor presided over a very happy New Year's feast with her senior ladies, younger children, her sister, and little Edmund of Cornwall who was now used to being named Ed. She thought she had never been so happy.

If only her children never had to grow up. The older boys were dining in the Great Hall with Earl Richard and the noisy court. As Ailenor bit into a fruit pastry, she thought of how Edward had wept like a small child as Henry sailed off to Gascony, protesting he was old enough to go and fight. He had watched Henry's ship sail into the distance until eventually he could no longer see its sails and they had to persuade him away.

He will grow up soon enough and be married to Lenora of Castile. A server poured wine into her glass goblet. She waved him over to Sancha who presided over the other end of the long table and retreated into her musings. Not for long. Musicians burst into the chamber to play for them. Arranging the sleeves of her gown over the arms of her great chair she sat back, leaning into her cushions, and listened to Christmas melodies. Her ladies rose from their benches to strum their lutes.

The children behaved with dignity fitting the sons and daughters of princes. Ailenor held onto the moment as if a cruel spirit would slip in from outside and steal it from her. Their children were their kingdom's future, God's gift to Henry and herself, a gift to the realm. She loved them with all her heart. Margaret, she thought to herself, Margaret will come home to visit us soon, soon as we can arrange it. We shall always be a close family.

She presented her ladies and children with gifts, calling out their names one by one as she handed them belts, purses, and little velvet-covered books containing a set of poems she had composed. These were tales of elves and goblins, fairy folk and giants, knights and ladies and, to the children's delight, dragons with fiery smoke, treasures with tiny illuminated capitals and miniature illustrations.

In January Ailenor celebrated her purification. The whole court attended, all aware she held enormous power. When the council convened again, Richard and Ailenor united to manage the magnates they had summoned to Westminster and appealed for funds to help win the King's war. For once, they met with success.

'It is admirable that despite the snow, they have come again for our Parliament and have agreed food, horses, and ships for Gascony,' Ailenor said to Sancha, nibbling at a piece of marchpane left over from her purification feast.

'Is there news from Castile?' Sancha said.

Richard frowned at Ailenor. 'The Castilian marriage will be costly. The Council won't grant further funds.'

Ailenor pushed her cup away and said with firmness, 'This marriage is important for lasting peace in Gascony. We'll collect a tax from the Jews and the religious orders – as much as we can.'

Richard stared down at his jewelled eating knife. 'There goes Henry's crusading collection. We can't ask for money for troops and for a royal wedding. The City will rebel, the barons will rebel, and the Church will tell you it's time we had an inquisition against the Jews.' He frowned at Ailenor. 'I believe you have paid Earl Simon three thousand marks to return to Gascony to help Henry, *and* you promised the rest of the money outstanding from his previous work there?'

'Earl Simon is worth it all, every mark. When Henry wrote how he needed him, I had to beg Nell to persuade him to return to Gascony.'

Richard leaned back and laughed. 'Earl Simon knows how to strike a hard bargain.'

'As do you.' She pushed her plate away, sweetmeats abandoned. Rising from her chair, she sent a servant to fetch Lady Mary and Domina Willelma. 'We must collect coin from wherever, Jews, merchants, nobles, and even the poor.' She narrowed her eyes. 'And I am sure you, Richard, will want to organise your own contribution.'

She swept from the chamber without another word, leaving Richard playing with his eating knife. Sancha looked adrift as if she could not decide whether to follow Ailenor or remain with her husband. She remained seated.

Richard, after all, was the wealthiest earl in the land, wealthier than Henry. He was so rich that when the Emperor of the Romans died, the Pope offered Richard the crown of Sicily and he refused. Richard might not want Sicily but Edmund, their second son, could become King of Sicily instead. Gascony for Edward. Sicily for Edmund. She must suggest this idea to Henry though it would be an expensive venture. It would not be popular with the King's council.

In February, a letter arrived from Gascony with good news. Ailenor was in her chapel praying, as she did daily, for Henry's safety.

Dropping her beads, she left the altar, Sancha scurrying behind her, desperately trying to keep up.

She read the letter slowly in the painted chamber where a fire blazed in the hearth. Glancing up, she said in an excited voice, 'It's happening at last. They want Edward to travel to Castile for the wedding. And, Alfonso wants to knight my son.' She let the letter drop onto her lap. 'But that will disappoint Henry. He had hoped to knight Edward himself.'

Her fingers rapped a small table by her chair. She felt her brow creasing. 'Alfonso wants a huge dower for his sister. He doesn't offer a marriage portion for Lenora himself.'

Sancha's face coloured as she said, 'Henry had nothing from *our* father.'

'Well, marriages are expensive.' Ailenor said. 'Alfonso knows we need this union with his House to persuade Castile to drop claims to Gascony.'

She glanced at the letter again. 'He wants Edward to be in possession of his own lands. They must be valued at ten thousand a year.' She shook her head. 'It's demanding.'

'Has the King agreed the terms?' Sancha asked.

'Apparently Henry *has* agreed terms.' She sighed. 'Alfonso wants Edward to be richer than his father. Navarre is the real problem.'

'Why is Navarre an issue?' Sancha's brow wrinkled.

'You see, Sancha. It's difficult. Theobald of Navarre is another suitor for Lenora of Castile. If Navarre joins with Castile to claim Gascony we are undone. With this marriage, we settle with Castile and prevent Gaston de Bearn from securing his own alliance with either state. Cousin Gaston would be outmanoeuvred.' She read on, her mouth breaking into a smile. 'It goes well for Henry in Gascony. Earl Simon has put down a rebellion.' She placed the letter on her table. 'Where is Richard today, Sancha?'

'Hunting.'

'In this weather?'

'He chases rabbits over in the warrens across the river.'

Ailenor thought for a moment. 'Don't tell Richard what I have

327

told you. I'll call a council meeting tonight and tell them about our success in Gascony and that negotiations for Lord Edward's wedding are going ahead as my husband wishes. As soon as Richard returns, Sancha, send him to me. I shall read him Henry's letter myself.' Sancha nodded. Ailenor stood and took her sister's arm. 'Now, shall we go and see how our children are? They might enjoy skating on the monk's fish pond. I need exercise.'

'Edmund loves the skates you had made for his Name Day. Remember how we could never skate in Provence. Well, only if we journeyed to the mountains.'

'That was a rare treat. Uncle William spun us around and around.' She felt tears gather in her eyes at the memory. 'God rest his soul.' She crossed herself.

It was these moments with Sancha that Ailenor enjoyed most, occasions when they shared recollections of their family history.

By April, ships sailed for Gascony. Ailenor ensured they were well-provisioned. Henry enjoyed English beef so she sent six cows, plus eight sheep and a gift which was a sleek black Arab stallion called Samson. Henry enjoyed pigs' trotters so she sent them pickled in brine. For his wardrobe she packed new tunics she embroidered herself with a chequered design whilst resting after Katherine's birth. She included an oaken chest with family gifts – soap from Beatrice, a pen and ink horn from Edmund, a jewelled dagger from Edward, and a Saxon cross set with garnets from herself. She wondered if now he would ever depart on a crusade since poor Louis had met with terrible disasters in Egypt and was imprisoned, though thankfully ransomed – at enormous cost to France. Marguerite had birthed two children in the Holy Land. They were back in Paris but Louis was ill almost to death.

John Mansel returned to Castile. The official announcement of the marriage contract followed.

Henry wrote: *Edward's marriage will take place in Castile in October. Accompany our son to Gascony. He is to continue to Castile with his own retinue as these are Alfonso's terms.*

By the time she had finished reading Henry's letter she was flushed, pleased and excited.

'Willelma, bring cooling waters for my face. My heart is racing.' Lady Mary held her whilst Willelma dabbed at her face. She took deep breaths. 'Lord Edward is to be married.' Her ladies congratulated her by cheering. If anyone had passed the painted chamber they would have seen the Queen swirl around with Lady Willelma, a letter in one hand and the other gesticulating wildly.

Ailenor summoned Edward to her side.

She heard his nailed boots clattering up the winding outside staircase from the practice yard. He entered breathless, smelling of hay and sweat. Ailenor stood in the middle of the room by the long oak table.

'Sit,' she said, gesturing to a chair placed by the fireplace. Edward swept his damp hair back and mopped his perspiring forehead with a linen cloth. He removed his gambeson and threw it over a bench.

'Mother, I know I stink, but your messenger said to come to you with haste. Is all well? My father . . .'

She took one chair and he sat in the other. She pointedly held a small ball of dried lavender to her nose. Removing it she said, 'That's better. Edward, I did not intend to frighten you. All is well in Gascony. Your father has written with good news. Alliance with Castile has been announced. John Mansel is on his way to fetch us to Gascony.'

'I really *am* to marry Lenora of Castile.' His face was filled with joy. 'I am to be a husband. When?'

'We travel to Gascony soon as it is possible. You will continue to Castile without me but you'll be accompanied by a retinue suitable for a great prince. You are to have great lands of your own.'

'Gascony, of course, but other lands?'

'Yes.' She found she was crying tears of joy for her son.

'Where?'

She drew breath. 'Wales and Ireland.' She saw how his eyes opened wide, even though he had inherited the accursed drooping eyelid. 'Chester as well. It is a very important city. Here, see for yourself. Your father has been generous.' She passed Henry's letter to him.

Edward slowly read. 'He doesn't say I am to be called Earl of Chester or Lord of Ireland. I should have those titles, should I not?'

Ailenor folded her hands. 'Henry still has those titles, but you will claim the revenues.'

'The war in Gascony will end at last. Lenora's brother won't support the rebels any more. He won't claim my duchy, just because my great-grandmother of Aquitaine was his great-grandmother also.'

'Quite so. You must reach Castile by the thirteenth day of October so that gives us time to plan. We shall pass summer in Bordeaux with your father. How do you like this?'

'Very much. Can Henry of Almain come with me?'

'If your Uncle Richard agrees. You might like young Hal de Montfort as a companion as well?'

'Yes.' Edward thought for a moment. 'Perhaps Father will allow me to join him in the fighting.'

'I hope, by now, he has the rebels subdued. It must be safe for you to travel south to Burgos for your wedding.'

'Without you both?'

She smiled broadly at her son. 'Enough of this. We have planning ahead. I'll consult with the tailors because your wedding garments must do us all honour.' She studied him. 'I hope you are not planning to grow taller by October. You are as long-legged as the antelope that dwells in Henry's zoo. It seems no time at all since you were a child and now, my son, you are to be a great lord and rule Gascony. The future is yours and Lenora's. Come closer. Let me give you my blessing.'

After she said a brief prayer over her kneeling son's head, her hands placed over his long waving locks which were beginning to darken, Edward rose, leaning down and embracing his mother, his head touching hers.

'No wonder they call you Longshanks,' she said.

Gascony stopped simmering with discontent. Earl Simon returned to England. He was, at last, a wealthy man.

That September, as the leaves began to loosen from trees, golden, brown and crisp, Ailenor with Henry at her side, watched Edward leave for Castile. Swifts circled overhead flitting back and forth from nests in the castle walls. Edward sat proudly on the Arab stallion, Samson, which Henry had given to his son for his journey south. Hal and Harry rode by Edward's side on equally handsome mounts. A glittering cavalcade of nobles and men at arms trotted into line behind the three young English lords.

'I hope, my love,' Henry said grinning at her, his eyes filling with moisture, 'Edward discovers as much joy in his marriage as we have in our union.' He took her hand. 'And now, I have a surprise for you.'

'How do you intend to surprise me?'

'Louis and Marguerite have returned to Paris. Louis's health has recovered. How would you like to visit your sister?'

Ailenor clasped her hands in front of her mouth, a young girl again for all her two score and ten years. 'We are to visit Louis's court? I am to see my sister?'

'Both sisters: Beatrice too. And I have suggested Richard and Sancha join us.'

Tears welled up in her own eyes. She had not seen two of her three sisters since they grew up in her father's castles. How they must have changed. She might not even recognise Beatrice, who had been a small girl when Ailenor had ridden all those years before to an unknown, hardly imagined future with a bridegroom who was by far her senior and whom she had loved from the beginning. Much time had shifted since Ailenor set out long ago on that winter journey to England. Her son was older now than she was then and today he had ridden off to *his* wedding. Ailenor glanced at the sundial in the courtyard. Time played tricks because *so much time* felt *no time at all*.

Henry tugged on his beard. He smiled. 'You will see your mother too, my love. She is in Paris with Beatrice and Charles.' He was gazing towards the sky where clouds were scudding over the castle, 'I'll visit Louis's soaring cathedrals. I shall see the Crown of Thorns at last, the holiest of all holy relics.' He clasped his hands in ecstasy. His blue eyes glazed over. 'Our Houses Capet and Plantagenet will unite after so many years of dispute. We'll make a long-lasting treaty.'

'I never dreamed I would see my sisters and mother again.' As they turned to climb the steps to the Great Hall, she added, 'Paris is very fashionable. We must all have new clothes. Will there be time? I wonder would Lady Rosalind be able to visit?'

'Our journey to Paris is planned for next year. You have plenty of time to send for her. We shall pass Christmastide in Gascony, bring Beatrice, Edmund, and baby Katherine here and travel to Paris in January. I have not seen this beautiful child. We may find a cure for Katherine's inability to hear. You may ask Lady Rosalind and Sir Thomas. Simon must join us too.' She smiled at that suggestion. 'We shall return for Alix's wedding next year. I think her betrothed will have had his tenth birthday by then.'

'I think Alix can wait for a ten-year-old to reach maturity. She should remain with us until he is fourteen.'

'As you wish.'

Ailenor, to her complete amazement, had become fond of Alix of Lusignan. She would suggest she joined her train of ladies when they visited Paris. The spirited Alix would not look forward to marriage with a boy so much younger than she, a difference of seven years, though no doubt she would manage him. Still, Paris would hearten her.

That night, Henry encased her hands in his own and whispered to her. 'I was most fortunate, my dearest love, when Richard brought me that poem you wrote -'

'Of King Arthur . . .do you have it?'

'I do,' Henry took her in his arms and stroked her long black hair. 'And once he had discovered you as a beautiful bride for me, I wanted none other. You are my enchantress.'

'God destined us to be together,' she said, drowsy with happiness.

The candle guttered and blew out. Windows rattled. A storm was on its way.

Author's Note

I began researching *The Silken Rose* in 2016. It is the first in a trilogy concerning medieval queens who were regarded by many contemporary barons and chroniclers as 'she-wolves'. All three were foreign. They were powerful queens. They upset elements of the nobility in different ways. Ailenor of Provence stands accused of nepotism. Eleanor of Castile stands accused of greed. And Isabella of France was 'not one of us'. These women have, in various ways, not enjoyed untainted historical reputations. I feel they have been misjudged and in *The Rose Trilogy* my aim is to bring these three medieval queens out of History's shadows and animate significant parts of their lives. In the novels you will discover their personalities, the medieval world they inhabited, and the plots and intrigues that influenced their lives.

Ailenor of Provence is the first of these foreign queens. She is followed by her daughter-in-law, Eleanor of Castile, whose skill at acquiring and developing property was frowned upon by the barons who lost properties to her. She provoked complaints from the Church because of her methods such as taking on debts from money lenders and foreclosing on debtors' lands. The third queen in the trilogy is Isabella of France who was Eleanor of Castile's daughter-in-law. Ailenor of Provence outlived her daughter-in-law, but Eleanor of Castile died long before her son Edward II married Isabella of France.

Why was Ailenor of Provence considered a 'she-wolf'? She was twelve or thirteen years old on her marriage to Henry III. The actual year of her birth is not set in stone; I allowed her thirteen years which may be authorial licence. She seems to have been determined to embrace queenship, giving alms to the poor, endowing abbeys, and being a good mother and devoted wife. She came from a poor country, yet Henry was astute when he made this alliance with Provence and Savoy because although impoverished, Provence was strategically important. Provence and Savoy guarded routes south into Italy and the Mediterranean. It was a romantic territory, a land of the troubadour culture popular during the High Medieval period of the magnificent thirteenth century.

Ailenor never brought Henry a dowry and was not from the 'top drawer' of European nobility. However, she was alleged to be beautiful, educated, intelligent, and fashionable. Margaret Howell writes in her biography about Ailenor of Provence:

Eleanor of Provence, her mother, her sisters and her daughters were all described as beautiful. What did it mean? Superficially it seems that medieval chroniclers were entirely uncritical in attributing beauty to any young woman of high birth. Here one must avoid anachronisms. Thirteenth-century chroniclers frequently mention beauty and manner in close association, and the second might powerfully reinforce the first . . . from Matthew Paris's superlatives it seems likely that Beatrice of Provence and her daughters had a generous measure of natural advantage.

Henry was happy to send a request to Ailenor's father, Raymond of Provence, for his second daughter's hand in marriage and to break off his marriage alliance with Jeanne of Ponthieu, a betrothal that had run into problems because, encouraged by France, the Pope would not give Henry his permission to marry Jeanne, on the grounds of consanguinity. France did not like the alliance between England and Ponthieu, one that could potentially strengthen Henry strategically and threaten French territories. Jeanne was heir to her mother's territory of Ponthieu and also to Aumale, which lay within Normandy. The French King Philip Augustus had seized Normandy from King John of England in 1205 and Philip's heirs could not risk England recovering land in the area and re-establishing control of Normandy. In fact, Jeanne's father had promised that he would not marry off his daughters without the permission of the

King of France. Queen Regent, Blanche of Castile, invoked that promise on behalf of her son Louis IX.

Jeanne of Ponthieu later married Ferdinand III of Castile. Her daughter was Eleanor of Castile, who in this novel is betrothed to Ailenor and Henry's son, Edward I.

Ailenor arrived in January 1236 with her uncle, William of Savoy. He was the first of Ailenor's Provencal relatives to be advanced by Henry III. William of Savoy, a bishop, became one of Henry's chief counsellors. Another uncle, the charming Peter of Savoy, later arrived, and was made an advisor and given property, the Honour of Richmond in Yorkshire. Peter built the Savoy Palace in London. Handsome, reforming Uncle Boniface became Archbishop of Canterbury.

Many talented clerks arrived in England from Savoy and Provence. They were employed in the treasury and other areas of government that had traditionally been the prerogative of the English barons. The barons felt such jobs were theirs to distribute and control. Moreover, as Savoyard marriages were made with English heirs and heiresses, it limited the field for the English aristocracy. Matthew Paris, chronicler, wrote at the time:

Before the said council was broken up Peter of Savoy, earl of Richmond, came to the royal court at London bringing with him some unknown women from his distant homeland in order to marry them to the English nobles who were royal wards. To many native and indigenous Englishmen this seemed unpleasant and absurd, for they felt that they were being despised.

This situation as illustrated in the novel was further exacerbated when Henry brought his half-brothers and two half-nieces to England after the death of his mother, Isabella of Angouleme, in June 1246. Spectacular marriages were made for his relatives, in particular that of Joan, the granddaughter of William Marshal and the Marshal heiress, to his half-brother William of Valence. Again, Matthew Paris wrote in 1247:

In the same year on the ides of August, on the lord king's advice and recommendation, Joan, daughter of Warin de Muntchensi, was married to William of Valence, the lord king's uterine brother. Since the eldest son and

heir of the above Warin was dead, his daughter Joan, the only one still alive,
was due for a very rich inheritance. Thus the nobility of England devolved in
a large measure to unknown foreigners. Moreover Alesia, half-sister to the
king, was married to John, the young earl of Warenne.

Henry's half-niece, Alix, married Gilbert de Clare. This was not to
be a happy union. The presence of Henry's half-brothers and -nieces
in England did bring a degree of conflict between him and Ailenor.
For a time, as historians write, it was King's men and Queen's men. It
seems they resolved the situation, so I adhered to this within the
novel. Just outside the novel's timeline, Henry made peace with
France. He and Ailenor visited Paris. She was for a time reunited with
her sisters and mother.

It is also fact that Ailenor was supportive of Simon de Montfort, at
least until the 1260s when conflict in England between the King and
his barons became imminent. Ailenor then spent years in France,
separated from Henry, loyally raising mercenaries to fight for her
husband. The civil strife was provoked by Henry's persistent demands
for extra finances but it was more because of a general dissatisfaction
with Henry's methods of government exacerbated by widespread
famine. The relationship between Simon de Montfort and Henry
reached crisis point at the time of Earl Simon's trial in the 1250s.

Henry enjoyed fashion as did Ailenor. He was extravagant, a lover
of pageantry and expensive building works such as Westminster
Abbey. They as did their children, loved the Arthurian legends and
believed in them. Ailenor came from Provence which had a troubadour following as had Aquitaine. She believed in the stories and in
the tradition of courtly romance popular during the twelfth century.
Like Henry's grandmother, Eleanor of Aquitaine, she would conduct
intellectual discussions on the subject of love. She was, I suggest, a
romantic queen who saw herself as a latter day Guinevere. Unlike
Guinevere and Arthur, she remained totally loyal to Henry and there
is no evidence that he was other than loyal to Ailenor throughout the
marriage.

The barons' desire to control Henry's spending, challenge his deter-
mination to protect Gascony – an expensive project – along with

Ailenor's and Henry's nepotism, were factors that contributed to the Barons' War of the next decade. Henry flouted the rules laid down in the Magna Carta. He made promises to his barons to curb his spending over and over again. The specific events leading up to the conflict are omitted from *The Silken Rose* because I had to make choices about what to include. Therefore I ended this book with Edward's betrothal to Eleanor of Castile because she will be the subject of the second novel, *The Damask Rose*, which opens in 1264 during the conflict.

Outside the remit of this book, Henry became embroiled in a war against the Hohenstaufen Dynasty in Sicily on behalf of Pope Innocent IV, in return for the title of King of Sicily for his son Edmund. When Henry's treasury dried up Innocent withdrew the title and offered it to Charles of Anjou. Finally, Simon de Montfort became the leader of those who wanted to uphold the Magna Carta and ensure that the king surrender more power to the baronial council. Earl Simon and the barons supporting him initiated a move towards reform. The Provisions of Oxford of 1258 abolished absolute monarchy, giving power to a council of twenty-four barons to administer the business of government and provide a Parliament. Henry made the oath to adhere to the Provisions, but bought the support of France by relinquishing claims to Normandy and with French support won a papal bull to release him from his oath. By April 1263, Simon de Montfort returned to England and gathered dissident barons together at Oxford. Fighting broke out in the Welsh Marches and by the autumn of 1263 both sides had raised large armies.

For *The Silken Rose*, I decided to introduce a subplot, the story of an imagined character, Rosalind. Her narrative intersects with that of Ailenor. My purpose was to view Ailenor through another lens; to introduce City craftsmen and women; to give the story another dimension highlighting the importance of English embroidery during the thirteenth century.

Finally, where there is historical fact, I have used it as a framework for this novel. However, as I am writing historical fiction I invent as well, fill in the white spaces, and hopefully animate historical personalities. Thank you for reading *The Silken Rose*. Without readers, this historical novel would never see the light of day. I thoroughly enjoyed my time living with my characters, real and invented, and enthusiastically researching and writing about their lives, both real and imagined. I hope you have enjoyed reading their stories.

If you are interested in further reading here are a few titles I recommend:

The Illustrated Chronicles of Matthew Paris, translated, edited and with an introduction by Richard Vaughan, Alan Sutton Publishing.
Henry III, The Great King England Never Knew it Had, Darren Baker, The History Press
Eleanor of Provence, Margaret Howell, Blackwell Publishers
Henry III, Matthew Lewis, Amberley Press
Four Queens, Nancy Goldstone, Phoenix Press
The Subversive Stitch, Rozsika Parker, I.B. Tauris & Co Ltd.
Taste, Kate Colquhoun, Bloomsbury

Many, many other books and chronicles informed this story. However, in particular I enjoyed the above, especially *Taste* as I love recipes and information about cooking in the past.

Acknowledgements

An author may write a book but there is a group of talented people behind that author helping to bring it to you, the reader. I would like to thank the Headline Group for publishing *The Silken Rose*, in particular my publisher and editor at Headline, Eleanor Dryden, and Rosanna Hildyard, her assistant. My thanks also go to editors Greg Rees and Jay Dixon, who both worked on editing this novel.

My thanks also to my patient family, especially my husband, Patrick. His support is amazing. Thanks also to my critique group, Sue, Gail and Denise. Thank you to Dee Swift, one of my beta readers along with Sue and Denise. Thanks also to Katrin Lloyd, Liz, Charlotte, Mel and Theresa who read and commented on various chapters of this book's first draft.

Importantly, I wish to thank you, my readers, because without you my books might never see the light of day.

Carol McGrath

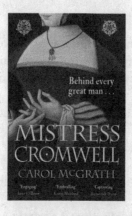

For the latest news, updates and exclusive content from Carol McGrath, sign up to her newsletter at:
www.CarolCMcGrath.co.uk

You can also find Carol McGrath on social media . . .

Like her on Facebook: facebook.com/mcgrathauthor

Follow her on Twitter: @carolmcgrath

And follow Headline Accent: @AccentPress

ACCENT